Knuckle Supper

The ultimate Gutter Fix Edition

By Drew Stepek

BLOOD BOUND BOOKS

ISBN 978-1-940250-30-4

Edited by Andrea Dawn

Interior Layout by Black Heart Edits
www.blackheartedits.com

Printed in the United States of America

Third Edition

Visit us online at
www.bloodboundbooks.net

CHILDREN of the NIGHT

Children of the Night is a private, non-profit, tax-exempt organization founded in 1979. They are dedicated to assisting children between the ages of 11 and 17 who are forced to prostitute on the streets for food to eat and a place to sleep. They have rescued girls and boys from prostitution and the domination of vicious pimps, and they provide all programs with the support of private donations.

They are making a difference in the lives of hundreds of children each year. Their commitment to rescuing these children from the ravages of prostitution is shared with a small but committed group of detectives, FBI agents, and prosecutors in Los Angeles, Hollywood, Santa Ana, Anaheim, San Diego, other areas of California, Las Vegas, Portland, Billings, Montana; Seattle, Washington; Miami, New York, Minneapolis, Atlanta, Phoenix, Hawaii, and Washington D.C.—all stops on the child prostitution circuit. And their numbers keep growing as more and more dedicated individuals become concerned about the welfare of these desperate children.

Child prostitutes require specialized care for effective intervention. Most of the children victimized by prostitution were first victimized by a parent or early caregiver. Most have been tortured by treacherous pimps, and many testify in lengthy court proceedings against the pimps who have forced them to work as prostitutes.

In most cases these children do not have appropriate homes to return to, and the only relative who is a suitable guardian may live far away from the child's hometown. For many the only option is an out of home placement, college dorm, maternity home, or mental health program. For those who reach 18 and need additional time to prepare to enter the mainstream society, independent living programs are recommended; special education programs are advised for those who need extra help with school, and alcohol or drug recovery homes are suggested for those with substance abuse problems.

Children of the Night is in demand to assist other agencies across the country and around the world to develop similar programs.

www.childrenofthenight.org

Up to 10% of the revenue from *Knuckle Supper* will be donated to Children of the Night.

FOREWORD

Knuckle Supper is a dish that ain't for the squeamish, that's for sure. But if you've got an appetite for vampire business that goes steps beyond the pale, then Drew Stepek may have your bloody number. Forget the neutered, neurotic undead that pop-culture's been feeding you. The dirty, amoral gangs of bloodsuckers that roam the streets of Los Angeles in *Knuckle Supper* are unsentimental, unrepentant killers, preying on anybody who gets in their way (and a lot of other folks, too). It's a hell of a ride, but like I said before, it ain't for everyone. Part satire, part gore fest, part gut-punch, *Knuckle Supper* is a brutal book, complete with a horrific, streets-eye view of the grimy and gory lives of a new breed of Los Angeles gangster. The jaded, drug-addicted vampires whose unpleasant un-lives are so violent and mean, they barely live out a regular human lifespan, much less make it anywhere close to sainted immortality.

There's no philosophy and no lofty proclamations about what it MEANS to live so long and be so different from the herd. No, the vamps in *Knuckle Supper* are so animal-like in their behavior, their lives are brutish and short.... their reality so grimy and dank, the book reads like a nature special about psychopaths. In some strange alternate reality, Iceberg Slim wrote a splatterpunk riff in *Less than Zero* and *Knuckle Supper* was the unholy spawn.

As you're about to find out, Drew Stepek is one sick fuck. I've known that since our days together roaming the halls of Larry Flynt Publications. If you ever have the chance to meet him, don't be fooled by his relaxed, easy-does-it California bonhomie. The Dude's got issues. Sure: you could fill a nice-sized suburban pool with the blood that's spilled during the course of this book, but despite all that (or maybe because of it all), he's doing something with *Knuckle Supper* that's been kinda lacking as of late in vampire lit…he's fusing good ol' blood and guts with a mighty conscience, exploring real issues and not coming up with any easy answers. Queasy answers, maybe, but no, nothing easy. Nothing pat. Nothing remotely safe for the mall vamps and their ilk. And bless his dark little heart for it.

So yeah, like I said before, *Knuckle Supper* is a dish that ain't for the squeamish. But if you're ready for a new kind of vampire and a new kind of vampire tale, you've found your sanguinary Shangri-La. But a word of warning: you might want to start flipping the pages on an empty stomach lest you find yourself getting a bit overwhelmed by what's about to follow.

Tighten your seatbelts, kids – it's gonna be a bloody read.

~ Gabe Soria / Author of *Life Sucks*

Man is the only creature that consumes without producing. He does not give milk, he does not lay eggs, he is too weak to pull the plough, he cannot run fast enough to catch rabbits.

Yet he is lord of all the animals.

~ **George Orwell**

1
MERCHANTS

Every once in a while, things went horribly wrong.

"Dez, get her in the fucking bathroom, you asshole!" I screamed, subduing the pimp by rapping him across the neck with a crowbar. He dropped, and snot from his jughead splashed all over the hardwood floor.

The dogs went into a frenzy in the backyard.

"And tell the dogs to shut up," I added.

Dez ran his fingers through his hair, trying to get it out of his face. I always wished he'd cut that shit hair of his. While licking gel off his index finger, he whispered, "What the hell, bro?"

The pimp squirmed around. He was still alive. Our little blood theater wasn't a wrap... yet. He struggled to his feet and made a run for the door, but I tripped him by chucking the crowbar at his legs. It was enough to send him nosediving back to the floor. Unfortunately, I only managed to bone-out one of his legs.

I looked at Dez, who was restraining the little girl. She wasn't shaking. I think she was just shocked. She probably figured we were going to rape her. "Just get her in the bathroom, dumbass. She's fucking twelve."

Dez shot me a salute, opened the bathroom door, and shoved the girl inside. He bolted it from the outside. "You can be a real pussy sometimes, RJ," he said.

You'd think that more junkies would find it strange that our bathroom had not one, but three deadbolts that locked from the outside. Then again, I took some mean smashes. My diet didn't exactly consist of low-fat chicken breasts stir-fried lightly with organic veggies. That being said, I wouldn't envy anyone locked up with me in close quarters.

Without acknowledging that once I got high I was going to beat the shit out of Dez for his stupidity, I proceeded to the pimp. While brushing the blood from his nose and out of his mouth, he crawled to our front door, trying to get at the locks that prevented him from establishing contact with the outside world. The bathroom wasn't the only door with deadbolts. His yellowed, chipped nails dug into the wood like he was holding onto the side of Mount Everest without a rope, a carabineer, or a spotter. Trembling, he got halfway up the door. His compounded left leg dangled sideways, more hindrance at this point than a method of propping him up. He felt around the first lock and dropped a little bit.

I ripped off a stainless-steel security chain from around my neck. "Looking for these?" I unhooked the clasp on the homemade necklace and let it unravel to my waist, revealing three keys on the end. The pimp looked at me, stunned. It was one of those moments when someone realizes that they're fucked. Dez ran from the bathroom door and snatched the key and chain out of my hand.

The pimp cried as his head rested on the door. "Please, bro, don't kill me. I'm nobody."

He slid down to where his ascension began, defeated. They were always defeated in the end.

Dez walked over to him. "You are nobody, bitch, and now you're gonna get me high for the rest of the night."

I grabbed Dez on the shoulder. "Don't kill him, idiot. You know that's not what we want."

He shrugged off my hand and proceeded toward the bitch-beater who was crying against his last hope to escape.

"Wait a minute," the pimp whimpered. "I know who you are." He braced himself up slightly by planting his palms onto the floor. "What are you? BBP? Sangre? Battlesnakes?" His words stumbled as he pleaded. "I... I... I can help you."

Dez continued his trek. "Wrong, motherfucker. Do I look like a Beverly Hills shithead to you? Do I look like a Mexican? Am I a fucking Rasta? We're Knucklers."

He stood over the trapped rat and kicked at his almost emancipated leg. The pimp slid backward on his mitts. Then, without even hesitating, my snaky friend began thumping the chain and keys down on his head, using them as a weapon.

"Stop, Dez." In all reality, I didn't care if this piece of shit was mortally injured, but he had to be alive. We both knew that even a douche like this guy wasn't any good to us "quiet".

I nabbed Dez's wrist before the chain collided with his skull for the fifth time. "Don't be a psycho. Do you want to get high or not?" I ripped the chain out of his hand, tossed it into the dining room and added, "I get

2

first dibs."

He flicked a blood droplet off his girly eyelashes. "You always get first dibs."

The pimp grabbed his leg and ran his tongue across his toothless gums. I walked back toward the coffee table, grabbed two loaded syringes, and wiped off all the asshole goop that had landed on them, noticing for the first time that the viscous beating had pitched his gore over most of the room.

I put one syringe in my front pocket. "Hold him still."

I looked at the bathroom door. Not a sound. Either the pre-teen girl behind it was scared, assuming she was next, or she didn't care whether or not we killed the asshole that dropkicked her down Sunset Boulevard on a nightly basis.

Dez got behind the pimp, secured him in a headlock and extended his forearm toward me with the wrist held upright. "Why did we have to go through all that? We should have just killed both of them at the same time. She's a junkie, RJ."

"Just hold him still," I commanded. "You know there isn't another way to do this. You wanna end up back on Skid Row eating rats?" I bent down on one knee, inhaled the warmth of human and grabbed the pimp about halfway up his forearm.

Dez freed up his arms from the headlock and popped both of the pimp's ears, causing the scumbag's head to waver around like a cartoon cat who took a frying pan to the face. Without wasting a beat, Dez replaced his restraint with his legs by crossing them over the dude's torso and then looped his feet around back.

With his hands now free, Dez yelled, "Hand me the needle."

I did as he asked. His hand was jittery as he accepted it.

"Don't fuck this up for me, dude," I insisted. "Stay steady. Shit, you act like this is the first time something went wrong. Remember when that one homeless guy started squirting shit and piss all over the house? This is nothin'."

"Me?" he squealed and he flippantly tapped on the cylinder and pushed the air out of the syringe. He tightened his leg lock and the pimp's eyes rolled up, showing nothing but white. I was pretty sure the guy wasn't going anywhere. We have superhuman strength and all that. "I knew this was going to be more of a problem than it was worth. You and these fucking cattle. Like they give two jogs about you." He shuffled his hand with the syringe, emulating jerking off.

Brown blood bubbled out of the pimp's mouth. He tried to chew on his lip, but he came up with nothing but gums and crust. The chain sprayed his teeth all over the carpet like we were playing fifty-two pick up in a dentist's office.

My grip tightened on the forearm. I felt his heartbeat and an orgasmic flush swept through my body.

"Whatever." I grabbed onto the pimp's middle finger, pushing the other fingers down and out of the way. "You really need to get that hair out of your eyes, Dez." I laughed and made a weepy emo face. "What? Are you a fifteen-year-old kid, angry because his pussy hurts?"

Dez laughed a little and tapped at the needle again with the hand that was locked around the pimp's neck. "Someday, you're gonna thank me for always being here. You could never do this alone."

I held up the pimp's middle finger. "Fuck you. Get it done. One... two... Spike this asshole!"

Laughing, Dez sunk the needle into the pimp's wrist. As soon as all the heroin was in his blood, I cranked the elbow quickly to the left and then to the right. Knowing the arm was loose by feeling the already-brittle bone give, I commanded, "Pull the plug!"

Without hesitation Dez pulled the spike from the wrist and I tore the forearm from the pimp's body and held it vertically in the air. I quickly snapped off the "fuck you" finger directly at the knuckle. Then I sucked and allowed the blood to flow into my mouth like some deranged beer bong.

As I drank the nectar, I scuttled across the floor, back to the coffee table. I searched around with one eye and my hand and grabbed a powdery new latex glove. I stretched out the glove with my hand and capped the end of the severed arm.

"Hurry up, RJ, this grit is going into shock and losing a lot of blood. If his heart stops, it's your ass."

Both Dez's arms were now taming the squirming body of the pimp.

Knowing time was running out, I kicked over a glass bong and then inched the bong stand toward me with my right foot.

"Hurry!" Dez screamed.

Finally, I spit the knuckle out of my mouth, placed the arm in the bong holder and dragged my rapidly fading ass across the floor. Dez released his legs and reversed his position swiftly so he was facing his prey. He laid the body down on its back. I grabbed what remained of the already trashed arm, cranked it toward the sternum and rested it above his heart. Dez dropped his weight onto the pimp's chest.

Trying to prevent more blood from coming out of the torn appendage, I wrapped a towel around the break point, then massaged my leg against his chest, toward the still attached arm, hoping to redirect the blood flow. Dez hopped to the intact arm and more sloppily than I had, he severed it at the forearm.

I nabbed the needle from my front pocket, forced out the air and tapped at it as I tried to hold in blood from the other arm. Keeping the dying pimp still, I took the needle and plunged it into a vein on the wrist. When the syringe was empty, Dez cracked off the knuckle with his teeth.

As he started sucking away, I moved over to the top of the armless pimp, hugged his neck like a strangler without the element of surprise and with one turn to the right and one turn to the left, I removed his head from what still remained of his torso. The chest plate sucked in one last time and gassed out from his five open holes. He pissed and shit himself. Dez managed to make it over to the coffee table to get his latex cap. I tossed the head aside and went back toward the bong display.

"That's a mess," Dez joked. His eyes rolled back and forth from the heroin.

I held up my arm-bong for cheers. He just fell backward on a beanbag chair.

"Fuck you then," I said, turning the arm up to my mouth. "Call one of your little Deziens to come clean this up." Deziens. That's what I called his pussy-ass followers.

The dope began flowing with the blood of the pimp through the dust inside me. It felt nice, warm, comforting. My head nodded back and forth and bobbed side-to-side. The feeling was so comforting because it was the only thing I ever knew how to feel. Heroin meant more to me than my body, my face, my words, and my brain.

Dez and I are in a pack called the Knucklers. Yeah, I suppose we're vampires but more importantly, we're junkies and gangster motherfuckers.

"RJ?"

"Yeah?"

"What are we going to do about the girl in the bathroom?"

"Good question, Dez."

Usually after Dez went to go fade for a few hours, I listened to music in my own daze. I was a collector of old school British and American vinyl seven-inch punk rock records. Something about the sound was so raw and so shitily recorded that it always put me in a really good vaporous state. It was kind of like being in a slow-motion scene in a movie where you faintly hear music, but it sounds like a single speaker boom box being broadcast through a tin can. Adding to the majesty of my circulatory antifreeze, my dogs howled at the Los Angeles wind chimes outside—police sirens.

I worshipped the smell and taste of the heroin that summer night. The drug was always quite a bit more pleasant than the blood that I had to use to bulldoze it into my system. I always have some blood in my body, but it's more like a small reserve of canteen water being carefully monitored by someone lost in the desert. It depletes and doesn't come back.

I spent hours (probably more like minutes) sifting through my stacks upon stacks of records, spreading them out all over the floor and looking at the artwork on the front that was more often than not a Xeroxed paper. The biggest pain in the ass when I was in a state of fucked-upness was switching out the little yellow spindle adapters that go in the middle. I thought for a long time that I'd just buy a thousand of those things and just put them inside all my records to make things a lot easier. For me though, that took time away from killing people and doing drugs and shit. After all, I led the Knucklers.

I tried to be careful not to bust any of my 45s because they were collector's items. Sad thing is that I often flopped around the floor like a fish that just landed on the deck of a fisherman's boat. As I sipped away on the pimp's arm filled with the garbage nectar, I dropped my knee onto a record and cracked it. It sounded like a bone breaking. Pissed off, I flung it across the living room into the kitchen. I didn't look at what it was. I hoped when I woke from my glaze that it wasn't one of the expensive ones. They were hard to replace because when they originally came out, the bands only printed about a hundred of them.

It was always a great thing to be wasted… at least while it was going on. I sat on a cloud and convinced myself for the longest time that I'd remember everything in the morning. I rarely did, though. I looked in the direction of the record I shot like skeet. I went to see what it said on the label and whether or not the wax was fixable. Then, I tripped on my own feet, knocking my arm bong onto the records.

"Goddammit!" I yelled at myself.

I picked up the bong and grabbed a Herrington jacket off the couch to dab away the mess. Thankfully, most of the records were in plastic sleeves, but the dust that collected on them was mixed with blood, urine, phlegm, and whatever else was in the pimp's dislodged arms and head that turned into this atrocious, gelatinous concoction that made me vomit.

Barfing made things much worse. I tried to suck it back down my esophagus but as soon as the barf retreated back toward my stomach, it snowballed and came back up bigger, stronger, and smellier.

Stymied, I slumped my back against the entertainment center behind me and crossed my arms like a frustrated little baby, bumping the needle on the player across the entire record. Then, I scratched my forehead. I immediately realized that I was rubbing retch, combined with the pimp's special sauce, all over my head and hair. I tilted my head sideways, let out a big "Hmmfff," and asked myself rather impolitely: "What the fuck is wrong with you?"

Looking around the room filled with heroin needles, body parts, shit, piss, vomit, records, blood, and a stiff pimp, I answered my own question. "Oh yeah."

Old RJ was never defeated, though. Like I told Dez earlier, one of his little Deziens should come over and clean the mess. So, I picked myself up, cautiously, and made my way past my bedroom and knocked on his door.

"Dez?" I asked.

No response.

"Dez? Can you call one of your little pussy shits to come over here and clean up my mess?" I opened the door a crack. Dez was sprawled out on my guest bed, covered in blood and narcotics, hugging his chunk of the pimp like a woobie.

"Hey, Dez?"

He rolled away from facing the door and let out a high-pitched wheeze. "What the fuck do you want, RJ?"

My face cringed a little. His winey voice stabbed my ears. I stayed out of the light in the hallway. I didn't want him to see what a mess I had made of myself. Pig Pen from the Peanuts Gang would have been ashamed to hang out with me.

I brought my negativity down a notch. "I was wondering," I began as I picked a chunk of puke off the side of my nose, "if you can call your friends to come clean up. The house is a disaster."

Dez shot up in bed. "Close the fucking door, you junkie. We'll have them clean it tomorrow. Fuck, dude, the heroin wasn't that good!" He threw his portion of the pimp at the door. The severed arm slammed across my face, creating a wind pocket that blew my own stench directly up my nose. I put my hands up to my mouth but it was too late. Spunk bombed through the alleys between my fingers and drooled down my arms to my elbows.

Seemingly forgetting everything that had happened in the past hour, I quickly unbolted the bathroom door and took off my shirt. After throwing it in the shower, I headed toward the sink, cranked on the faucets, and began cupping water all over the upper half of my body. I swear that I saw stink lines and squiggles emanating from my head. It was pretty rare that I gave myself a full sink bath, but turning on the shower at that point seemed like more of a chore. If the sink is good enough for the French, then it was good enough for me.

After I was somewhat satisfied, I turned off the water flow and dragged my feet back to the living room. I figured I'd start cleaning. I blacked out instead.

About an hour later, I woke up. I looked over to my right. All my records were stacked nicely. I take that back, They were stacked, sure… but, in between each one, sludge dripped over the sides, making the mound look like a shit sandwich with all the fixings.

"That's funny," I said to myself. "I don't remember doing that." I had never, in fact, ever stacked my records until the morning because I always wound up in a situation like the bodily chaos I created earlier that night.

I eyeballed the room to see if Dez had called one of his Deziens to come over and clean while I was passed out. No one was there. Hmmm. I knew Dez didn't clean it up.

Like a kid on a pogo stick, I suddenly bounced to my feet and ran down the hallway toward the bathroom. I tried to reassure myself that I had stacked the records, but it was pointless. Even that fucked up I wouldn't have left the puke and sludge all over them.

Sure enough, when I reached the shitter, all the bolts were unlocked. Still too wasted to use my brain enough to decide what I was going to do about the little whore in there, I swiftly and discreetly locked all the deadbolts. The last thing I wanted to do was explain to Dez how she got out of the bathroom. On top of that, she had been in our living room… stacking my records for some reason.

1
DELINQUENTS

While the rancid stench from our dance with the devil still encased the living room, *I* on the other hand smelled like Irish Spring. After shaking off my buzz and having taken a proper shower in the master bathroom, I decided it was time to figure out what to do about the twelve-year-old whore in the community bathroom. Thankfully, Dez was still in bed. Typical of him. In his defense, it was my fault the girl wasn't dead yet.

I knocked on the shitter door. "Are you okay in there?" No response.

I unlocked the first bolt. "I'm coming in. If you are thinking about ambushing me when I open the door, I wouldn't recommend it."

Clink. I heard what I imagined was the towel bar dropping to the tile.

I unlocked the second deadbolt and spoke calmly as I peered into the bathroom. "Smart move."

The brittle girl was standing on the edge of the tub with her toes curled over the porcelain edge like a gargoyle. Her body looked shaken, but her eyes told another story. The little human seemed indebted that we had offed the pimp and spared her life.

"I'm coming in, and I don't *think* I'm going to hurt you." I opened the door to its full extent and propped both my arms up against either side of the door frame, blocking any escape. "I know you're probably a little freaked out here. It's kind of difficult to explain."

She locked onto my eyes and boldly said, "Not really. Pimps owe people money."

She smirked as she brushed her greasy skunk-streaked hair out of her young face. Her blistered bottom lip quivered slightly and her piggy nostrils flared: open-closed-open-open-closed. Her squinty, blood-cracked eyes rolled around slowly, trying to hatch her escape route.

"So, are you gonna fuck me or kill me, or fuck me then kill me, or kill me then fuck me? You sure didn't seem interested when you came in here earlier to wash all that shit off in the sink." She started to pull down her ripped jeans shorts.

"Jesus, keep your pants on," I said, dropping my guard to cover my eyes. As quickly as I covered my face, I was belted in the nuts with my stainless-steel shower radio. "Owwww!" I yelled, doubling over in pain.

She booked past me and headed toward the front room. In an aggravated state, I attempted to appeal to any sense that this little whore might have. "You can't get out, stupid." Reflecting, that probably wasn't the smartest thing to say.

She ran back over to me and unleashed a barrage of blows to my neck and back with the radio as it dialed through three or four Latino stations. "No shit, asshole."

After about ten blows, I caught the radio with my right hand and nabbed her wrist with my left. I could've snapped that thing off so easily. For some dumb reason, I didn't.

"Relax." I slid the radio across the room on the hardwood floor and grabbed her other wrist. Oh man, did I want to break both her arms backwards, crack them off and just beat the shit out of her.

She felt my power. She tried to get me to release. "Don't you fucking touch me, creep," she yelled.

I nudged her with my eyes. "There's your pimp." And then threw her down next to him.

"I know, fucktard," she roared. "I saw him earlier when I came out here to try to steal some of your heroin and see if I could sneak out. You were passed out with your hand in your pants, queer."

"Do you really want to end up like that? You aren't going anywhere until we figure this all out."

She shoved herself away from the corpse. "What do we need to figure out? Are you going to kill me or what?" She backed herself into the corner. Her head twitched and she covered her face with her hair as she tried to avoid looking at the pimp. "Who are you psychos?"

I cracked my neck and fully stood up. Walking cautiously like a child trying to feed a deer, I moved in a little closer. "I come in peace." I put up my arms to show her that I wasn't planning any shenanigans. "Kinda."

She shoved herself farther into the corner and her hardened eyes started to swell. "What the fuck are you?"

I hesitated, unsure how to answer the question. Then, I blurted out, "I'm a gangster."

"You don't look like a gangster." Her eyes focused on my chest. My eyes inched down to see what she was looking at. I already knew, even though I was wearing a shirt. On my chest was my ink: A Batman symbol. In my defense, it was actually the symbol for skater Steve Caballero's band, The Faction. The thing was that I had the band's name written on top of the black bat in dark blue ink. In other words, you couldn't really see it.

I grabbed for a shirt thrown on the back of a chair and casually buttoned it up. "What do you know about the gangs in Hollywood, anyway? You're like twelve."

She smirked; obviously she knew I was embarrassed by the dumb tattoo. "Gee, I don't know. I've been on the streets, turned out, for over a year now."

I didn't understand how she was staying so relatively calm with the shredded corpse on the floor about six feet away from her or why she didn't try to kill me when she stacked the crud records.

"Your name's RJ, right? I heard your lovers' quarrel with your friend earlier."

"'Lovers' quarrel?' What does that mean?" Stunned by her ease in my slaughterhouse, I finally asked. "Why aren't you freaking out at all?"

"You just killed my pimp. Now answer the question, Batman: What are you?"

I scratched at the tattoo through my shirt. "I guess you could call me a vampire."

"You're kinda out of shape for a vampire," she chortled.

She was right. I stood just under six feet and had fried hair that I'd call a rat's nest if it wasn't an insult to vermin everywhere. I didn't have a lot of body tone because most of my flesh seemed bloated from narcotics and alcohol. I had a big lower lip and an even bigger nose. I tried to brush the tobacco off my teeth as much as possible but since they were contained inside a walking carcass, they never really shined like chompers on a toothpaste commercial.

I had nice eyes though, so that could be considered a double helping of cherries on top of a turd. At least that's what I looked like the last time I stood face-to-face with my own reflection. Contrary to popular belief, we have always been able to see our reflections. No matter. I didn't like looking at myself. The only thing I ever saw was a serial killer looking back at me and laughing at me for somehow being able to live.

Finally, I said, "Thanks, I know I'm out of shape."

Thud! Thud! Thud!

I looked at the front door and then at the little skunk girl.

Thud! Thud! Thud!

"Shit."

I grabbed her by the back of her striped halter top and rushed her back to the bathroom and threw her in. I put my index finger to my mouth. "Shhhhh," I whispered. Down the hall, I heard Dez fumbling his way out of bed. I snapped the outer bathroom locks in place and ran to his door to greet him just as he opened it. "Heeeeeeeey!" I said with a smile.

Thud! Thud! Thud!

Dez looked up at me and squinted. "What the fuck is wrong with you? Answer the damn door, RJ."

I improvised. "I came by to get you first. Is someone supposed to come by here?"

He squinted at me a second time. "No." He shoved me aside and headed toward the front door as I kept my eye on the bathroom. Aloof, I followed him down the hall. He put his face against the door; I got into a grappling position, as if I was about to enter a wrestling ring. Dez looked over at me again. "Hey, retard. What in the hell is wrong with you?"

I looked at myself in the mirror next to the door. I did look like an idiot. "Ummmm, I did some blow."

"How?"

I kicked what was left of the pimp on the floor in the ribs. "I just mixed it in with the blood from this asshole."

"That was a waste." He re-pressed his head against the door. "Who is it?" he asked.

"It's Linnwood Perry," the voice on the other side returned.

"What do you want?"

"Copper told me to come over here. I need something taken care of."

Dez looked at me as if I had an answer for the intentions of our visitor. I simply shrugged my shoulders.

The illustrious Linnwood Perry was the leader of a vampire gang who ran the Beverly Hills and Bel Air area: The BBPs, or the Blue Blooded Perrys. They were a bunch of wannabe rich kids who loved coke and all dressed similarly in Fred Perry tennis sweaters, stack haircuts, and white leather tennis shoes. All of them had the last name Perry: Linnwood Perry, Greg Perry, Lance Perry, et cetera. We thought it was pretty lame, but truth be told, they were a ruthless bunch. The name and look came from a gang of soccer hooligans in England called the Perry Boys. The originators were these poor kids from the streets that stole clothing and put out this vibe that they were these normal preppy kids and then they'd just kick the shit out of people.

Linnwood surveyed the room. "Looks like some partying went on here tonight. Wow, look at this loser."

He wandered over to the pimp.

"Damn, you Knucklers sure are dirtbags."

"So, what's the deal, Linn?" I asked as I yawned, dipped a cigarette in the pimp's eye socket and lit it. For some reason the blood from the eye mixed with a cigarette and fire was tastier than just dipping it in blood. If Perry wasn't a vampire like Dez and me, I guess he might have found it intimidating.

"We have a snitch." Perry produced a pack of Dunhills from the pocket of his button down that was nicely pressed under his V-neck sweater. Covering his nose with a monogrammed hanky, he bent down to the pimp, pressed the filter end of the cigarette into one of the missing tooth craters in the mouth and then lit it with a Zippo by torching the roof of the pimp's mouth. I'm not going to lie, it was pretty cool.

Dez wasn't so impressed. "Yeah, and?"

"Well, since the Knucklers have become the Battlesnakes's whipping bitches since the—hmmm—how do I say this... incident—" he looked at Dez and then back at me, "—we all feel it would be better if you took care of the problem."

I arched my back to tower over Linnwood. "Who is we?"

With his cigarette dripping between his index finger and his middle finger like a pretentious asshole, he took a drag. "Me. Copperhead. That's who *we* is."

I popped my thumb in and out of my mouth. "Copperhead? He has no say over what we do in our area."

Dez moved a little closer to me. "RJ. He kind of does now. King Cobra doesn't bother with this low-level shit anymore."

I flashed Dez a shit look. He was friends with Copperhead and I didn't trust any of those Rasta fucks. I looked back toward Perry. "So, if that's the case, what's the story? Is this guy a Perry?"

"Yes. Apparently, Gavin—"

I looked back at Dez and giggled a little, made a limp wristed gesture and mouthed the name Gavin. Dez turned away from me to hide his face. He was laughing.

"Real funny, RJ," Linnwood said, shoving me. "How about I just leave now and let you deal with the Snakes?"

I wiped my smirk clean. "Okay, dude. Relax."

"Anyway, this asshole has been blabbing to these two slices of bacon for a boatload of coke. It's all confiscated from high-level busts. He's giving the pigs maps of the city and where all of us run things, and also giving them locations of exact compounds. The guy is a pussy and he would rather have the coke and the cadavers handed to him by the cops than deal with our way of doing things."

I smacked myself on the side of the head. "Are you fucking kidding me? Linn, you gotta control your boys. What's in it for the cops? Did your rat tell them that they could be turned?"

Perry nodded his head. "I guess. That is unless the LAPD is planning some kind of bust. I sincerely doubt that, though."

My mouth dropped. When were people going to realize that isn't the way all this vampire shit worked? "What I don't get is why we have to take care of this problem."

"Simple: the Snakes don't want to get everyone all freaked out over the cops knowing everything about the territories and the gangs. That being said, Gavin meets with these cops in your area so they don't get busted by us. In all honesty, your territory, your problem."

I looked at Dez again and shrugged my shoulders. "I suppose that makes sense. Killing another idiot is killing another idiot. Where and when? Is there anything we should know about this Gavin?"

Dez giggled.

"I mean is there anything special about him?"

"Not very big. Typical BBP. He's meeting these guys in an hour over behind the Samsung building on Wilshire. Do you know where that is?"

"It's only the biggest fucking building in the area with a huge, neon-blue sign on top. Consider it done," I assured Linnwood. "But let's make things clear: you go tell Copperhead that this isn't going to be a regular thing. This is your mess, Linn." I swept my hand down the shoulder of his white, cable-knit sweater. "I've always been curious, where do you guys buy all these expensive threads anyway?"

Linnwood plucked my hand off his arm and dropped it back to my side as if he was discarding a plastic bag full of dog crap. "Posers on Melrose, idiot." He shoved me on the chest. "You should shop there. 'Who Farted?'" he said, reading my bleached t-shirt out loud. "Classy. You should really learn how to do your laundry."

Rather than furthering our runway model fashion fight, I tapped Dez on the back. "Dez, see him out of here and around the block." And then, I flicked Linnwood on the chin. "You're lucky that a random Knuckler didn't pop you for being over here."

As soon as I shuffled them out, I headed back to the bathroom, unlocked all the deadbolts, and grabbed the whore from her new stoop atop of the toilet. "Shhhh," I reminded her.

Throwing her over my shoulder, I rushed her down the hall and into my bedroom. I quickly opened my closet and threw her in there. I nabbed a pair of handcuffs that were for some reason hanging from a belt loop on a pair of old jeans, cuffed her hands and then locked her around a hanger bar. Frumpily, she dropped flat-footed and broke the hanger bar in the center. My clothes dumped off the bar and all over her.

"Stay quiet or you're dead."

"I got nowhere to go," she said falling into the mound of shit she dumped everywhere.

I can't tell you to this day why I didn't throw her out the window to deal with my dogs in the backyard. Regretfully, I just didn't.

✂

"This is lame. Why didn't you tell me that the Battlesnakes were going to start using us for this vice principal bullshit, Dez?"

"Let's not get into this, RJ. You know why."

I left it at that. I did know why we owed them. I just liked to try and forget the fact that I indebted myself to the most dangerous thugs in Los Angeles. They were the faux-Rasta, drug-running leaders of the vampy underworld. Regrettably, I had to bow down to a bunch of dingbats who couldn't have come up with a better name than the Battlesnakes.

We both sat on a fire escape on the side of the building, overlooking the alley where Linnwood told us the snitch was gonna be waiting for his pig buddies.

Dez and I dangled our legs over the railing, trying to be quiet. Along with the super strength, vampires have an acute sense of hearing, so we didn't want to set off any alarms for this Gavin Perry to know that his jig was up.

I pointed to a billboard across the street for a vampire film called *The Chronicles of Nightshayde: Our Darkness.* "Your boy," I said to Dez. On the advertisement was Hollywood's latest vampire pin-up tool, holding hands with a teenage girl. A red moon separated them. He was flexing his muscles toward the shadow of a werewolf that appeared to supernaturally cradle the girl.

"I prefer the books," he admitted.

I cocked my head toward him. "Really? You prefer the books? So, you're admitting you've read them?"

He lashed back, becoming uppity. "Hasn't everyone?"

"Ummm. No."

"God, RJ. Leave me alone. So I read some vampire books."

I put my arm around Dez. It was better to leave him alone sometimes than to constantly bag on him for his idiotic pastimes and behavior. This wasn't one of those times.

"'Ello, Gavin. Would you like to take down your knickers and let me

15

give your cock a good flogging?"

He shoved me away, laughing. "Get off!"

In all honesty, I always gave Dez a lot of shit. He tried to put out this aura that he was this chosen god among living-dead people, but he was just another street shmuck trying to swindle the next sucker waiting in line to be killed.

I guess if I were to call someone my little brother, it would be him. Hard to say who was older though, I suppose. None of us really knew our ages. I did guess that I was about thirty-something and that he was about twenty-something, but there was never any real way to tell. We simply couldn't remember where we came from or who we were. I know that I was found on the street, eating rats by an older member of the current Knucklers named Pico. I didn't know much beyond that. That's where I found Dez, too: vermin feasting on the urine-flooded streets of a dead city.

"Dude, quiet," Dez whispered as he pointed below.

Two cops pulled up about a block away and walked down the alley. One of them was carrying a duffle bag. It wasn't like a gym bag. It was one of those bags you see the SWAT team unloading after a huge bust.

"Bingo," I said. Using the front bar of the rusted fire escape, Dez and I slowly pulled ourselves up. When he was halfway, I kicked out his left foot. In a wimpy voice, I mocked him. "I prefer the books."

"Let it go, RJ," he said, as he grabbed onto the rail of the jiggling fire escape.

As predicted, a tennis sweater-wearing BBP sashayed from the other end of the alley toward the cops. Dez and I crept down a flight of stairs in an attempt to get our super ears within reach of the conversation.

Gavin went over and fist bumped the cops. "Zup, Rogers? Zup, Picky?"

"Not much, Gavin. Whatchu got for us?"

I nudged Dez and went limp wristed like I had before, mouthing the name Gavin in a negative fruity way.

"Something big is about to go down," Gavin returned. He was being honest. My ears smelled sincerity. Even a rat tells the truth sometimes.

One of the cops rolled back his sleeve and cut through a vein on his wrist almost up to his elbow.

"Wanna taste?" He took out a little baggy from his pocket and handed it to Gavin.

"Where did this shit come from anyway?" Gavin asked as he lifted the arm up, smeared the blood around a little and then shook some powder into the open wound. The numbing cut to the wrist, combined with the pain, made the cop shiver and shake like a wet hound. I figured the whole production was Gavin's way of convincing the nitwit detectives that they could be "turned".

Gavin ran his nose directly up the arm and swiftly brushed his head up at the end of the line. He stood upright for a second, the arm remained steady like a table. He closed his eyes, put his fingers up to both sides of his nose and snorted all the blood and drugs in like a vacuum. Gavin's etiquette was sloppy at best. Then again, I never got into snorting. I preferred the instantaneous rush of mainlining.

He shook off the split-second satisfaction and his eye bulged out.

"Goddamn, boys! That isn't coke."

"Nope, it isn't," one of the officers returned.

"Me likey, boys." Perry continued as he pushed the mystery powder into his brain with his index and middle fingers. "Like I was saying, some big shit is gonna happen."

"Like what?" one of the cops asked, holding back the duffle bag. I rolled my eyes. Even a shit like Gavin could have just swiped the thing from them and torn them to pieces.

Dez whispered in my ear. "Let's go now, get this over with."

"Shut the fuck up, Dez. I wanna hear this."

"Come on, dude!"

I held Dez back by grabbing his devil lock, and then cracked my fist with the back of his head in tow against the wall behind us. Stupid move. Gavin's ears picked up the sound. "Shit, Dez. He heard. Move!"

We both leapt down five flights from our perch. On the way down I instructed, "You take the fat one."

"They're both fat."

"Then... wherever you land, brother."

Dez shot me a wink. "I'll take the cops." He was hungry for swine. Like two starving Valkyries, we swam through the air toward our prey.

Dez landed on one of the weight-challenged cops as I subdued Gavin. I snatched his head and ripped off his sweater.

"You don't even deserve this, motherfucker. Your gang is lame, but you're just a rat." I quickly began pounding his head against a discarded toilet in the alley, still shit-covered by vagrants who used it as a port-a-potty.

I looked over at Dez who was having a good time with his first pig. He ripped the asshole's hands off by snapping the bones and stretching them loose from the veins. Then, he shoved them down his pants, one in front and one in back. Always light on his feet, Dez shuffled steadily and swept the leg completely off the other cop who was trying to make a break for it. The cop tripped, face first. The sound of his nose breaking sideways as the rest of his face splattered like a bum's diarrhea on a curb made my eyes light up.

I went back to work on Gavin Perry. The snitch. He was after all, another vampire. I shoved his head into the bowl of the toilet. His ears crushed through the porcelain as they were cut loose by smashed shards from the seat. Furiously, I bounced him face first into the bottom of the basin. I don't want to seem overly romantic about my kills, but he wasn't going down easily. I had to use all of my strength. We had the element of surprise, which worked for us... even when dealing with a coke head.

I looked at Dez, who broke the arms backwards on his original puppet-cop. Dez discarded him by throwing him to the ground and proceeded to the second cop, who was crying with his face still buried in gravel.

He tore the law enforcement-issued pants off and yelled, "Damn, RJ, what cop goes commando?" He picked up the first cop by his neck while he took his boot and smashed the head of the other poor fuck on the ground. "This is gonna be hilarious."

I went back to Gavin. I lifted his head out of the empty toilet. "What's the big deal about to happen?"

He spat in my face. "Fuck you, junkie."

"Really?" I palmed his head with my right hand and beat it against the bottom of the toilet bowl again until my hand went completely through the front of his face. I opened my clenched hand, poked his eyeballs outward and swiped out his brain. After extracting his mind, I grabbed his neck, thrust my other arm up to the elbow through the face-cave and disconnected his skullcap. I spun around like a college hippie playing ultimate Frisbee and whizzed it toward Dez.

Why get rid of it? It probably wouldn't have tasted good. Vampire body parts all tasted like Mexican water. They were generally more dirt parts than liquid. Only the real desperate sickos liked the taste of human transfused to vamp blood... the real psychos.

"Whew." I sat down for a second and looked at Dez's flesh sculpture. "Come on, Dez." I figured my "head games" would surely overshadow anything Dez had to offer up artistically.

"Do you think I'm a pussy for reading books now?" He had taken the cops and put them on top of each other with their pants down. He might have even put the top cop's dick in the other cop's ass. Body parts from his showpiece covered the scene, but Dez lined them up as if he were delivering some sort of Al Capone-like message.

"Get your friend to pull the stolen car around; we gotta get rid of—" I made the limp wristed gesture again, "—Gaaaaaavin's body."

Dez snatched the hand out of the pitcher-cop's pants and threw it at me. "High five!"

I batted the hand away and picked up the duffle bag. It was heavier than I expected.

"Well, open it." Dez licked his lips and skipped over next to me. I'm serious, he skipped. That was how excited he got for a fix.

Slowly, I zipped back the top of the bag. Dez's eyes ignited.

"Holy shit, Dez." I looked over at him. "There is like fifty pounds of Charlie in here."

He dug his hand down to the bottom of the bag and felt around. Then, he pulled out a brick and slit the top open with his bullet fingernail, scooped up a little taste tester and dabbed it on his lip. He used his tongue to roll it around on his gums. After that, he picked out another dollop and sucked it into both of his nostrils. Immediately, his face puckered up so that his top lip touched the point on his ratty nose.

"Fuck." He sneezed, catching a handful of his own bloody snot. His mouth opened up as he gasped for air and he cranked his head around in a circle.

"RJ. This ain't Charlie, motherfucker. This is heroin, dude."

"What are you talking about? Why would Gavin Perry be getting a big duffle bag full of heroin? We run that shit."

"I don't know. Maybe these pigs made a mistake when they stole the evidence. I guess I don't care. We just scored enough H to last us months."

"Dez, are you nuts? King Cobra is gonna want this shit hand delivered to him, like tomorrow."

"Fuck him, RJ. We'll tell him that the cops didn't bring shit. Tell him there was some kind of mix-up. We cleaned up their mess and we should be paid for it."

I looked at the bag and licked my gums with my mouth closed. "That has to be the dumbest idea I've ever heard."

Just then, the Dezien's stolen car pulled around so we could haul off Gavin's body and destroy the evidence of a vampire walking around and talking to cops. Dez threw the duffle bag at me and tapped me on the shoulder.

"It's your call. Free heroin is free heroin. Cobra will never find out, dude. These are the only ones who saw us, the two pigs and that snitch." He pointed at the cops buttfucking then at Gavin, whose mangled face was somewhat supported by his toilet seat necklace. Dez then pointed upward with his index finger. "Someone up there might have seen the bag." He switched fingers and flipped off the sky. "But since there is no God... he's got nothin' to say."

III
PROSTITUTES

Dez dropped me off with Gavin's corpse. I dumped the body on top of the pimp and threw the duffle bag in the corner. This time I didn't forget. I headed over to my room to see if the weird little girl was still there. Besides, The Deziens would be over at any time to start the cleanup process and they didn't interact a whole lot with humans. The last thing I wanted was some dumb, dead kid on my hands.

I shook off the feeling of carnage and tapped on the door to my closet.

"Hello? Little whore girl? Are you still here?"

She cautiously poked the closet door open with her huge prostitute shoes. "Yeah," she replied.

I opened the door a little more so I could see her hazel eyes and sun-freckled face. "Do you want to come out and talk about all of this? All the bad people are gone. I'm not going to kill you," I assured her.

"All of the bad people? Then what are you?" She held up the handcuffs. They weren't on her wrists anymore.

"Fair enough. I guess I'm a bad person, too." I looked down at her platform shoes, expecting a nut shot at any minute. "Please don't kick me in the sack."

She kicked at the door and started to stand up.

"Do you want coffee or something?" I asked.

"Is it going to have blood in it?"

"Normally, yes. I think I can brew you up a cup that doesn't have any blood in it though."

I started walking toward the kitchen. I turned my head slightly to see her peering back toward the closet. A grin quickly came and went on my face as she picked up her tasseled, silver purse and started following me.

✂

She sipped on the coffee that I told the Dezien to make for her. She had showered and got most of the grossness off her body. I was still somewhat bewildered that she was so calm.

"So, explain this to me, RJ. Don't you think you're gonna get caught killing people and selling drugs?"

I pointed across the room at the bottom feeder who was doing his job filleting and disposing of the pimp's and Gavin's bodies. "As far as getting busted for slaughtering a bunch of junkies, pimps, and lowlifes, not really. That's his job."

She flicked at her puffy, little cheeks. "Well, how do you live in this house?"

"I guess you could say I'm housesitting." The truth was that I lived in a washed-up child actress' house. She ran into some hard times when her tweeny show *Dag Nabbit* got cancelled and she turned to heroin.

To avoid being caught in the act by the lecherous paparazzi—who seemed set on driving her to suicide by dubbing her "Drug Habit", a play on the title of her show—she bought a heroin den in Hancock Park. The only people who knew about the place were her accountant and me. I paid the bills and everything that came in the mail, so by chance it became my house. I figured she forgot about it... and about me. I doubted that I would ever see that bitch again. It turns out she kind of fucked me over and made me an open target to all my enemies.

The bottom feeder surveyed a nice prime cut and then threw it in a bucket.

"Hey, what's-yer-face, let the dogs in and feed them," I instructed him, as if he were a fraternity pledge.

The maudlin, teenager vampire did as he was told, but not without shuffling his feet across the floor like he was walking through a foot of maple syrup.

"That kid can't be any older than me." The tartness of the black coffee made her almost nonexistent lip cringe. "Do you have any sugar?"

"Yeah. Don't try and go anywhere. If you think that I won't kill you, someone like him will." I pointed again at the bottom feeder that was mid-quest, progressing only ten feet across my living room. "Let's just say he's anxious to make his first human kill."

She opened her legs in the direction of the dork. I took the liberty of kicking them closed before he saw her. I walked into the kitchen backwards, continuing to watch her. "He's actually only thirteen. His balls haven't dropped yet."

"Meaning?"

"We haven't jumped him in yet. He's Dez's big progeny."

I returned to the corner. The girl had slowly glided her way onto the couch.

My Great Dane and French Mastiff came bounding into the house with the slug lord kid trailing them at a turtle's pace. First, the dogs came to me in the kitchen, sniffed around a little, licked my hands and then proceeded to introduce themselves to my guest.

"What are their names?" She scratched the top of the Mastiff's head, causing a leg tantrum. The dog tried to give the girl his paw as the Dane leapt on the couch and started salivating all over her shoulder.

"The big one drooling on you is Leroy and the littler one trying desperately to have you shake his hand is Skillet."

Leroy stretched out his long legs and dropped himself into her lap to which she gasped.

She put both her hands on both the dogs' heads and compared their sizes. She looked at me, avoiding eye contact. "Why don't they attack you? Did you hypnotize them?"

Skillet somehow managed to sniff his way into the girl's crotch. Both dogs' tails were wagging frantically. The little whore was, after all, their first real human interaction in a long time. Deziens didn't count as humans either; for all intents and purposes, they were vampires as well.

"That's a misconception about... well... vampires. I figure they like us so much because they think we're hurt. You know. Technically we're dead."

"Lame," she said, as Leroy leaned against her. "Okay, so I guess you're in a gang. Can I ask you more about the other thing?"

"First tell me your name."

"Well, my real name is Bailia. But that asshole you're cutting up over there called me 'Jailbait', seeing as how I was the youngest trick he ever put to the street." She dumped half of the sugar shaker into her coffee.

"Ask away, Bait," I said, smiling.

"Okay." She clung onto a crucifix around her neck as if she was in control. "Does this scare you, monster?"

I snatched it in my hand. "Yes. Religion scares me. Can this hurt me? No."

She let out a defeated puff onto her hot coffee. Skillet, not alarmed by her sudden movements, gave up looking for attention and walked over by the door and sat down. Leroy had given up seconds before that and was fast asleep in Bait's lap.

"What about garlic?" She scratched at her temple. "Can it kill you?"

"That depends. It can probably kill my chances of getting laid."

She laughed and her tightened shoulders dropped a little. Her eyes widened a bit. "How does it work? Can you be killed?"

"Okay, rather than go through a million back-and-forth questions, I'll explain it to you in the simplest of terms."

I grabbed the pimp's arm and took a sip. "I can't live forever and even if I could I would choose not to. Most of us are killed or last as long as the average human." I belched and a little squirt of the junk blood shot back into my mouth. The blood was getting stale quickly. "We are more powerful than regular people, but we can't fly or anything like that. On top of that, we have this insane healing ability."

"Huh?"

"Yeah, if I get stabbed or shot or something my body rejuvenates and heals pretty quickly."

"Then how do you die?"

"I imagine that you'd probably have to pull our heads off to put us down."

"Can you turn into a bat, Batman?"

Leroy looked up at her and yawned. Then, without hesitation, put his monstrous noggin and mite-infested floppy ears back in her lap and moaned as if even he was sick of the conversation.

I lit a cigarette to get the rancid taste of the arm out of my mouth. "No, that's all bullshit, smartass. Being whatever it is we are—and there are hundreds of us—is more of a blood disorder, I guess, that makes us hypersensitive to light. If I went outside during the day, I wouldn't melt or turn to dust or anything like that, but I would be in a great deal of pain after about a minute. From what I read online it's called photophobia. Beyond that, I don't know who my parents were. I don't know if I have some weird disease or not. I do know we can walk and talk and think. But I don't know why we're here."

"So, wouldn't that make you a zombie?"

I hadn't explained this to anyone besides a peewee in a long time. I shook my head. "Not really. I can function. I do need nourishment though. That's where the blood comes in. We can eat raw flesh, but blood from a beating heart is the best because the blood in our bodies always dries up. We need to replenish it to keep us walking."

"What about the heroin?"

"Well, Bait, that's called addiction." I looked at her arms and couldn't tell if she was familiar with scag like most Hollywood hookers. As far as I knew, it was the easiest way to get a tween to turn tricks: get them hooked.

"The thing is that you can't inject it into a bloodstream that doesn't have enough blood to support it. I tried it. It's kind of worthless and the buzz doesn't last."

She tickled Leroy's ears. "Hmmmm."

"We don't have fangs, except for a couple of sets who have metal fangs made for them. So, we came up with this system to get high. It's really a variation on what several others have done over time to enjoy wine, ferment blood, snort speed, whatever."

"You want this?" The bottom feeder interrupted, holding up a watch. "Looks pretty nice." Skillet lifted his head off the floor and snarled a little.

"What is it?"

He looked at the faceplate. "Seiko."

"Keep it." I looked back at Bait. "See, this is how we make money. We sell drugs, loot suckers; take their money and their drugs. Not a great life."

She hid behind her hair. "Kind of like being a hooker?"

Against my better judgement, I got closer. I wanted to brush her hair out of the way but pulled back before I made contact with her. "Yeah."

She sneezed on my hand that dangled a few feet away from her face. "You seem pretty smart. Did you go to college?"

I wiped my hand on the back of my jeans and moved away. I didn't know if she sneezed at me to signal that she didn't like to be touched, but I didn't want to touch her anyway. The hair thing was just annoying me. "What part of not being out during the day didn't you understand? Our choices are pretty much night school, University of Phoenix or learn from the street. The resources are much limited to nothing. The only thing that we know is how to be hustlers and what some of us learn from reading. That's why we sell drugs and steal."

Bait sipped her coffee; she looked happy with the sugary sweetness that warmed her tongue. "So, how many of these vampire gangs are there?"

"In Hollywood, all the sets are divided into different neighborhoods. I'd say there are around ten or so. It's a lot like the gangs in South Central, and the streets are clearly defined. We're the Knucklers. Our area, and the heroin area, runs from La Brea to Fairfax and from Sunset to Wilshire. There are some smaller sets mixed in the area but they don't interfere with our business. The Batwangers are in our area."

Trying to be inconspicuous, she wiped her nose with her hand and then brushed it into Leroy's back hair. "The Batwangers?"

"Wait. Did you just wipe a fucking booger on my dog?" I pushed a box of tissues on the table in front of her.

She ignored the Kleenex. "Whatever. I have a cold."

I pulled a tissue out of the box and wiped off Leroy's back.

"Whatever? Leroy doesn't want your sniffles."

"What are the Batwangers?" she asked.

I crumpled the rag in my hand and discarded it over my shoulder. "Batwangers. Yeah, chicks with dicks… a tree and tits."

"Holy shit!" She spat her coffee across the room. "I see them every night at Carl's Jr. on the corner of La Brea and Santa Monica."

"They don't give us any trouble. I guess we've always figured that if anyone is that desperate to fuck a bitch with a bad weave and shoulders like a linebacker, they should just have it."

"How do they…"

"They aren't snobs about drugs. They'll do anything. Most important, they suck cock and then when the John starts shooting his wad, they bite off their dicks and essentially eat them alive." I sucked my cigarette down to the filter and put it out on the coffee table.

"Ewww."

"Yeah, it's pretty nasty. All the gangs are pretty peaceful with each other, and all the action is delegated by a stoner gang of Rastas called the Battlesnakes."

"Seriously? The Battlesnakes? That's the best name they could come up with? That has to be the lamest name I've ever heard. The Battlesnakes? Like rattlesnakes? You're kidding me, right?"

"I did say they were stoners. Not exactly known for their intelligence. They're some brutal badass fucks though. I just stay out of their way."

Truth be told about my relationship with the Battlesnakes, no matter how far I go to avoid them, they always manage to plow into me.

"So, what about all this blood after you kill someone? Do you just clean it up?"

I stood up and walked to the opposite corner of the room. The dogs both got up and followed me. Leroy shook the foundation of my house as he leapt from Bait's side.

"See this?" I grabbed the bottom feeder by the shoulder. "Little peewees like this kid come over and collect all the blood for us—at least what they can salvage." I walked over to the fridge, opened it, and pulled out a bottle. Both dogs sat in front of me in the kitchen, expecting a treat. They smelled meat everywhere. "Then, we ferment it to make beer and wine. It's pretty much shit." I took a swig off the bottle. "But it helps take the edge off on a night like tonight. Then, they take what's left of the bodies and bury them."

"You're a slob. I thought vampires were s'pose to be all romantic and musical and stuff."

I put the bottle back in the fridge. "Fuck that. I've never worn a ruffled shirt and I've never played the harpsichord."

She picked up a CD off the table and brushed away a rock of base that Dez was saving for later. "Can you play any music?"

"I can play a couple chords on a guitar, but that's about it."

She squinted and bit her lip. "L. Byron Nightshayde is a classically trained music guy. He writes songs for his girlfriends all the time. I heard his album at a record store. It was pretty dark."

"Bait, that's all bullshit. Nightshayde is some character from a bunch of crap books. It's no more real than—"

"Batman," she said.

I slammed the fridge shut. "For your information, the tattoo is for The Faction. They're a punk band. You sure are a mean little bitch, aren't you? I should be asking your story, but to tell you the truth you're about a dime a dozen in L.A. Runaway. Turning ass for junk. Typical. Did you come to L.A. to become a big movie star?"

"No, asshole, I came here to get away from being raped every night. As for the junkie hooker, I heard that young ass makes a lot of money. Jeez. At least I don't have a Batman tattoo. You got any other crappy ink?"

I subtly rubbed my ass. I didn't want to make it too obvious that I had something even worse. So, rather than make a dick of myself yet again, I avoided the question.

"Hey, who's-yer-name," I said to the bottom feeder. "Would you give these dogs something to eat? They're annoying the fuck out of me." I pointed to Skillet who was sniffing and licking Leroy's ass. Not uncommon.

The bottom feeder went into the meatpacking fridge at the other end of the kitchen and pulled out two steaks. The dogs strutted over to him and sat at his feet.

"Cook them up a little bit. I don't want my family getting worms."

"Yes, master," he said, almost belittling me.

I rubbed the dog drool off my right hand and went back to the living room.

"How old are you, RJ?"

"I'm not totally positive. I imagine around thirty."

"Pretty cool. Thirty-year-old gangster/vampire with a Batman tattoo."

"Enough, you little shit. I should have listened to Dez and jacked your ass up when I had the chance. I'm a fucking killer. I can kill you."

The door unbolted and flew open from behind me.

"Yeah, RJ, you should have killed her." Dez walked in and stumbled over to Bait, grabbing a lock of her greasy hair. "You are such a pussy."

"You can't keep me locked in this bathroom forever," Bait squealed.

"Shut the fuck up, whore," Dez yelled back. "You'll be dead soon enough." He turned to me with his hand in an L shape and brushed his devil lock out of his dilated eyes. "How stupid are you, RJ?"

"If I remember correctly, Dez, you were about that age when I decided to jump you in, bitch. I let you off easy because you're such a little pussy. Remember?"

His head titled to the side and he let out a disgusted sigh, almost as if he just farted. "That's not the same thing. I'm like you. She's not."

Bait's muffled voice interrupted. "I can be like you though, right? I mean you can bite my neck, right?"

"Shut up before I kick this door down and bite your neck off."

"Be quiet, Bait, and let the big kids talk now," I said.

"Bait? RJ, what the fuck is Bait? Did you name it? What is wrong with you?"

"Me. I'm Bait," she said from behind the bathroom door. "So, you can bite my neck and make me a vampire, right?"

"Shut up!" Dez and I both yelled at the door. "There are no girl vampires."

"Listen, Dez, I'm not about killing kids. Humans are cattle and all that, but I really can't bring myself to kill anyone who's twelve. Maybe I should have killed your ass before your balls dropped."

"Dude, you're being so stupid. What are we going to do, keep her around and bang her until she dies?"

"Will that make me a vampire? In the *Nightshayde* movies, L. Byron bit Amethyst Rose and turned her to save her from the Elders."

"Bait!" I shook the doorknob. "Seriously, shut up. You can't make someone a vampire. That's another dumb myth. It's horseshit."

"Bummer," she whispered.

"You seriously can't think that we're going to keep this little girl around. Do you know how much trouble we would get in?"

"With the elders?" Bait said.

I pounded on the bathroom door. "Christ! There are no elders. Be quiet for one second, please."

"Whatever, Batman."

"Jesus, RJ, you showed her your gay tattoo?"

"He didn't show me the one on his ass."

"So, you didn't show her your ass. You didn't even screw her? It's a tattoo of the Tasmanian Devil."

"Bwaaa-ha-ha-ha! God, RJ, you sure can pick 'em."

I rubbed my ass a little, but acted like I was picking a wedgie. "Both of you: fuck off."

The bottom feeder walked over and handed Dez a wallet. "Looks pretty filled, Dez."

Dez snapped it out of his hands. "It better all be there. You have your shit meat, now finish cleaning up and get out of here before the sun comes up." Dez then spit in the kid's face.

"Thank you," the bottom feeder said.

I heard Bait move close to the door. "Is this some kind of club?" she teased.

Without even hesitating a second, Dez kicked the door off the hinges, knocking Bait on her back. "I'm gonna enjoy ripping your sarcastic little ass to pieces, whore."

She was terrified for the first time that night.

Dez lifted the door out of his way and bent down. "What's it going to be?" He drilled his heel into her stomach. "Do you want me to just flat out pull your head off? Nah, that would be much too easy. I'll just take off one limb at a time, starting with your tongue."

"Leave her, Dez! And a tongue isn't a limb." I lunged at him, knocking him against the broken door. I shoved his face into the bathroom mirror and then smashed it into the sink a couple of times. It didn't hurt him at all, but he got the message.

"This is your fuck up, RJ. This is all you, asshole."

I pointed down the hall to the front door. "*Vamonos.*"

He pointed at Bait. "Bitch, you'd better hope this faggot never leaves your side. I wouldn't give a drop of diarrhea for you." Then he stomped away.

I threw her a towel to use as a tow rope to help her up off the bathroom linoleum. She stroked a chipped tooth; it was a small price to pay for Dez plowing over her with the door. For some asinine reason, I felt partly responsible.

As much as I would like to say that I taught Dez a lesson, the fact was, I didn't. He was constantly insubordinate to my leadership because he thought of us as "bros". But the fact was I was the leader of the Knucklers. It wasn't him and it never would be. Until I died, he was nothing more than a little brother and a kick around.

IV
CHILDREN

I looked at Dez across the kitchen table. The duffle bag full of heroin sat in the middle. "Okay, tool, what's your big super-duper plan?"

"Don't be a dick," he said as he dug into his teeth with a toothpick and then flung his hair out of his eyes. "The way I see it, no matter what I come up with, it's better than that." He pointed to Bait who was sitting on the couch, flipping through the channels with a remote. Leroy and Skillet sat on both sides of her, dead asleep. They were protecting her from Dez, nonetheless.

"I'm not going to tell you again. She's staying here for now until I can figure out what to do with her."

Dez picked up a knife from the table and put it to his neck. "How about—" he dragged the knife across his throat, "—we kill the bitch."

I stood up and knocked the knife out of his hand, scraping his ear. "How about I kill you?"

Dez threw up his arms, surrendering. "I'm just goofing around, brotha."

His shitty attitude was starting to get old. "What's your awesome plan, Dez?"

"Jesus, RJ." Dez picked up one of the dog's tennis balls and lobbed it across the room.

"Ouch," Bait squeaked as the ball pelted her in the jaw.

I slapped him across the head. "That was totally unnecessary."

"What? I was trying to throw it to the dogs."

"The dogs are sleeping and they hate you anyway," I reminded him.

Dez looked over at Bait. "Hey, little whore thing."

"What?" Bait said, annoyed, as she massaged her jawbone.

Dez swiveled his fists over his eyes and in a baby voice added, "Sowwy."

Bait tapped at the remote control, turning up the volume on the TV. "Whatever, jerk," she said under her breath.

I patted the duffle bag at the cloth handles. "Get on with it, Dez."

"Fine. Well, we both know that no one saw us kill that BBP and those cops, right?"

I kicked my chair back and put my feet on the table. "Yeah."

"Then, why don't we just take this and move it ourselves?"

"Where do you want me to start, Dez? First of all, Linnwood Perry knows what we did. Secondly, he was sent to us from the Battlesnakes. Thirdly, how are we going to sell fifty pounds of H around here without anyone being suspicious about where the hell it came from?"

Dez became animated like a TV pitchman delighting an audience of retirement home suckers. "That's the beauty. They don't even know this heroin exists. They were expecting coke."

"So, they think we traded the coke for heroin. Either way, we'd be screwed. I'm sure Linnwood and King Cobra are expecting us to deliver whatever we stole from the gathering back there in the alley."

"We lie. Where are we going to trade fifty pounds of heroin for coke and fly under the radar? The Snakes control all the drugs. They'd know."

"Exactly my point, dildo. How are we going to sneak out that much extra junk onto the streets?"

"We don't sell it on our streets. We sell this shit in Culver City."

"De Sangre territory? Are you fucking crazy?"

"Who cares about those spics? Listen, I get all the bottom feeders to go down there and sell like low-life peddlers. They know the territory, and all they have to do is stay away from the areas with El Reinado De Sangre tags. We let them sell the dope like they are just nobodies and bring the money back to us. It's not like we're sending them out with pounds. We give each of them a couple of twenty-bags a day."

I thought about it for a second. I'd never tell him straight up, but it *was* a great idea. I stroked my fingers down my chin. "I don't know, Dez. If we miscalculate even a little bit, we'll be dead as shit. You know as well as I do that if we even fuck up slightly, King Cobra is going to have our nuts."

"I'm going to do all the legwork, pussy. Start acting like a leader and not—" he pointed to Bait, who was petting Leroy and Skillet, "—a babysitter."

"Watch what you say, Dez. I'm dead serious. There is a line not even you can cross and you're getting really fucking close to it."

"It's just—"

"It's just what? You're a nobody in the Knucklers, bro. You're a nobody on the streets. If you disappeared, nobody would care. At all. The Battlesnakes have it out for us."

"According to Copperhead—"

I bounced back into the conversation. "Okay, that right there. When did you and Copperhead become boyfriends? Even mentioning his name during a conversation about stealing drugs from his gang shows your complete lack of understanding. They hate us. We're lucky to be alive—"

"You're not alive," Bait interjected from across the room.

I kept my eyes deadlocked on Dez's. "Shut up, Bait," I grunted from the side of my mouth.

"Come on, RJ. Let me do this. I mean, you're going to get most of the money anyway and you won't be doing any work at all."

I grabbed the duffle bag and excused myself from the table. "Get your hair cut."

Dez sprung up from his chair. "So? It's on?"

"Call a meeting at the garage. I'm in, but I have to know that everyone else is cool with this."

Just as Dez was about to show me some love, the remote control rapped him in the face.

"Fuck no," he yelled as he started toward Bait. "You're dead, whore."

Bait backpedaled on the couch. Leroy and Skillet jumped in front of her, grimacing like they were rabid. They emitted warning snaps at Dez, broadening their parameter around Bait by moving their dense frames sideways, walling her in.

Dez stepped back to the table, seizing his black army battalion jacket off the back of his chair. "So, this is how it's going to be, huh?" He walked over my imaginary line that I told him not to ever cross and simply said, "Thanks, brother."

I stood my ground over him. "Make the call if you want this to happen. Don't say a word to Copperhead. I'll sell your ass down with him and not even bat an eye. Don't even think about fucking with me, Dez. I will ship your ass back to skid row COD with all your pussy followers."

Without saying another word, he moved past me, bumping my shoulder, staring Bait down the whole time.

Bait scrunched up in the corner of the couch and mimicked his fake crying. "Sowwy," she mocked.

The door slammed behind him.

"Why?" I asked her.

"What better stuff do I have to do with my life?" Bait said.

"Why not go home to your family? You have that choice. Dez and I don't. We have no families."

"Well, then how did you get here? How did you get on the streets?"

I scratched at my temple. "Not sure exactly."

"Anyway, this is a free ride for me. I don't like living on the streets either."

"I've already told you that we can't make vampires. Look, Bait, you've been here for a week now and although you lock yourself in the bathroom with your shower mat while Dez and I do our—"

"Vampy stuff?"

"Yeah, vampy stuff."

"I'm never in the way. I sleep on the bathroom floor."

"Shower mat," I corrected her.

"Shower mat," she agreed. "Do you really want me to go back out there and find another pimp? Maybe I can go hang out with those assholes at Hollywood High. I wanna see what you do."

"It's not real pretty. We are way more dangerous than any pimp you could ever find."

She frowned and tugged on my arm. "Think of it this way. I can lead pimps and Johns and frat boys back here for you to kill."

I thought about it for a second. "It's dangerous and kind of evil. The last thing I want to do is subject a twelve-year-old—"

"Whore," she inserted.

"That's not what I was going to say."

"I can be one of those peewee guys. I can, like, get my haircut all in my face and act all mysterious." She rambled on, jumping from one situation to another. "I don't like being in the bathroom. It sounds like you guys have a good time out here. I mean, I like heroin too."

I scratched my head. "Bait. Listen to me. You can't become a vampire. I assure you that it isn't a fun life, if you can even call it that."

"Then, I'll be a gangster. Or, I can be like a churro."

"First of all, it's *chola*. Secondly, no one in the Knucklers is Hispanic." I was close to throwing my arms up in frustration. How could someone who has been on the street for a year be so clueless?

"*Chola*, churro; what's the diff?"

"The 'diff' is that those kinds of gangsters are different from us. When they jump someone into one of their gangs, they just beat the shit out of them or make them shoot someone. We maim people. You saw what was left of your pimp and you saw one of our peewees clean that shit up."

She yanked my shirt off my shoulder. "I can clean the house."

I batted her hand away and straightened my shirt. "What are you, the hooker Cinderella? The answer is no. Go grab your overnight bag and go back to your life."

"RJ, I just thought—"

"You fucking thought wrong. Go back to school. Go home."

She started to well up, hid her freckly face behind her hair and pouted.

"Jesus, don't do that. Why would you cry? Did you ever think your parents might be concerned about you? You've been on the run for a long time now."

"They don't give a fuck at all, RJ. They don't care about me at all. My parents hate me. I wanna live here and do what you do."

"Goddammit, Bait."

She looked up from her skunky hair and blinked her eyes.

"Has that shit ever worked?" I asked her. "If you wanted a doll or a toy, maybe."

"It did work when I asked my pimp if I could get a pair of higher heeled shoes. It didn't work when I asked my mom to get my stepfather off me." She smiled a little bit.

I wanted to return the laugh but the fact was, it just wasn't funny. "This isn't a joke."

She reached over to me and gave me a quick hug. "Thanks, RJ."

The room felt like it shrunk as I became limp. I looked over her shoulder for an escape. Human touch. Yuck.

From a table behind her, she grabbed a shot glass. "I made you this."

I took it from her. "What's this?"

"It's some of my blood."

"Why?"

"Come on, vampire man. Will you just drink it?"

I didn't want to know where she drew the blood from. I guessed she was just a cutter or something. What a weird little kid.

"Okay."

I lifted the shot glass, cheered her and slammed it down.

She squealed and ran into her bathroom. Just as quickly as her whore shoes had reached the bathroom, I heard them clogging back. She poked her rosy-red face around the corner. "One more thing: can I sleep on your floor?"

"No."

"Cool. I want to meet the gang. Need to get ready." She fluffed up her hair. "Can you give me some money to go shopping on Melrose?"

"No."

She hopped back and forth on her feet. "Whyyyyyyy?"

"What's wrong with you?"

"You wanna know what's wrong with me? Fine. My stepfather used to make me finger myself in front of him while he jerked off. When he was about to blow his load, he'd press my head up against the corner of the room, drill it into the wall and open up my asshole so he could cum inside of me. He used to pin my younger sister down and make her lick his balls while he shoved his hand inside of her. He called her 'Pinball' and came in her face. You're a vampire, so why would you care?"

The room became silent. For the second time, I looked at the door for an escape. But rather than deal with anything, I pulled a bunch of blood-stained wadded bills from my jeans. "Take it. Go to Melrose. Go wherever you want."

She nabbed the money out of my hand and turned off the tantrum like it never occurred.

"Thanks."

V

COLLEAGUES

Bait and I turned the corner to the front of the Knuckler's garage. I spun a sign on the corner wall that had once said something about smog certification before the garage went up in flames.

"Home," I said to myself.

Bait pulled something out of the front pocket of her sock and started fiddling with a touchscreen.

"Wait. I didn't give you enough money for an iPod," I said as soon as I realized what she was playing with. "Where did you get this?"

Bait rolled her eyes up to me and crinkled her lip, playing tough. "Stole it."

I grabbed Bait's wrist, yanked the earbud out of her ear and looked her sternly in the eyes. "This isn't going to be easy at all, you know."

"Whatever," she spat back, grabbing the earbud cord from my hand and plugging it back into her head.

We were late to the meeting. Much to my dismay, Bait spent too much time picking out a "hardcore" introduction outfit that consisted of a black corset, spiked heels, a pair of skull-printed tights, a pleather mini-skirt, and a scarf/knee-high sock ensemble that matched the aforementioned tights. It was ridiculous.

So, we were late to a meeting that I called. As we walked in, everyone grew silent as if my entrance comically scratched a record. A wrench dropped somewhere in the middle of the gang. Not only was every Knuckler already there, but our tardiness gave Dez the opportunity to tell everyone in the gang about RJ and his dumb human prostitute.

The smell of musty towels, fried wood, and Bondo putty rose up from the floor and through my nose inside the dilapidated building where the

Knucklers met. It used to be Al's Body Shop until it burned down. The Friars Club it wasn't.

"See, I told you." Dez pointed at Bait. She slid behind my arm. No outfit could have made her look hardcore in the eyes of those asshole derelicts.

"What's up his ass," she said, tugging on the back of my belt.

I ground my teeth. "Shut up, Bait. I warned you about the hearing."

She shot me a thumbs up.

"Everyone, I asked you here to talk about something that could put us all in a shitload of danger," I said.

Crannnng!

A socket wrench beat against the blackened brick of the building, causing a snowstorm of torched building innards to fill the air.

Dez lowered the wrench, hacked up and spit a huge phlegm ball onto the floor. "Aren't any of you going to say anything about him bringing a human to the meeting?"

His eyes scanned the room for support. Knucklers gathered in a circle, scratched at their necks and flinched around trying to avoid making eye contact with him. It was nice to see Dez's ill-planned *coup d'état* going nowhere. The kid didn't have an ounce of leadership in him. I knew that nothing made him happier than the dream to overthrow my rule and then rape and suck down all of Bait's blood. Yeah, a badass bunch of vampires that team up on a twelve-year-old junkie girl.

Feeling good that the mutiny lasted less than a minute, I decided to push him back into the corner where he belonged. I looked at my wrist to the watch I didn't have. "Oh, are you here for the Girl Scout meeting, little girl?" I cracked with a sarcastic jeer. "That was at six."

The garage instantly erupted.

"Fuck you, RJ," Dez shot back.

"I called this meeting for you, jerk. I'm here to tell everyone about your stupid plan and then, if we unanimously agree, we'll do it." They all looked over to Dez. "This has nothing to do with the little girl, Dez. This is about you, and I'm giving you the chance. So... speak."

He cleared his throat. It was the first time that he ever had the chance to really propose anything important to the Knucklers. "The other night, RJ and I took down some Perry snitch who was getting drugs from the cops. Turns out that they were moving about forty pounds of H. I want to put it back on the streets and sell it."

"Does Cobra know about it?" someone asked.

"We're not sure," Dez continued. "We were supposed to intercept a bunch of coke. I figure we just tell the Snakes that there were no drugs there. Maybe say that the snitch was double crossed by the cops or something."

The gang whispered amongst themselves.

I called across the garage. "Pico. Beer."

Pico dragged his leg over to the cooler. He had been out already that night hunting. His stalking gimmick was brilliant. He'd snap his leg backward and act like he was a vagrant. He constantly spent his time reading medical journals so he knew exactly where to break himself so that it wouldn't cause any lasting damage. I guess you could say the old man was our doctor.

At night, he'd collect change and then devour what he considered the best suckees, drag them down an alley and have at them. He looked older and grumpier than the rest of us. His Shar-Pei-wrinkled face was filled with gray whiskers. He stood crippled in his mid-fives and his body was made more awkward by his enormous forearms. The old bastard looked like Popeye's dad after a violent tour in Vietnam.

Pico handed me a beer that he bottled himself. "So, are you going to introduce us, RJ?" He bit at his cracked lips and shot me a wink.

I snapped the beer from his hand. "Pico, you dirtbag, she's twelve."

"A twelve-year-old whore, junkie," Dez interrupted, drifting away from the conversation about the heroin.

"What the fuck is your problem, Dez?"

Big Tahoe walked over and put his elbow on Dez's head to rest. "He's jealous because he thought he was your only bitch," the mammoth mocked.

Dez shook him off and whipped a machete out that was tucked into the back of his belt. Always with the weapons.

"Whose bitch do you wanna be, 'Hoe? This is just another one of our fearless leader's shit ideas, just like The Habit. We all know how that turned out."

"Dez," I said, "calm down and tell everyone the rest of your plan. Then, we'll decide."

He looked at Bait and then started again. "We sell the heroin in Culver City. My boys will move little bits of the product every night."

"Sounds fucking dumb," another Knuckler yelled from the corner of the garage.

"It's not dumb," Dez insisted. "It's called free money. This heroin is *free*."

Most of the Knucklers cleared out, except for those of us who made the decisions. It turns out that many of the members were more concerned about Bait being around than Dez's heroin plan.

"You know that you have to talk to King Cobra, RJ," Tahoe reminded me as he dead-lifted the front of an abandoned Nova.

I looked over at Bait who was being babysat by Pico. "Can we just not tell them about her?"

She seemed entertained. He was snapping his limbs back-and-forth and flailing around like a human puppet. It was pretty gross.

"Dude, are you nuts?" Dez took a shot of whiskey and blood. "No matter what, this whole thing you have cooking up is a horrible idea, and if you don't tell them, they are going to find out. That's just what we need, the Battlesnakes calling for an all-out turf war against us. I hate to tell you this, RJ, but our land claim gets smaller and smaller every day." Dez brushed his hair out of his face with his machete.

"Turf war? Seriously, turf war? What are you talking about, Dez? If there is going to be an issue between us and the Snakes it's going to be because we decided to sell their heroin under their noses."

Tahoe broke in. "As stupid as it sounds, you should tell Cobra about the girl. It might make him forget about the drugs."

"Look, RJ," Dez said. "I don't think I need to remind you how pissed off Cobra was when things went wrong with The Habit. Shit, I wanted to fuck her too. It didn't go well; she exposed all of us to The Cloth."

"The Cloth," I scoffed. "Do you all really still believe that fairytale? Do you really believe that there is a group of renegade Catholic priests whose only mission is to create a vampire Holocaust? Are you kidding me? No one has ever seen these guys. It's bullshit created by the Snakes to scare you. Stupid."

"I don't know. A lot of gang members from every set have gone missing," Tahoe declared, dropping the Nova to the garage floor.

"Copperhead told me—" Dez began.

"Copperhead? Great, your little alliance with these assholes just confirms everything I've said. The Habit was never working for some mercenary God group bent on vampire genocide. She was just some washed up loser who wanted to see what it was like to kill people and it just happens to turn out that she was a junkie. I got a free house out of the deal.

"You guys really need to start thinking about what you're saying. We aren't in some big good versus evil battle with anyone. You know what our battle is, Dez? We battle to get high. So, some gang of Rastas thinks they are running something that's bigger than it is. It isn't." I blew smoke in his face. "The Cloth? Are you kidding me?"

"Hey, RJ, check this out," Bait yelled across the garage. The few

Knucklers left had gathered to watch her. I couldn't tell if they were sizing her up because they wanted to drain her or if they were sincerely entertained by her childish antics. She cracked one of Pico's legs out. "Broken," she said. She cracked it back in. "Fixed."

I looked back at Dez and Tahoe, who seemed completely miffed by her display, and shrugged my shoulders.

"RJ," Dez said, turning away from the Romper Room, "you've completely lost your mind. Not us. Listen to me. I know you took my ass in when I was living on the streets, trying to shoot heroin and sucking rat blood."

"You're just that lucky aren't you, Dez? I took you in because you were pathetic. I took you under my wing because you seemed like a good enough kid. Are you jealous that I'm doing the same thing for her? You are such the fucking bastard kid here and you know it. You should be glad that we accepted you then and that we accept you now. Do you think your buddy Copperhead would think highly of you if he got a look at you on the skids, picking through people's feces, hoping to find some blood?" I grabbed him by his shirt. "Don't be a little bitch. Call your friend and set up some face time between me and Cobra if that makes you happy. Just remember, little man: you aren't all that different from her."

Dez flipped his hair over his head. "What about the drugs?"

"I say we do it," Tahoe answered.

I pushed Dez back into his chair. His eyes glossed over with stone as he nodded that he'd get it done. I stared at him. I didn't want to hurt his feelings, since I knew his pussy-emo ass actually *had* feelings, but he had to know that pissing on my leadership and trying to make a joke out of me wasn't his right.

"This is hilarious," Tahoe chuckled.

I patted Dez on the shoulder, trying to mend the rift growing between us, then turned back to Tahoe. "What's hilarious?"

He pointed back to the Bait show.

"Hey, RJ, RJ, RJ!" She was spazzing out like she had just found the greatest toy in the world. "Look at this. Broken. Fixed. Broken. Fixed."

The Knucklers continued to observe her like she was a new pet.

That's when I agreed to tell Cobra that Bait was staying with me, and we all agreed that we would sell the heroin.

The next day, back at the RJ Estates, Dez and I divvied out small bags of junk to his followers. One-by-one, they lined up, all looking like Dez—

desperate, hair in their eyes, mopey with their backpacks open.

I locked Bait in my room with her new iPod, a stolen computer and her pimp's Discover card. Yes, Big Daddy Badass had a Discover card.

As Dez distributed the little Ziploc bags of Mexican Mud-like rations, I looked through a Thomas Guide that I had spent the previous night dividing into sections, clearly defining the lines of rival gangs. I had all the pages of Culver City earmarked, and I flipped back-and-forth trying to figure out a somewhat centralized yet widely distributed area that only fringed on the Sangre territory. Personally, I didn't care whether or not Dez's followers got torched. Unfortunately, they had such a clearly distinct and similar look that all paths would surely lead back to the Knucklers.

"Is there any way we can shave these kids' heads and give them like Slayer shirts or something?" I asked. "You know, get them out of those tight pants. Make them more…"

"More what?" Dez asked.

"You know," I said. "More Mexican." I grabbed a kid by his choker and dragged him in front of Dez. "Throw a black Carcass shirt on this kid or something." I shoved him to the floor.

Dez's lowly secretary whispered into his ear, hiding behind his bangs that almost touched his shoulder in the front.

I snapped the kid over to me. "No whispering, dork," I said. "I need to know everything about this. There is more on the line here than you seem to understand." I started pointing around the room. "Your wellbeing, your wellbeing." I finished on Dez. "And even yours."

The kid cleared his throat. "I was just telling Dez that it was a good idea to move into Culver City unrecognized, but rather than shaving our heads, I thought maybe we can tuck our hair into caps."

"Are you done?" I asked, turning back to Dez. "C'mon, Dez, this isn't about being fashionable and looking hip. Mexicali vamp teens that skate and listen to Slayer will destroy these—" I pointed at his followers again, "—losers."

For some reason, when they heard "losers", their faces lifted from the profoundly depressed to the slightly sad. Even though their eyes showed hope, they seemed destined to be forever on suicide watch.

Besides, I didn't intend calling them losers as a compliment.

"We don't want them to look exactly like the Sangre," Dez rationalized. "If any of them do get busted, we all get busted for trying to take over their area." He questioned his drones. "There aren't going to be any fuck ups with this… right?"

Surprisingly, Dez's reasoning was well-founded. After all, why draw any attention to ourselves?

"The hats will be good enough," I concluded. "But try and blend in a bit more."

One of the Deziens raised his hand. "What do you mean, 'blend'?"

"Jesus, poser. You know what it means," I said. "Wear baseball caps on the side or whatever. Don't wear eye makeup or bowlers. Try not to look like you think you're in a gothic fairytale."

The Dezien smirked to his friend on his right. The friend added, "But that *is* the norm now."

Damn. Was I really the old fart in the room? Before I slung myself on the kid, I looked to Dez for reassurance that they were the norm. Dez nodded his head yes. To my surprise, these shits were more dime-a-dozen than the jocks, skaters, and dorks I watched on network TV.

"You'd be surprised, sir," the boy said. "The kids my age dress like vampires."

"And what does a vampire dress like?" I asked.

He pointed to the back of the line at the only somewhat unique individual in the bunch. He was the kid I heard them calling "Piglet". He was fatter than the rest of them and instead of the covered eyes look, he apparently opted for the disgusting, stringy, black hair look. Topped off with a German Iron Cross broach thing, his satin button-up shirt looked like it was going to pop because it was packed like a sausage casing with his chins and his neck. At the bottom of his look was a pair of not-so-tight black latex pants. He looked like the shorter and plumper bastard son of the L. Byron actor I pointed out to Dez on the billboard for the *Nightshayde* movie.

"That's real nice, guys," I said. "If this kid is so lame then why do you roll with him?" I looked to Dez. He shrugged his shoulders, setting off a chain reaction of more shrugging, puzzled looks and raised eyebrows from his pupils.

The secretary kid, who up until his next sentence I figured had leadership skills, finally blurted out, "He knows where to—" he cleared his throat, "—he knows where to get the coolest clothes."

"Are you kidding me?" A voice said from the hall behind me. "This is what you call a gang, RJ?" All the Deziens panted like starving wolves as I spun around.

I thought for a second before speaking because I was pretty ashamed by the clothing statement as well. After a long pause, "Get back in the room, Bait," finally came out.

"Told you," Dez said to his clan.

I pivoted back to him and got in his grill. "Told them what, Dez?"

"I told them that you let this little whore run the house." He mimicked Bait's voice: "Here's your shot of blood, RJ. Here's your dog food, RJ."

Leroy and Skillet came out of my room into the hall and joined Bait as her guardians.

Dez grabbed his nuts. "Here's your balls, RJ." Inconspicuously, the drones elbowed each other.

"Why are you nerds laughing? You're the ones talking about what's cool to wear. You're acting a lot more like a bunch of little girls than me." Bait flung her stare back to Dez. "I hate to tell you, but *that* is way lamer than me bringing back dudes for you guys to eat and get high on."

Dez looked at his watch. "How long has it been now, whore girl? You haven't brought us shit yet except for a pain in my ass."

"Would all of you shut up!" I yelled. "When did this house become a junior fucking high school?"

Silence filled our living room. Bait grabbed onto her stomach as a wet burp came up in her mouth. She immediately made a beeline to the bathroom, slamming the door behind her. I heard her turn on the bath water, but it didn't cover up the thundering sound of her retching. From what I made out, she managed to hit all four walls, including the shower curtain, the floor, and the sink. In seconds, some semi-chunky, yellow fluid ran out from under the door.

Thankfully, Leroy and Skillet were standing guard so they could lick it up as it exited the bathroom.

"What was all that about?" I asked Bait. Her hair was a Medusa mess on top of her head. I thought about gently patting the mess out but I didn't do anything. I didn't want to take the chance of getting her kid mange on my hands.

Her swollen eyes looked up at me and she tried to speak through her bloated cheeks and glands. "It's the smell of this place."

"I've told you several times that our lifestyle is gross. It's not going to smell like a room at the Ritz."

"I know, I just think that when Dez and his friends teamed up on me… well… it just reminded me of when I went to school."

"I don't understand."

She sipped her coffee; it added to the hideous nature of her breath that I was trying to avoid direct contact with by turning my nose sideways.

"Well, before I ran away, I had just started junior high."

My mind began to wander. I never went to school, I never cared about it, and it seemed so far from my world and my reality. However, I said, "Go on."

"In my elementary school, I was like popular and had all sorts of friends and stuff."

"Yeah?" I continued to listen but my interest faded as quickly as I heard the word "popular". The word and its connotations were all foreign. Her entire story became completely inconsequential to me. I wasn't very popular when I was twelve. All I remembered was being in an alley dumpster, only living to score heroin and find rats. I'm sure my smell alone was taken into consideration when my eligibility for popularity came into question.

"Anyway, over the summer, before I went to this new junior high school, I told my best friend, Brianna about what Thomas was doing to me and my sister."

"Thomas? Thomas the Train?"

"Thomas the stepdad."

I salvaged the conversation. "Oh yeah, and your sister is Pinball, right?"

"Hey, you remembered." She smirked inside her inflated shell. She looked like a marshmallow dropped in a cat box that ended up sticking to all the discarded hair, turds, and litter inside.

"How can I forget a name like Pinball?" I said. "I love pinball." Her smile dropped and she went cold.

"What is it now, Bait?"

She picked a barf biscuit out of her front teeth, using the plastic lid of her coffee cup as a toothpick. She proceeded to wipe the discharge on the arm of the couch. "Nothing. If you don't want to hear the story, then I don't care. It's lame anyway."

I stood up, pretending to get something from across the room while she closed her eyes. Unnoticed, I grabbed a tissue and gathered up the asteroid that came out of her mouth. I shot a quick basket across the room. *Swish.*

"C'mon, Bait," I said as I fell back on the couch next to her. "I like the game of pinball. I'm sure if I got the chance to meet your sister, I'd find her to be a very nice young lady as well."

She chippered up a little bit. I could tell she was nervous about having the conversation with me as she gnawed on the Styrofoam cup that she was drinking from. "Okay," she agreed, spitting a half-moon shaped piece of the cup onto my coffee table. I ignored it.

"So, I told this girl—"

"Brianna?"

"Who's telling the story here?" she moaned and jumped to her feet, acting like she was going to stomp out and go back to her bathroom. "Fuck. I'm trying to tell you something important."

I caught her wrist. "I'm sorry, Bait. Sit back down. I want to hear the rest of the story."

"Where was I?" She sat down and started again. "Oh, yeah. So, I told this girl Brianna what Thomas…"

"Your stepfather."

"Shut the fuck up. Yes, my stepdad. I told her that my stepdad was having sex with me because she told me that she broke her hymen over the summer while she was riding her horse."

I closed my mouth and made an uncomfortably surprised expression. I couldn't help but think about how absolutely inappropriate the conversation was. Rather than cut her off again, I simply sewed my lips shut, bulged my eyes and started nodding my head.

"Brianna and I pinky swore these were our secrets and stuff. When she asked me if I liked how it felt, I might have said that I did because I think I was trying to show off about how mature I was compared to her or something. That night was a week before school started and my family went to Disneyland for vacation."

"Mmmhmm," I hummed.

"Well, I got back the night before school started and I was like all tan and stuff from vacation in California," she continued. "The next day, I got to my first day of junior high school and everyone was ignoring me."

"Even Brianna?"

She nodded with a pout on her lips.

"The nerve," I managed to get out as I coaxed the discussion along.

"Right? That day at lunch no one sat by me. I sat alone at a table near the back and this boy I liked came over to me and yelled, "Hey, everyone. Bailia fucks her dad and she likes it. Slut!" Then, everyone in the lunchroom, led by Brianna, started chanting it. "Bailia fucked her dad. Bailia fucked her dad." She began clapping her hands as she remembered the chant. "Bailia fucked her dad."

My face morphed from a sarcastic, uninterested jerk to the look of a concerned parent, and not her shit parents. My posture straightened. "Shhh," I said, comforting her. "Bait, what did you do next? Did you run away to California right then?"

"No, this is where the story gets good."

I didn't tell her that there was nothing inherently good about it. Actually, it probably ranked in the top three of the saddest stories I'd ever heard.

"So, I had gym class right after lunch and I didn't go to the class at all. Instead, I sat in the shower and cried. But I waited. I waited the entire period for them to get back from class. The second Brianna got to her locker I jumped her and took out a sock with my gym lock inside of it.

Then, I beat her halfway to death."

She jumped up from the couch like she was a cheerleader, swung her arms around and kicked her boney legs in the air. "Go Bait!" She cheered. "B-A-I-T! What's that spell? GOOOOOOOOOO Bait!"

Leroy and Skillet howled and jumped up and down with her, causing Bait to stumble over Leroy and hit her chin on the coffee table. I tried to break her fall but she nailed it anyway. Not leaving anyone short changed, she hugged the dogs and they both licked her bulging face. Then she finally sat down next to me, giving me a hug.

"Isn't that part awesome?"

"Umm, I guess." I tried to shuffle as close to the arm rest as I could get but she intensified her vise-grip squeeze. Go figure, I was terrified of a twelve-year-old psychopath.

"Hey, RJ?"

"Yes," I answered.

"Can I sleep on your floor tonight?"

"Yeah."

"Can I bring my shower mat in your room?"

"Yeah."

"Can you wash it for me?"

"Yeah."

"'Cause you know my bathroom smells like barf really bad."

"Yeah, I know, Bait."

THESPIANS

Bait pulled a shot of her blood out of her backpack. "Here," she said, handing me a container.

"A Sponge Bob sippy cup?"

"Sorry. It's the only way I could figure out how to get it here without dumping it everywhere in my backpack."

Reluctantly, I took the shot. "Okay, Bait," I said, tapping the brass werewolf knocker against the heavily-weathered black wood door. "This guy is a little weird." I gripped tightly to the heavy duffle bag filled with smack.

"Weird how?" She wiped her nose on her sleeve, dragging the front of her hair out of her face as she pulled her arm away. "How much weirder can he be than the rest of the losers you've introduced me to?" She blew at the strand of hair in an attempt to get it to return to the rest of her messy mop. I had no right to say anyone was unkempt, but yeah... Bait was pretty much a pig.

"Just be quiet until he gets the chance to pick up your scent. I'm sure he'll like you. As far as people like us go, he's very tame."

"Okay, what's his name?" She crossed her eyes. The lock of hair was now sticking straight out from her face. She blew more profusely, but since the hard-boiled hair hunk refused to comply (and because it had somehow managed to mix with snot), it just shot further and further up like a unicorn's horn.

I licked my hand. "Goddammit, Bait!"

Not wanting to touch her, I quickly pushed the hair down and back into place as best I could. "His name is Eldritch. Would you stop being such a—"

She bucked out her teeth and shook her head. "Twelve-year-old?"

"Yeah. You talk about how 'street' you are. You act like—"

Before I could finish my lecture on booger wiping in public, the large door crept open on its own to reveal an oversized, and overpriced, high-ceilinged loft. The main room was only lit by a few candles.

Without missing a beat, Bait bravely stepped in and looked behind the door to see who had opened it. "I thought he knew we were coming." She turned back and surveyed the room that was decorated with bad vampire-movie clichés.

"Oh, he knows we're coming all right." I sighed.

She stepped in a little further, cupped her hands around her mouth and shouted, "Heeeeellooooo!" Her voice, combined with lame Goth music, echoed and bounced off the cathedral ceilings.

I put my hand over her mouth. "Shut up. Go sit over there." I pointed across the room to an area with red Victorian couches. Frustrated, she stomped across the hardwood floor of the loft to the couches like a brat whose mother wouldn't buy her a pack of Gummy Bears while waiting in line at the supermarket.

Being the megalomaniac that he was, Eldritch had his acting sizzle reel playing on several TVs that were framed and set up like magic mirrors around the room. The reel was synced on all the TVs. It pathetically showed him acting in bit parts, intermixed with him playing with swords, shooting fireballs from his eyes, and vigilantly overlooking Los Angeles from the tops of old, gothic buildings.

Feeling a migraine developing, I massaged my temples as I walked over to the spiral marble staircase leading to the master's suite. "Eldritch," I called up the stairs. "It's RJ."

I looked back at Bait, who, in the ten seconds that I wasn't scolding her, had managed to make her way across the room to a large structure that was covered by an embroidered scarlet, velvet drape. She bent over and lifted the drape in a half-assed attempt to see what was hidden underneath.

I clapped my hands and hissed, "Get back on the couch!"

Startled, she dropped the drape and returned to her upright position. Shooting knives at me with her stare, she mouthed, "What?"

I pointed back to the couch, this time snapping my fingers to show authority.

She decided to give me the finger. How this little shit wasn't killed by a pimp or a John was mind numbing.

Just then, the music in the room intensified at the crescendo before the chorus. Hundreds of candles flared up around the room. Startled by a living human shrine that lit up last in the corner, Bait scurried back to the couch and sat up straight. Knowing the "curtain" had been lifted and the show was about to begin, I followed her lead and plopped myself onto the couch next to her.

She pointed to the lethargic body in the corner. "What is that?" she whispered.

"Just shut up and watch."

Incense and smoke—I'd guess originating from a fan blowing a dry ice machine—materialized from an open doorway at the top of the stairs. A growing shadow, broadcasting from a red lightbulb, engulfed the room as Eldritch's white, high-cheekboned face appeared from what he must have figured was the "beyond". The pulsating sound of a Vox organ followed his steps as he seemingly floated from the perched room. I tried to close my eyes so their blatant rolling at the spectacle would go largely unnoticed. Train wreck. Half-assed. Overdramatic. None of those words properly described Eldritch.

Eldritch stood about six-foot-six. Not the biggest guy I had ever seen, but big enough. Still hovering, he floated down the winding stairs, candles to his left and right illuminating as he passed them. His medieval metal fingernails clamped onto each of his digits, including his thumbs, brushed the faux-antiqued handrails of the staircase, reflecting small rays of light that were being projected out of motion-controlled tract lasers.

I looked down at Bait to get a feel for how she was accepting the production. She rubbed her eyes, probably trying to get the overpowering density of patchouli and the sting of street urchin incense out, and looked up at me. "He's hot," she whispered.

Eldritch continued his descent into the living room. Over his shoulders was a coat made from a white wolf that puffed up so that the eyes of the dead animal covered his own. The only thing not covered on his face was his jaw and carved chin line. Almost in tempo with the music, he smirked, dragging his tongue across his metallic fangs. The front of the fur opened to reveal every boney protrusion and muscle on his lanky but carved torso and waist. Just below his hip bones he wore a pair of skin tight leather pants that looked aged enough to be an auction item from Jim Morrison's estate, but I figured they came from the Jim Morrison collection at an Armani Exchange. As the rest of his body came out of the smoke, a pair of bondage strap creepers finished off his ensemble that could only be described as counterfeit, at best.

He walked over to us, withdrawing the wolf's head from his face. His long, ebony hair swirled around him and then fell perfectly down to the middle of his back. "Greetings, my friend," his bottomless voice boomed.

I stood up as he reached us, kicking Bait to do the same. She seemed to be under a spell, fixated on his greasy pecs, while she ascended slowly; her head barely reached Eldritch's abdomen. He moved toward me for an embrace. Derailing him before he got too close to my personal space, I put up my hand to shake.

Dumbfounded, but used to the treatment, Eldritch grabbed my hand. Rather than bringing me in for a full European-style reception, he settled for the less-touchy "chest-to-chest" bump. I didn't find it too disrespectful. After all, I just sat through a spectacle that combined the resurrection of Christ with *The Rocky Horror Picture Show*. I'm sure the vampy teens that aligned themselves in Eldritch's "legion", The Nightcrawlers, thought it was pretty awesome. I knew better. I was there at least once a month, and this was the first time I had ever seen that particular production.

Eldritch turned his attention to Bait, who was still enchanted by his theatrics.

"And this must be the young damsel you spoke of." With one clawed-hand, he lifted her chin and with his other hand he brought her downturned hand upward. He bent over and kissed it. Controlling her like a marionette, he brushed her hand down his makeup-emphasized cheekbone and pulled her close. Lifting her so her ear was close to his mouth, he whispered, "Are you the trick… or the treat?" Bait's eyes rolled back and her open mouth panted.

"Jesus! Come on!" I grabbed Bait's arm and dragged her closer to me. "What the fuck, dude?" I yelled, trying to stabilize Bait as she stumbled back to her feet. "She's got fucking snot in her hair."

"Why are you so mean?" she shrieked, pulling from my grip. "I'm pretty, RJ!" She kicked her foot up in back and pulled off her whore shoe. Then, she started thumping away at my crotch with it. The joke was on her. I invested in a cup immediately after I told her she could move in.

As if I needed Eldritch's help to fend off a hundred-pound-when-soaking-wet little girl, he heroically came to my rescue by tranquilly placing his hand on her shoulder, his signature spellbinder. He lit a clove cigarette that materialized out of nowhere in his mouth. "It is nothing to fight about, young temptress. Sir RJ is simply marking his territory." Bait calmed and returned the shoe to her foot.

I rolled my head back and closed my eyes. The combination of smoke, red lights, incense, and overall gayness were making my head throb more. I exhaled as much of the bullshit in the room as I could and bounced my head back into position. First, I looked down at Bait.

"Calm the fuck down, please. I'm sorry that I don't get excited when a grown man makes sexy talk with a little girl." Then, I proceeded to Eldritch, who towered over me. "As for you, can we get to business here? This isn't a casting call for your next wannabe victim, dude."

Eldritch stood his ground, snarling with his steel fangs. Not really wanting to have the guy rip me in half, I turned away from his stare and looked down at Bait. In an attempt to look threatening, she snarled as she pawed at me. She looked more like a kitten batting at a moth than any creature from the streets of Los Angeles.

I laid the duffle bag on the elaborate coffee table that separated us. "Can you take this for me or would you rather have no part in this?"

Eldritch extended his long arm to the handles and placed the bag on his lap. Using the end of one of his talons, he unzipped the bag revealing the contents. He looked up at me and smirked. "Coke?"

"Have a sample."

He split one of the ten-pound bags open, slit some blood out of his finger and let it drip into his claw. He then scooped out a dollop and raised it to his nose for a sniff. He set his head back slightly and clinched the opposite nostril and sucked it into his throat. He waited a minute and then shook his head. "Heroin? You say this came from the Blue Blood Perrys?"

"Kind of."

"What are you wearing?" Bait interrupted as she petted Eldritch's fur cloak, still on his shoulders.

He turned away from our adult conversation and rebooted his charade. "It is the pelt of the Arctic Wolf. I was raised by this victim's enemy pack in the northern-most mountains of Canada. I took his hide as a trophy when we took his pack's den." He brought the pelt in around his shoulders as if the phony flashback was traumatizing. "It was during the coldest of Arctic winters."

Bait curled her feet under her and her eyes lit up. "You were raised by wolves?"

"Some say I'm part Lycan," he boasted.

"No one has ever said that, Eldritch. Ever."

Bait put her finger to her lips and faintly shushed me. She stroked the fake pelt and sang out the word. "Lycan."

I didn't have the heart to take away her excitement. Truth be told, Eldritch was born and raised in a cabin outside of Duluth. He moved to L.A. to become an actor. Unfortunately for him, he was so terrified of the light that he could never make it to any auditions other than the few Z-Grade monster movies and standard cable shit-fests I saw on his dumb sizzle reel when we walked in.

"Bait, can you give us a few minutes, please? This is somewhat important," I said.

Eldritch returned his attention to me. "Okay, RJ. What does 'kind of'

50

mean?"

"Well, you know how I 'kind of' owe King Cobra... for the Habit burning down his place and all?"

"Yes."

I flicked at my thumb. "Well, Dez and I were 'kind of' told by the Snakes to kill this BBP dude and the two cops he was snitching to."

Eldritch threw the bag back on the table, creating a small poof of heroin that drifted through the air like a light snowstorm. He crossed his legs tightly, placed his elbow on his knee and his face in his hand. He scratched at his right cheekbone with his index claw, smearing some of his makeup.

"So, I assume this pillaged bag of heroin was supposed to go to the Battlesnakes after you disposed of the snitch? Are you are telling me that you and your comrade, Dez, have decided to stiff them? Have you gone mad, man?"

"It's not what you think, Eldritch," I assured him as I attempted to catch some of the smack floating around the air on my tongue. "They have no idea this BBP jackass was asking for heroin from the pigs instead of coke."

"Here is a question, RJ: why would a BBP be getting so much?" He retreated from his relaxed, listening position and opened the bag again and counted. "One... two... three...?" He looked back up at me.

A dreamy-eyed Bait continued to pet Eldritch's pelt. "It's fifty," she said.

"Fifty pounds." Eldritch shook his head and pointed his index claw at me. "Why would the BBPs or the Battlesnakes want fifty pounds of heroin? Have you even begun to think about that? They have no use for it. What happened to the rest of it? Did the Knucklers have a party I wasn't invited to?"

"Well, we've been dealing it in Culver City. As far as why it isn't coke, I figured maybe it was a mistake. Maybe that's all the cops could swipe from the evidence room."

Eldritch searched his thoughts. "Or maybe, the Battlesnakes are thinking about getting into the heroin business and disposing of the Knucklers altogether. What is their take from the Knucklers' dealing?"

I counted on my fingers. "I don't know, fifty, sixty percent."

"Well, seeing as how you have such an outstanding relationship with King Cobra—you know, the burning of his home and friends and all—I think it is safe to say that the Knucklers have seen their last hurrah on the streets of Los Angeles. Why don't they just bring that forty or fifty percent in house? You have been set up, RJ."

"How do you see it?" I lugged the duffle bag off the table. "We have the drugs. Besides, there is a code of conduct on the streets. We all live somewhat in harmony, right?"

Bait interrupted again. "I knew there was a vampire law."

"Shaddup, Bait. Go fuck off somewhere."

Bait propelled herself from Eldritch's side. "Hmmmf!" She started looking around the room filled with romantic oil paintings in baroque frames and religious statues that he splattered with blood or red paint. I couldn't really tell which, but I'd bet it was paint.

Eldritch closed his eyes and got to his feet. "Foolish. They wanted you to steal the drugs. That way, the Battlesnakes have a reason to kill all of you without having them look like they have broken any rules." He began walking toward his shrine in the corner and looked back. "Besides, you and I both know there are no rules."

Sitting in the corner on a throne-type chair that matched the rest of the décor in the room was a young man with his eyes rolled back. The figure's lips quivered every so often, but it was clear that he was in a comatose state. Drool dripped from his lips down to his chest and connected with one of the many flexible snake pipes that were plugged into all his major veins. Hooked to his arm was an IV drip of opium. Eldritch knelt in front of his semi-living victim and lit a water-filled sphere embedded in the chest cavity.

As he heated up the blood and opium, he placed one of the hoses in his mouth, flipping a valve that was placed halfway down the pipe. He sucked and smoke manifested from the corners of his lips. He smiled, sucked the toxin into his lungs, waited a second and then puffed smoke rings straight into the air.

Bait had made her way over to the coma victim. She waved her hands in front of his eyes and mushed his mouth around with her thumb. "Is this guy alive?" she finally asked.

Ignoring her, Eldritch looked back to me. "You genuinely want me to hide these drugs that you have taken from the most dangerous gang in Los Angeles. I regretfully decline, RJ."

"What?" I threw my arms up in frustration. "Don't be such a pussy, Eldritch."

"I like pussy," he said, extending his tongue out between his fangs. "I am what I eat." He winked at Bait.

Bait's right leg sprung up behind her and she began to blush.

"She's twelve, molestro!" I yelled across the room as I stood up and started walking over to them. I grabbed the pipe out of Eldritch's hand and toked away. The taste was putrid, almost as if he had filtered the opium-filled blood with perfume before it entered the bowl.

"Please do this for me," I let out with a hookah load and blew it in his face.

Eldritch grabbed the hose back from me and took a quick hit. "Because I call you friend," he said, "we will decide on this matter like men." He inhaled the smoke.

Bait's hand nodded the comatose victim's head around like a bobble-head toy and excitedly said: "A fight! You're so dead, RJ!"

Eldritch dropped the hose and blew out his last drag. He ethereally clamped onto Bait's wrist to settle her down. "It is actually more a duel than a fight, young one." He dropped her arm to her side. "It is the duel of gentlemen."

Her eyes widened as she followed him across the room, only to look back at me and stick her tongue out. She clinched onto a piece of Eldritch's wolf coat thing like he had her on a leash.

"Do you fight with swords or axes or something?" She pointed to one of the monitors showing his sizzle reel. "Can I use that big sword?" Eldritch arrived at the red cloth-covered object in the room.

Bait daintily bounced on her toes. "Is this your coffin?" she asked. Eldritch simply smiled and romantically stripped the shroud into the air with one hand as he used his other to spotlight his showpiece. Lights turned on as a faint humming sound rumbled at our feet. The majesty of the professional-sized, brushed metal phenomenon was open for all eyes to see. As the cover fell behind him, he announced: "Air hockey."

I never thought many of Eldritch's things were cool, but this was the sole reason I came to his place all the time. There was nothing better than getting wasted for free and playing ghetto hockey on his ginormous table. To prevent it from getting demolished up by our vampy power, he reinforced the frame with steel which also fit the other furnishings in the house. Although I didn't think one way or the other about all that garbage, I loved this table. It was perfectly level and he always kept it in top shape so that the hover-ability of the pucks never died out or got sticky.

Disappointed, Bait turned to study a picture of Eldritch dressed as Count Crackula.

I flipped my personal paddle out of my back pocket and whirled it around in front of me. Eldritch opened an old safe cloaked behind a painting of him naked and covered in blood with a bunch of white wolves. In the safe were half a dozen paddles that he had tailored for his large hands.

"I will go with Mozart today," he announced, plucking his paddle from the safe.

We played air hockey for about four hours while Bait slept upstairs on Eldritch's elephant coffin waterbed. For the record, I beat him thirteen games to twelve. In about the middle of the third game, he decided he'd hide the drugs for me and make drops for Bait to pick up.

VI

IMPOSTERS

It was Halloween in Los Angeles. Contrary to popular belief, it got really fall-like that time of year. The leaves changed color and the wind picked up on most nights, so much so that thick tree limbs lined the streets. It never made for a solid sewage system during rainy winters because most of the shit filled the drains, causing neighborhood flooding everywhere.

From what I read and had seen on TV and the Internet, I only guessed what winter and fall were like in the rest of the world. I'd never seen real snow, and despite my physical aversion to the sun and heat, I hated the cold. My body was always cold enough for me.

Bait had been staying with me for around four months, and although the plan was to have her lead Johns back to my place, it didn't end up that way.

I tried to justify her being alive, saying that she had become quite a housekeeper. In all reality, her version of upkeep and labor involved running a vacuum across the hardwood floors only long enough to carelessly chip and scratch them. It was hardly worthy of room and board. But, she was doing her part with the stolen drugs. She had become a solid go-between, and her involvement seemingly kept us off the Battlesnakes's radar.

Dez didn't see the point of her being able to breathe another day at all. As the antagonism grew between them, the questions about her relevance increased and drove Dez and me further apart. Beyond anything else, he was pissed off that I never asked him to stay with me unless he was too faded to get out before daylight rolled around. I truly felt bad because, after all, he was like a brother to me. However, what didn't seem to register with him was that Bait was a brittle, human girl living on the streets. He, on the other hand, was this otherworldly street hustler who always managed to land on his feet, especially when killing to get ahead was involved. I was only worried about Dez surviving when he was first jumped in. After that, he seemed fine once off the rat blood and on his own.

As for Halloween, I guess I didn't have the right to comment on the holiday much at all because I never remembered being a kid. But I never liked Halloween. It wasn't as much about me getting angry about a bunch of punkasses around the world mocking my disease as much as it was the spectacle of Halloween in Hollywood. However, they didn't irritate me as much as the holiday being hijacked by adults. When did little girls dressing as princesses become abused porn stars dressed as drunken whores?

Chances were pretty good that I would never have to answer the door to a gaggle of kids to give them candy, because they didn't trick or treat in my neighborhood anyway. Seeing how I lived in a predominantly Orthodox Jewish area, Halloween was frowned upon. Besides, for all intents and purposes, I was a serial killer, so it was better they just stayed away. I had enough stupid kids in my life.

The Jewish version of Halloween in my area was called Purim and it took place in mid-March. When it rolled around yearly, it was less about dressing as box-office superheroes, demons, wizards, and vamps and more about them celebrating their religion. Sure, it always involved getting wasted, dressing up and feasting, but I always likened it more to Mardi Gras. I was never sure if it was a recognized part of the Jewish holiday calendar, because it seemed unorthodox.

I saw the conventional Jewish people more like vampires than Christians because of their strict adherence to the following of the Shabbat from sundown on Friday to sundown on Saturday, their closeness with their family, and their overall demeanor. The Orthodox traditions for the most part generated internally and to some extent so are vampire/gang traditions. Fact: our existence depends on drugs and blood. Also a fact: their existence is based on their spirituality.

Although I would never consider a religion a gang, they still follow a pack system much like we do. The most obvious comparison would be that you can't make someone an Orthodox Jew. Marrying an outsider is considerably frowned upon. With us, we can't bite someone's neck and make them vamp out. Which brings us back to Bait... she doesn't belong. Not so much that it's a private club or that we think we're too good for her. She just didn't belong.

Bait stood in the hallway while I cut and packed some meat in the kitchen. Her arms were behind her back so I didn't know what to expect from her. I wasn't afraid she was going to try and kill me, but I sometimes wished she would put me out of my misery. Always full of childish surprises, the end result more often than not turned out to be something preposterous like a friendship bracelet. She pouted and scratched her legs together like a cricket. I tried to ignore her but she began clearing her throat to get my undivided attention.

Without turning toward her, I asked, "Can I help you? I'm busy; whatever it is that you want, I'm hoping that it can wait."

I licked some *au jus* off a cutlet that I had just spent the better part of a half hour carefully filleting. She stayed in the hallway, remaining silent, only grunting every so often to remind me that she needed to be the center of attention. After about two more minutes of becoming increasingly provoked, I accidentally sliced through my finger. I stuffed the digit in my mouth. "Shit!" I then wrapped a paper towel around the cut. "What, Bait? What do you want?"

While staring at the ground, Bait mumbled in a baby voice. "What awe you doing? Awe you cawving a pumpkin?"

I lifted the butcher knife and licked the blade. "Does it look like I'm carving a pumpkin? Is there a pumpkin anywhere in this house? Please tell me you're not hiding a pumpkin behind your back."

With her face still fixated on the floor, she murmured, "I don't know."

Her baby voice was much more exaggerated than usual. Somehow, between when I spoke to her earlier that day and this conversation, she had managed to develop several speech disorders including those of, but not limited to, Porky Pig, Elmer Fudd and Daffy Duck. When anyone, namely a twelve-year-old, replaces an "R" with a "W" it's enough to drive any parent to homicide.

"What do you mean, 'I don't know'?"

She rubbed her nose on her shoulder, as not to reveal the mind-bending secret she concealed behind her back.

I dropped the knife on the counter to which she curled a slight smirk out of the corner of her dopey mouth. The pale moats that surrounded her freckles went flush. Unbeknownst to her, I put down the knife not because she had won the war, but because I was afraid she might lose her life if she continued.

"What, Bait? What in the hell do you want?"

She pulled one of her arms out from behind her back. "You haven't done your shot yet today."

I eyeballed the knife. It was so close. "Is that what this is all about?

Who cares?"

"I care," she whimpered. "And I have something else."

I ignored the knife and walked to her. I bent down, took the shot from her hand, and downed it. "Cheers. Delicious, Bait." I handed her back the empty shot glass.

"Are you starting to feel more human?" she asked.

"Not really how it works. I eat human blood all the time."

Truth be told, her blood was becoming a cleansing addition to my days, but comparing it to a regular person drinking water or juicing would be a stretch. Even if it was just a thirst quencher, it was a good one. "So, what's the big to do? What's the other secret?"

She wiped her nose on her sleeve. "It's just…"

"Let's have it, Bait," I insisted, wanting desperately to get back to chopping meat.

"Today is my birfday."

"First of all, enough with the baby talk. Secondly, happy birthday. You're what? Fourteen or something today?" I never celebrated my birthday because frankly, I never had any idea when I was born, if you can even call how I ended up walking around being born. Maybe I was the result of some experiment where a redneck fucked a raccoon.

"I am thirteen."

"Your birthday is on Halloween? That's cool, I suppose. Do you want some candy or something?"

She pulled the other hand from behind her back and thrust it in my face. "I got this for you." It was the iPod.

"That's your iPod. I don't want that. Besides, you didn't get it for me. You best keep it. It's the only way I know how to get you to shut up."

She scuffed her slippers across the floor that she trashed with the vacuum on a weekly basis and put the iPod in my hand.

I looked at it for a second and then returned it to her hand. "I don't want this, Bait. You stole it, so it belongs to you. You know, 'finders keepers' law and all that."

"Well, I did get it for you. I took all of your records and made them into MP3s." She handed it to me again. "Now you don't have to make a huge mess all over the floor."

"God forbid I should make a mess that requires cleaning from a guest in my house whose job it is to clean up." I put the ear bud in and scrolled to a song. "How did you do this?"

"I figured out how to do it on your computer, and I've been putting your records on it for the past month while you've been sleeping."

The songs were intact. I scrolled to another that I knew was particularly battered and pushed play. All of the snaps and pops and grain were there. It was my turn to smile.

"I don't know what to say. This is awesome."

She lit up. "I also found this website where you can download a bunch of this stuff for free. I bookmarked it on your computer."

"But, it's your birthday." I fumbled around in my back pockets, hoping to find some money. Instead I found a losing lottery scratcher and for some weird reason a guitar pick. I couldn't for the life of me remember where I got it. I had no use for it. I never learned to play the guitar so I guessed the victim I got the jeans from was a rad hatchet dude.

Coming up empty, I fixated into her eyes, trying to figure out what she wanted in return. She wasn't as easy to read as I thought. "I don't really have anything to give you. I'm sorry."

"I took this." From under her shirt, she pulled out a necklace she'd made from my favorite titanium 45 adapter and a piece of string that I used to securely wrap my meat after I covered it in paper grocery bags.

I should have been pissed because I hated using the yellow plastic inserts but rather than act ungrateful, I realized that I had no use for it any longer.

"That's super cool. Is there anything else you want?" I asked, not expecting anything more. I was suddenly preoccupied with my new toy. She had not only transferred all my 45s, including the B sides, onto the iPod, but she also found all the cover art for the records and put them all in by name and categorized the singles by bands. I later realized that the iPod does all that shit automatically, but it seemed like a big deal at the time. "Seriously. Anything you want."

For a third time, she reached behind her back and pulled out a crumpled page from the *LA Weekly* and handed it to me. Not automatically noticing the advertisement that she circled with a marker, I studied the ad. The entire page was filled with commercials for medical marijuana, escort services, and strip clubs. Seeing how vampires can't read minds, the first ignorant thing that came out of my mouth was: "I think you need to be eighteen to work at a strip club. Not twelve."

She corrected me. "Thirteen."

"Right. You're still too young."

"Not that." She came up to the page and pointed to the ad she circled. "This."

I closed my eyes and exhaled. I didn't want to disappoint her after all the trouble she went through, but it was asking more than I wanted to give. "I can't do this," I stammered.

She tapped her index finger up and down on the newsprint.

I read the ad again.

Club Thirst Presents:
The First Annual Vampire Samhain Ball
Goth. Fetish. Darkwave. Industrial.

Surrounded by a frame of skulls, there was a picture of a romantic looking vampire, peering over the shoulder of a woman wearing a Victorian dress. His fangs dripped with blood and he was winking to all the suckers who read the ad.

"Forty-fucking dollars?" I yelled, reading the small print located at the bottom of the page. "Are you kidding me?"

"Come on, RJ," she pleaded. "It's my birthday and I gave you a cool gift. Besides, I know I can get in. I was told that they don't card people."

"No. These places bug the shit out of me. Besides, Halloween night will just be that much worse than any other stupid night."

She got on her knees and placed her hands together as if she were praying. "Pretty please. Look," she said, pointing to another part of the ad. "One-dollar blood shooters."

I couldn't bear to read another word in the ad. "I'll bet that is either a Bloody Mary in a shot glass or grenadine and booze in a test tube."

"Please give it a chance. I want to see real vampires."

I crumpled up the page and threw it at her nose. "Real vampires are me."

The ad clung onto the white-dyed streak in the front of her hair like Velcro. She swatted it away.

"How many times do I have to tell you that I am a real vampire?"

"But I want to see more vampires like Eldritch. You know, romantic and clean."

Thankfully, the phone rang. I sniffed my armpit on my way to pick it up. I was clean. Wasn't I? I answered the phone, happy to escape the current conversation.

"Hello."

"Hey, RJ, it's Tahoe. What are you doing for Halloween? Wanna go kill people?"

I went back to avoiding eye contact with Bait. I knew she was back to her forgotten birthday moping.

"Don't really feel like killing or going out at all. I hate Halloween." Like a girl left dateless on Valentine's Day, I usually stayed in. Instead of a love story and a pint of ice cream however, I usually had some microwaved blood and heroin. Maybe I'd watch a horror movie.

Bait started tugging on my shirt and for some unlikely reason—or maybe guilt because she had given me such a thoughtful gift—I gave in.

"Goddammit. I'm thinking about going to this stupid club in

Hollywood called Club Thirst."

I heard whatever Tahoe had in his mouth spit across the room. "You're kidding, right?"

"Unfortunately, no. Bait has some desire to see what real vampires are like."

"You dummy, RJ. That's the stupid place where your butt-buddy Eldritch recruits members for the Nightcrawlers."

I covered the phone and signaled for Bait to get ready. She chirped away delighted, kicking the newspaper page in front of her. She banged her hands on the wall like she was a drill sergeant waking up a bunch of recruits at boot camp. Halfway down the hall, she lost her balance and slipped on the floor that remained un-mopped. She bounced back up as quickly as she hit the floor and crawled into the bathroom.

"You're kidding me, Tahoe."

"I shit you not."

"I thought he picked those kids up off the street or the mall."

"No way, bro," Tahoe said. "Once he convinces them he's the real deal, he brings them back to his place. He either hooks them up to that hookah thing or he has them be his slaves."

Trying to trick the big ox, I injected, "You wanna come with us?"

"Fuck no."

"Then, don't tell anyone I'm going. Bait hasn't gotten us any victims yet and I'm sure you know better than me that the shit talking about my leadership is running rampant."

"That's actually why I called. Dez has been talking a lot of smack."

"What's he saying? And stop talking with your mouth full of food."

"It's all his chest pounding about the money he and the Deziens are bringing in with the Battlesnakes' heroin in Culver."

"Really. Just a second."

I beat the earpiece on the kitchen counter, shaking off my anger but not before getting a good "fuck" out of my mouth.

"Take it easy, RJ. No one is listening to him."

"It's not that. If he has the balls to talk shit about me to you guys, how long is it going to be before he slips to someone else? How long before he confides in his good pal Copperhead and lets everyone know what we're doing? Jesus, why doesn't that scrawny little bitch just start his own gang with those idiot followers of his and the Battlefakes?"

"Like I said, no one is listening."

"Not the point, Tahoe."

"Well, why are you taking the kid to a club tonight? I think she's cool and all, but—"

"It's her fucking birthday, dude." I hung up the phone only to be sprayed from behind. I turned around and saw Bait holding a blood drop shaped glass bottle. I wiped the liquid off my neck.

"Ewwww. What is this? It smells rancid."

She read me the bottle. "It's NightShayde: The Essence of L. Byron Nightshayde."

I shook my head.

She rubbed her thumb on the bottle. "He's that hot vampire from the *Nightshayde* series."

I snatched the bottle out of her hand and smelled the syrup she violated me with. The red bottle had a pyramid spiked wristband around the neck and the product name was written in a gothic typeface. In the center on the back was the silhouette of the same messy-haired asshole that I kidded Dez about on the Samsung fire escape. I gagged.

"Oh God. This smells like ass and a Phish concert. I smell like a stinky, rotten hippy." I felt the stench coming out of all my pores as it stung my nose like I was snorting a line of bees.

Bait grabbed the bottle back and put it in her pocket. "I like it. It's what all the vampires wear."

✂

As we waited in line to get in, I remembered what Club Thirst used to be back in the day. In the early eighties, it was a roller boogie rink called TJ Hustler's. I think I may have killed some jackass in there back when I was still aimlessly wandering around the streets. Somewhat ashamed that my legacy and traditions had been reduced to a fading and distorted trend perpetuated by pop culture movies, TV shows, and books, I elected to grin and bear it rather than slaughtering everyone around.

Bait—done up in another of her outfits bought with my hard-earned money—rubbernecked while we waited, taking in every word and mannerism of the carnival of blockheads. This outfit was more risqué than her last. A tight-laced dress was accentuated by a pair of knee-high, stiletto-heeled boots. It was a disgusting outfit for a thirteen-year-old, and I decided that if I did run into Eldritch that I was going to borrow whatever ridiculous coat he was wearing to cover her.

I wasn't sure, but I think she might have washed her hair and blown her nose before we left the house because her hair was combed out of its usual frantic, matted shit style and as far as I could tell, there wasn't a build-up of snot on her naked arm.

After she had her hand stamped—I still have no idea to this day how she got into the club—Bait clomped her way into the bar.

The doorman then frisked me and shouted, "Dress code required."

I guessed that like many of the other bar patrons, he had recently made the transition from white-ass hip-hopper to vampire.

I brushed any lint off the front of my body. "What are you talking about, bro?"

He decided to get all hard ass on me. "I'm not your bro, friend."

"Okay. What are you referring to?" I took a second look at my outfit. There weren't any rips. I wasn't wearing a hoodie. I wasn't wearing a bandana. Nothing gang-related. As a matter of fact, I was wearing a yellow Cramps shirt and a new pair of stolen jeans. I was even wearing shoes rather than flip-flops, which was rare for me.

Desperately flexing his bicep under his mesh Danzig shirt, he pointed to a sign above the entrance and then read it aloud, dictating his authority. "Vampire, gothic and fetish attire required. Strictly enforced—read the last part, friend." He brushed strands from a long, black wig out of his face.

"Strictly enforced," I replied. "Here, dick. Here's fifty large. Take the extra ten and go buy yourself some vitamins or something."

He stepped up to me. "You got something to say?"

I didn't stand down. "How do you know what a vampire dresses like, you troglodyte?"

Probably not knowing what "troglodyte" meant, he opted to grab my shirt by the collar. He then backed up his fist to punch me or scare me or something. I shook him off as a voice from behind him called out, "Hey, Mazzuco. The boss wants to see you."

Being the tough guy that he was, the doorman went in for a punch but retracted by saying, "Psyche." Before the pop reached my jaw, he flattened his palm as if to instruct me to "talk to the hand".

"You're lucky this time, faggot," he added, snatching the fifty bucks out of my hand. To his dismay, no one in the long line behind me was cheering him on. Even those fakes realized what a douche he was. I was going to remember that name, Mazzuco, and the stench of chili-cheese fries that accompanied it.

The other bouncer relieved him and stamped my hand. "Don't worry about him," he assured me with a pat on the back. "'Zucco gets all roid raged sometimes."

I patted him back and winked. "Shocker."

"Yeah. Have a good time, mate." He handed me some plastic fangs. "This will help your costume."

"Thanks."

I unwrapped the novelty teeth, put them in my mouth, and then grabbed a pair of earplugs out of my pockets. The music was clearly too damn loud for my delicate ears. The edges of the bridge of the teeth cut into my gums and almost instantaneously, my mouth filled with spit. I was glad that being a dead person didn't involve having fangs. As I put my wallet back into my pants, the self-appointed leader of a gaggle of Halloweenies bumped into me.

"Hey," I said.

He snorted at me like a dandy. "Hey, what, buddy?" His face was painted white with blackened cheekbones and runny eye makeup. "Nice costume... jerk."

Sighing, I smiled. "It's pretty lame, huh?"

One of the gang joined in. "Spit much? What's up with the ear plugs, gramps?"

After a flurry of high-fives, they entered the ballroom of Club Thirst in a single file line.

Calves to the slaughter, I thought. I followed them with a mission to track down Bait. I disbanded my fangs in a potted plant that appropriately housed a dead rose bush.

The inside of TJ Hustler's had changed drastically from its original roller boogie décor. It was still round, only they took out the roller rink floor and replaced it with black tile. The wall that was used as a safety net for those not so light on their skates looked like it was smashed with a sledgehammer to emulate decay and painted headstone gray. The seats, which I imagined used to be the plastic side-by-side seating that surrounded the rink behind the walls, were torn out and replaced by tables and chairs that matched the re-envisioned spurious design. On both sides of the room, where the snack bars and videogames used to be, there were now two bars. They served up fake absinthe and vodka cranberries.

TJ Hustler's, I thought. *God was that a great name.*

Instead of Shooting the Duck, the dance moves of the week were something recycled from another eighties staple, "Dead Can Dance". The new abomination dance combined Washing Windows, Changing the Lightbulb and being stuck in a coffin. It was all so mundane that I wanted to plow through the clones doing the Gorilla, but I remembered it wasn't my day. Killing some wannabees who had no idea who or what they wanted to be other than what they were told wasn't in my cards.

I scanned the club through the sea of fucktards and saw Bait already dancing with some idiot. Unlike the more traditional camp and trampers, he was rolling in the newer breed regalia. He was a brooding young cover boy with a pompadour tuft. His dark eyes looked like they were ready to burst into tears at any moment, but his confident arrogance said he could handle his demons. I looked at his shirt, strategically ripped and bleached, convinced that it wouldn't fit around my thigh. Tying up the outfit was a pair of nicely pressed pinstriped suit pants.

"It's almost Sunday," a flamboyant kid yelled into my ear. "I'm going to be up all night. I'm totally rolling my ass off." He fanned himself with his hands. His fluffy black hair stuck to his face that was smeared from a horrible dye job. I was probably the only one in the club without black hair. My hair was shit short and dirty blond. I looked like no one in The Cure, past or present.

"Me too," said a bigger gal in a corset who fought against the rhythm of the song blaring on the sound system. It was difficult to tell if she had no sense of timing or if it was as simple as she was on so much E that her mind was playing a completely different tune altogether. If that was the case, I'm sure the song sucked.

Giggling echoed from across the room. My attention returned to Bait, as I was sure she was the perfect outsider for this tribe to team up on and mock. I was correct. Unbeknownst to her, a bunch of them, including the dreamy doofus she was dancing with, encircled her on the dance floor as she robotically powered her way through one tween-absorbed hip hop dance after another. Was she really a hooker? It was truly pathetic. I figured I'd let it continue a bit longer, to teach her a lesson, as if she didn't already know how mean people were from her single day of junior high.

I cautiously walked toward her spotlight dance. As I was about to terminate the spectacle, however, I was stopped in my tracks by the reverberating sound of a finger snap. Without questioning the source, the crowd dispersed as Bait continued her stomping Running Man that wouldn't have been acceptable if it were performed as a joke to show how dumb white people are on a sitcom. Behind Bait on an elevated table was the source of the snap.

Eldritch.

He glanced at me as his talons tickled the arms of the catbird seat he aloofly fell into. I nodded at him and he nodded back, letting me know that he had everything under control.

As soon as I was reassured that he had Bait's back, pretty boy Johnny Darko crept up behind and tripped her. Quickly, before either Eldritch or I could have swallowed the guy up, he made his way over to the bar. Not to be easily defeated by the embarrassment of busting ass or by the pointing and giggling whispers of the dead-for-the-weekend USC students, she tromped up behind him and grabbed his gelled hair.

She slammed him into the bar. "What the fuck, asshole?" His stomach smashed into a tray full of what was almost surely the alchemistic "blood shooter" I had read about in the modern Necronomicon known as the *LA Weekly*.

With his perfectly messed hair filled with plastic test tube shards, he lashed back, sweeping her leg a second time, sending her back to the floor.

I didn't hesitate. I made my way over to the scene, bumping off of the girls spinning to the latest Darkwave dreck that DJ Destitute spun on the wheels of surreal. I picked Bait off the ground. She was about to burst into tears.

"I thought he liked me."

"It's cool, Bait. The guy is an asshole."

Johnny Darko spat bar drippings in my ear. "Who are you calling asshole, old man?" Behind him was a gang of his own deciding to take a night away from video games, and who felt pushing buttons on a controller entitled them to act tough in the real world. My world.

I spun Bait behind me. "Let it go, pal," I said.

"Yeah, this time," he concluded. "This time. She's just a dumb kid, anyway."

Bait tried to paw and scratch past me with her painted black press-on nails. "I'm not a kid, motherfucker. Kill him, RJ. Show him what you're really like."

I pulled her back to me and cupped my hand over her mouth. "Giddy up, boys. Nothing to see here."

They turned as instructed and Johnny dismissed us with a flutter of his hand. "Dumb," he said.

"Have you had enough, Bait?"

"You were right, RJ. Can we go home now?"

"Yeah."

I looked over to Eldritch, nodded at him and then again at Johnny Darko. Eldritch nodded back. It was almost certain that idiot wouldn't be returning to his dorm room early on November first to take notes from vampire TV shows in his quest to impress young women with the darkest depths of his soul. His soul was either going to be splashed all over the alley behind the club or become a month-long fixture in Eldritch's veins. Either way, the kid was getting exactly what he deserved.

Bait latched on to my arm as we made our way out of the metamorphosed roller skating rink to unauthentic vampire crypt.

It wasn't so much that I disliked humans. It was more that I disliked followers who covered themselves in a façade of loneliness because of a fad transmitted into their tiny, little brains. Everything I believed was confirmed for Bait. These were the same cocksuckers who called her a whore on her first day of junior high school. The only difference was their costumes. They were true monsters.

I tapped the doorman on the shoulder as we exited. "Have a nice night, 'Zucco. I'll be seeing you real soon."

"Yeah, I'll see you, friend… in Hell." He chortled oafishly to the oblivious and self-consumed Goths waiting in line.

"Whatever you say, champ. See ya in Hell."

Before I had the chance to pat myself on the back, I was suddenly face-to-face with Dez. Four of the younger Battlesnakes stood behind him.

I made sure I was seeing things correctly. "How did you know I was here?" I asked.

"Tahoe told me. I didn't go in because those people make me sick. I thought they made you sick too."

It was easy for him to brag about how much cooler he was than the losers inside Club Thirst. Unfortunately, I was starting to see that Dez was substantially more like them than I was, and maybe even more so than Lord Eldritch.

Dez remained quiet, waiting for me to make any move. He signaled the Battlesnakes behind him with his eyes. I rolled mine back at him, as if I couldn't see that he was five deep, four of which not being Knucklers.

One of the Snakes inched in front of Dez. "King Cobra wants to speak with you."

I shoved my hand into my pocket, pulled out a wad of bills and the key to my house. I handed the package to Bait. "Take a cab back to the house."

The Rasta parted our hands before the exchange took place. "He wants to see her too."

A black Escalade rounded the valet booth. One of the heavies opened the door as another made its way around. As the Snake talking to me retrieved the keys, he pushed the parking attendant to the ground by his head.

Bait grabbed my arm. All the talk about the Battlesnakes and how much they hated me since she lived under my roof suddenly became reality to her.

As we walked to our chariot, I whispered to Dez. "What the fuck are you thinking?"

"You told me to set up a meeting."

"Tonight, Dez? Why would you blindside me like this?"

"It's your fault for coming here on Halloween."

Not fully realizing the dark days ahead, I simply ended the conversation with a snide, "Thanks, little bro."

VIII

SERPENTS

"Why are we here?" Bait asked me. Her eyes were opened wide with fear and she was breathing like she had just finished a marathon.

We were told to wait just outside the Battlesnakes' compound after being shanghaied outside of Club Thirst by baby Snakes and Dez.

"Yeah, RJ. Please share."

"Dez, I don't want to have this conversation again. What in the hell did you say to Copperhead? Couldn't this have waited?"

"I talked to him, as instructed by you. I told him that you wanted to meet with Cobra. No matter how lame I think you're being, I'm not gonna let you show up here unannounced or without me. If I wanted you dead this second, then maybe I should have sent you here alone."

"Whatever that means. Thanks, though. I need your anorexic ass to back me up against a horde of monstrous black guys. Is your plan to beat them with your purse?"

Dez's mouth dropped as if my tone urinated in his face. Is it possible that he was dumb enough to think he was doing me a favor?

"I can tell you this much. Cobra ain't happy about this at all." Dez put a cigarette out on his tongue. "You can't push him around like you do to me."

"Ummm, back to me." Bait shoved herself between the two of us. "Why are we doing this, RJ?"

"It's hard to explain. Remember when you were asking about elders?"

"So, there are elders?"

Dez huffed. "Yeah, you little whore, a bunch of mass-murdering Rasta elders."

"Dez, shut the fuck up. Look, Bait, I described these guys to you before. They are kind of like the lead gang. They set up the territories; they control the money, the drugs and the action." I pushed Bait aside. "As for you, Dez, I hope to Christ your little followers aren't getting all diarrhea mouthed about what's going on in Culver City."

"Pfft," Dez snarked, discrediting my accusations.

The Battlesnakes' compound was on an old string of row houses in downtown L.A. that they had gutted and connected. They used to have a warehouse close to Koreatown, but someone burned that down along with a couple of members. The cops never bothered them because King Cobra had allegedly made a deal with them to keep traditional Los Angeles bangers and other undesirables off the streets. In that sense, they were lucky. I suppose the cops had been convinced that at one point they could be turned and become eternal. Sometimes humans are so dumb. But to the Snakes' credit, they were in charge.

I hated dealing with the Battlesnakes, especially face-to-face. Usually Dez and Copperhead, Cobra's vice principal, figured out all the details of what we owed and where we were allowed to hunt. Now it was the three of us against them. Seeing as how I was always nervous around these jokers, I wished a little muscle like Tahoe were with us. I was pissed off at him too. His fucking big ass mouth—that was most likely filled with food—was the reason we were in this predicament to begin with.

"This is bad, RJ."

"Then why did you do it? Quit being melodramatic. You're making the kid nervous. Besides, the stealing of drugs was your idea, genius."

"I could swear that you're the one who's nervous."

"Just avoid any conversation about The Habit. The last thing we want to do is set off any alarms or remind these assholes about that."

"You think they don't remember? Are you nuts?"

I grabbed Dez by the hair and knocked on the door three times with his head. "Thank you," I added.

"Nice, RJ," Dez said, rubbing his forehead.

Bait tugged on my shirt sleeve. "What's The Habit?"

"Oh, you haven't told her." Dez fluffed Bait's hair around like she was an infant. "Don't worry, you'll find out soon enough, you little fucking whore."

Bait scrunched her face and walloped Dez in the nuts with her knee.

He buckled over slightly and grabbed a wrench from the front pocket of his girlie jeans. "What the fuck?" Dez whispered. "You are so dead, little whore."

I grabbed the wrench from his hand and snapped his wrist backwards. I whispered, "Why the hell did you bring a weapon, dude? Do you know how stupid that is? There are three of us here: two junkies and one Bait.

There are over thirty of these guys."

I threw the wrench across the open lot so that it was out of the line of the floodlights that surrounded the compound.

Bait chimed in, wanting to be a part of the conversation. "All this talk about The Habit, whatever that is, is making me hungry. I want a hamburger from The Habit."

"What is wrong with the both of you? Jesus Christ. Stop. This isn't a joke."

"What are you looking at, you faggot?" Bait got up toward Dez's chest. He looked down at her and stared, licking his lips.

"Bait, take this and stop." I handed her the iPod she gave me.

She held the iPod back toward me and pinched her nose. "I don't like your music."

"I'm serious now. These guys aren't like the Knucklers, and they aren't like Eldritch."

Reluctantly, she did as she was told.

The door to the compound flew open. Carrying Tek Nines, Copperhead and two other Snakes came out and began patting us down.

"Sorry 'bout dis Dez, you know da deal," he said. Copperhead was tall and gangly. With his short, awful, orange-colored dreads sticking up everywhere, he looked like a palm tree. You could barely see his eyes because they were always beat red and filled with pot and blood. Dez had gone through a big stoner period, and that's when they started hanging out.

"Is dis the whore, Dez?" He put his hand under Bait's chin and directed it toward his eyes. "She don' look like much. KC is not gonna be happy." I stood there nervous, hoping Bait didn't think it was a good time to make one of her stupid faces. Luckily, she seemed too frightened.

Dez tried to smooth things out before they got miserable right out of the gate. "That's her, Cop. What kind of mood is KC in?"

The two guards finished patting me down. Copperhead shot me a wink. "RJ."

"What's up, Cop?"

"Seems like we already been trew dis, huh, RJ? Come on in." The stink weed permanently on his breath swirled around. It made me want to vomit. "Take off dem shoes, Knucklers."

I tapped Bait on the shoulder and signaled for her to ditch her boots. She mouthed, "Why?" I made a fist, insisted with my eyes, and snarled. Reluctant, she took them off. Her socks had skulls on them. Jesus.

We followed Copperhead through the sparkling gold of the main foyer. Paintings of King Cobra covered the walls, and throne-type chairs shaped like snakes materialized every few steps. Peter Tosh's music quietly filled the foyer halls like waiting room Muzak. Battlesnakes, who

70

seemed to get bigger and blacker the further we made it through, whispered to each other and laughed. I made out *Knucklers*, *The Habit*, *Crackers*, and *Punkasses*. Yeah, I wasn't loved inside the Battlesnakes Compound.

We reached the center of two marble staircases that were woven like snakes into the main chamber. Copperhead led us to the very back of a room that looked too big to be inside the compound at all. Only one of the Snake henchmen was present.

"Sit down," King Cobra commanded. We obliged. A massive being, he stood close to seven feet. He never wore a shirt when I saw him so he could show off how shredded his body was. If his mind was as big as his body, I'd be much more uncomfortable around him.

It seemed obvious to me that anyone that would name a gang "Battlesnakes" was not the brightest businessman in the world. Then again, I was told he started the gang from scratch in the late seventies. I wouldn't call the guy a visionary, but the Battlesnakes, without a doubt, were the first of their kind.

In front of King Cobra was a girl strapped down securely in a steel chair. Her mouth was gagged, and although she tried to flinch loose, it was pretty obvious they had already beaten the resistance out of her.

I grabbed Bait and whispered, "Don't watch this."

Copperhead moved behind Bait, ripped out the earbuds and held her head straight forward toward King Cobra's throne.

Bait watched. She had no choice.

From a gold bowl next to his throne, King Cobra plucked out an enormous bud. He picked the leaves off the stem with his manicured fingers, creating two, perfectly even balls.

His voice knocked off the walls of the throne room, deep and loud enough to suspect that he was wearing a microphone. "This is good bud, huh, Cop?"

"Is sticky," Cop answered. "Some of dem Finks got a nice grow house."

The victim shook as King Cobra packed the bud into both of her bottom eyelids. The song "Mystic Man" by Tosh intensified as Copperhead used a remote control to increase the volume. Cobra sang along. He thought he was a mystic man. He bobbed his head back and forth, his dreads catching the light of the red, yellow and green track lighting above him. Don't know if the modern vampire's propensity to stage a show was in the lack of blood or if it was tribal. I thought it was dumb.

Loudly, he sang, "I don't take no heroin. No, no, no." It was a direct dig at the Knucklers. Sure, he claimed he didn't do anything besides smoking bud, but he sure wasn't afraid to sell those other drugs. Like most criminals who try to justify their actions, Cobra was a hypocrite.

The girl in the chair blinked to get the bud out of her eyes that was packed in there so tightly that they looked like the cheeks of a chipmunk filled with nuts. She tried to cry, but the herb blocked her tear ducts.

Cobra continued to bob his head, extending the performance, making it more affected than his typical, daily bud ritual. From behind his kingly throne, he grabbed a two-foot glass cylinder. One end of it was comfortably shaped and cushioned to fit flawlessly around his mouth. The other circular end of the pipe was tipped with a sharp steel blade. Without losing the rhythm of Tosh, he brought the modified bong up behind his head and unceremoniously buried it directly into the top of the girl's skull.

Bait flinched as blood shot out of the victim's head, covering Cobra's face. Copperhead held her steady as he snickered and blew smoke from his nostrils into her eyes.

King Cobra, still dancing with himself, placed his lips inside the mouthpiece and grabbed the girl's neck. Then, from his lap, he produced a blowtorch, fired it up and sent the flame right into the eyes. Charred blood streamed from the eye but stopped short of dropping on her shoulder because it congealed from the heat and built up like dry cement on her cheeks.

The girl's body went into a seizure. Smoke puffed from her sightless sockets as Cobra sucked on the bong. The girl's cornea melted, followed by her iris and then her pupil. The bubbling of the blood in her brain spun out of control in cadence with Tosh.

After a giant bong load, Cobra extracted the glass apparatus from his victim's head, creating a slurp and crackle as the suction was released from the skull. Pointing the pipe upward like a bugle, he sucked down all the smoke. The girl's head fell forward, revealing an atrocious gash in her skull. A smoggy twirl of marijuana smoke floated from the noodle hole all the way to the ceiling.

Copperhead was using his fingers to pry Bait's eyes open as if she were being brainwashed. She was crying, her tears spilling over his fingers.

Cobra stood up from his throne, put his arms over his head and kicked the victim's chair over in front of him.

"Reynolds, as I live and breathe. You got big ass balls."

After peacefully shaking hands with Dez, Cobra told him and

Copperhead to leave the room. Cobra handed Copperhead the remote control after he turned down the music. I'm sure Dez and Copper had business transactions to talk about anyway. The business was how to scare the shit out of me on Halloween and the price was my life. Bait stared at Cobra; she was about a third his size.

Cobra ran his many-ringed fingers through Bait's hair. "This is the one, huh?" He grabbed Bait by the back of the neck. The only noise she made was the nervous tapping of her shoes on the floor. "She's no good to me. Her head is too small," he added.

"Hear me out," I started.

Unlike Copperhead, Cobra elected against the fake Jamaican accent. Nonetheless, every word that came out of his mouth was painfully direct. "Before you say something you're gonna regret, answer me this question: Why in the fucking world would you think I'd let this happen? Do you know what I lost last time you wanted to bring a little white bitch around?" He kicked over my chair and planted his bare foot into my neck. He grappled Bait's head and lifted her up like a moppet. She dangled in the air.

"KC, she's just a dumb hooker who has already seen the operation. Look how small she is; she can't do anything to any of us."

"Really, RJ, just like The Habit."

"Sir," Bait interrupted.

"Not the right time, Bait." The words barely escaped my lips, my trachea nearly crushed under King Cobra's foot.

Cobra pulled her toward him and coughed in her face. "RJ, tell her to shut the fuck up if she doesn't want to die right now."

He lifted his foot from my throat.

"Bait, shut up."

"Sir," she continued, "what's The Habit?" Her stomach growled. "I'm kind of hungry. Can you get Habit hamburgers delivered over here?"

Meanwhile, I was on the floor approaching a pant leg full of shit.

Cobra returned his foot and almost smashed my throat. Then, he chuckled and released his foot again. He lowered Bait to the floor. "What the shit is this, Reynolds? Is this some kind of joke? Get up." Doing what I was told, I stood up and cracked my neck. I heard Dez and Copperhead laughing in the shadows of the musty room.

"Get outta here, motherfuckers!" Cobra bellowed.

He plucked the chair up off the ground and shoved me into the seat. He picked up the other chair next to it and swept Bait into it.

"Let me tell you a story, little white whore. The Habit almost destroyed everything that I built. She was another white bitch who my butler friend Reynolds here brought to me just like this. 'I need help getting my fix,' he said. 'We need a human on our team,' he cried. 'I'm a lazy junkie motherfuckin' idiot,' he pleaded. You wanna know what happened when I allowed this bitch in? She fucking torched my home and killed a bunch of my brothers. What did Reynolds get out of it? A new house."

He smacked me in the face. "Isn't that what happened, Reynolds? Because you wanted to get your dick inside of a human and a roof over your head, you cost me a lot of money and a lot of friends."

"In my defense—"

Cobra raised his finger to my face. "Don't." He knelt down to Bait, not taking his finger out of my face. "Your friend Reynolds here didn't understand that there are people who want to destroy this operation and my way of life. You see, this pussy ass would rather see himself in charge of L.A. than me. You're a big man, aren't you, Reynolds? Don't be mistaken little girl: Reynolds will never be in charge of anything more than a small bunch of disgusting junkies because he makes fucked up mistakes. He also fails to recognize that changes are happening all around us. He doesn't listen to anyone but the junkie voices in his head."

"So…" she hesitated, "can I have something to eat?"

Defeated, Cobra stretched his frame upright. "I'll let you do this, Reynolds. If anything goes wrong, anything at all, you're one dead motherfucking Knuckler. We're watching you."

Time stood still for a second and I wished that being a vampire endowed me with the gift of time travel. That duffle bag full of heroin never would have seen the inside of my house.

"Fuck," Dez said to Copperhead from the shadows.

"Bitch," Cobra yelled. "Get the fuck in here; bring that queer ass with you."

Dez and Copperhead shuffled into the room.

"You motherfuckers wanna get us all something to eat?"

"Get some macaroni and cheese, bitch," Cobra shouted as he kicked at the leg of another Snake. He pointed to Bait. "That little bitch can't eat this shit."

He opened his arms to display his feast. Up and down the table were gold serving dishes piled high with prime cuts of fresh humans. Some of the food was cooked to his liking, but most of it was raw and drenched in blood. One thing I never said about Cobra was that he wasn't a gracious host. That was, at least, if you weren't the one on the menu.

Bait held up a fried, human finger and dipped it in some BBQ sauce. "Can I try this? It looks like a chicken nugget."

I seized the appetizer from her and crunched into it. "Mmmm," I said praising the light batter. "No nails."

"What are you talking about nails? I make sure that the nails are taken out." He gaped at Copperhead who was next to Dez at the opposite end of the large, black lacquer reception table. Unsuspecting, they laughed it up as Bait gnawed on small portions of drenched liver.

Cobra sang out: "Isn't that right, Copper?"

Copperhead didn't ignore the question but he didn't acknowledge it either. It seemed there was just as much dissention within the Battlesnakes compound as there was within the Knuckler garage.

King Cobra continued. "That son-a-bitch used to run my kitchen, talking about reading cookbooks and watching the Food Network and shit. About two months ago, I'm eating this piece of meat that is stuffed with these round things that bulged out of the top. 'What's in there?' I asked him. 'Try it out, you'll like it,' he says. So, not thinking, I bit into it."

Copperhead hid his face behind the large candelabra that separated the authority from the peons. Dez's nudging and chuckling ended. He knew better than to coax the volleying between the two. Frankly, Dez was probably just as surprised as I was that things were going so well between Cobra and I that he didn't want to unintentionally mess up our peace mission. He was probably just as surprised that Bait was still among us.

Not knowing the outcome of the story, but not necessarily wanting to further Copperhead's unease—even though he sent out his boys to pick me up at Club Thirst—I tried to put a freeze on the conversation. "Well, I'm a pretty bad cook, too."

Rejecting my attempt to change topics, Cobra pointed his carving knife directly at Copperhead's cock.

"After I take a bite, this motherfucker says, 'It's testicles and ovaries.'"

With the memory of his humiliation still fresh, Cobra flipped the knife up and caught it blade side. Without missing a beat, he slung the blade at Copperhead. Unfortunately, he missed. Not so unfortunately, he caused Copper to clumsily dump his plate all over his lap and splash it on Dez.

The big man sneered. "That's the problem with these younger ones, Reynolds. They have no respect and they're into all sorts of wild ass silly shit."

"I know what you mean," I said.

He gripped my shoulder. "I bet your boy hands are full with those little shits and now with this little whore. You practically got a goddamn orphanage over there."

Confessing without thinking, I blurted out, "I know. A few months ago, Dez mauled these two cops and then left them in an alley. He left them to be found like they were butt fucking."

Across the table, Dez's face tensed up. His white face became whiter and he looked to be having difficulty swallowing his food. I realized the grave mistake my mouth had made as I saw the horror in Dez's eyes. I tried to suck it into my body to drop it through my sphincter, where the rest of my insides were currently in a holding pattern to be delivered out of my body. It was as if I was a ventriloquist dummy being controlled by a blabbermouth. In my attempt to gain acceptance, I led us all into a conversation that I specifically told Dez not to bring up.

Cobra leaned on the table, using both his forearms as support. He grabbed the stem on his chalice full of blood between his pinky and his second to last finger. "Oh really." He twirled the cup. "These were the cops that the BBP was snitching to, correct?" He seemed exceedingly relaxed. "The reason I know about this is because I read it on the front page of the goddamn *LA Times*."

"I read it too." Dez checked in to defend his actions. "The cops thought it was a gang slaying."

Cobra hurled his chalice at Dez, accidently pegging Copperhead in the face.

"Do you know how stupid you sound? What are the Battlesnakes? What are the Knuckleheads?"

"Gangs," Bait answered.

"Shut up, whore," Dez hissed. "The cops thought it was a *real* gang."

Cobra shot to his feet. "Are you saying that we're—" he spun his finger around the room, "—not real gangs, motherfucker?"

"No..." Dez stammered. "It's just... they figured it's like... the Crips or the Bloods."

The gargantuan Snake leader started pacing back and forth, waiting for Dez to continue his shoveling. As far as I could tell, we had both made it about five feet and eleven inches toward six feet under. The visibility out of our graves was becoming more and more blurry as they filled with dirt.

In a last-ditch attempt to diffuse the situation, I said, "KC, seriously, he doesn't know what he's talking about. Stupid kid, right?"

He stopped marching and closed his eyes. "You brought it up, Reynolds. You all wonder why you fucking work for me. But none of you listen to me."

Bait tugged on my sleeve. "Elders?" she whispered.

"Shut her up, Reynolds."

Taking the advice of the butcher who was about to kill me, I shoved a human finger in Bait's mouth. "Be quiet."

"Cobra, I'm sorry. I got carried away," Dez apologized.

You know how ashamed parents feel when their kids are running around and screaming in an expensive restaurant? That's how I felt, like the A-hole dad who wished he had worn a rubber.

Cobra soared across the room, touching down on Dez and burying him backward on his seat, which broke into kindle on his back and ass. "Carried away, little boy? *Carried away?* Motherfucker, just like all of you... you, Tahoe, Pico, and that fucking Habit bitch. I wait for you all to fuck up and let your guard down. You're not doing the Battlesnakes or me any favors. All you do is your lowly job being my bitches. *You're* especially a nobody."

Feeling Cobra's impending wrath, Copperhead began inching away from the table.

"Where the fuck do you think you're going?" Cobra panned over to him and coaxed him back to the table with his all-authoritative finger. "We're going to play a little game here, boys."

Cobra flipped Dez over, grabbing him as if he was preparing for a high school wrestling match. He steadied Dez in a doggie style position. As Copperhead moved like a slug toward the scene, Cobra reached up, threw him on Dez's back, taking his position.

"Hold him tightly. Dez, pull your pants down." Twitching from fright, Dez did as he was told.

"Good. See, boy, you can do as you're told. Copper, rub his body and kiss his neck."

Scared and twitchy, Copperhead submitted.

I wanted to get up and stop the demonstration but my hands were pretty much tied down by my pussy when it came to Cobra.

"Hey, Egon," Cobra said to the Battlesnake who came in undetected to deliver Bait a bowl of mac and cheese. "Go get my new camera."

Cobra then wedged his size twenty-two foot between Copperhead's shoulder blades and dragged it down to his tailbone.

"Move, motherfucker," he barked.

Copperhead complied like this was a reoccurring role for him. He started dry-humping Dez. I couldn't see Dez's face, but I could hear his disgusted snorts and whimpers.

Bait started chowing down, uninterested in anything beside her mac and cheese. Thankfully, she was at a loss for words.

Egon rushed back into the dining hall with a camera. Cobra took his foot off Copperhead, grabbed the camera, and began shouting directions. "C'mon, motherfuckers. Show me how much you love each other."

I got up and mouthed *Stay* to Bait.

"Sit down, Reynolds. Enjoy the show."

His amusement was extenuated by tee-hees and hiss-like cackles. "Have you ever seen them shoot a porno out in Chatsworth?"

"No," I mumbled as I back-stepped to my chair.

Cobra started snapping pictures. He even went as far as to alter his voice to that of a clichéd flamboyant fashion photographer. "More action. More love. Be sexy for the camera. Be sexy for me." He kicked Dez in the ribs. "Where's your passion, motherfucker?"

Dez kept quiet.

"Make some noise," Cobra continued, transposing his voice back to its original bloodcurdling strength.

Almost as if that one sentence triggered a bad memory with her, Bait put down her fork, pushed out her chair and stared silently at the ground between her legs.

"Come on, bitches, make some noise!"

With no other option, Dez and Copperhead moaned and groaned, caressed and made sexy eyes at each other.

"Louder!"

They complied again.

No one in the room was laughing or having a good time other than Cobra. As a matter of fact, it was almost as painfully uncomfortable for the spectators as it was for Dez and Copperhead.

With a thunderous boom from his bare feet, Cobra grabbed Copperhead and launched him off Dez's back and then hopped into a huddle stance over Dez. "What were you saying about real gangs, motherfucker?"

Shame clogged Dez's throat. "I… I… I'm sorry. I never know what I'm saying or doing… too fucked up on drugs all the time."

"You're damn right, Knuckler. You don't know Jack or Shit." Cobra pressed the camera against Dez's cheek and snapped one last picture. The light agitated him. Bloody tears ran down his face. In large doses and close to the skin, artificial light can still be hurtful to people with photophobia.

Cobra offered his hand to help him. "Get up."

Dez accepted the help and got up from the banquet room floor. He looked around as he pulled up his pants. Cobra helped him and then rubbed salt in his wounds by pulling the pants so far up that he gave Dez a wedgie. Then, being the host of the night, he swung a new chair under Dez's ass and sat him down. Copperhead walked back to his seat and sat down, quiet as a mouse.

Bait, on the other hand, continued looking at the floor. I snapped my fingers at her, announcing the end and hopefully not the intermission to Cobra's twisted program. She returned to her mac and cheese.

On the way back to his roost at the head of the table next to me, Cobra handed Egon the camera. "Go put these on my computer." He looked over to me. "And email them to my good friend, Reynolds."

"What's his email?" Egon asked.

"Does it really fucking matter?" Cobra fumed, causing poor Egon to lose his balance and almost drop the camera.

Then, as if his show had given him the endorphins of running ten miles, Cobra sat back down and sucked the meat off a human finger. "Now, Reynolds. Where were we?"

I said nothing.

"Oh yeah. So, this motherfucker." Cobra pointed to a distressed Copperhead, who was as still as an ice sculpture, erase-faced behind the table's centerpiece. "Since he served me some motherfucker's balls... wait... let him tell you. Hey, Copper, what do you do in the kitchen now?"

Copperhead's slit-stoned eyes snuck around the candles. "I wash the dishes."

"That's right, bitch. You see, Reynolds, it doesn't take much to get demoted around here." He slapped me on the shoulder again. "So, take away whatever you want from tonight. It's not going to take you much more of these mistakes to get deaded out there."

Trying to act focused on the meal, yet clearly understanding the conditions of our new agreement, I said, "I hear you."

"You know what's still a little funny and confusing to me about that night you and that jackass were sent to kill that snitch, before you made front page headlines for icing two decorated cops?"

Shit, I thought. He knew.

He cleared his throat. "Where in the fuck is my cocaine?"

Trying not to reveal my tell and be an unconvincing liar, I simply said, "Wasn't any coke there, dude."

Like we were playing poker, Cobra read my face for any abnormalities. Luckily for me, I was telling the truth. There wasn't any coke there that night. I wished my brain had told my heart that though, because it was thumping so hard I could feel it inside my earlobes.

"Yeah, that's what I figured because that pussy—" he pointed at Dez, "—told that pussy—" he panned over to Copperhead, "—that there wasn't any coke. The thing is, Reynolds, the BBPs were expecting fifty pounds or so of yeyo. So, not only did your fucking dumb Knuckler show raise some eyebrows to my business, I'm also out a bunch of money."

Rather than state what everyone else in the room was thinking about the fantasy cocaine, I elected to simply state, "We were sent there by Linnwood Perry to kill a snitch and some cops. There was never any talk about recovering and bringing back any coke at all." I got a little bold.

"We did everyone a favor and even though Dez was stupid, we got it done. No coke anywhere."

As much as I disliked intentionally throwing Dez under the bus, I was readily reminded that it was his idea to steal the drugs. I knew it was stupid, and if we walked away alive from that Halloween feast, I was going to make sure Dez realized that.

In all honestly though, it didn't seem like Cobra or Copperhead had any idea that we fell into a huge duffle bag of heroin. Whether or not we were dealing it outside of our designated area didn't seem to matter.

Cobra gripped my shoulder with his giant hand and dug his nails into me. "Besides, Reynolds, you would never betray or steal from me. There is no way you could possibly be that fucking stupid... especially after burning down my home and killing a bunch of my brothers." He scanned me one last time, making sure I was telling the truth.

"There was no coke, Cobra. I promise."

His hand regressed to its less intimidating pat. "That's what I figured," he said. "No one is that dumb."

With a mouth full of runny instant pasta, Bait finally spoke up. "He's pretty fucking stupid. He has a Batman tattoo."

Cobra pounded his fist on the table as he erupted in laughter. "I do like the whore, Reynolds. Don't make me kill her."

After we finished dinner and said our goodbyes, Egon escorted us home. Not one word was said and the radio was off. Halfway home, the silence was lifted by the buzzing of my cell phone. Cobra had sent me the pictures of Dez and Copperhead.

IX

SACRIFICES

My anxiety was at an all-time high after Cobra's threats toward the Knucklers. Even though he said that he believed me, I kind of had a bad feeling that he knew about the drugs we stole from the cops. However, we were moving the drugs undetected, and after one near confrontation with El Reinado de Sangre, Dez got his followers to start wearing red bandanas like the Culver City Boys 13.

In an attempt to throw them off the trail of us infringing on their territory, the Deziens also started carrying spray cans and dropping the CXC13 tag everywhere. We all figured it was smarter to start a neighborhood war rather than a vampire war.

I tapped Bait on her bony shoulder. "Before we start in with you bringing Johns back to us, you need to know how this works. I need to show you what we do, and I also have to make sure you have the stomach for killing."

"I don't think my stomach can get more grossed out than it was when we went to The Snake Pit or whatever it was called. 'Reynolds'. Why does he call you that?"

"We aren't born with any names, so we create our own names based on products, things we see, stuff like that."

It went farther than that though. Cobra called me Reynolds because it was a constant reminder to me that I opened up the Battlesnakes to The Habit. Although Cobra didn't put two-and-two together at the time when I introduced The Habit to him, her burning down his compound was about more than killing vampires. Her kiddie TV show, *Dag Nabbit*, had a stereotypical butler character on it named Reynolds. Essentially, when the studio ignored the outrage from the black community over the modern-day equivalent of Stepin Fetchit, someone burned down the soundstage where they filmed the show. Those someones also left Snake symbols sprayed all over the studio lot. Well, since the show had reached its peak long before the arson, and little Dag Nabbit had grown up, the studio cancelled the show.

Typecast as this cutesy little girl, The Habit stopped getting jobs immediately. Two years later, she was a full-blown junkie whose camera time was limited to inflammatory muff shots of her falling down on Sunset Boulevard. The tabloids served up the pics ad nauseam with a yuck-yuck and a nudge-nudge to give working saps in America a good laugh. The show had a resurgence a few years later, but it became the children's show equivalent of watching a *Naked Gun* movie only to remind your friends that Nordberg is a murderer.

Of course, I knew none of this when I brought her to the original Battlesnakes compound. King Cobra simply didn't recognize her because she had fallen so far from her star.

I shuddered thinking about how Los Angeles tore her up, so I switched topics away from The Habit. "Dez has changed his name a lot. A few years ago, he named himself after this local artist Dez Einswell. He thinks he's pretty cool."

"Okay. Whatever."

"Not whatever. You have to be serious if you want to be involved in this. Trust me, I've told you before and I'll tell you again, Bait, I can't turn you into a vampire. So, the reason you're doing this is to kill and hunt people and do drugs. I'll protect you, but that's about all I can offer you. What if I'm faded and I let things get out of control?"

She sipped an iced coffee. "Like I care what the hell happens. It's free drugs." She started listing the positives on her fingers. "It's a free place to live and I'm not getting beaten up and I'm not fucking to make money for someone else."

When she reached her fourth finger, she made a fist and grunted. It was pathetic.

"And you don't think our pimp is the Battlesnakes?"

Bait giggled. "That name still cracks me up. It's so retarded."

I chuckled as well. "I know, it's like Ninja Turtles or some shit."

"I know, right?" She paused for a second. "Ninja Turtles? Is that another gang?"

"Ummm, no."

Bait put up her left hand for a high-five and put her right thumb down. "Battlesnakes. Lame."

I didn't have the heart to tell her that I didn't engage in the high-five, the fist bump or the shaka. She was a kid. I had to remember that. So I high-fived her.

"Anyway, if you think someone as stupid as me has some sneaky plan to burn down your house or burn down the snake guy's house, I don't."

"Well, good, because they will literally eat you alive. Don't forget what you saw in there. That was tame by their standards."

"What was the deal with this chick The Habit anyway? Did you love her or something? I mean can you even feel things like that? Do you have any feelings or anything?"

"I have something because I let you live, didn't I?" I slugged back some of Pico's beer and blood dipped a new cigarette, then lit it. "I guess I have feelings."

"Well, were you in love with her or something?"

"I don't know. I know I wanted to love her. I loved her house. It's pretty much my house now. No one knows about it and she's probably dead."

A jealous flush came across Bait's face. "So, how do you fuck anyway?"

"Do I have to answer that question?"

"I mean, isn't like your insides all filled with dust and dead shit?"

"No. There is blood in there, and my heart circulates it around. But there's not much, and we need a constant source of it. That's why the bottom feeders always keep some on hand for us. As far as sex... that's a little more difficult to explain and I'd rather not have this conversation with a twelve-year-old."

"Thirteen. Whatever, I'm a whore." She rubbed up against me.

"Dude, don't touch me. Don't do that. Don't ever do that!"

"Are you like gay or something? Why not? I'm a hooker."

I ashed my cigarette on the coffee table. "You're a child."

"I'm a child that you're willing to put at risk just for you to get high, you selfish cock. I bet your wiener doesn't even work."

"Enough. Get ready. Besides, what would be the point of having sex knowing that you can't reproduce?"

"Well, what about Dez? He's always talking about raping chicks and stuff."

I latched on to the back of her neck. "Stay the fuck away from Dez." I shoved her toward my room. "And get ready. Wear something stealth, please. I don't want to see a scarf with skulls on it unless you're hanging from it."

✂

Bait dragged on a dipped cigarette. "Gross!" She flicked the butt at my leg. "Why do you smoke like this? You should smoke cloves."

"You asked to try it," I said. "Shhhh."

She stood behind me. "Why are we here? There aren't any Johns at the gym at midnight."

We stood in the shadows, peering through the window that allowed everyone on Highland to see California's finest hardbodies show off their vanity.

"That's the fun of this. We aren't out to get Johns tonight. Watch and learn, little girl."

A stout jackoff walked by the display case with his shirt off. As he curled with both arms, he crossed right by us, put the weights down and said something to a very sweaty girl on a stationary bicycle.

"Hi again, Mazzuco," I whispered, remembering the bouncer from Halloween night.

"Who are these losers?"

"They would be the prey. She works here, closes up and lets him exercise after hours. He is just some douche bag who was working the door when I took you out for your birthday. He tried to start shit and I'm going to repay him for it. I could have torn the guy to shreds there, but there are some ethical codes involved about revealing ourselves in public places. So, I started following him around. Figured out his whole routine. When he gets done with work—"

"Where does he work?"

I shot her a look. "Do you listen at all? He's the doorman at Club Thirst."

She looked perplexed. "You mean that lame place we went for Halloween?"

"Yes, for God's sake... focus. When he gets done with work, he comes here and works out with his girlfriend. Anyway, since she has keys and is a personal trainer, she lets him work out and shower and shit for free."

The douche began egging his girlfriend on to do more reps. She was struggling.

"This guy is an asshole, huh? So, we're going to jump in there and just get high on this guy and share some with her?" Bait nodded her head up and down repeatedly and rounded her eyes. Her bucked teeth flickered yellow in the streetlight.

"No, we're not here to get high tonight. You'll never get high with me. I'm teaching you how this is done."

"But we're gonna sweep in from the ceiling and save her, right?"

"Fuck no, Bait. We're not a halfway house. We're going to kill both of them. What did I say to you before we left? I'm a killer, not a swashbuckler. This is to make sure you can deal with this. Whether innocent or guilty of being a fucktard means nothing to me. It shouldn't to you either. Focus."

Her nostrils flared out. She hid behind her skunked hair and started trembling.

I put my hand on her shoulder. "Bait, I knew that once you realized that this isn't about romance and writing poems that you wouldn't want to be involved. C'mon, let's go back."

Her shaking intensified. She shook the hair out of her face revealing that she was beaming. She began hopping up and down. "Are you kidding me? I want to kill that cunt so badly. I hate her and everyone who looks like her. Can I stab her in the face or play kickball with her head after you rip it off? Can I? Pleeeeaaaase?" She swatted me with the back of her hand on the chest. "Oh look, they're heading back to the showers. How do we get in?"

I hadn't noticed until now that she pieced together a makeshift stealth outfit with a pair of Dez's black girly jeans and an old Youth Brigade sweatshirt. She grinned and tied her hair back in a ponytail with a garbage bag twisty and tightened the strap on her backpack.

I licked a little bit of leftover flesh out of my back teeth that had been in there for a few days. I looked south toward my house down by Melrose. I looked back at Bait. Still beaming. Then, confused, I push the door open. "It's not locked."

"Awesome. No need to crawl through the ceiling or anything, right.?"

I continued to look at her with concern and confusion.

"Come on." She walked in front of me, sliding across the floor sideways.

I reached into my pocket and grabbed a handful of change. "Okay, Bait. We rarely just hunt people for the hunt, but if we're going to, why not make it fun? Now watch. You'll get the same reaction every time."

I lifted a couple of pennies and threw them over the stalls. They landed one shower before her and spun into the drain.

Cling. Cling.

Nothing. I held Bait back with my forearm. "Wait for it."

Still nothing.

Bait reached into her bag of tricks and before I could stop her, she winged a handful of rocks into the shower with the girl.

"Owww!" the girl screamed.

I looked at Bait and shook my head, mouthing *Why?* She devilishly bit into her palm and snickered.

We heard the echoing voice of the personal trainer. "What the fuck, Mazzuco? I've got fucking shampoo in my eyes. What, you haven't gotten enough of coaching my 'fat ass'?"

Bait couldn't contain herself. She pulled my ear down to her mouth. "He called her a fat ass." Bait snorted.

My cheeks filled with laughter and I closed my eyes. I waved my hand at her to stop and pushed myself back up on her head.

She attempted to lower her voice and shouted, "Clean your pussy, fatso."

I smacked her on the back of the head. "Shut up."

"What's so funny, you asshole?" the girl yelled. "That hurt. What are these? Rocks? Nice. Much better than your dick, you limp shit."

Bait and I looked at each other in surprise.

Playing along at this point, I whispered to Bait, "Listen to this."

I cupped my hand over my mouth and tried to make an Italian, Mazzuco-sounding voice. "Gets backs to da weights, tubby." It probably sounded more like someone from Transylvania than New Jersey.

Bait fell over in the shower next to us, hysterical. I grabbed the iPod she gave me out of my pocket and threw the earbuds into my ears. I loved having aggressive music playing when I pounced on a human. Cobra liked Tosh, I liked 7 Seconds. I flicked the touch screen.

"What the fuck, Mazzuco?" The personal trainer turned off the shower and stepped out of the shower, rubbing the water out of her eyes with a towel and scratching her ass.

I sped toward her like a Greyhound bus, passing five showers on both of my sides. I jumped. As soon as the towel was off her face, I was on her like a beast. I didn't have time to turn around to see if Bait had gotten up to witness what I was about to do. This bitch had to be taken care of immediately as not to alarm Mazzuco... yet.

I pried her mouth open with my right hand and quickly ripped off her bottom jaw, tongue intact, so she couldn't scream very easily. I immediately put my left foot into the portion of her face where the mouth used to be and pressed my foot down hard. She squirmed around. Her defined arms reached toward my face. She tried to lash around with her ultra-cheesy, jewel encrusted French manicure.

I kicked my boot up into her skull, busting through her nose and blowing out her eyes. Her arms dropped, and as I held her head down, I grabbed both her arms and twisted them outward, breaking them off entirely. I chucked both arms into the showers at my sides. To end the job, I stood up in the boot I had in her mouth, lifted my other leg, and just crushed right through her sternum. If there was even a second of life left in her, it was done after that. A successful workout: she lost some of that extra weight Mazzuco obsessed about.

I dug my face into her chest, and while picking the bone slivers left from her ribcage out of the way, I tugged out her pulmonary veins and sucked the life directly out of her heart. In the middle of the carnage, I spun my head around. I made sure that my face was drenched in blood and that heart parts were hanging out of my mouth.

I even growled like a monster.

I saw Bait, standing underneath the low lights of the gym shower back at the end of the hall where we began. Her face wasn't beaming anymore and her backpack spilled from her shoulders to the middle of her back.

I shook the veins and grabbed the personal trainer by her hair, ripping off what was left of her crown.

Bait looked at me in shock and tears rolled down her eyes. Another handful of rocks that she had prepared fell from her hand.

"RJ," she whimpered.

I howled again. If she didn't know yet, now it was clear that I was a monster.

"That was… totally… fucking… awesome!" She reached toward a rack next to her. "Do you need a towel, dude?"

Pieces of heart fell out of my mouth as I slam-dunked the head to the tiles, splashing it everywhere. I secretly wished the more noble Eldritch were there to perform my public service announcement about the inherent dangers of vampirism. I knew that if I saw myself in the mirror that it would have been laughable.

"Bait you can't look like you're afraid of blood," I insisted. "You need to look sweet."

I ripped the twisty out of her hair and broke it into two pieces with my teeth. I grabbed her greasy skunk hair on both sides and tied them off into pigtails. Mazzuco's "bro-jams" of Korn and Drowning Pool filled the men's shower. I looked at the Youth Brigade sweatshirt that Bait was wearing for a second, then I spun her around. I figured it would work.

"What if he comes after me? He's a big guy."

"I've got your back, don't worry. I promise."

The corners of Bait's face curled upward around her buckteeth. "Really?"

"No, stupid. We're doing this so I can have some meathead named

Mazzuco attack and kill you. Get rid of that smile. It looks too forced. Try to look confused and alone or something." I handed her the iPod.

She put the earbuds in her ears. "What's this shit?"

"Come on. Go with it. You need music to be a lunatic." I shoved her toward the shower. "Besides, the music he's listening to is totally wrong."

She walked two steps, sideways with her arms extended like she was running a defensive basketball drill.

"Stop."

Bait took an earbud out. "What?"

"Walk normal," I commanded with my finger pointing toward Mazzuco's shower. "Act terrified." Reluctantly, she continued her trek.

When she had gotten right to Mazzuco's stall, she turned back. I nodded my head, assuring her that everything was going to be cool. Then, I leapt to the top of the mold-lacquered, once-blue-tiled stalls and held my finger up to my mouth, letting out another subtle "Shhhhh".

Bait curled her little piggy nose in excitement and shot me a thumbs-up. Then, as if she were about to audition for a part in a B-movie, she put her flattened hand in front of her eyes, moved it down her face and changed her expression from one of excitement to one of dread.

I smoothly kept stride across the tops of the shower stalls. Bait kept her eyes on me. I stopped right above her. With my fingers, I signaled: *1... 2... 3*.

Bait tore back the shower curtain, looked up at Mazzuco and sweetly said, "Is this yours, mister?" She lifted the personal trainer's annihilated skull up with her left hand.

I gave the meathead a second to take it in. He shrieked like the bitch he was. The cry was my signal to plunge down from on top of the shower and grab him from behind. Without delay, I ripped off a hollow, metal rack inside the shower that was bolted to the wall with my left arm and subdued the Guido with my right.

As quick as the rack came off the wall, I pierced it directly through the center of his chest and started fucking his sternum with it, trying to eat away at as much insides as I could. You could hear the chorus of innards squishing around and bursting, mixed with the rhythm of the shower dripping into the drain. You could hear bones cracking. Great sounds compared to his lame music.

"Holy shit," Bait yelled frantically. "He was fucking jerking off."

Mazzuco's screams gargled with blood and throat lining. He tried to cough, but all the air in his chest was purging out through his gashed lungs.

Bait bounced from side-to-side, seemingly skipping in place. "RJ! He was jerking off! RJ! RJ! He was *jerking off*!"

The meathead began losing consciousness. I pulled the rack from his chest and lanced him directly through the heart. Using the rack like a crazy straw, I put the opposite end in my mouth and sucked the life out of the guy. With my left arm still restraining his chest, I pumped it like I was giving him CPR.

Out of life, Mazzuco slumped to the floor. As he fell, I saw Bait. She stood with the personal trainer's head in her left hand and a shit-eating grimace on her face. "Watch this," she said. She lifted back her boot and stomped on Mazzuco's cock.

I coughed some of his blood out of my mouth. "Dude, Bait! He's dead. No need to kick his dick! What's wrong with you?"

She pushed her head trophy toward my face. "Pretty fucking sweet… right?"

I shuttered a little more and swatted it out of her hand. "No."

"Hey, asshole, wake up."

I felt the sunlight fry my skin. "Owww! Dez, close the curtains. What are you doing?" I howled, pulling the comforter over my body.

"Where were you last night? Copperhead and I were up in Hollywood. I thought we were gonna get high last night."

"Close the curtains," I said. "It might hurt me like shit, but I can still jump out of this bed and kick your ass."

Dez had already moved on to where Bait lay. "Owww," a tired Bait grunted. "Why are you kicking me? Oh, it's you."

"Get up off the floor, little whore. The men need to talk right now."

"Dez, close the curtains," I insisted again.

"Dude, that hurt. You kicked me in the stomach," Bait squealed.

I felt the warmth of the room return to dark and I threw the comforter off. "You better have a really good explanation for doing that, Dez."

Bait left the room and headed into the bathroom. I think she was crying.

"Sorry, I just thought maybe you wanted to tell me what you were doing last night."

"Seriously, what is wrong with you? Why would I want to hang out with Copperhead? Why are you hanging out with Copperhead?"

"He's my friend. He's a lot better of a friend to me than you have been lately."

"Okay, let me explain this in a way you can understand because obviously you're way too dense to get it. I took Bait out last night for a hunt. You know, we have this big plan to lure assholes back here so we can get high whenever we want. Remember?"

"That was never my plan, RJ."

"What are you talking about? This is something that is going to benefit the Knucklers. This is less work. This is cleaner. This is a way for us not to have to deal with any police."

"Too bad everyone else just thinks you're soft."

"Soft how? When was the last time you went out and just hunted someone, Dez?" I rubbed off the dry skin that had fried when Dez exposed me to the light.

"Did you happen to clean up the bodies?" Dez threw me the *LA Times*. "At a health club? RJ, what are you doing? It's all over the news and it's the biggest story in the world right now."

I read the headline out loud. "A Man and Woman Mutilated at Local Fitness Club."

Dez punched a hole through the wall. "Do you think that Cobra is going to like that at all? He's going to kill us."

I jumped to my feet and snatched Dez's head with my hands. "Please tell me—*Please* tell me—that you didn't tell Copperhead about this."

Dez tried to shake his head loose from my grip.

"Dez. Please don't tell me that you told Copperhead about this."

He shoved me away. "No, dude. I haven't said shit. I wasn't even sure it was you. I actually figured that it was some invalid in Hollywood, since that far up Highland isn't where we're allowed to hunt anyway."

I pointed to the chair in the corner of the room. "Sit down." Dez did as he was told. "And wipe that look off your face, you smug little bastard. What right do you have to tell me how to handle my business?"

"We're gonna get in a lot of trouble. Everyone thinks that this whole thing with the whore is a huge mistake. They think you care more about her than you do about us. You're the leader of the Knucklers. You aren't acting like a leader at all. It's a complete repeat of what happened with The Habit. This time, it's worse. Don't you think that this sends out a huge red alert to The Cloth? Humans don't kill other people like that. It's being called the most despicable murders since Richard Ramirez. This isn't gang violence or killing some pimp or drug dealer and then getting the halfwits to clean up our mess in our house or on our territory. You specifically went against every single law that we have lived by since I can remember."

I sighed. "Call everyone. We need to have an emergency meeting tonight."

Dez stayed in the chair and looked at me with his mouth open.

"Well, what are you waiting for? Go."

He got up and shoved the chair across the room.

Bait appeared from the bathroom and Dez strutted by her, shoving her into the bathroom door. "I wish you would've stayed in there," he yelled.

Shuffling her feet, Bait walked into my doorway. "I'm sorry," she moaned as her face collapsed into her hands.

X

VIOLATORS

Christmas rolled around, which was a good thing for all of us. Dumb people carry more cash around during the happiest time of the year, so it was really easy to make money being a stick-up kid. It was also a cleaner way to stay alive and not so many people had to die.

The heroin operation was running smoothly too. Bait took the money the Deziens made selling the heroin to a drop box we set up with Eldritch. He, in return, dropped a reasonable amount of uncut, stolen H for her to pick up and bring back to my house. Then, Dez and I weighed and cut the heroin with baby laxatives and ephedrine. Finally, Bait divided the stolen heroin out to the undercover Deziens who dealt it in Culver City. The process went full circle and the money came back to me. I counted it and bundled it, called Eldridge and the cycle continued. Sure, Bait wasn't fulfilling her role of bringing me Johns to kill and eat and get high on, but I decided that this was a better way for her to earn her keep. After her sadistic performance at the gym, I rethought stealing her humanity.

As far as we knew, the Battlesnakes had no idea about what we were doing under their noses, and the only gang getting screwed was the Mexicans because they weren't paying King Cobra as much as they were supposed to.

Bait shook my shoulder as I sprawled out on the couch, half asleep, listening to some motivational music by Johnny Thunders. "RJ, wake up."

I snorted and rolled over. "Can it wait until later?" I didn't know why I was so tired; I hadn't been doing any real work for a long time other than counting bills. "Put the money on the table, Bait. I'll deal with it later."

She bit down on her lip as her face slid behind her hair. "That's the thing. I think some of Dez's friends are mad at us."

"Us? There is no us."

I wiped my eyes with my palms and flossed some nap plaque out of my teeth with my fingernail. Shaky at first, I sat up, grabbed a silver spoon off the coffee table, and fired up some leftover dust and blood using a pen and wrinkled tinfoil. Groggily, I wheezed, "What are you talking about?"

"Well…" Her left eye parted out of the center of her hair-fort and twitched erratically. "People aren't paying all the money they owe this week."

"Why? Didn't they sell all the shit?"

"I don't know, they just told me to bring more."

"So, where's the money? Are those little shits using all the heroin?"

The bad idea of putting a little girl in charge of the day-to-day affairs of our covert operation suddenly made me feel claustrophobic in my own skin. Whether the Deziens were pussy vampires or not, they were much stronger than Bait would ever be. And with me not directly in the equation, they were starting to overstep their bounds.

"No, they're selling it."

I lofted a huge cloud of bodily exhaust into her face, causing her to cough.

"This is really simple, Bait. It's a point A to point B process." I put the pen back in my mouth and returned to the foil. Out of the side of my mouth, I asked again, "Where is the money?"

She looked upset. "They said they want to get paid."

I huffed in a huge mouthful of vapor. Realizing that I bit off more than I could chew, I coughed it back into Bait's face. Some goop torpedoed out and splashed on her chin.

She sneezed and wiped it off. "Why are you spitting on me?" She knocked the poor man's chalice out of my hand.

Giggly and high but irritated, I jumped to react. I extended my arm, grabbed her by the straps of her overalls and threw her to the floor, holding her down. "Clean it up, whore," I demanded, too dizzy to focus on what I was doing.

Leroy and Skillet, who I thought were outside, shot up from behind the couch and growled.

I grabbed a tabloid with my free hand and waved it at them. "Piss off. Both of you." They stood steadfast and put their front paws on the back pillows of the couch. They flip-flopped between growling and panting like the spasmodic animals they were. Leroy let out a furious bark.

Somehow, Bait managed to rotate her head and submerge her Chiclet teeth into my wrist, causing me to let go and lose my balance while I attempted to get to my feet to face off against the disobedient hounds.

I fell back on the couch and she made a run for it. No longer simply being mischievous, Leroy and Skillet blitzed me and held me down. Skillet locked onto my wrist like a shark snapping at chum as Leroy pinned my shoulders down and bumped my forehead with his like a rhinoceros. As if I had just stubbed my toe or smacked my head on a cabinet, my kneejerk reaction discharged my rage. I flipped Leroy over at his gut and volleyed him across the room. He slammed into the turntable; the needle dragged across the record for a split second and then ceased to emit any power whatsoever. The dog fluttered on his back a little like a turtle and then bounced himself back up to a full stance. He snarled at me with a droopy-eyed look of disgust and then pranced down the hall, following Bait.

I tore my arm away from Skillet's grip; he licked at the tearing arm hair and flesh out of the corner of his mouth as it stretched away from my body like a tug rope. He gnawed at it, then shook his head in disapproval. Before I got situated again on the couch, Skillet smacked me in the face with his tail as he followed his unruly canine co-conspirator.

I sunk down into the couch cushion, grabbed a t-shirt and wrapped it around my arm. "Get back here!" I bellowed at the three of them.

Rather than locking herself into the bathroom with Leroy and Skillet as expected, Bait, followed by both dogs, returned. They barreled toward me like they were on the front line at the beaches of Normandy. Bait emulated the dogs and began growling, twirling the shower radio over her head like she was wielding a mace. Then, standing over me, she pounded the radio against my sternum.

As if it were a planned attack, Leroy and Skillet both jumped and scratched my chest with their robust paws.

"Stop," I begged.

The power of all three soldiers caused a wet fart to seep out of my ass. I felt diarrhea slink down my thigh, onto my calf and then on to the floor. Sidetracked, the dumb Great Dane started licking the shit up. It was no wonder his breath always smelled like Long Beach contaminated shrimp that had been stewing in a pool of vomit inside a pig carcass in the sun for a week.

The distraction gave me the opportunity to reverse and overtake the onslaught. I rotated my body off the couch and dropped onto the floor. I arched my back to try and stand, as my right foot sloshed around in 'rhea still inside my pant leg.

Before I could tell the three musketeers to desist again, they all retreated. The bathroom door slammed closed. Not to be defeated by a little girl and the two dumbest, most uncoordinated dogs on the face of the earth, I stomped down the hall toward them, spattering my runny poop everywhere. Stopping at the door, I took a deep breath, placed my cold fingertips over my closed eyelids and massaged my temples with my thumbs. Trying to release some of my anger, I bit as hard as I could into the t-shirt that was wrapped around my arm.

Calmly, I asked, "Bait? What's going on?"

She said nothing. The only sound coming from the other side of the door was her playing bumper boat in the tub with the hounds and them panting uncontrollably.

"Bait?"

"No!"

"No what?" I returned as I continued to rub my face. "It wasn't a question that required a yes or no response." I took my fingers off my eyes and gripped the door handle.

She sucked some agitated snot back into her throat and swallowed it. "No!" She yelled again, this time with a little more punch.

I turned the knob cautiously and I cracked the door open, only far enough to peek inside. A half-corroded battery, that I assumed fell out of my shattered shower radio, beamed me in the eyebrow. I counted backward in my head to remain cool. My anger, mixed with the dizzying effect of the drugs, whispered coaxing messages to my brain, reminding me that the sword of a little girl had just anally lanced me.

I blinked the corrosive particles out of my eye. The three of them were packed into the tub like it was a miniature submarine. I dragged my poo-foot into the door and slowly opened it with my left arm. I slid into the bathroom sideways and made my way to the throne. No projectiles were catapulted at me. Leroy and Skillet, bushed from all the exercise, shook off and let their guards down.

I dunked my gross foot into the toilet and sloshed it around in a sad attempt to wash off my mess. Without looking at the lot of them, I reached over and put my hand on Bait's wet head. Spray-on black hair dye was smeared all over her face and shoulders. I wiped it off my hand onto my pant leg. Leroy extended a peace offering by licking my hand, signifying that the war was over.

"Tell me what's going on, Bait, and why you didn't come home with my money."

"You're just gonna be mad at me."

Continuing not to make eye contact with her, fearing I would rip her skull from her body, I said, "So beating the hell out of me, getting my dogs all riled up and turned against me, this was something you thought would make me happy?" I spoke slowly, like a parent trying to further investigate unsatisfactory behavior.

I placed my hand back on her head.

She shook me away. "You were the one who was about to hit me."

"I wasn't going to hit you. You knocked the last little bit of drugs I had out of my hand."

"Oh, so your drugs are more important to you than I am?" She pushed herself against the soap dish in the tub.

I reached further toward her and placed my hand back on her head. For all intents and purposes, yes, the drugs were more important to me than she was. After all, they helped keep me alive, another question in itself. Rather than get into a circular argument about why I existed, I played to her neediness.

"No, Bait. You're more important than the drugs." I dipped a half-wet cigarette into a claw-induced laceration on the back of my neck and flicked it into my mouth. "Do you mind if I smoke?"

"I don't care," she huffed as she started petting the dogs. "It's your house. Or is it that bitch's?"

Although I continued to avoid locking eyes with her, I heard her voice starting to give way to whimpering.

"Bait, please answer the question. Why aren't they going to pay me? I thought we all discussed how the system was going to work. No one was going to get paid until we refunneled the cash we made from the heroin into buying new heroin that wasn't stolen from the Battlesnakes." I stepped back. "I'm not blaming you, but that is what we all agreed on. It was all really simple."

She hugged Leroy's big, hairy mane. "I've been getting high with them. For a while now. They've been giving me heroin."

My eyes shut. Concerned, I continued to calm the conversation.

"I thought we agreed that you wouldn't use if I let you live here. You told me that since you'd been on the street, you didn't use that much and that you didn't even really like it."

Trying to camouflage her response under the thundering tongues of Leroy and Skillet guzzling bathwater, she quietly admitted, "I lied."

Petting her head, I asked, "So, you've been using this whole time?"

"That's not what I lied about."

Remembering why I hated kids, I steadied my hand. "Okay, what did you lie about?"

Figuring that a day full of surprises had come to an end, I looked over to her.

Nonchalantly, she answered, "Pretty much everything."

"Huh?"

"That first night I came over here... you remember, right?"

"Yes," I exhaled. "How could I forget?"

"You were supposed to be my first screw. I had just met the pimp you killed that day. I only ran away from home at the beginning of the summer."

My forehead dropped into my hand that wasn't straddling her skull. "Dammit, Bait." I should have known that someone who was so lacking in any kind of street smarts could never have been on the streets for two years.

"I'm sorry, RJ. I didn't have anywhere to go."

"So, you chose here? Here, of all places in the world. So, now you're going to tell me that Dez's little assholes have been paying and that you've been stealing my money. Right?"

Her whimpering built into bulbous teardrops that plopped into the half-full bath. She shrugged away from me and snuck behind her dog guardians. "No."

"No, what? Fine, you lied to me so you could go on some romantic vampire adventures that you read about in some dumb books. See, it's not glamorous in any way. Are you satisfied?" As much as I regretted what I said next, at that moment, it felt like all there was to say. "Now dry off and take the money you stole to the bus station or airport or wherever and go home to your mommy and daddy."

"I didn't steal your money!" she said. "Instead of giving me the money, I've been asking them to get me high." She clutched onto Leroy, almost strangling him. "Then, I let them fuck me."

"What?" I shouted as I smashed my t-shirt-covered arm back into the mirror.

"I'm sorry. I wanted to feel like one of you. I thought if I got high and fucked them that maybe they would bite me and turn me into a vampire."

I plucked my hand out of the smashed glass and the rest of the wall behind the vanity. I nabbed my cell phone out of the sink and opened it to call Dez.

She lunged toward me, trying to grab the phone. "Don't tell them I told you," she pleaded frantically. "Don't call them."

Dez's voicemail picked up. "Dez, it's RJ. Did you know that your little idiots are raping Bait? What's going on? We agreed that she would help us and that none of this could ever happen." I hung up the phone and tossed it back into the sink.

"Dez knows."

"What do you mean Dez knows?"

"Dez was the first one to fuck me."

Too mad to think, much less speak, I raced to the door, grabbed my phone again and called Tahoe.

He picked up. "Yo, RJ."

"Tell everyone to get to the goddamn garage now!" I screamed.

"Relax."

"Relax nothing. Make sure every one of you sorry-ass motherfuckers are there. Now!"

"But…"

"No buts! Dez isn't picking up his phone. Make sure that little twat and all his lemmings are there."

I hung up and furiously stomped and huffed and puffed around, looking for a sweatshirt.

Bait lifted herself out of the tub, using Skillet's head. "There's more."

"Like what? Like all that isn't enough?" I yelled. "You little liar!"

I stormed out of the house. Whatever other lies she had in store for me would have to wait until after I dealt with Dez.

⚸

"I think we all know why we're here," I said to a packed garage of Knucklers. Dez was the only one missing. I left Bait at home. The meeting was no place for children.

Nobody spoke. They all just looked down. "So, no one has anything to say to me?"

They continued to look at the silt-covered cement.

I walked over to Tahoe. "Nothing to say, huh, big man?"

"It's just…"

I fired into his ear like a drill sergeant. "What the fuck is wrong with you all? You big retarded twat! You have killed hundreds of people you didn't like. As a matter of fact, I saw you rip a guy to pieces, that's right, *pieces* for giving you a cooked-up bag full of ephedrine. That's nice. Who was there to clean up your mess that time?" I swatted Tahoe on the back of the head and continued down the line.

"Parker? How many family pets have you shredded and filled with heroin? No red flags there. Most fucking coyotes leave syringes next to their prey." I stood over him and shoved him into the ground. I held his face to the floor. "Who cleaned up your stupid, little ass when you were passed out in some old lady's backyard? I guess we can just say that you're lucky that the sun didn't come up."

Struggling to talk, he hacked out, "You."

Pico laughed.

I jumped across the room. "Did you just laugh, you twisted old fuck?"

I grabbed both his legs and pulled them out from under him. When his back hit the ground, I flicked my arms outward and snapped both his femurs.

"Why don't you tell everyone here about when you tried to anally rape a Batwanger? Feel free. Who saved your ass that time? No red flags there, either. We had to kill it and ditch its body." I picked him up by one of his broken limbs and launched him through the windshield of the Nova.

"And the rest of you ungrateful pissants. I have a story for every single one of you. That would be except for you hyped bottom-feeding nobodies who somehow managed to sneak into my gang without my knowledge. That's right. *My* gang."

The peewees stood in the corner. They all had their faces hidden behind their wannabe Dez emo hair.

"Not for long," one of them whispered.

I knew who it was. The one who had been cleaning our house. It was the little prick that wised up to me all the time.

"I hope I didn't just hear something from you, kid. This isn't a fraternity." I jumped over to him. "Do you and all your buddies think that I would give a squirt of shit for you at all? This isn't about being in some clubhouse with your fudge friends. This is about survival."

The kid looked up from his gloomy daze. "Dez says you're soft."

"Don't do anything, RJ," Tahoe yelled from across the garage.

I grabbed the kid by his hands. A fury went through my body that was different than knocking someone off to get high. "I'm not sure what Dez has taught you about being a vampire, but there is something that I'm pretty sure he was too lazy to teach you."

The other Deziens stepped backward.

"What's the matter, boys? I'm sure you don't know either."

They took another step back.

"I guess we can all learn a lesson today, can't we?"

Tahoe yelled again, "RJ, don't do this. We can get through this. Cobra and Copperhead don't know anything."

I turned to him. "Shut up." I pinned the kid's head down on a table. "There is this funny thing that you can't learn from Hollywood movies about what you are. Even more so, you can't learn it from drug addicts you see on TV," I told him, and shoved his left hand into his own mouth.

"I'm a drug addict. I'm a drug dealer. I'm a gang member."

With his chin pinned like a vice, I used the top of his head to crush and chew through his own fingers, digit by digit. Directly through his hand to the wrist.

"Please... God, stop," the bastard begged and screamed, choking as he forced pieces of flesh and bone out of his mouth.

"I can't understand you. Are you still hungry?" I pulled his right arm away, breaking it behind his back. Then, I shoved that hand in and used his teeth again, even though some were falling out due to the strength of the bone. I hammered away at the top of his head with my palm. Gore flew everywhere. His choking intensified and once I got him down to his second nub, I chucked his ass across the room.

I wiped my hands off on my pants. Tahoe looked at me shocked. "You have something to say, Tahoe? Does anyone else have something to fucking say to me?"

The big man looked at his shoes. "No."

"Why don't you tell everyone here the big secret that you have apparently all forgotten to pass on to these disrespectful children?"

Tahoe mumbled.

"Again. I can hear you, but let's make sure they can hear you too."

"Limbs don't grow back."

I looked at the kid in the corner. One of his boys tried desperately to wrap his stumps with grease rags. "Not much of a badass Knuckler anymore, are you, big mouth? Pico, when your legs heal, go drop this wiseass off in an alley. He didn't make the cut. Let him starve to death."

I surveyed the rest of the Deziens and pointed at them with my index finger and my pinky. "You don't rape little girls. If you think that I'm soft, then so be it. Step up and tell me how big of a pussy I am."

They all looked at their friend in the corner and then back to the floor.

XI

MUTES

I felt that I might have acted a little impulsively by crippling the Dezien. At the end of the day, it should have been Dez who caught the brunt of my anger. It was just like him not to show up, knowing how pissed off I was. He was always such a chicken shit when it came to facing the music. Chicken shit kid. He sent his peasants to feel my wrath rather than admit to me that he was fucking Bait. The way I looked at it, the line at that point was clearly drawn between the young and old in the Knucklers. They fucked with one of mine and I fucked with one of theirs. The kid would eventually die. If a vampire wasn't able to feast, stalk and kill to support their habits, they dried up.

I had to face the facts: what right did Dez have to live more than Bait? After all, she actually was a legitimate living creature. We just… were.

I opened the front door to my place and wasn't greeted with the usual slobber hose from Leroy and Skillet. I hoped Bait hadn't taken everything I said to heart. Just then, a funny image went through my mind: Bait being pulled around Union Station by the two dumb dogs, trying desperately to purchase tickets out of Dodge for the three of them.

I called out as I locked the door behind me. "Bait?" I rounded the hallway toward the bathroom. The two dogs, their tremendous bodies fully stretched across the floor, scrunched their snouts under the bathroom door. They had scratched the hell out of the white door to get in, but obviously Bait was too tied up in her web of lies to let them in.

As I got closer, I noticed that both dogs were also frantically licking the floor. I wasn't shocked, nor did I find anything out of the ordinary about their behavior, as they proved earlier that they had no problem tongue kissing my diarrhea-soaked pant leg. It was safe to say that they would drink and eat anything.

I crossed my bedroom and saw her precious bathmat on the floor, next to my bed, empty. "Bait? Where are you?"

I dropped some change and a handful of the Dezien's fingertips on my dresser and proceeded back down the hall to my bathroom. Was I too hard on her? Hardly, I told myself; she put herself in danger's way from day one. Everything about her living with me and mooching off me was a lie.

I looked down at the dogs before I politely knocked on the bathroom door. I slid Leroy and Skillet out of the way with the outsides of my boots. They weren't licking water or poop at all. It was blood.

"Bait, what are you doing?"

"Go away," she faintly huffed.

I snapped the knob off and slid the door open. And there she was sitting upright with her back against the tub. She had her pants down to her ankles and between her legs were the remains of a smashed two-liter bottle of Pepsi, drenched in blood. On top of the bottle was a cinder block that came from the backyard. The bathtub overflowed, funneling the mess into the mouths of the two junkyard hounds on the other side of the door. They didn't immediately run to save the day. They were far too stupid and scared.

I grabbed the cinder block and heaved it down the hallway behind me, past the dogs. Instantly, I bent down to pull the bottle out of her. Blood and what appeared to be some lining from her uterus bubbled out. When it was removed, the carbonation created a chemical reaction causing a science fair explosion.

"Stop." She grabbed at the bottle, trying to reinsert it.

I nabbed a bunch of towels from under the sink. "Stop what? What are you doing?"

I started patting at the area, trying desperately to dam the floodgates and prevent the continual blood loss. I didn't have time to think about what she was trying to accomplish, but I was sure it wasn't a clichéd teenaged suicide attempt. It was beyond a cry for attention. I wrapped her entire body in towels like a mummy after I ripped off her pants and her drenched shirt.

"Out of here," I snapped at the dogs. They obliged and headed to the living room, knocking each other against the walls in an attempt to clinch the alpha dog position. When they got there, they peered around the corner into the hall as if they'd done something wrong.

Carefully, I slid my right arm under Bait's neck. Her eyes rolled back into her head as she started choking a little bit on blood and soda that had somehow made its way up into her windpipe. My phone rang. I looked over at the toilet. It was the child molester, Dez. I didn't answer it. I'd deal with him later.

"Don't," she pleaded, falling in and out of consciousness.

"Don't what, Bait? I need to get you out of here." I bridged her back. "What did you do?"

"Just let me be."

"What are you doing in here, Bait?" I placed my left arm under her bent legs. "What is all this?"

Her eyes floated around in their sockets as her breathing became louder and louder. She snorted through her nose and tear ducts, an alternative to the clogged passageway to her lungs. I bent her head upright and firmly pressed on her chest cavity with my palm. I pressed every three seconds, angling upward, trying to dislodge the congestion. After my fifth try, a bubble popped out of her mouth and the wheezing settled. At the same time, I felt the soda's bottle cap spin out of her and smack me on the knee.

She began blinking furiously as her skunky hair got stuck in her eyes. "Just leave."

I brushed the hair clear and put my arm back under her knees.

"Just leave me alone," she insisted.

Slowly, I lifted her up and delicately sidestepped my way out of the bathroom. "What are you... what *were* you doing? Are you trying to kill yourself?"

She didn't respond immediately. I reached the bedroom and laid her out on top of my bed and covered her with my comforter. Finally, she said, "Not me... it."

Pico signaled me into the living room as he injected some heroin into Bait's thigh. I patted Bait on the forehead with a warm washcloth and wiped dried blood from her mouth.

"Are you sure we can leave her?"

Dragging his gimpy leg, Pico ignored the question and walked into the other room. After I made sure Bait was sleeping and breathing, I followed.

I fell back onto the couch, exhausted. "What is that?"

For the previous three hours, we had gone through the constant ups and downs of an emergency room that consisted of Bait screaming in pain, not breathing and hemorrhaging from every orifice on her brittle body. Luckily for Bait and me, old Pico was quite a seasoned physician.

I suppose that's how he knew how to break himself in all the right spots whenever he went out on the streets to hunt.

"She gave herself an abortion, RJ."

"What? With a soda bottle and a cinder block?"

"Yeah. I had to clean out what was left of it, but she definitely terminated the pregnancy. She almost terminated herself in the process."

I was shocked. "Are you serious? Where the hell did she learn to do something that stupid?"

Pico lit a cigarette and threw one to me. "I imagine she learned it on the Internet. It's pretty common for desperate kids to do dumb things like that... or at least contemplate it."

I lit my grit off a candle I was using to try and get the smells of the day out of my house. "Wait. How did she get pregnant?"

"Come on, RJ. Don't be so naïve. She's a hooker."

"That's the thing. She told me right before I left for the meeting that she never actually hooked. Wait. Is that the right word? Hooked?"

"Well, she got pregnant somehow."

"She told me that she's been fucking Dez and the kids to get a fix. But that couldn't get her knocked up..."

Pico rolled his eyes.

"So, that's why you crippled that little prick at the meeting? He wasn't just fucking little girls. He was fucking Bait. What's gotten into you? I like the little girl just as much as you do but you can't just go around and kill your own. She's not a pet, RJ."

"Our own what, Pico? What are we? Do you even know where we come from? You've been around longer than me. At least that's what I've been led to believe. Right is right and wrong is wrong. I told all of them that Bait was not to be killed, fucked or fucked with. She was doing our job for us."

"Our job? You mean our deceit. The drugs aren't ours. They were stolen from the cops and that means they were the property of the Battlesnakes."

I tilted my head in disbelief. "And you think now is a good time to speak out against all of this? We all met and agreed we were going to give that little shit Dez his chance. This was his idea. Not mine."

Pico dragged hard on his cigarette. "You're the leader, RJ." He blew out a smoke ring. "Therefore, it was your idea and your decision as far as everyone else was concerned."

I slumped back further into the couch, almost attempting to hide. I wished that none of that day... the day Linnwood Perry came over and the day Dez and I killed the cops and stole the heroin ever existed. As much as I hated to admit it, Pico was right. Who was I to put all of us in so much jeopardy because some dumb, human girl and an even dumber emo-sidekick told me to? Nothing would ever be the same again.

On top of being completely overwhelmed by the scope of everything, something still itched at the back of my neck. "So, Pico, if she was only fucking the Deziens, then how did she get knocked up? I mean, I think it's pretty much a known fact that we can't breed. Sure, with a little help we can get hard and cum and all that, but I know we can't reproduce. It's impossible. Isn't it?"

"Well, most people will tell you that it's impossible for us to be walking around at all. But, you and I both know that we exist. We think, we move and we feel."

"Tell me something I don't know. All that these cherished emotions have done for me is cause me to make horrible decisions."

"There are two possible scenarios here. Either one of Dez's friends isn't a vampire or one of them has evolved."

I ashed my butt at him. "Horseshit."

"Horseshit, what? That's the only plausible explanation unless the girl is lying to you. She said something to me while I was stitching her up."

"Which was?"

"She said, 'You're right, RJ. The world doesn't need any more monsters.'"

"Meaning what? I never said anything like that."

"It means that she was definitely impregnated by one of us. To her, we're the monsters."

I discounted him again with a wave. "Horseshit. The world is filled with monsters. So not every one of them kills other people to get high. How far along was she? Like that even matters. She could be out hooking when I sleep. Stupid kid is probably too dumb to use condoms."

He cupped his cigarette into his hand. "I have no idea how far along she was. Her insides looked like a casserole. Why would she lie to you? What could she possibly achieve by getting you to cripple the Dezien? She knows you have a temper. She risked getting thrown back out on the streets by telling you her secret."

"Ash on the floor, you cripple. It's not like this place can get anymore jacked up."

Pico flicked his cigarette. "Anyway, one of us got the girl pregnant."

"Okay, let's just say that some of us can reproduce. Wouldn't that mean that there would be some girl vampire-things out there somewhere? Shit, the odds say so."

"Like I said, this is something new."

"Uggghhh!" Bait moaned from the bedroom. Pico and I both shot up and rushed down the hall, bumping each other just like Leroy and Skillet, who thankfully had been outside enjoying their meals from earlier that day.

Bait was turned on her side, reaching for the bath mat that was rolled up on the floor, next to the bed.

Pico ran to the far side of the bed and rolled her on her back as I grabbed her hand.

"I want my blanket," she exhaled. At that moment, I felt ashamed that I made a little girl sleep on a rubber bathmat while the person who raped her crashed on a bed in the bedroom next to her. I was just as much a monster as any other Knuckler, vampire, gangster, or drug addict.

She faded back out as Pico filled her up with more heroin. It was clear that Bait couldn't stay at my house any longer... especially after what I did to the Dezien back at the garage.

XII

HEALERS

The old man helped Bait sip some soup. "You know you can't keep her here anymore."

She hadn't spoken much since I found her laid out. I didn't blame her.

"Maybe you can let Eldritch babysit… I mean… take care of her," Pico suggested.

I pulled the blanket up to her neck. "That isn't gonna happen."

As he pulled a thermometer out of her mouth Pico said, "But you said he liked her."

"Don't get me wrong. It's not that I don't trust him; I just know that will be the first place Dez will go looking for her. I've already put Eldritch in enough jeopardy by using him to traffic the drugs and money."

I handed Bait a magazine. She nodded her approval. The actor who played her vampire darling, L. Byron Nightshayde, was on the cover. He was shirtless. His hair was a mess. He had some smug look on his face and he was wiping blood off his fangs with the back of a gloved hand. It was ridiculous. I hadn't decided at that point if I necessarily wronged her or not, but since I felt like a dick, I figured why not be nice to her.

I grabbed the thermometer and inspected it, as if I had any idea what I was doing or what was the normal temperature for a human being for that matter. I put it down on the nightstand. Bait flipped through the magazine, seemingly oblivious to the danger she faced. I hadn't gotten any response from Dez other than a hang up. It was now clear that all trust and allegiance between the two of us had dissipated. I was as dead to him as he was to me.

"Would you be willing to go with her and watch out for her until she's able to get around by herself?"

Pico scratched his head. "Gee, I don't know, RJ…"

"Let me rephrase that. You will stick by her side and you'll get Tahoe to help you."

"They're gonna find her at my place or Tahoe's place just as easily as they would find her here."

I slugged him in the arm. "You don't think I know that? The Knucklers are separated now. I can't take back what I did to that kid and the Deziens can't take back what they did to Bait. I'm still unclear as to how she got pregnant."

Bait tugged on my sleeve.

I looked at her. "Yes."

She turned the magazine around so it faced me and with a trembling finger she pointed to an outfit. "Can you get me this, RJ?"

Doing everything in my power not to slap the magazine out of my face, I looked at Pico. "How much heroin did you give her?"

He held up the empty syringe. "A lot."

I turned back to Bait. "Can you let the grown-ups talk now?"

She dropped the magazine and grabbed her abdomen. Bait furthered the performance by grunting like she had been holding in a deuce for three days.

"Fine, fine, fine," I agreed. "I'll get you the outfit when you get better."

Without thanking me, she dog-eared the magazine page and continued browsing.

I returned to Pico, who looked to be debating whether or not to flee Bait's bedside so he wouldn't be automatically elected to be responsible for her. "Anyway, Pico, I need you and Tahoe to watch over her and hide out at one of the suites with the Batwangers."

"Are you kidding me?"

"Not at all. I can trust them. For Christ's sake, I let them sell drugs and bite cocks off in my neighborhood. It's the least they can do for me. I trust Nomi. What could a group of transsexual weirdos do to you, Tahoe, or me?"

"Why can't you just do this?" He minimized his voice. "And why do you care?"

"There's no need to whisper. She can't hear us." I waved my hand in front of Bait's face. "And I care because I care. End of story. She's a little girl. Don't you care about anything?"

He rubbed his arms. "Getting high."

"That's what I figured. This isn't about being a hero or a savior. It's about what's right. I'm telling you this now…" I pointed at Bait's stomach. "This should never have happened."

I didn't know where my concern for humanity or my sudden humility came from. I guessed it was the price I had to pay for taking daily shots of blood from a naïve and silly little girl.

Pico looked down, almost ashamed. I slapped him back into the conversation.

"Owww," he cried.

"Those slaps didn't hurt, you pussy. Look, I've decided on this. I don't know what else to do."

He rubbed his jaw like I'd just beaten him with a frying pan. Exaggeration was contagious in the room. "You know what you were like when I found you on the street in a garbage bin, RJ? A little twelve-year-old, starving baby. If it weren't for me, you would be nothing more than a bag of bones sitting in a landfill somewhere. The same can be said about all you ungrateful pricks. You, Tahoe, the rest of them. You all wouldn't even exist if it weren't for me."

I pulled him toward me by his shirt and yelled into his eyes. "And where were we before that, Pico? Where did we come from to be left on the streets?"

He avoided my eyes. "I don't know," he answered.

"You don't lie very well, old man. To be honest with you, I don't care where we came from at this point."

"It's my turn to speak, little boy. Please don't lecture me on the right or wrong thing to do. I know." He shook himself loose from my grip. "I know more than all of you self-indulgent pricks. Not one of you has ever thanked me for saving your lives."

"Thanked you? Thanked you for what? Gee, Pico, thanks for bringing me into a world where I am sentenced to being a drug-addicted killer who is sensitive to light, can't get a hard-on, or live a normal life."

I snatched his chin, drew him close to my face so he could see my anger. "Look at me. All of us. We survive on the blood of our disgusting victims and fucking narcotics. Tell me, Pico, how is it that the drugs seem so much more important than the blood? I've never seen a vampire movie where drugs keep them alive. Rather than ask these questions or even think about them, we simply settle into this justification that 'it's just the way we are'. Well, what is that? What are we? Where do we come from?"

I took my other palm from the magazine that was pinned to Bait's face. I ran my hand up and down my torso. "Do you think I like, this? You know what, Pico? I wish you left us all on the streets to die. As a matter of fact—" I pointed between Bait's legs, "—I wish that my mother, if I ever had one, which I'll never know, had the good sense to jam a fucking soda bottle up inside herself and drop a cinder block on it. Wouldn't that have solved all this misery?"

He didn't answer.

I sighed and patted Bait on the head. "Sorry, Bait." She was fast asleep with the magazine covering her face. "I'm going to call Nomi. Do me a favor and call Tahoe. All of this isn't going away and I'm one hundred percent sure that Dez already ratted us out to Copperhead. Guess what that means, old man: Cobra knows we stole from him by now. I couldn't be happier that someone who has searched high and low for a reason to kill me for years now knows I stole a lot of money from him. The safest place for you to be right now is away from me."

Pico did as he was told and began dialing Tahoe's number. "He knows more than you think, RJ," he sneered under his breath.

Rather than continue my tirade about being a fake-human, I dialed Nomi's number.

XIII

ANGELS

Wrapped in a blanket and not a bathmat, Bait snored in Tahoe's arms. I rang the doorbell.

"Are you sure you want us to do this, RJ?" Tahoe whispered, trying not wake Bait.

Before I got the chance to respond, Pico chimed in. "It's the right thing to do, 'Hoe."

Rather than challenge the plan, the big man nodded his head. Sure, he'd rather have been out hunting, lifting weights, or whatever he did in his spare time, but I think I did a concrete job convincing them both that we all had a certain obligation. It was something beyond the self-serving addiction that kept us alive.

One of the Batwangers answered the Christmas light-covered steel door. Leave it to the Batwangers to be seasonally festive.

I extended my hand to shake. "I'm here to see Nomi."

He ignored my gesture and invited us inside. Decorated top-to-bottom like an oddball, sixties science fiction movie, circa *Barbarella*, The 'Wangers's lair—or brothel—was action-packed with characters for the set.

We were escorted toward Nomi's queen's den. Filling the hallways was the strange reverberation of operatic new wave and techno music. It sounded more like whale mating sampled over breakbeats than cohesive music. Pulsating buttons and control panels lined the walls. As we passed rooms, Batwangers came out in silver and gold stretch cat suits, winking and making passing comments at Tahoe.

"Did you bring room service, big man?" one of them asked.

Tahoe responded, "She's not food," referring to the sleeping Bait.

"Tuck it back in your pants."

I commended him by slapping him on the ass. "Good job, Tahoe. That's what you say until you hear otherwise."

As the halls warped and webbed toward the end, Nomi's door slid open like an airlock on a spaceship. Darker than the rest of the house, the room sat as the centralized decorative parasite, seemingly infecting everything else it touched. Cables dripping with green ooze and neon and plastic-encased wiring sprouted out into the hall like the limbs of alien creatures. Knowing of Nomi's multiple connections to the Hollywood world, I wouldn't have been surprised if his portion of the house was designed by a special effects artist who happened to go missing when the interior design was complete.

Our greeter stopped at the door and gracefully ushered us in. "Please, have a seat. Nomi is expecting you." He then pointed us to a fabricated, Martian tentacle that crossed the room and beveled near our end of Nomi's centerpiece, his bed. The four of us did as we were instructed and sat down.

Nomi's bed was truly something to behold. Obviously playing off the giant, foreign insect theme while keeping the whole H.R. Giger décor intact, the bed was an enormous canopy. Spinning around the black support poles were more living cables that were using hydraulics to create a breathing effect. It didn't look like anything was bought from Home Depot. The canopy top was more of a web that pulsated inward and outward and wove itself in a circular pattern as if it were powered by a motor. It was the most unique piece in the room because although I was sure it wasn't a projection, I had no earthly idea how it was spinning itself from nothing to a fully woven web and then back to nothing. I think that Tahoe was trying to peek behind the bed to get the upper hand on any giant, trained tarantulas that were planning a surprise attack.

Even though I thought it was indeed unique and cool, it just seemed like more of the Eldritch and King Cobra pyrotechnics and theatrics than anything else. But in Nomi's defense, he was a very high-priced transgender prostitute, and I always gave his grandiose stagecraft a free pass. Eldritch and Cobra, on the other hand, had no excuse beyond being failed performers.

Bait woke up and rubbed her eyes. "What the hell is this?" She tightened into Tahoe's cradle. "Are we dead, RJ?"

"No, you're not dead."

Nomi appeared from a second room off to the side of the bed. Judging from his elaborate outfit, I guessed he was appearing magically from the wardrobe where he was going to make changes between performances. In reality, it was a walk-in closet he was hiding in so he could make an extravagant entrance after he knew we had a minute to take in the mothership.

"This is cool," Bait said, trying desperately to glance at every piece in the room.

Nomi walked over to Bait and Tahoe and ran his fingers through Bait's greasy, blood-encrusted hair. He wore a leather, form-fitted battle suit that left none of his curves to the imagination, including his boobs and cock. The futuristic witch garb was accentuated with an enormous collar that reflected the interwoven webbing on top of the bed and ended in a lengthy train of steel worms. He wore spiked gloves and buckled moon boots that lit up with bright red lights on the soles. His eyelashes were also spiked, and they popped out from the light blue makeup covering his face. In the center of the makeup, one sparkling silver stripe crossed the tip of his nose at an angle from the bottom of one ear to the fake pointed tip of the other. His lipstick was the same shade as the stripe, though it was difficult to judge the pallet due to the chappy aftereffects of collagen abuse.

"Light," he called out. Our greeter scampered over and lit a bright red cigarette that was extended six inches by a holder. "Leave us," Nomi instructed the concierge, who bowed to each of us then backed out of the room through a secret entrance; his mirrored platform shoes clunked across the disco throbbing floor.

Nomi's hands moved to Bait's breasts. He cupped them; shook off his hands almost immediately and then proceeded to measure Bait's arm tone using a skin fold caliper around her bicep.

Pico looked at me puzzled and wriggled his shoulders. "What?" he mouthed.

I ignored him. I suppose I should have told him and Tahoe how I arranged the meeting.

"Okay, biggins," Nomi said to Tahoe. "Now let's see his rocket."

Tahoe looked at Bait who looked back at him.

"C'mon, big boy, let's see the dick."

As Nomi reached over to unwrap the blanket, Bait swatted at his twirling, neon fingernails. "I ain't got no dick," Bait yelled.

Nomi spiraled around to address me. "RJ..." Before he reached my line of view, his leather and steel train got stuck in one of the canopy poles. He immediately tugged it free, almost causing him to lose his balance. "RJ! What is this? This little boy won't do."

Bait yelled again. "I ain't got a dick because I ain't—"

Taking a cue from me, Tahoe covered her mouth. Pico started to look around the room for an escape route. He fixated on the hidden wall that the helper exited from. Too bad for all of us we were already trapped in my perpetual laundry list of lies.

Nomi hovered backward then took a seat on the bed; he sat as gently as he walked. "Does anyone want to tell me what the fuck is going on here?"

Pico, Bait, and Tahoe looked to me for answers. Bait waved at me. She was still in pain and completely jacked up on drugs.

Nomi snapped his fingers. "Anyone answer... besides RJ Reynolds." He stood up and began pacing in front of us like a schoolhouse principal that was disciplining a gang of unruly hooligans. He pressed a button on the glove of his left hand that flicked out a Swiss Army, cyborg-like ashtray. Impressed, Pico nodded his head.

After ashing his smoke, Nomi continued. "How is it that RJ Reynolds called me a few hours ago and told me that he found a new member for my—" he stopped and took a drag of the long fire stick, "—group?"

He started pacing again. "How is it that you three idiots walked into my house with a human teenager? Not just any human teenager, mind you... a female human teenager."

Bait managed to inch out through a gap in Tahoe's fingers. "Oh yeah, you're one of them dick eaters."

Ignoring the ridiculous child, Nomi stopped directly in front of me and puffed away. "Correct her," he advised.

I cleared my throat. It might have been a laughable situation if we weren't sitting in the dead center of twenty, bloodthirsty she-males. "Ahem. Bait, it's Batwangers."

Nomi shuffled back to me. "Since they won't talk, this brings me back to you, RJ Reynolds."

I tickled my chin with the back of my hand. "Funny thing, Nomi..."

He bent down and touched noses with me. His eyelashes batted mine. Before I had the chance to stand up, he spit his cigarette across the room and planted his strong hands on my knees. As the ashtray retracted into its home within the wrist of his glove, two sharp spikes popped out of his thumbs. He leaned forward with his hands and the blades edged my penis.

His hot breath let out his last drag. "What thing?"

His low, smooth voice belted my ears and made me wonder: *Who could ever think this was a woman?*

"The funny thing is that I lied," I confessed. "I need your help." He fluttered his eyelashes again, dragging them down my cheeks.

Bait, who I could always count on to say the wrong thing at the wrong time, sang out: "I'm not a boy."

The steel thumbnails inched closer to my stick, ready to shish kabob it at any second.

"Shut up, Miss Thing," Nomi lashed back, unfazed by Bait's babbling. He stared into my eyes, looking for another lie.

"Why do you need my help, RJ?"

"I had to lie, Nomi." I put my hands up to surrender. "Let me get something out of my bag."

He stalled for a minute and then retracted the spikes. The sweat from my brow mixed with his mascara and slid down my face onto my neck. He stood up and instructed me to do the same. Keeping my hands visible at all times to prove I had nothing up my sleeve, I pulled my backpack off my shoulders and then dropped it to my feet.

"Proceed," Nomi allowed.

I bent down and unzipped the bag.

Nomi extended his long neck over to try and catch a glimpse of the contents. "There better not be a gun in there or my bitches will be in here—"

"No gun or weapon. I assure you." I reached down into the bag. Out of the corner of my eye I saw Tahoe and Pico also trying to get a birds-eye view of the mystery the backpack contained. I pulled it out and lofted it to Nomi.

He flinched and the bag landed on the bed next to him. He pressed it to his nose and sniffed it. "Heroin?"

I rested my elbow on my knee and felt around my crotch to make sure everything was still intact. "Yeah, that's a pound of the cleanest shit I've ever come across."

First, Nomi judged the weight by balancing the bag between both of his hands, and then he sliced open the corner for a little taste of the pony. He swished it around in his mouth like he was in wine country and then swallowed. "It's good," he concluded. "What do I want with this?"

"It's a pound of heroin. With it, I give you and the rest of your crew free reign to distribute anywhere you want in Knuckler territory. You've always wanted in on the action."

"What?" Tahoe and Pico yelled in unison.

"RJ, what the hell are you doing?" Tahoe added.

I put my hand up to silence their concerns.

Nomi's face showed signs of warming. A barely visible smirk could almost be seen behind his bloated lips. "And what do I have to do for you to be honored with such a privilege?"

I sensed cynicism in his voice, but I needed his help. Besides, the Batwangers could eat the four of us alive. I played to his female side, pointing to Bait. "This little girl was raped and she gave herself an abortion with a soda bottle. She's thirteen years old and I'm concerned that she'll get killed if she stays with me any longer."

Bait waved at Nomi.

Nomi walked back over to Bait. "As if that weren't obvious when you walked in here. This must be that hooker you brought to King Cobra on

Halloween. The one you begged and pleaded for with him. How humane of you, RJ." Nomi put his hands around Bait's head and cupped her ears. Then, he moved down to her thighs like he had with me. He didn't bother with the blades. "Go on."

I cleared my throat. A snot rocket was whistling up and down inside my face. "Just please, let them—"

"Them?"

"Yeah, Pico, Tahoe, and the girl. Please let them stay here, out of sight until I can get this nightmare sorted out."

Nomi patted Bait on the hips and got back up. "I need to make sure we're all on the same page here, RJ. You want me to take in this fruity old man, the 'roided-out retard, and this thirteen-year-old hooker—*human* hooker—and in return I get to deal the heroin you stole from King Cobra and have been hiding with Eldritch and dealing not very secretly in Culver City?"

A jittery feeling of surprise slammed through my neck and titillated my armpits. Rather than respond to the reading of my death certificate, I remained fossilized with my elbow on my knee.

"Come on, RJ. Don't be so shocked. You didn't think I knew all of that?" Nomi put his hands up like puppets and made them talk to each other.

"How could I possibly know that?" one hand said.

"I don't know. Aren't you just some stupid faggot bitch?" the other hand responded.

He slapped them together, making boom sounds with his mouth. "Isn't that right? Isn't that what you Knucklefuckers have called me for years?"

More ashamed at that moment than surprised that our extra-stealth operation had been exposed, I simply admitted to him, "Yes."

"You," he dragged his finger down the line, starting with me, to Pico and finally to Tahoe. "You all think you're doing us a favor by letting us live and hunt in your precious territory. You are the most hurtful and evil of all of us. You simply don't care at all. When you need something though, you come crying to us with stories of the inhumanity you suffer beside us. Well guess what bitches: I'm a vampire too. I don't want it." He threw the heroin back to me. "I will let them hide here and I won't turn the little whore out."

"Meeeeee," Bait waved again, smiling.

"I don't want your pity drugs, RJ."

"Nomi, please let me pay you back somehow."

He surged back into my face. "What's the matter? Does the big, badass RJ Reynolds have feelings?" He shoved me on the shoulders. "Don't act like you care. If it's not the Knucklers who'll wipe us out, it will be BBP.

If not those dandies, it'll be the Battlesnakes. It doesn't mean anything. Besides, you already paid for this favor."

"How so?" Pico asked.

Nomi rolled around one of the bedposts until he landed flat out on the bed. The metal tails followed him, slithering around the room. "Are you really that dumb, old man?"

I stood up. "I'm not following either."

Nomi pulled a stainless-steel compact from his pocket and tugged out a nose hair. "You don't really think I'm the only one who knows about your mystery powder? Do you?"

I looked at him confused.

"Oh, come on, RJ. I thought you were a little smarter than that. Surely you must have had some inkling in your bloated belly that King Cobra knew about all this."

I swallowed the snot rocket. Fear unlocked it from my nasal passage. "Actually, no."

"The way I look at it, your territory becomes our territory pretty soon. Those drugs will make their pretty little way into my house soon enough."

XIV

MONGRELS

Copperhead's Escalade sat purring in my front yard. Not in front of my house. Not in the driveway where you'd expect a guest to park. Not even at the curb in front of my house. It was literally in the front yard.

Rather than confront my enemies without a plan—knowing how well my plans came together—I hid across the street, out of the range of eyes and ears behind two garbage bins and a blue recycling bin. I'd been frozen in that same position for the better part of a half hour, waiting for him and whoever else tagged along with him to realize that the drugs and money weren't anywhere to be found inside.

They must have pulled in quick, expecting to catch me off guard.

I didn't know why they picked today, of all days, to collect their stolen property. What an amazing and uplifting week I was having.

After about fifteen or so minutes longer, four of them burst out of the front door, kicked down my mailbox after checking it, hopped in the car and peeled out down the street. Not that I had a yard crew, but they left my front yard looking worse than usual—like the track at a demolition derby. Once I saw their taillights blaze down Melrose going east, I prowled around the house to see if they left someone to ambush me from inside. The dogs were quiet, and after I felt safe enough that there were no Snakes rattling around in my house, I entered through the front door since it was nicely kicked off the hinges for me.

My place was beyond trashed. I bent over right near the entrance to survey what was left of my 45 collection. Nothing but jagged pieces, empty syringes and record adapters. All the couches were shredded and stuffing littered the floor. My kitchen, which normally remained clean from Dezien diligence, exceeded disarray. Whatever kind of tough shit life

I led, if it could even be called life, was rampaged by my enemies.

As I entered my room exhausted, I felt that maybe I still wasn't even with the Battlesnakes. After all, because of me, their whole compound got torched and a lot of their people got killed. My dumb collectables weren't worth as much as solid-gold chairs and wall-sized murals…or lives.

My room seemed to follow the same theme of destruction. The only thing still intact, and that didn't rest on the edge of the newly formed sinkhole in the middle of the room, was Bait's stupid bathmat. On top of the mat was the necklace she made after she helped herself to my titanium 45 adapter and her junior high identification card. Her picture on the card was fuzzy and her face was hidden behind her hair. It read:

Bailia Jenkins
Seventh Grade
Skyline Jr. High School
Peoria, Arizona

I stuffed both the ID card and the necklace into my back pocket. When she woke up from her abortion daze, she'd want them. Why not give them back to her? After all, I had nothing left anyway.

And then…when I didn't think I could possibly feel any worse about myself, I opened Bait's bathroom door.

There they were.

My dogs, my friends, were both left in my bathroom like two sacks of shit, the belts still tight around their necks. The force of the strangulation unlatched Skillet's eyes from their sockets, and I believe he chewed through his tongue in an attempt to get at the belt and gnaw it free from his neck. His body was contorted and still. The only part of him moving was the grumbling of his burst internal organs.

Leroy, the much larger and longer of the two, being that he was a Great Dane, suffered a worse fate. His ribcage was smashed from the first bone down to the last. In the middle of his chest was a Timberland boot print that sank all the way through his body, crushing the skin of his chest against that of his back. The thick tread of the boots actually wore completely through parts of Leroy's skin, and I could see the pattern of the floor tile through his blood.

Probably because he kicked and fought with his long legs, the Snakes broke them all and then folded them to the floor like he was a card table left on the curb for a garbage man.

Being more torturous than necessary, they poked around in his head for some reason after they gouged his eyes inward. After I figured out which parts of their bodies went where, it became clear to me that the killer strangled Leroy with so much hatred that his force twisted the poor dog's head around backward and crumbled every bone in his neck. The neck didn't support his huge head anymore, causing it to fall wherever it landed.

I dropped to the same floor where just days earlier I found the bloodied Bait. I pulled both dogs toward me as I pleaded with them not to be dead. I scratched them both behind the ears and petted them on their backs, trying to get them to scratch at their special spots. I put Leroy's head in my lap but it slipped between my legs, getting no support from his rubbery neck. I cradled Skillet close and put my palm on his heart, hoping that he would scratch or snore or thump or something. All I could think about was every time I did something mean to them, like pretending to throw a stuffed animal so I could get a cheap laugh at how dumb they were to chase something that was still in my hand.

I pulled out from under their corpses and for some reason, I ran down the decimated hallway, hoping they would follow me. They didn't. They were gone. What I would have given to hear one of them whine, bark or gallop around. I wanted them to anxiously sit as they waited for a treat.

I stared at them from the end of the hall. I kept telling myself that if I looked at them long enough, they would roll over, stand up and pant as they blinked their doughy eyes. I knelt on my butt begging. "Please get up, Leroy. I have a steak for you, Skillet. Skillet. My little monster. Please, come get the steak. Leroy, you uncoordinated dingbat, come wrestle."

As I tried to turn away, I noticed a piece of paper speared by one of Leroy's long broken legs. I took my time walking back, knowing it was the last time I would ever see either of them. The memory of Skillet's yelp when I smashed him into the turntable volleyed back and forth between my heart and my eardrum. The image of him scampering to follow Bait into the bathroom played, paused on him shooting me a disgusted look, then rewound and played again. It was now a loop of my last living memory I had with the two sweetest gentle giants that had ever walked the face of the earth.

I got on my knees one last time and patted each of them on the snout. I grabbed the note.

We know you have Cobra and we know you stole our drugs.
Get it, Knuckler?

Without spending a second thinking about why the Battlesnakes thought I "had" Cobra, I went out to the tool shed and got four five-gallon cans of gas. I poured it everywhere in my house... wait... her house. It was the first thing I ever took that signaled I was off the streets. I lit it up. I was back to being a city rat. No home. No friends.

No life.

XV

JESTERS

I jumped on the closest MTA as three fire engines roared by. I needed to head back to West Hollywood. I called Tahoe in route.

"What?" he asked.

"They killed my dogs."

"The other part."

"What other part, fucker? They killed Leroy and Skillet."

I scooted my butt to the very end of the plastic bus seat because the great, big fat person next to me was taking up more than his fare of room. Not only should he have paid for two people, he was chowing on fast food, which was also looked down on when riding Los Angeles' top-notch public transport.

"They left a note that said they know we have Cobra," I continued to tell Tahoe, barely avoiding hanging up my phone as my co-chair lifted his arm to grab a bite of his burrito.

Tahoe thought on the other end of the line for a minute, then dumbly asked, "Do we?"

"What do you think, you huge dumbass? How in the hell could I have possibly kidnapped a massive Rastafarian who is closely guarded in a compound? Better question: Why would I kidnap him at all? Besides, I've been with you losers for the last few days."

"Oh yeah, right."

My phone buzzed. "Just a second. Someone is trying to call me." I clicked over. "Hello."

"It's me." *Dez.*

"Where the fuck have you been, asshole? I am going to fucking kill you when I find your little ass. Your goddamn friends killed my dogs, motherfucker. *They killed my dogs.* I can't wait to kill them. I can't wait to look in your eyes as I tear off your cock and then pound it into your mouth. Do you think that it's cool to rape a little girl? Did you think—"

"I think we need to put that on the back burner," he said.

The phone shuffled around on his end.

Copperhead spoke. "Reynolds. Did you get da message?"

"Yes, assface. What reason did you have to kill my dogs? Jesus, dude, I have no idea where Cobra is. You killed my dogs!"

He paused to suck on what I imagined was a joint and then exhaled. "We know you 'ave him."

"I seriously don't have him. What would I do with him?"

"You 'ave our drugs and our money."

"Are you serious? You killed my dogs over some drugs that never even belonged to you. Listen—"

"I'd tink long and 'ard before you use any words. We want Cobra back and den we'll give you Dez back."

I called his bluff. "I don't want Dez." The only reason I still wanted Dez around was to kill that little asshole myself.

"We'll see you, wit Cobra, our money and what's left of our 'eroin in an hour. Here."

The bus announced my stop. Trying to hold on to my phone and get past the humongoloid sitting next to me, I accidentally dumped a large box of fries on the floor.

"Hey," he cried out as his tennis racquet-sized hands fluttered around trying to beat the five-second floor rule. He shoved a handful of dirt-covered potatoes into his mouth.

"Hey what, fatboy?" I jammed his head into a sign that clearly said that there was no boomboxes, food, drink, or smoking permitted on the bus. Next to everything else prohibited was a picture of a dog. That sign said *No Pets*.

"Who you callin' 'fatboy,' motherfucker?" Copperhead yelled in my ear.

"Some jackass on the bus."

"Listen, Reynolds. We want Cobra and all our prop'ty in an hour."

A shuffling sound, and then Dez got back on, his voice trembling. "What did you do with Cobra?"

"I didn't do anything with him. Maybe if you bothered to come to our meeting the other night, you would have known that, you chicken shit little asshole. The longer this lasts, the worse it's gonna be for you."

"Look, bro, they are about to kill me and they already torched the garage."

"What? Was anybody there?"

"I don't know. They picked me up on Sunset yesterday. Where have you been for the past few days? No one has heard anything from you."

"Never mind, asshole," I told him, hiding my involvement with Bait and her abortion.

"Who are you with?" he asked. "I haven't seen anyone for days."

"Like I'm going to tell you that when you're sitting right in front of them. Tahoe and Pico are fine. I don't know about any of the others."

"Get here, RJ. This is bad. They've known about the stolen drugs the entire time."

"Thanks, fucker. I'm not going to turn you over to them anyway. That would be far too nice of me. They killed my dogs."

I hung up.

The fat ass that was sitting next to me had a fast food napkin shoved into his nose.

I patted him on the back. "Sorry, mate. You caught me on a very bad day."

"Jerk," he said as the bus started to slow to my stop. I looked at him, flinched at him with my fist and then exited the bus.

The Battlesnakes had known about the drugs the entire time. It must have been fun for them to see us scramble around and sell drugs just so they could sweep in at the end and grab all the profit. The only thing that left me baffled was the whereabouts of Cobra. The only person I knew who could even put up anything that resembled a fight with Cobra was Eldritch. Hopefully, the Battlesnakes didn't know about his involvement at all.

Pico and Tahoe greeted me outside the mothership that was the Batwangers whorehouse.

Pico ran his fingers through what was left of his hair on the sides of his head. "Where do you think Cobra is hiding?"

I fought thinking about my murdered dogs so I wouldn't give in to my softness. It was time for me to put on a leader's face. "I have no idea. The only two people I know who are strong enough to get him on the ground are you or Eldritch." I slapped Tahoe on the butt. Judging from the eyeliner and blush on his face, I guessed that Batwangers were having a good time with him. "Since Tahoe is here and Eldritch is an enormous pussy, I don't have a clue where he is."

Strained by the situation, Tahoe grumbled, probably hoping I wouldn't take note of his glittering lip-gloss. "Then where is he? Sounds like a setup."

"No shit it's a setup." I rubbed my palm down his face. "For God's sake, you look like a female body builder."

He buffed his forearms across his face. "We were just having some fun with the kid."

"Thank you, but dress up is over," I said. "Now clean it off. You're coming with me."

"But I don't wanna die."

I shoved him back toward the door and kicked him in the rump. "Go clean it off. If I have to die, then so do you. Besides, you're already dead, juicehead. Think of it this way, you'll be putting your simple brain to rest."

"But—"

"But nothing. Go wipe it off."

He spit on his hand and wiped his face. "It won't come off."

"Jesus! Go ask one of the queers for makeup remover or something."

With his face half-covered by the collar of his t-shirt, Tahoe reluctantly headed back into the house.

"This is a bad idea, RJ. I agree with the big man. This is the most obvious trap ever. Who cares about Dez? You said this whole fiasco was his idea to begin with. Let him suffer the consequences. Let's get the Knucklers together and go over there full force. At least we'd have a fighting chance."

I smacked the old man on the back of the head. "They destroyed my house and the garage. Who knows if any Knucklers even exist anymore aside from Dez and the three of us? Besides, I agreed to steal the drugs, and like you said, I'm the leader. It's just as much my fault. I want to kill Dez myself. Forget all this brother bullshit. They killed my dogs, Pico. He raped a little girl. This kid has become more than a thorn in my side. I want him dead and leaving him to the Snakes isn't my idea of justice."

"You're not going to make it out."

"Maybe. If I give them this." I shook the bag on my back that had the last pound of stolen heroin in it. "And tell them that I'll get the money. Do me a huge favor, try and get a hold of Eldritch and tell him to drop all the money."

"Should I tell him the situation?" Pico asked.

"Don't tell him anything. Just tell him to drop the money. His involvement in this is nothing beyond helping me out. He knew this was a horrible idea to begin with."

Relatively passive about the situation, he asked, "What if you don't come back?"

"I am coming back, but thanks for the concern. Do you really think I'm going to leave your pedophile ass with a thirteen-year-old girl? Oh, and give Bait this." I grabbed the 45-insert necklace out of my pocket and dropped it in his hand. I kept her school ID card.

"What's this?"

"It's some dumb thing she made. I found it back at what was my house."

"Well, what should I tell her, you know, if you don't come back?"

"Don't tell her anything. And please, Pico, don't let the Batwangers turn her out or anything."

"Okay, but why?"

"Just don't. If we don't come back, grab the little shit and get out of here. Go see Eldritch. I don't care. If I get killed and all the rest of us are dead, then the 'Wangers can do whatever they want. Take her and leave."

Pico reached in for a hug. "I promise."

I crossed my arms over my chest, avoiding his attempt to cuddle. "C'mon, dude. I'm coming back. They want their money more than anything else. Surely, they will have no problem handing Dez over to me. They don't care about him."

"What are you going to tell them about Cobra?"

"Shit, I might as well tell them that I have him in a safe place or something."

He massaged the sides of his head. "Do you think they'll believe that?"

"Who cares? Besides, the money is the only bargaining chip I really have. I refuse to believe that Copperhead cares if Cobra is missing or not. If Cobra is dead, that makes Copper in charge of Los Angeles. That snaky little tool probably killed him in his sleep and dumped him in the L.A. River. Let me just focus on getting Dez back and then give them their money. If they don't kill us right away, we'll have the opportunity to man up and leave town or whatever."

He pulled on his hair. "Where will we go?"

"There are forty-nine other states. Each of those states has drugs, streets, and crooks. We'll be fine."

Tahoe came out of the whorehouse. His face was rubbed-red from trying to strip the makeup off and smeared with a Mondrian of colors and sparkles. He rolled his shoulders and ripped the sleeves off his shirt. While discarding the sleeves on the ground, he flexed his biceps.

I picked a plastic star off his cheek. "That ain't gonna make you look tough, dude."

⚔

"Are you sure you don't have any change, Tahoe?"

He tried to dig his big flapjack hands into his tight jeans. Evaluating from the back, I decided that all of his pockets had holes in them. Coming up empty, he said, "I don't have any money."

"Shocking." I dumped five bones into the bus's pay station. That's the great thing about the Los Angeles transit system. If you don't have exact change, you're pretty much ass-fucked.

Tahoe and I headed to the back of the nearly empty bus that took us directly down Santa Monica Boulevard. At first Tahoe tried to sit next to me on the two-seater, metal and plastic seat.

"What are you doing? This isn't a loveseat." I shoved him off and pointed to the front of the bus. "There is barely anyone on here."

He broke his fall with a handrail. "I figured you wanted to talk."

"We can talk across the aisle. Are you five years old? You're like three hundred pounds and you have sexy alien makeup smeared all over your face. We're already drawing way too much attention to ourselves."

"Fine, I'll stand."

"If that's what you want, crybaby."

He thumped his left bicep with his index finger and then in a huff, he chose a seat. "Do you have any heroin?"

I patted the backpack. "Yeah, I've got a pound still in my bag that we're gonna use to trade for Dez."

"I feel really weak."

So did I. I needed to get high to replenish my body fluids. "We don't have any blood or anything," I pointed out.

Tahoe pointed with his head up the entirety of the bus. "Errr," he grunted. On my side of the bus sat a mid-twenties Hispanic chick listening to her iPod and reading a book and the driver. On Tahoe's side, there was an Orthodox Jewish couple and a vagrant with a handheld pocket radio firmly pressed against his ear.

"There really isn't anyone to kill on here." I told him. "I'm not killing the girl... looks like she just got off work." I pointed to the apron on her lap. "I'm not killing the Jews. They are way too old and dusty." I eyeballed the bum. "Him? Maybe. He looks weak but—"

Before I could finish my sentence, he pulled the cord, signifying that he was getting off the bus. If he only knew how lucky he was.

Tahoe began standing. "Should we get off?"

I grabbed him by his t-shirt and pulled him back down to his seat. "Sit down. We just got on the bus. We have to go downtown. I'm not going to get off and kill this guy and then stand around waiting for another bus."

"You have gotten soft."

I slapped him from his chest up to his chin. "Soft how? Soft because I don't want to kill some girl who just worked like twenty hours to support her family or soft because I don't want to kill some crusty, old couple who want to get home after temple?"

He relaxed in his seat. "Just soft. The old RJ would have killed all of them for fun."

"We'll find some rats or something once we get downtown."

He cracked his knuckles. "I ain't eating no rats."

"What choice do we have, asshole?"

He nodded toward the front of the bus again. I surveyed the vehicle. "The driver?"

"Yeah."

Justification for killing was always such a curious thing. I always validated killing people to support my habit—my life force—by seeking out the slimiest cocksuckers I could. It was usually an honor bestowed upon thieves, pimps, gangsters, and the like. I didn't regularly just kill anyone unless they wronged me or the rest of the world in some way. Mazzuco and Brianna at the gym were a little different. He deserved to die for being an A-hole and I suppose she was guilty by association. So, I guessed by association, technically, the bus driver was guilty of working with the Mass Transit Authority and dicking me out of two-fifty. After all, he could have at least tried to make change for me when he saw Tahoe and me scrambling through our pockets.

Setting some conditions, I told Tahoe, "I'm not soft. He's yours. But we have to ride the bus until everyone gets off. If we hit the end of the line and there are people on the bus, we're eating rats."

He agreed as he pulled a handgrip wrist and forearm exerciser out of the front of his pants. I was amazed that he had room for them considering his jeans appeared to be sprayed on.

Astonished, I asked him, "They still make those things?"

He pressed the grip with his right hand and then flipped it over to his left and pressed it again as if he had been waiting for this moment in front of a mirror his entire life. "Yeah," he said casually. "What of it?"

"No reason really. I just didn't think they made those cheeseball things anymore."

He stopped pumping, swung the circle part of the device around his finger and then re-gripped it like he was a gunslinger. "Yup. They still make 'em. It gets me totally psyched."

I laughed. "All that growth hormone you shoot is really messing up your brain, man." I grabbed the toy out of his hand and squeezed it. "These things don't even do anything."

He nabbed it back. "Gets me pumped."

We remained silent as the Jewish couple got off the bus just outside of Hancock Park, followed by the Hispanic girl in K-Town. We waited to see if anyone else got on the bus and as soon as we started to see the projects on the skirts of downtown, I signaled to Tahoe.

"Arrrggg!" he blasted out as he fell over into the center aisle. He grabbed his stomach and belted again. "Ohhhh!"

Startled, the bus driver looked into the huge rearview mirror. "What's going on back there?"

"This guy is hurt," I shouted back as if I didn't know Tahoe. It should have been pretty obvious to the driver that we did indeed know each other since we'd been sitting next to each other talking for the better part of a half hour.

Stupidly, he pulled the bus to the side of the road between Figueroa and Grand. Unlike most cities, Los Angeles' downtown area was completely vacant on most nights after the sun went down, unless there was a Lakers or Kings game or a big concert at the Staples Center. We were lucky; it wasn't one of those nights.

"Help, mister," Tahoe cried out as he started to crawl to the front of the bus. I had to give him credit, his acting performance was pretty convincing—must have been all the prep work he did with his masturbation machine-thing.

Without bothering to call dispatch, the driver rushed back to Tahoe. As he bent over to see what all the ruckus was about, he was snapped underneath Tahoe like a rat in a trap. The big man put his left hand over the driver's mouth as he shoved his index finger up to his own mouth. "Shhhhhh," Tahoe whispered.

More than overpowered, the scrawny bus driver lay under Tahoe and shivered. Quietly, he said, "We don't carry any money. Please. I have a family."

As the one-man wrecking crew turned the driver over so he was face down, he planted his face into the grimy and moldy bus floor. All the driver could do was kiss a day's worth of shoe sludge.

I cooked up some powder on my spoon as quickly as possible and threw in a cotton ball to soak up the sugar.

Tahoe spoke smoothly into the driver's ear, reassuring him that everything was going to be fine.

Jumping the gun a little, as the drugs weren't fully cooked, I slurped as much liquid into my needle and threw it to Tahoe, which, of course, he caught with his teeth like a pirate. Knowing that he didn't need my help to get his desserts, I let him take care of the driver himself as I cooked up my share.

Before the driver had a chance to call out for help, Tahoe manhandled his arms like a doll by bending them backwards until they unhinged from the torso. Tahoe firmly pressed his knee into the man's neck and snapped it sideways. He was dead instantly and while we normally kept our prey alive until we were both high, drastic times called for drastic measures. While the driver's heart let out a few last beats, I sipped my heroin into another syringe and grabbed my arm bong from Tahoe just as he adjusted his weight, injected his drugs into the arm and snapped the knuckle off with his teeth. I turned my arm upright, so as not to spill the blood everywhere, injected my needle into the wrist, snapped the knuckle off and followed suit. Knowing time wasn't something we had on our side, we took a seat next to each other and slugged away at our arms. Feeling too guilty to cheer Tahoe for his hard work, I went about finishing the deed. There was no time to sit back and enjoy the nectar.

I looked at the limp body of the driver spilling blood all over the center of the bus. "Shit," I said. "It was either him or us? Right? I mean… kinda?"

Tahoe didn't answer.

After we were satisfied and refreshed, we turned off the bus's hazard lights, shut it down, and closed the doors behind us. The rest of the journey to the Battlesnakes compound was on foot.

XVI

GHOSTS

Tahoe looked around the grounds of the Battlesnakes's compound from a perch on top of the brick fortress wall. "This is weird."

I reached the top of the barricade and looked around as well. There wasn't one guard or a King Cobra bootlicker in sight. "Gives you kind of a bad feeling, doesn't it?"

Usually, the place was crawling outside with the biggest and baddest Snakes in the gang. If it weren't for the presence of the always alert guards in front of the compound, the Battlesnakes would have been abolished years ago by some disgruntled gang, tired of the tyranny they posed.

"Makes me feel a little oogy," Tahoe said.

If I didn't feel a little "oogy" as well, I would have taken a moment to point out the lameness of Tahoe's choice of words.

Investigating the area further, we rounded the wall's parameter.

"Tahoe, they know we're not this dumb. What's the point of this? I mean it's pretty obvious we're walking into a trap. We were, after all, invited to walk into the trap."

I ground my teeth a little and stopped to think. Was it sheer obnoxious arrogance of the Snakes that led them to believe we'd break into their house to be killed? Anyone would have brought a weapon to their own funeral... Better we be frisked before we're let inside.

"What else did they say to you?"

"I told you. Copperhead said, 'Bring the drugs, the money, and King Cobra.' Only it was in that lame Jamaican accent."

"I don't like this, bro. We need to go now."

I grabbed Tahoe by what was remaining of his recently shredded sleeve top. "As far as we know, the Knucklers are all dead. There's just me, you, Pico, and Dez. And Dez is somewhere inside that building. If they want their money, their drugs, and their leader, I find it hard to believe a scavenger hunt is what they have in mind."

"You think it's a surprise party?"

I released my grip from the frayed shirt and tapped Tahoe on his bulky arm.

"Yeah, buddy. It's a surprise party." I felt bad for the guy, but sometimes the absolute ignorance in his questions made me wonder if he was even conscious. "Get down there."

I shoved him over the barbed wire into the cement parking lot below us. He looked around nervously and then looked back to me, only answering questions by shrugging his shoulders. For some reason, the motion-sensitive floodlights that blazed from every corner of the building reminded me that he still had that ridiculous Ziggy Stardust makeup smeared all over his face. Not in any mood to laugh at the poor steer or knee him in the nuts for his clowndom, I opted to jump down and take his side.

As I landed, a few more lights shot on. It was then that I expected an entire platoon of Battlesnakes to pop out of the ground, covered in camo and leaves to go commando on us. The question at that point wasn't so much why didn't something that theatrical happen, it was where the hell were they at all.

I pointed to the eerie, uninviting front door of the compound. "I suppose we should…"

"Are you sure, RJ? This isn't good. There is always an army of folks out here."

"What choice do we have, Tahoe? Besides getting Dez out of there, we need to stop all the butchering that's been going on. We're going to have to face the music at some point and better it be on our terms than them hunting us down and killing us." I grabbed him. "You didn't see what they did to Leroy and Skillet. If that is any measure of what they have planned for us, then they will find us and destroy us. This is much more to them than us kidnapping Cobra, stealing their drugs, and cheating them out of money. Also, having these fools simply kill Dez is much too gentle for him."

Even though I didn't have any idea what my punishment was going to be when I did have that little shit in my hands, my loyalty to him as a friend and a brother remained for some reason. Conflicted, I knew that I was beyond the point of a tongue-lashing, but I also knew that it was going to be difficult for me to kill him.

"I am going to teach that prick a lesson," I said.

I coerced Tahoe to the door. Ignoring the huge gold snake that covered it from top to bottom, I knocked. There was no response on the other end. Only the faintest sound of Reggae "riddims" could be heard. I knocked a little bit louder with both my fists. Still getting no response, I rattled the door latch of first Battlesnakes security measure: the thick, steel front door. As I predicted, it was locked.

"Tahoe," I said resorting to his steroid strength. "Ram it." At that point, the thought of breaking into our own cemetery and not even making out like poor-ass grave robbers seemed secondary to the mystery of the meeting.

Reluctant, Tahoe stepped in front of me and braced himself sideways. He closed his eyes, hiding the fear of being blitzed by an arsenal of weapons under his mascara. He plowed into the door once with his shoulder and compounded the steel. It only crumpled inwards lightly because his half-power and hesitance weren't enough to disengage the lock. After shaking his shoulder, Tahoe backed up further on the front stoop and switched sides. He looked at me, hoping I was going to give up and call it a day.

I said, "We need to do this, dude."

He wheezed a few times, unsatisfied by my persistence, and rammed into the door again. This time, the door latch fell off and I heard a distinct click that signified that it was unlocked. Getting into berserker mode, Tahoe and I both hacked away at the compound door with the soles of our boots until it flung open, and then stopped midway after the top hinge fell off.

Lights flickered on and off inside and the tawdry gold fixtures, stairs, and chairs were dull with the blood of what we could already tell was a Battlesnake holocaust. I moved Tahoe aside and took the lead. At first glance, all we could make out were dreadlocked heads and body parts throughout the foyer and lining the ostentatious staircase. As I walked further, I noticed much more.

Not only were heads decapitated everywhere, the brains and internal organs were completely, almost surgically, removed from the Rasta corpses. It was as if whoever killed them wanted to make absolutely sure they were dead. Apparently, they didn't get the memo that all it took to kill a vampire was taking off the head, ceasing any brain activity.

We sidestepped over body parts and innards to pass through the entrance and into the dining hall.

Tahoe stopped at one of the pompous paintings of King Cobra that was framed inside thick, solid gold. "RJ? Why didn't they take any of this expensive stuff?"

"I don't think that's the real question, Tahoe."

"Why? I want some of this stuff."

I slapped his hand off the picture frame that he was giving a Thai Massage to. "The question is who they are. No gang did this."

I looked over toward the doorway to the banquet room and saw a white head stuck under part of the sweep. Responding immediately and somewhat hoping it wasn't Dez, I rushed over.

With my boot, I kicked the head over. It wasn't Dez. He was still mine. It wasn't even a gang member; at least this guy wasn't from any gang that I was familiar with. He was an older man with gray hair, smashed wireframe glasses and bushy eyebrows.

"Who's that?" Tahoe asked as he paced around the proximity of the head looking for a possible matching body.

"I don't have any earthly idea," I answered. Jokingly, I added, "Maybe the Snakes were having problems with the IRS."

Either Tahoe didn't get my attempt at a joke or he was scared shitless by the aftermath we walked into. Rather than explain the one-liner, I instructed him to follow me into the banquet room. If anyone was still there, our cover was far blown after we barreled through the front door.

Cobra's table was filled with a true feast reminiscent of the Last Supper. As in the foyer, more corpses were left in pieces. Some were still in chairs and others under the table. And again, there wasn't any sign of the attackers. All we had to suggest that it wasn't the impact of a civil war eruption between Cobra's Snakes and Copperhead's younger followers was the head of some middle-aged nobody.

I caught Tahoe licking his chops after eating one of Cobra's finger snacks off the table.

I gripped the straps of my backpack tightly. "Come on," I said.

With a mouthful of digits, he gasped and shrugged and said, "You always talk about how awesome these are. I've never really been invited over here for dinner. Besides, I love soul food."

"Quit fucking around. Come on." I led him toward the throne room where Cobra loved to put on his little Reggae Sunsplash concerts, like the one he had performed for Bait and me on Halloween.

Well, I told myself, *at least we wouldn't have to worry about these assholes ever again.* We shoved our way through the electric wall that opened the throne room/theater into the dining hall. Before I had the chance to investigate the area and clear it for entry, Tahoe beelined to the center of the room where several white corpses were laid in a line as if they were being prepped to be bagged and removed. They were all wearing Catholic priest garments.

The Cloth.

"Tahoe! No!"

One. Two. Three. Four. Five. Six. Seven. Eight. Nine. That was the number of Christmas lights that I counted in a split second that popped up on the back of Tahoe's head.

He turned around to look at me like an excited little boy who had been playing in his mommy's makeup to tell me he'd unraveled the mystery. A finger hung from his mouth like a lollipop.

When he realized his face was nearly covered in red lights, the smile dropped, as did the finger. He brushed at the target lasers on his sleeveless arms and chest. He then looked at me and blinked one last time with bewildered eyes as gunfire erupted and his face was torn off, section by section, leaving only the top of his spine peeping out from his Gold's Gym t-shirt. At first his arms whipped around and his hands fluttered uncontrollably, then his immense shoulders released and his knees buckled, and he fell to the floor. As his entire torso collapsed, the line of corpses behind him bounced around like jumping beans as they were riddled with bullets.

Slipping at first, I ran back the way I came in, through the banquet hall and into the foyer. I squashed the head of the bodiless enigma outside the dining room as I rounded the corner toward the door. I leap-frogged from body to body in an attempt to exit. And then… I stopped dead in my tracks.

"Hey, RJ," she said, coughing into her hand and using the broken door for support. She lifted a double-barrel shotgun at my face.

It wasn't so much that I was confused, in shock or in denial as it was the overall feeling of defeat. It took that fucking junkie whore bitch a couple of years, but she got the last laugh in her personal vendetta with the Battlesnakes.

As I started getting pistol whipped and stock-socked on the back of the head, I fell to my knees only to be rained on by a dozen or so cattle prods.

"Fat Mac wants him. Don't kill him," she said.

Then one of the prods hammered me across the eyes, and my world went black.

XVII

ADVERSARIES

"Reynolds, wake up."

My head seemed to be ballooning in and out and my body ached like I smoked a bunch of rocket fuel and launched myself head-first into a telephone pole. Rusted springs from a cheap cot prickled into my back.

"Reynolds, get up, you dumb white bitch."

The memory of being beaten down propelled me up on the bed. The rocket fuel dropped into my lower bowels. Sickened, I laid back down. I struggled to open my eyes only to realize they were covered in bandages. I felt the sides of my head. I hacked only to have phlegm rejected halfway up my esophagus and sent back down to my lungs to fester. Sliding my fingers down past my ears, I stopped at a metal collar bolted around my neck. I didn't bother trying to rip it off. The tight noose was there to stay.

My nose picked up the smell of rat droppings, Ajax, and pig blood. My ears picked up the sound of a distant choir.

"Damn, Reynolds. They messed you up, fool."

Carefully, I unwrapped the dressing that covered my eyes to reveal the vagueness of a dank room lit by a single bulb. I didn't do it to see who was yapping at me. I already knew. "What's up, Cobra. I thought you were dead or kidnapped or something."

My eyes started adjusting to the dark room, painfully un-blurring my environment.

"Oh shit."

We were both in cells right next to each other. He was facing me, bound on his stomach to a plexiglass slab that was pressed up against the jail bars. He was practically crucified. One of his eyes dangled down, bringing attention to his smashed-out gold teeth. His dreads and the top of his head were cleanly chopped off. A few pins stuck out of his brain that had Post-Its adhered to the balls on the ends. His entire body was pot-holed and scaly as if his enemies had tortured him with massive amounts of high-energy light. Around his neck was a collar. I'm sure it was the same as the one I felt around mine.

His tongue lapped out of his mouth. "Bitch, I wish I was dead."

"Man, if you're telling me I'm jacked up, I must be the walking dead."

"Heh," he coughed. "Don't make me laugh. It only hurts."

In all my years of fighting with Cobra and as many times as I dreamed about seeing him dead, I never expected to see the seven-foot monster so banged up. It wasn't quite as sweet as I envisioned it.

I squinted my eyes and scratched some goop off the roof of my mouth. "Where are we?"

"Where do you think, you dumb fuck? The Cloth is real and your pyro ex-girlfriend is working for them. Did you ever stop and think for a second that I ran things the way I did for a reason? Shit, Reynolds, even your stupid, albino ass should have seen this coming."

"What happened? The last thing I remember was Tahoe—"

"Your muscle is dead. I heard some of the guards giving props to each other for shooting his head off."

"How were you caught?"

"Are you dense? We were fed to these bastards by Dez and Copperhead. The Snakes are gone—"

"I saw."

"The Knucklers are gone too. We were popped by those bitches."

My eyesight started to reach full clarity. Cobra was not a sight for sore ass eyes. Cuts and slices covered his body, and they were infected. For some reason they weren't healing properly. By the time it took for the wounds to get infected even his skull should have healed. As far as the power of healing went, Cobra usually regenerated at an alarming rate compared to the rest of us, as if his antibodies were in a constant spiral. His internal strength was directly related to his street strength. There wasn't another one like him.

Looking around our cells more closely, I saw each had a toilet, a sink, and a locker. Next to the plastic-covered pillows on each bed was a bible. There were no sheets on the rotten, molding mattresses that were secured into the corroded cots, which were bolted to concrete floor. Next to my cot, like a bed pan, was a bucket full of blood and chum. The smell was swine. I grunted and edged my way off the bed, barely able to stand from the severe drubbing I took at the Battlesnakes compound.

"*Ah-choo!*" Cobra sneezed. "Fuck," he said, pressing his nose into the glass, trying to wipe. Essentially a quadriplegic, he reluctantly smeared snot all over his face.

"Need a tissue?" I joked.

"You little bitch." A tooth fell out of his mouth and stuck to his lip. "If I were over there, you'd already be dead."

"I guess it's convenient for me then, huh?"

I surveyed the cells further. The fronts were composed of metal bars. The back and sides opposite each other were brick walls, with the metal bars between us. The bars themselves were spaced out about six inches apart. I could tell that there wasn't a whole lot of give, but it wasn't going to be impossible to escape from.

"Shit, Cobra. I'll be over there to un-strap you in a second. How you haven't gotten out of here yet is beyond me."

"What are you doing, Reynolds?" Cobra wiggled his head around, further drenching his face with sneeze.

"Dude, do they really think they can keep us in here with steel bars? These assholes need to do their homework on super strength and vampires."

"No, Reynolds," he said. "Don't do it!"

I dropped my fingers between two of the bars. "This is nothing. I can feel the give, Cobra."

"Reynolds, no!" He coughed.

Just as soon as I began to feel the bars bending, two giant infrared lamps slipped on directly outside the front of the room and light up Cobra's and my cell.

The intensity sent me rushing backward against the far end of the cell. I landed back on my bed. Frantically, I searched for a blanket, a sheet, or any kind of shield. Coming up empty, I sank my face into the synthetic pillow and tried to bury the rest of my exposed skin into the mattress. I felt smoke rising from my shoulders. The smell of burnt flesh engulfed the room. This was much more powerful than the effects of regular sunlight on our skin. It was as if the sun was a mere mile from the Earth.

Trying to drown out the screams of Cobra's pain, I yelled to him over the deadly hum of the lamps. "How long does it last?"

His screaming stopped as he passed out from shock.

I crawled and rolled around my mattress like a salamander being chased in an attempt to avoid the light.

I peered out from behind my pillow to see Cobra's convulsions shaking the glass plank he was secured to. Liquefied portions of his skin gobbed off the corners of the table. I shared his pain as my veins began boiling like I was being cooked inside out. Even with the pillow bound to my face, I felt my sensitive corneas adhering to my torched eyelids.

Finally, the beams powered down.

I hugged my pillow as I fell off the bed and rolled around on the floor, attempting to douse any flames on my skin. I grabbed for the bucket of pig stuff and I began lathering my body like I was applying aloe to sunburn. My hull began to foam as I rolled around trying to stop the pain. I looked next door to Cobra whose skin was clumping off his body like he was shedding.

I guessed he was falling into cardiac arrest because I made out his booger decoration mixing with the blood he was vomiting. Then he started beating his head against the table, probably to divert the pain from his back that smoldered and crusted.

Breathing heavily, I stopped fidgeting around and reached into the bucket for what was left. I tossed it through the bars onto his back. Enough slop made it through the small bars to absorb and dampen much of the fire. Cobra's erratic breathing mellowed as his spasms slowed. After I was sure the worst was over and that Cobra wasn't dying, I crept under the bed and passed out.

That night, they shut off the lights completely, except for—I counted—ten red motion detectors that continuously scanned both cells.

I was hungry. I was hungry for heroin, but since I used my bucket of pig slop to save our lives and because I was still recovering from my beat down at the compound, I was much more in need of blood.

A neon clock that centered on the back wall between us helped light up our cells. When the clock hit midnight, a looped, soothing female voice recited the Lord's Prayer.

In the relative tranquility, I thought about Bait and all the horror I had gotten her involved in. I pulled her ID out of my back pocket. *Skyline Junior High. Peoria, Arizona.* I only hoped that Pico took Tahoe's death and my disappearance as a signal to take her from the Batwangers and get out of Los Angeles. If the 'Wangers didn't turn her out, I feared somehow that Dez and whatever crew he was rolling with would get their hands on her. Most likely, Dez figured The Cloth just killed us. If he and Copperhead had a brain to share between them, they would stay clear. It was pretty lame that the two most protected and revered bangers in Los Angeles ended up where Cobra and I were. I never should have let Dez hang out with Copperhead, and Cobra shouldn't have either. Rather than bringing our two syndicates together, they tore us inside out.

We Need Heroin.

I looked through the smoke that projected the red security beams.

"What did you say?"

Cobra was almost too faint to hear as he tried to speak. "I didn't say shit."

"I must be hearing things."

"You *should have heard* what I told you." His tongue clicked around in his mouth. "You gonna listen to me next time? I've been in here a few more days than you. I know the deal."

"How are you feeling?"

"How do you think I feel?" He coughed. "Dammit. I'm strapped down you… you stupid, white bitch."

I ripped the cover off the bible next to my bed and began brushing dead skin off my body. "Even if you weren't, I think I could kick your ass. You're messed up."

"Hmmmfff," he breathed.

"How long was I out before you woke me up?" I asked, scraping the corners of my bucket for leftover blood. I took the scarce amount and rubbed it into my eyes, trying to get my eyeballs free from my eyelids.

"I haven't been keeping track. A few days. They kept you sedated with a slow drip of some kind of sedatives, water, and a small amount of blood. They also run those high beams over there on low frequency to drain our energy. They never want you strong enough to get out of here. I'm not healing at all because they keep firing me up."

A few dAYS without heroiN.

There is was again. It was no surprise that I was hearing weird things, considering my predicament, but this was different. As if my withdrawal was talking to me. I blinked my gooey eyes free. "Why? Why don't they just kill us?"

He groaned. "Exactly."

I limped over to my sink and splashed warm water on my face. Then, I tilted my head back and swished some more water around my eyes. "How did you end up on that table?"

"I'm tougher than you. They can't really keep me down with anything. From the get go they tried a couple of different things that didn't do nothin'. At one point, I ripped one of the guard's arms off. That's when they brought in about ten assholes with cattle prods and started the tanning lights. After I was weak enough, they stuck me to this table."

I tried to pull a paper towel out of the dispenser next to my sink, but it was empty. "Come on," I griped. I wiped my hands on my jeans and walked across the motion detectors.

"Don't worry, they don't do anything," he said. "I think they're just monitoring our movement or studying us or some shit."

I moved closer to him to get a bird's eye view. A portion of his brain was visibly absent.

"When did they scalp you?" I asked.

"They didn't scalp me, bitch. Your little asshole friend and Copperhead did this to me. They came at me like forty deep. They fucked me up and left my body on the doorstep of this place with a note. That's when these psychos started in on me."

I bent my neck and studied him.

"Hey. What are you looking at, Reynolds? Get back to bed."

I conceded and returned to the mattress. I was happy he couldn't see himself because he was an awful specimen to observe. "What are these clowns doing to us?"

"I don't know... saving us maybe?"

The amplified Lord's Prayer being piped into our cells grew louder.

I tried to talk over the prayer. "Why?" I asked.

"Don't you know where you are, Reynolds? This is where you were born."

"Yeah, right. I was born on the streets."

He coughed a little more and swallowed another loose tooth. "You weren't born on no streets, fool. None of us were. We were all born here and we were kept alive in a coma until they thought we were ready to be on the streets."

"Whatever. How would you know all that?"

"Because I'm the one who dumped most of you out there. I set up the territories. They made us. We're some kind of experiment. I don't know much, but what I do know... you don't wanna know."

As unconvinced as I was, I couldn't help but believe him. It made sense in a lot of different ways and it answered the most basic question of why didn't we remember being kids.

"Why?"

"I don't know. I just did as I was told. I rarely talked to anyone. I'd get a delivery time. I'd come out to the alley behind the church we're in right now and then go dump people on skid row or in any shitty alley. If the kid looked queer, I'd dump him near you. If not, I'd dump him near me or just take him back. All I know. You're going to have to ask them."

"When did it stop?"

"About fifteen years ago."

"Well, how long have you been around, Cobra? Wait, is there any chance I can call you something other than 'Cobra' or 'King Cobra?' I feel weird calling you that. I always have."

His voice dropped. "I ain't got no other name, bitch. That's the name I gave myself."

141

"It's just that…" I slowed down to think through how to approach the lameness of the Battlesnakes's name. He was nailed to a table; there was no better time. "It seems kind of comic book-y. Obviously it came from somewhere."

"Are you that dumb, Reynolds? I'm not going to give you a history lesson. It's simple. It sounds like 'Rattlesnakes'. It sounds badass and it commands respect."

"Maybe in the seventies," I said.

"What did you just say?"

"You heard me. If you guys are such hardcore Rastas, why wouldn't your name be like The Judah Lions or something?"

He paused for a minute and confessed, "We weren't always Rastafarians. In the seventies, we wanted to be more about Black Power and shit. We wore berets with snakes on the front."

"Then, why not the Black Mambas or something?"

He paused again. "After that we rolled into the Blaxploitation Petey Wheatstraw shit."

I tilted my head. "Hey, I saw that movie. I named my dogs after Leroy and Skillet, those two comedians from *Sanford and Son*."

"You named your dogs after black people? Fucking cracker ass."

"What does it matter now, asshole? Copperhead and your boys killed them."

"Everyone in my gang is an adult, bitch. There ain't no boys."

"What's your problem? Don't you think we should be worrying about more than me naming my dogs after comedians?"

"You started this shit. We're the Battlesnakes. Deal."

"The whole thing is so cheesy, dude."

"You better check yourself, bitch. You're named after a brand of cigarettes and your gang name reminds me of a bunch of skinny, little white assholes jerking off in a circle."

"What about Herman?"

"What about Herman? What, motherfucker?"

I pointed at him.

"You must be out of your goddamn mind, Reynolds. Shut up and try to get some sleep. They're gonna come down here tomorrow to fucking feed us. If we're lucky they'll tell us what we want to know."

"Battlesnakes… weak."

He coughed up the tooth he swallowed earlier but rather than spitting it out, he sucked on it like a throat lozenge.

"I'm not even about to listen to you anymore, fool. I'm also gonna kick the living shit out of you if we ever get outta here."

"G'night, Herman," I yelled over the Lord's Prayer.

"You're a dead ass bitch, Reynolds. Dead ass bitch."

Goodnight, RJ.

Goodnight, weird creepy voice.

XVIII

CLERICS

The Lord's Prayer finally concluded its broadcast at six a.m. Our alarm clock was a quick flash of the sun lamps.

"Look out, Reynolds."

"Dammit." I tried to take cover, but my skin was still attacked by the UV rays. "C'mon, man."

"Heh," Herman laughed.

It only lasted a few seconds and I rushed to the sink and splashed some water on my chest. "You could have warned me about the wakeup call, dick."

"Yeah, but I have to suck it up every morning because I don't have the luxury of a pillow to hide behind like a little girl. Besides, I'm getting used to it. Damn, you should have seen your face."

Forgetting that the custodian didn't refill my paper towel dispenser, I tugged on the lever, only to come up empty. "Well, you should see your face, you gross ass."

"There ain't no towels. They know better than to give you a bum's blanket."

I punched in the dispenser. Obviously, they were never going to give me anything to dry my hands on, so my jeans would have to do.

"Hey, Reynolds, check this out." Herman closed his left eye and inhaled. Slowly, his right eye began squirming up the table back into its socket. With one last "pop," it went back in. For the record, it went in crossed, but at least it was in its home.

Impressed, I asked, "How did you do that?"

"They didn't knock my eye out; I did it myself. Figured the worse I looked; the easier they'd be on me. They are religious folk, after all." He through the pain, obviously congratulating himself for his cleverness.

The sound of a bank vault door being cranked open down the walkway from our cells was followed by the sound of combat boots clomping their way on the cement toward us.

I jumped back onto the bed like a little boy playing video games after bedtime and closed my eyes.

"That's not going to do you any good, fool. They've been watching us all night and all morning. You're so stupid sometimes. They know you're awake so get up and get ready for breakfast."

My stomach boomed. "What's for breakfast? Denny's?"

"Pig slop. The same stuff you wasted last night."

"I didn't waste it, Herman. I used it to save your life."

"My name ain't Herman," he growled.

"Good morning, boys."

I peeked out from under my pillow. Two guards dressed in Gestapo vestments stood in front of our cells. One of them held two buckets and an I.V. bag. The other held a cattle prod and a Gat.

The guard with the gun leaned up to my cell bars. "I know you're awake, white guy. That's a pretty cool tattoo you have there."

I rushed the front of my cell but restrained myself before I reached it.

The guard with the buckets and the I.V. snickered. "He must be confused and thinks you're The Riddler, Tim."

The other guard chimed in, "Go for it, junkie."

Tim nudged him with his elbow. "Yeah, do you need to be reminded of what happened last night, demon?"

"Just do what they say, Reynolds. Take a good look at me." Herman rolled his eyes around. "It's just a matter of time before you end up like this."

Even though his advice didn't necessarily calm me, I was reminded that both of us were in this predicament because of my awful decisions.

I looked at both priests. "Demon? What are you talking about?" I figured if I played along they might cough up some information.

Not Tim walked toward me. "You're a demon who shouldn't be alive."

I inched my face by extending my neck as close to the bars without setting off the sun lamps.

"What's your definition of alive, friend? I'm walking and talking, aren't I?"

Real Tim jumped back into the conversation. "You're walking now. We'll see how long that lasts."

Herman sighed. "Christ, just let them give you some food, Reynolds. Face it, your tattoo is gay. Let's move on."

I snapped my fingers at Herman. "Wait a second. I deserve an explanation." I looked back to Real Tim and Not Tim. "Why are we here?"

"You'll find out soon enough, demon."

After patting Real Tim on the neck, Not Tim went back by Herman's cell and hit a button on a car alarm key ring. The cell door slid open. Cautiously, he walked in and exchanged the I.V. bag on the stand next to Herman's legs on the table. "Damn, you stink, Cobra."

Herman lay crippled as the adventurous guard moved close behind the Rasta's head. "Check this out." He put his finger in Herman's brain, causing his legs to jolt. "Dance."

Both guards laughed. All Herman could do was lay there and try to enjoy the pig's blood they fed him intravenously. Not Tim exited the cell, clicked his key chain again and then walked back toward me. He pressed another button, and a small doorway opened up at the front base of my cell.

Real Tim observed my curiosity and fired up his cattle prod. "Keep staring at it. Even if you broke every bone in your body, you'll never be able to get through that opening." He tapped the UV lamps behind him with the prod.

Not Tim walked up to the hole, dropped his bucket and kicked it in toward my feet. The top of the food bin skimmed the edge of the hatch but it didn't trigger the sun lamps. Satisfied he'd fed the stray dog, he clicked the key chain one last time and the cubbyhole closed.

"Mac says, 'Have a nice breakfast,'" Real Tim added. The two priests bumped arms again. "Hey, Cobra. Tell him who Fat Mac is."

After shooting me sarcastic sad faces, complete with pantomimed tear rubbing, Real Tim and Not Tim yucked their way back down the hall. I think I might have heard a high-five when they reached the door at the end of the hall.

"Herman, what kind of priests are these guys? Some kind of religious militia?"

"Don't call me Herman anymore."

I picked up my bucket and began shoveling guts into my mouth. "Well, since I've made it clear that I refuse to call you King Cobra; get over it and deal with it. What are you going to do about it anyway?"

As the energy dripped back into his body via the blood bag, the crust on his back started to heal, becoming a taffy-like, yellow puss. "I already told you, Reynolds. They're The Cloth. We're in a basement of their goddamn church. I think it's where we were born."

I flipped a morsel of a pig liver out of my cell and onto Herman's table.

He snorted and inched his head up. With the aid of his forehead and nose, he slipped it into his mouth. "Look," he said as he consumed the food with his near-toothless gums, "I don't know the whole story, but I'm almost sure this is why we're the way we are."

I threw him another piece, hoping that if I gave him more treats he would tell me more. "And…"

Using the same head-to-nose trick, he inched the food into his mouth. "And nothing. That's all I know."

"Then why didn't you ever tell anybody, Herman?"

"I did." He chomped on the pig, trying to prevent choking on a big piece that he couldn't decompose without teeth. "The old man… Pico. He knows just as much as me. He might know other things. More please."

"More what?" I held a long string of intestine up to his face. Rather than play SeaWorld with me, he just closed his eyes. Feeling bad, I threw it to him. Unfortunately, it landed on his brain. "Oh shit, Herman. I'm sorry."

He bent his head sideways and tossed the food like a burger patty from the top of his head onto the table. He extended his tongue, latched onto it, and rolled it up into his mouth.

I actually didn't think he knew anything else so I switched subjects. "Do you think that clock is right?"

"Probably not, but who cares? They're giving me some kind of lobotomy over here."

I walked over to my toilet and looked for a seat. There wasn't one. I doubt if they knew toilets were one of my favorite weapons, but their ability to vamp-proof my cell was an A-plus effort nonetheless. "Yeah, I can see that, Herman." I pulled my pants down and sat on the cold rim.

"Don't you dare take a shit, Reynolds."

"What do you want me to do? I haven't gone since I got here."

I dropped a big loaf. A clean exit, it shot water back up my sphincter like a trailer park bidet. The splash felt good.

Herman closed his eyes. "Like I want to see your little white man dick."

"Sorry I'm not a seven-foot tall black dude, asshole. Shit, where's the toilet paper?"

"You're going to have to use your hand."

I looked up to a camera on the wall. "Hey, I need some TP in here."

"They're not going to give you any paper, Reynolds. Use your hand and then wash it off after."

I eyeballed Herman's colostomy bag resting on the floor next to his bed.

"At least when I lived on skid row, there was always something to wipe with."

Making a sour face by scrunching his eyes and nose together, Herman tried to avoid my stench. "Deal with it."

I waited until I was finished and then wiped myself. I flushed, walked over to the sink and used almost half of the pink juice in the soup dispenser. My hand smelled like free grooming at incontinence dog park.

"So, who is this Fat Mac I keep hearing about?"

Herman relaxed his scrunched face. "Goddamn, you stink. He's their leader. He was the only one I've ever spoken to before I got caught."

I took some innards out of my bucket, walked back to my cot, and then placed the pieces over my seared eyes like cucumbers. "So, let me get this straight: Mac is the leader of a crew of lunatic priests. Come on. That's almost as asinine as a gang of pothead vampires called the Battlesnakes."

"I told you where that came from, Reynolds."

"Not really. You told me a bunch of stories about Black Panthers and Superflies. Now you're telling me a crazy story about us being part of some experiment. Do you even have any idea where you come from or are you just throwing bullshit my way to annoy me?"

"I know where I'm from, bitch. The only one of us that's older than me, and knows more, is the old gimp."

"Did Pico save you too?"

"Hell no. I didn't even know he existed until I saw an old ass man runnin' with your junkie crew. Look, Reynolds. We exist, we do drugs and we kill people. What more is there to know? I don't even care what I am or where I come from right now. All I do care about is being jacked up on this table with my head cracked open."

The steel door latched open at the end of the hall and then closed again.

"Those pricks again?" I asked.

Herman licked his lips. "We should be so lucky."

A single pair of soft-soled shoes squeaked down the hall. They didn't clomp like the boots the guards were wearing.

They stopped directly in front of my cell.

"Hello, Mr. Reynolds," the priest began. "Low lights." He then whispered into a lavaliere microphone hanging near the center of the white square on the collar of his standard-issue clerical uniform.

The sun lamps hummed to life. They weren't on a high enough frequency to burn me, but they were powerful enough to deplete all my energy.

I rubbed the pig parts on my eyes. Although the lights didn't bother me too much, I didn't have enough energy to get up and take cover. And the warbling heat massaged me almost into a daze.

"Open cell," he said into the mic. The cell door popped open. He grabbed a wooden chair from the hall and dragged it into my cell. Having difficulty moving, I took my fleshy tanning specs off.

The priest pulled the chair into the center of my room and pointed to it.

"Do you mind?" he asked.

"Whatever," I said, unsuccessfully re-covering my eyes. As the pig parts slid down the sides of my face, my arms loosened and dropped to my sides.

He put out his hand to shake. "Well, Mr. Reynolds. It's a pleasure to meet you as an adult."

Too exhausted to shake, I said, "It's not mutual."

He lifted the lavaliere back up to his mouth. "Increase lights. Feed bible."

Per his demands, the lights intensified slightly and passages from the bible blared from the speakers. I tried to roll under my pillow for cover, but I was too weak to move.

He sat down on the chair and plucked an apple out of his pocket and brushed it off. Taking a bite, he said, "I'm not offended you won't shake my hand. I understand."

The only thing I wanted him to understand was that if I weren't incapacitated, I would strangle, mutilate, and kill him.

"My name is Father Martin McAteer. Most people call me Fat Mac."

I turned my head to get a closer look at him. Mac was a small man in his fifties or sixties. He had slicked back hair that mixed reds and browns with gray highlights. The hair tried valiantly to cover odd thinning patches all over his head. His eyes blinked constantly and were submerged in a strange population of freckles that fused together, almost forming a birthmark. The pigmentation blotches created a raccoon-like mask on his face. His bulbous nose started small at the bridge and ended in two huge nostrils that opened and closed erratically. It was a bizarre tick for someone who presented himself so calmly. He had extremely slight lips, which was unfortunate because his teeth were chipped away and riddled with gaps. Below the burst dam that was his mouth, sat his butt chin that swirled into a repulsive scab. Still lower, his liver-spotted, turkey neck sprouted from his priest outfit. Covered from that point to the floor, I didn't have to use my imagination to think about what other horrors were under the cloth.

He pulled a rubber hood over his head to protect him from the rays. "Hot enough for ya?"

"Fuck off," I squeezed out as I tried to shield myself from the sun lamps in the shadow of his oblong head.

"God bless you, my son," he said, standing up and making the sign of the cross. His eyes twinkled as they followed the movements of his hand. "Do you know who I represent?" He retook his seat.

The artificial sunlight blew across my body like an oscillating fan, blowing fire across my exposed flesh. "Cloth," I said.

He patted me on the leg, deepening my blistering pain.

"Correct. We are indeed men of the cloth. Did your adversary..." He produced a small notepad from a pocket as he took another bite from the now smoking apple. "Oh, here it is... Herman. Did Herman tell you that?" He looked over at Herman and waved. "Hi, Herman. That's a much better name. Don't you think?"

He chomped on the apple and licked the roof of his mouth. Having trouble reading through the sweat that rolled into his eyes, he produced a pair of reading glasses from yet another pocket. After he wiped off the lenses, he rested them on the end of his nose.

Herman stayed silent. The light was still dim in his cell and he wanted to keep it that way.

"You seem curious as to where you come from... more so than anyone else like you. Well, this is it." He raised his arms in praise. "This is where you were brought into the world."

I fell in and out of consciousness, wishing that I weren't subdued because I did want answers. This joker was pulling my dick to prove that he was in control.

"I can tell that you are tired from all the excitement, so I'll let you rest until you have more time to let this information sink in." As he stood up, wiped some sweat off his cheeks and littered his apple core on the ground of my cell, he closed his little notebook and placed it back in his pocket. Then he took off the reading glasses, folded them and placed them in the breast pocket on the front of his uniform. From the same pocket, he pulled out a bottle of holy water.

Pressing to overcome my nausea, I felt my gums getting weak and my teeth loosening. "Holy water doesn't do shit, old man," I said.

He unscrewed the top of the bottle. "Oh, I'm afraid this isn't holy water, my son."

Excited, he accidentally knocked over his chair.

"It's hydrochloric acid." He began reciting the Lord's Prayer. "Our Father, who art in Heaven, hallowed be thy name."

I grabbed the side of the bed, too weak to pull myself out of the way.

"Thy Kingdom Come, thy will be done, on earth as it is in heaven." Again, he made the sign of the cross. This time, however, he poured the acid, starting at the top of my chest and traveling all the way down to my pelvis. I didn't cry. I didn't move. I was nearly paralyzed. The only movement I made was to close my eyes as he opened me up like a Ziploc bag.

"Give us this day our daily bread," he continued. "And forgive us our trespasses, as we forgive those who trespass against us. And lead us not into temptation, but deliver us from evil."

As he dug into the last portion of the verse, he switched direction, going now from nipple to nipple. I felt the watered-down acid eating my skin away like he dropped a nest full of parasites on me and hung a sign under my chin that said *Welcome*.

"For thine is the Kingdom, the power and the glory. Forever and ever."

He threw a syringe on the floor next to my cot. I didn't open my eyes but I faintly heard him sashay his soft shoes out of my cell. I felt the ground rumble as the bars closed behind him. A piercing drone of pain tickled my ears and overloaded my brain.

"Amen," he concluded the prayer. "Lights off. Gospel off. Mr. Reynolds, there is blood and methadone in the syringe."

Fucking methadone.

My animal instincts demanded that I jump out of the bed and rip his balls off, but my spent body didn't respond. Instead, I slipped into a comatose state from a combination of the lights and the acid. My mind spoke louder than the fury too, telling me that if I rolled onto my side or sat up that my guts would splash all over the floor.

The lights went off and the motion sensors zapped on.

"Damn, son." Herman laughed. "You just got fucked by the fuck up."

It was a rough heal. I lay on my cot for endless hours, trying to gather enough energy to reach the floor and grab the syringe. Not long after my attack, Real Tim and Not Tim came in to my cell, hooked me up to an I.V. like Herman's and whispered threats into my ear. Making things worse, vomit from my heroin withdrawal burped-up out of my mouth and landed in the gaping caverns cut into my chest from the acid. Every time I stretched my arm out to grab for the syringe, I felt my insides waddle around, almost spilling over my skin. The withdrawal fevers didn't help my situation and were a constant reminder that I needed the heroin to survive.

"How does it feel, Reynolds?" Herman badgered every time he saw the needle eluding my reach.

I shook frantically. I grabbed onto the sides of the cot to steady the bowl containing my ingredients so none of them escaped. I was positive that everything would rejuvenate over time, but since I had never been in a situation like this, I felt it best to keep everything as stable as possible and intact while my shell pressed forward to mend itself.

I'd never felt withdrawal symptoms before. If I needed the fix, I went and took it. I stole drugs from dealers and then I took their lives to satisfy my needs. Even when I rummaged around in the gutter, I always somehow managed to score. I don't know exactly when my hunger began, but once I was aware of my needs, I smelled the heroin and sought it out.

I was now in my most desperate moment, and my existence seemed frail and useless compared to the power of the drugs, the torture from the acid and the constant exposure to the sun lamps.

Herman laughed away. "How does it feel, Reynolds?" In between his bouts with consciousness, he flung insults at me simply because he knew I could hear them but was unable to respond. To him, even as fragmented as he was, this was his way of reminding me that all our problems were my fault.

Every couple of hours that passed, I'd run a finger up and down and across the wound, checking for progress. The hours became days.

Fat Mac didn't pay us another visit. Our only visitors continued to be Real Tim and Not Tim. They came into our cells, made jabs at us, and switched out our I.V. and colostomy bags. They didn't bother dressing any of our wounds.

About two days after Fat Mac left, the Tims upped the sedatives on my blood bag. Either they were concerned about my slow heal or they just wanted me nice and loopy so they could hatch a more nefarious strike against me. The drip from the I.V. was slow, but it was comforting as it bombed into my bloodstream, only to be instantaneously devoured by the first lucky part of my body that needed it most.

It was a seemingly never-ending game to them. They laughed and drank wine while they flicked the sun lamps on and off. There wasn't a damn thing I could do about it.

I vaguely remembered a game that the Tims played called "Fireball" where they would turn on the lights and see which one of us stayed responsive the longest. Whomever picked the loser had to drink. They stopped playing the game after only a few matches because whichever one of them picked Herman always won.

I felt like I was hovering above my bed like some out of body experience; I was floating over the shit pile that was my life. Feeling the light bouncing off me, I would scratch at my butt making sure that Bait's I.D. was still there. It was my single motivation to escape. Before I met her, I never felt things like guilt or pain. I didn't know whether or not that was some sort of blessing or curse. Thinking about her made me feel nothing but guilt.

On the third day after my punishment at the hands of Fat Mac, my gash had healed just enough for me to get at the methadone syringe. Without sitting up on my bed, I carefully ripped off a shred of denim from the side of my jeans and tied off my arm.

"Is it worth it, lowlife?" Herman yelled over to me.

I tested the durability of my chest cavity and its contents. My arm trembled as I bent it to an upright position. Terrified, I started to prop myself up, attempting to keep my sternum as flat as possible. I used my free arm as a safety net just in case important organs manifested themselves into a wave and overflowed. Remaining vigilant but anxious, I let the brace of my arm down. The cross on my chest fizzled and oozed.

Although raw, it was secure enough. As I arched myself slightly further upward, I relaxed my shoulders. If I even yawned, I would have sprung open like a jack in the box.

Herman carried on. "Hey, hillbilly, they did you a favor. They torched that stupid-ass Batman ink. You should thank them."

I sunk the needle into my arm. The blood in the syringe was room temperature and the taste was putrid… nothing like the fresh blood hijacked from a beating heart. It felt sour in my body like I was just giving my dead veins a transfusion with urine.

My eyes rolled toward Herman's cell. "I wish it was worth it. This isn't even heroin. It's fucking methadone."

ASK for heroin.

The voice wasn't going away.

"I'm hearing a voice," I confessed.

"Yeah, I'm hearing your voice right now and it's pissing me off."

"Not like that, dude. I'm hearing a voice that keeps telling me to find heroin."

"Ha! What the hell does it sound like?"

"I don't know. Like a weird, scratchy whisper."

"Oh, you dumbass, Reynolds," he laughed. "That's just The Gooch."

"What's that?"

"It's the bully you never see, tellin' your dumbass what to do."

"I think it's withdrawal."

"Sure, it's that, too. On that TV show *Diff'rent Strokes*, Arnold was always pushed around by some big ass bully that we never, ever saw. That was The Gooch. Arnold was always bitchin' and moanin' about The Gooch. He was always the scapegoat, the reason for all his problems."

"That's really stupid, Herman."

"You sure about that? What's it telling you right now? Is it telling you to get some heroin, even though you're all fucked up in that cell?"

I didn't respond.

"Sucks for you. Pot ain't addictive. Ain't no Gooch runnin' my life."

I curled my dry tongue inside my mouth as I tried to enjoy my fix. "Cut the shit, Herman."

"I ain't cutting any shit, fool. We're both here because of you. If you would have listened to me… even once… we wouldn't be here. You bring me one washed up actress bitch that burns my house down. Then, you bring me another little bitch who steals my drugs and my money. Then, the first bitch comes back and kills everyone I know."

"Bait didn't play any part in it. It was just me and Dez."

"Bullshit, Reynolds. We had people following her back and forth from your drop. Do you think that I'm stupid? I knew she was involved the night you came over and sat there, looking me straight in the face, telling me that the cops didn't have any drugs."

"I said no coke."

"Dumbass. We made sure it was heroin because we knew you just couldn't pass up an opportunity to rip me off. Look around you. Can't you see they're beating us down for their enjoyment, fool? This isn't a mystery, Sherlock. We are two in a long-ass line of vampires who go missing every year. From the day we were born, all we've been is a big experiment."

Herman raised his head and propped his chin on the table. He spat a loogie into my cell.

"Fuck you too, Herman. You set us up for what reason? Because you hate us? Why didn't you just kill us? We played right into your test. Are you proud that you proved a junkie would take a duffle bag full of heroin?"

"The list just keeps getting longer every time you call me that name. I've kicked your ass more than once, and when the time comes, I'm going to finish the job."

"I can't wait."

He scratched his chin on the table. "Since we're talking about your bitches, that pyro, The Habit, she's the one who dragged your Raggedy Andy ass in here. She also came into my cell and shoved a hunting knife into my armpit. I can't even tell you how much I wish I could go back to that night you brought her over. I would have shoved both of you into my meat grinder, ate you, shit you out, and then fed you to the rest of your wangster-ass friends. I hope she was one awesome lay, Reynolds. You D-list star fucker."

I reached sideways and dug into my bucket for a piece of life. "I never banged her."

Herman's eyes lit up.

"Let me get this straight: you brought some psycho-ass bitch up into my shit, let her burn my house down and then I end up here with you, and you don't even have a decent anal story for me? You never even dipped it? Stupid, Reynolds. You never pay attention to what's going on right under your own nose because all you can think about is drugs. It's funny because Copperhead told me that every one of them tapped the ass on that little Bait girl."

"Piss off, Herman."

"You're kidding me. This is a comedy club in here. I'm serious, fool. You were the joke of the town. Dez came over to our place and showed us videos of him and his partners bangin' on that little girl in every single position you can imagine. All she did was sit there and frown. She had dead-ass eyes because she was all faded from the junk. Copperhead was in the videos too. This is priceless."

I rubbed the scar tissue on my torso.

"What do you mean, Dez was showing you videos?"

"Man, Reynolds. How do you think we were sure you took the drugs from the cops? Damn. That little bitch confessed the day after Halloween."

"Fuck," I screamed, folding both my arms over my chest to hold myself together. With my foot that was dangling off the bed, I kicked my bucket to the bars at the front of my cell. The lights blazed on. Gun shy to fully stand up, I tipped onto my cot on my back. Being mindful of my body, I rolled toward the back wall. Using my ass, my thighs and what power I had in my arms, I propped up the mattress.

"Enjoy the sun, asshole," I screamed as the light singed the tip of my tongue. "There's nothing you can do now, King-Fucking-Cobra!"

He didn't scream like before, meaning either he was developing a tolerance to the sun lamp or he didn't want me to hear how weak he'd become.

After a while, the lamps powered down and a smoky mess from Herman's cell wafted toward me.

"Remember, Reynolds," he snorted. "I'm keeping a list over here. I'm just the messenger. You and I both know they ain't gonna let either of us die in here. Like I said, they need us for something. If and when I get the chance to square up with you, it'll be much worse than anything that happened to that little girl. And when I finally do get my hands on that bitch that burned down my house… forget it."

I snuck out from behind my mattress. His seriousness made me realize that our survival was going to be decided not by us or our willingness to work together or apart. Our fate was in the hands of The Cloth.

The neckband tugged at my skin as it caught one of the exposed springs from the bed. After the smoke cleared, I looked into Herman's cell.

He winked.

It only made sense. If Cobra and I were ever going to see the light of day… scratch that… the outside world, at night, again, we would have to come together against a far more dangerous gang than the Snakes and the Knucklers combined.

His voice grew louder and more powerful. "It happened, Reynolds. We all hit that little girl. What do I have to gain by making that shit up? We had a hell of a time laughing at you back at the compound."

I scratched at where the Faction tattoo had been. The only thing left was puss.

"We should talk about building up our own cartel," he babbled on. "You know… so when we get out of here we can make our own dollars. You and me." He nodded his head, coaxing me to agree.

"I'm in. If we get out of here, we work together."

He winked at me again. "How bad do you want Dez?"

I thought for a second.

"There isn't even a scale that can weigh that question." Then, I turned the question to him. "How bad do you want Copperhead?"

"Oh, you don't even know."

Using a combination of budget sign language and camouflaged gang slangs that we both knew, Herman and I formed an alliance. We veiled it in discussions about the big plans we had after we got out of jail.

"Hey, Reynolds."

"Yeah?"

"That was a pretty dope move with the mattress. I didn't even see you break it off the frame."

Flattered, I smiled.

"It was pretty nice, wasn't it? I realized I was scratching away at the bindings the entire time I was healing without really paying attention. Right before I kicked the bucket, I noticed that both sides of the mattress were free."

I pressed my mouth up to one of the bricks behind my bed that I knew hid one of the many pinhole cameras used to observe us and yelled, "Okay, you dumb Catholic cunts, we want to know what you want."

XX

JEZEBELS

As the Hells Bells of the Lord's Prayer invaded our dreams, I heard the door at the end of the hall disengage and open. Herman slept and even if his hearing was fully intact, I doubted that he was interested in any late-night booty calls. The usual sound of combat boots and soft shoes coming down the hall was replaced by the heel-to-toe tap dance of stilettos. Halfway to our cells, the clicking was interrupted by the sound of a tumble.

"Shit," a female voice whispered. She then broke into a laughing hysteria. I heard her get up, brush herself off, and stabilize against the brick wall. Unbelievably, the process of a junkie picking herself up from a fall and making herself presentable without dozing off took an unsubstantial fifty-five seconds. Somewhat shuffling, probably because of a skinned knee, she made her way to the front of my cell.

"Hey, RJ," she spat with her perpetually laryngitic voice. The Habit stood around five-foot eight in her spiked heels. For some dumb reason she was wearing a nun's habit. Her blond hair was stringy and pushed behind her ears, revealing very little inside the emptiness of her pale, blue eyes. She was blessed with naturally mesmerizing eyes, but, since she chose the path of waste, her black pupils blanketed the color. Whenever I saw her, I expected her to say *I'm ready for my close-up, Mr. DeMille.*

When she scratched at the track marks under her robe, her shoulders compressed, causing her spine to bend. I don't know if she had scoliosis or if the constant cold spins from the drugs made her bend around like a hunchback. Her makeup was so poorly applied, it looked like someone literally took a clown, grabbed it by the hair, and pounded its made-up face onto hers.

She looked thinner than I remembered. The only part of her

appearance that seemed to be applied with any TLC was her lipstick, but since it was clumped on to conceal an outbreak of herpes in the corners, her lips could never be described as kissable. Punchable? Yes, but only if the fist was thoroughly disinfected and sanitized before and after contact was made.

She grabbed her outfit at her thighs, pulled it out at the sides and curtseyed. Sadly, her attempt to look like a lady appeared more like two anorexic weasels chasing each other around a scratching post. "Do you like my outfit?"

I didn't get off my cot. I lay there, shooting knives at her busted-up face with my eyes.

"You get it, RJ? It's a *habit*. A nun's habit." She fell against the bars to steady herself and exhaled like she just competed in a caber tossing tournament. I would storm the bars and slurp her into my cell piece-by-piece if I didn't know that the UV lamps would flip on and give Herman a fireman's wakeup call. However, I had no interest in touching that pile of contagion.

I yawned. "What do you want, Habit?"

"C'mon, RJ." She giggled. "Is that any way to greet your long-lost girlfriend? Don't you want my autograph?"

Her tone stung my ears and heart; it reminded me that not only did I never bed her, but that she used me solely for drugs. Her time on this planet was limited to being a price-slashed knockoff of Nancy Spungen. I should have killed her when I lived at her house with her, long before she burned down the original Battlesnakes compound. If I ever had anything written about me on a gravestone, it would have to say something about my inability to read females.

First it was The Habit, and then it was Bait. It seemed unfair that the bitch was standing in front of me, alive, while somewhere Bait was enduring some type of torture. All I could hope for was that Pico was doing right and getting her away from Nomi and the 'Wangers, who wouldn't think twice about handing her over to Dez.

I got out of bed. I made my way toward the front of the cell, wary of the threshold that triggered the lights. She backed away from me.

"Get her, Reynolds!" Herman said. "I can suffer through the lights. Kill that little washed-up bitch."

I didn't.

I rubbed my eyes.

"I burned down your fucking house," I confessed to her.

She thought for a minute. As I figured, she forgot that I lived in her secret heroin den. Then her eyes lit up. "Good, I'm not getting residuals like I used to. I can collect the insurance money. Totally forgot that place even existed. I thought you would have stopped paying the mortgage. Thanks."

"I wouldn't be thanking me. When they open that place up, they are going to find a shitload of remains buried in the floorboards. Good thing I don't have any record with the cops. Even better, everyone knows who you are."

"Whatever." She fell quiet for a minute. "No one knows who I am anymore."

"What do you want?" I asked her again.

She smirked and scratched her arms more fiercely under the robe.

"I just wanted to show you my outfit," she repeated. "Get it?" Her eyes swam with the effect of the heroin.

"Yes, I get it. It's stupid."

"Please kill her, you soft ass," Herman said.

"I said, what do you want! Why are you here?"

Struggling, she stood up, breaking off her heel in the process. "You're an asshole." She bent down and kicked her shoe off.

I turned around and headed back to my cot. "How did you get in here?"

Realizing that she had the upper hand because I wasn't going to kill her, she came closer to the bars and picked up her shoe. "They let me in to talk to you. They gave me all the security shit because I helped them find you. They know about our history and they figured I could convince you."

"Pffff," Herman scoffed.

She threw her nun's habit over her head and started scraping at her inner thighs with her broken heel. Her arms were beyond blotchy and black and blue from collapsed veins. Her left arm, her preferred shooting arm, looked like a tattooed sleeve of ominous thunderstorm clouds. I came to the conclusion that she was less of an asset to The Cloth at that point than she was a roadblock in their effort to get us to do their bidding. I felt kind of bad for her. Sure, she led them to us, but what was next for her?

I wiped my nose on the synthetic pillow. "Why would you lead them to us? Who are these guys? What the hell do they want?"

She tugged away at the skin on her arms and legs with the heel so hard that she started bleeding in numerous places. Usually, I quite enjoy the smell of blood. Her blood smelled like a sulfur mine and celluloid burned up inside an old movie projector. Heroin had not only killed her mind, it also digested her insides straight through to her soul. She was the next childhood actress waiting in line to one day get back on top. If Hollywood history foretold when that would be, her star wouldn't shine again until the day she died. Only then would her fans remember how "great" she was.

"She's just another worthless junkie," Herman said, dismissing the conversation. He definitely doubted she could deliver any insight to our captivity.

She stomped crookedly on one broken heel over to the front of Herman's cell. "You sure didn't feel I was too worthless when I burned down your house or when I killed all those assholes inside. That's right; I turned them inside out the last time I went over there. You ruined my career, you motherfucker. I had it all."

Herman rattled the table, trying to break out of the straps, cuffs, and chains that clamped him down.

The Habit ran her finger down one of his bars. "What's the matter?"

He turned his head away from her to the back of his cell. "Don't worry, girl. This ain't over. Not even close. Just so you know. The Battlesnakes didn't kill anyone when we burnt down that set. You killed my brothers. I'll never forget that."

She shivered. I don't know if she was being theatrical or just a junk rat. "Ooooo," she sang. "What are you going to do? Are you going to beat me with the leftover body parts of your gang?"

She clomped back to my cell like she was an uneven barstool.

"They aren't going to kill you, RJ." She pulled the nun's habit back over herself. "I think they plan to rehabilitate you or something."

I sat up against the bars on the back wall next to my bed. "Rehabilitate me? Are you sure that's what they want?"

"Something like that." The scraping with her heel resumed, and made its way to her neck and a big hickey near her jugular. "I don't know. I wasn't paying attention or anything like that."

"You never do," I said, frustrated. "You should have paid attention to your agent before you got kicked off TV."

She pointed back to Herman. "I lost my show because this motherfucker destroyed it."

Tired of playing charades with a dope fiend, I asked one final time, "So again, what do we owe the pleasure of this enlightening visit, Habit?"

She ran her finger over her lips and soothed the bedrock in her voice. "I wanted to see you, my little RJ."

"Why?"

"Because, I haven't seen you since I got back from rehab in Malibu. These priest guys paid for it. They said that they may be able to get me on some TBN show."

"I see it was successful. And here I was wishing that you'd fallen off the earth or died from an overdose. Is that where you went after you torched the Battlesnakes compound? You realize that they came really close to killing me for that, right? Where did you go after that?"

"I don't know. I did a couple porns."

Herman rotated his head back to her. "Get the fuck out of here. I've been tortured enough."

She picked a piece of crust out of the top of her nostril and flung it in Herman's direction. I stood back up and paced my cell with my head down, evaluating her claims. "Wait. Wait. Wait. So, you really did all this... orchestrated this elaborate revenge because you aren't a star anymore?" I pointed to Herman, blood vessels popped in his eyes, creating clotted tears. "You burned down his compound and killed his friends, thereby leading him to set me up with the cops a year later and then landing both of us in this fucking jail to be tortured." I stopped and swayed my head back to her. "All of this because you aren't a star anymore?" I hesitated for a second and then rushed toward her. As predicted, the lights didn't blaze on.

"Kill her, Reynolds! Kill that junkie whore!"

Somewhat prepared for my reaction, The Habit pushed herself out of my reach as I tried to snatch a strand of her fried hair. Again, she lost her balance because of her uneven shoe. She trembled as she pushed herself further and further from my reach. She seemed more surprised that The Cloth wasn't protecting her than she was at my reaction; she scanned the room for the lights to zap me.

She was worthless to The Cloth. She was nothing but a dry, smelly, bottomless sinkhole to dispose of needles and pour shit into. You could still turn on a standard cable channel to watch her show, but the canned laughter seemed all too fitting a mockery of what she'd become: another Hollywood nobody.

She thumped on the metal wall at her back, not taking her eyes off me. Knowing her depth perception was beveled and warped, she feared the dangers of stumbling an inch or two out of her safe zone. As she scooted her can up the wall, she continued to knock.

"I wanna leave now!" she cried.

She looked toward the speakers or cameras in the sky, trying to get the attention of her comrades. Still unsure of her location as to how it pertained to my reach, she glued herself to the wall as she side-stepped away. As soon as she reached the end of my cell, she dashed to the exit, sounding like a peg-leg fast breaking on a basketball court.

As she reached the door and clutched the handle, she hollered back.

"You're an abortion, RJ. A goddamn abortion."

The lovely music turned off as it had every day. However, we weren't greeted with the routine morning dose of artificial vitamin D. Nonetheless,

I was prepared. I had gotten in the practice of beating the lights every morning.

Seemingly bored by our predicament, Herman yawned. "You can come up from behind your mattress, Reynolds. I don't think they're going to hit us anymore."

Trying to play it cool rather than continuing to cower, I upended the mattress back onto the frame by using both hands. I might have even flexed. I dusted my hands against each other like I had done something productive. All in a pussy day's work, I suppose.

"Why are you frontin' like you just did something? You blew it."

I sat back down on the bed and cradled the back of my skull with my hands. The laceration on my sternum was almost fully healed and my body was beginning to feel cleansed from heroin. I ignored his badgering.

"Why are you saying stuff like 'frontin''? You're an educated man. Enough with the thug-life talk. It's only you and me in here. You have nothing to prove."

Knowing I was right and his mobster façade was useless inside, he simply said, "Whatever."

"Do you think the lights might be broken?"

Herman coughed and wiped his face on his table. "The lights aren't broken. It's back to more cat-and-mouse shit."

I shot him a glance and noticed that his body was noticeably more intact that it had been in weeks. He was starting to look normal again and less like a melting candle.

"Seriously, why didn't you kill her, Reynolds?"

"You should be thanking me, asshole." I pointed to the front of our cells. "No lights."

"I can stand the lights," he said. "And I'm not thanking you for anything. Ever. You brought that white trash bitch around to begin with. You brought a card-carrying member of the KKK into my house." He twirled his arms around, showing off his cell. "You're to blame for this."

I jumped from my bed. "Herman. Holy shit. Your restraints."

"What about them?"

"They're off," I said, pointing at his body.

Taking a second to adjust, he put his hands in front of his face. Then, he scratched his ass.

"Dammit, Reynolds. I have been waiting to get at that itch forever."

"Be careful, dude. Maybe you should grab the top of the table so you don't slide off."

When he satisfied his itch, he firmly latched on to the top of the table. Cautiously, always expecting a trick up The Cloth's almighty sleeve, I inched toward the bars that separated us. "Can you get up?"

He delicately rolled his torso from side-to-side. I could tell that his front hadn't been as viciously scalded by the lights and tortured as his back. "I don't know."

He tucked his legs up under his pelvis and then slipped back down. "Legs work." He tried again, getting similar results. Because the middle of his monstrous body was so weak, he was as reluctant as I was after the acid incident to test his body's durability. He was either afraid he was going to break in half, or he was afraid his insides were going to spill out of the paper-thin remains of his back. The once vicious gang leader and most notorious killer in Los Angeles had been reduced to a defeated and crumbled shell of his former self, reluctant to rediscover mobility.

Herman tugged his body up the span of the plexiglass table. As he wormed upward, globs of skin broke off like tightly secured twine snapping a Christmas tree from the roof of a car. He wiped a week's worth of sneezes and teeth off his face. Presumably more annoying than the constant reminder that his ass itched, he seemed relieved to release that diamond-encrusted gold tooth off his cheek. While supporting most of his weight with one arm, he tucked the tooth into his pocket.

"Why are you keeping that? The tooth fairy isn't going to visit you here," I joked.

"Hilarious." He brought his hand back to the table and redistributed his weight as he pulled himself toward my cell.

"Careful, Herman," I advised as he began arching his back. "I can't tell how solid that part of your body is. The last thing you want to do is have your guts drop out of you."

He attempted to get a look at his back. "Owww. What's this thing around my neck?"

I pointed to my collar. "I'm guessing it's probably some kind of shock collar."

"I have one of those around my neck? I thought you were trying to be punk rock or something."

I smirked. He thought I was a bigger poser than him.

Unable to drag himself any further without causing possible permanent damage, he lost his balance yet again and slipped back to where he started. "Shit."

He looked at both his hands and reset the process a third time. "Can you see my organs or anything, Reynolds?"

I stood on my tiptoes to look further down his body toward his lower back.

"It's mainly charred skin. I can't really tell if there is anything beneath it at all. Try and scrape some of it off so I can get a better idea of what's going on there."

He rolled his eyes. "You'd like that, wouldn't you?"

"Meaning?"

"You know what it means."

I felt that we had made a lot of progress being locked up next to each other. I guess I was wrong.

"Actually, Herman, I don't know what it means."

"Do I have to spell it out for you? You want me to open it up further. From what I can feel…" He pressed on the burn with the balls of his fingers, "there isn't anything there now except for charred-ass Tommy Burger."

I dropped down off my toes. "That's what it looks like from here."

He pulled himself up to the table's edge to create a little more support for the rest of his body. I could tell he was doing everything in his power to devise a scheme to somehow hopscotch onto the floor and then onto his bed without shaking up his innards and disturbing what little protective support his backside offered.

I looked around his cell for an answer, wishing there was a gurney for him to transfer onto and then push himself to the bed. There was his I.V. machine and a small metal surgeon's table next to that. There was nothing that would support his weight. However, there was a roll of duct tape on the table.

I turned away from being his lifeguard and headed back to my cot. "Wait a second, Herman."

In a rare showing of uncertainty, he blubbered, "Where are you going?"

I nabbed my bargain pillow and rushed back to the bars. "Here," I said, pushing the pillow toward him.

Herman's head was nearly at the side of my cell. "What do you want me to do with this? Take a nap?"

"No, jackass. Wrap it up as best as you can around your lower back with your free arm." I pointed to the small side table. "Push that over to me first."

Herman unenthusiastically followed my instructions. As he struggled to hold himself up on the table, he flicked the cart up to the bars between us. "Now what?"

I grabbed the tape and opened it with my teeth as Herman tried to tuck the pillow around his stomach without gliding back down the table onto the floor and his death. "Okay," he said.

"Pull yourself up a little farther."

Seeming defeated, he whined. "I can't."

"Shit," I said, reaching both of my hands into his cell. Extending my body as far over him as I could, I stuck the open end of the tape on one of his shoulder blades and then ran it across his back. "Inch up a little."

Herman pressed himself up slightly so I could run the tape roll under his chest. As I spun it back around for a second pass across his back, I felt how mushy his protection actually was. I didn't say anything. There wasn't any reason to alarm him before I gave my plan a try. "Up again," I said.

As carefully as if he was carrying a tray full of antique china, he arched himself up again. Quickly, I rolled the tape under him. His strength was fleeting. As soon as I signaled to him that the tape was clear, he thundered back onto his stomach. I stretched my arms further into his cell and threw the tape down to his side.

"I know this is going to be tricky, Herman, but you're going to have to try and secure the pillow on to your back. My arms won't reach in any further."

Looking toward me like a helpless child, he continued to whimper. "How?"

"You've got to do it slowly by switching arms and maneuvering the tape roll under you across the table."

"I can't, Reynolds."

Just as unsure as he was, I still tried to comfort him. "Yeah, you can do it."

Trembling and agitated, he sucked in the front of his body as he continued to grip on to the edge of the table. First, using his ribcage, he pressed the roll under him by lightly rocking his body back and forth.

As soon as he felt it pass through to the opposite side, he stuck it sticky side down so it wouldn't topple off the table. Then, he brought his right arm around to the back, grabbed the tape and pulled it over to the right side of his body. Seeing that he was about to drift down the table again, I reached back into his cell and anchored both my arms around his wrist. I dug my combat boots into the cracked cement to give him more support.

With me lending my strength to the equation, Herman started winding the tape around the pillow and his body as quickly as possible. At some point his carelessness caused the tape to twist so the gummy side wasn't sticking to the pillow.

"Tighter," I advised him.

Too busy to think about anything other than getting the chore done, he struggled furiously to get every inch of the sliver of tape around him until it ran out. His breath became heavy and sweat soaked his face.

"It's gone, Reynolds." The empty cardboard roll bounced off his floor into my cell. "I don't think I got enough tape on the bottom to hold."

Continuing to pull him up and myself backward on my heels, I tried to look over the hump on his back. "I can't tell," I told him. "How far down did you get?"

"I don't know," he gasped. "Maybe just past my kidneys."

Reluctantly, I said, "It'll have to do."

Herman gripped his loose hand back to the top of the table. I eased off some of my pull and stepped sideways, trying to bridge the gap between his table and his bed.

"Hold on really tightly for a second," I directed, switching my support from his left wrist to his right, one hand at a time. "Okay, I need you to do something now."

His throat rasped as he tried to pace his breathing. "I need to rest."

"Herman, if you rest, you're going to end up in a thousand pieces all over the floor. Listen to me." I let go of his wrist with my left hand and started dragging his other wrist off the table. I used all the strength I could muster as he let that arm off the table and into the security of my free hand. Once again rocking his torso, Herman shuffled across the table.

"Drop the leg now. I've got you." I squinted my eyes, preparing to have three hundred pounds of pressure yank me into the metal bars. "Be careful. As you hit the floor, continue arching your back. Keep your head upright too."

Without any comment, I steadied him as his first leg dropped toward the floor.

"Okay, now I'm going to pull you sideways so both of your legs can make contact with the ground." I pulled him around until I had turned his body about 45 degrees laterally. Then, I started to give him leeway as he wiggled his way down so that his bare toes touched the floor.

He looked at me from under squinted eyelids. "Are you sure?"

"We have nothing to lose," I half-assured him.

He shuffled down until his bottom half stabilized his top half. I let the wrist go slowly until he was standing on his own. His back hunched over as his neck stretched out like a hungry giraffe. It was the only thing supporting the bowl of chili that used to be his cranium.

"You can let go now," he said, still unsure.

I did.

One carefully plotted foot at a time, he made his way to the cot in his cell. He placed his hands on the mattress and collapsed his knees underneath him. As soon as his sternum was safely on the bed, he let the rest of his limbs loosen with the exception of his neck, which he propped up under his pillow to keep his head upright.

"I need this pillow, Reynolds," he said, letting out a convincing sigh of relief.

"Don't sweat it. I hated that pillow anyway."

XXXI

WIZARDS

Real Tim, Not Tim and a New Tim parked in front of my cell.

"White guy, wake up."

"I'm up," I responded.

"Get out of bed and turn towards the back wall," New Tim commanded.

Playing dumb, I pointed at them. "What's all that for?" Despite my confused behavior, I knew that the shackles, cattle prods, and shotguns were to remove me from my dungeon.

I got no answer and groggily did as they instructed. The car alarm sounded, my cell door unlocked and then opened behind me. Almost as instantly as the wheels that controlled the door began to click, I felt the barrels of both shotguns shoved into the back of my head.

"Don't move," Not Tim barked. Sparks from the prods tingled up and down my spine. The New Tim crouched to my feet and swatted at my boots. "Open your legs," he said.

"Do you want me to not move, or open my legs?"

Real Tim and Not Tim moaned. One of them eased a prod closer to my skin. "Open your legs, idiot."

As I separated my feet, New Tim clamped the shackle around my ankles and handed me the other end of the chain through the center of my legs. "Put these on."

I reached between my legs and dragged the connection upward as I clamped the metal cuffs around each wrist. "You know these can't hold me, don't you?" I said.

One of the barrels knocked at the back of my head. "We know. The chains are just another deterrent."

I picked a dry booger off the inside corner of my nose and flung it over my head. "Who's to say that I won't turn around, break the chains, disarm you and then rip the three of you to pieces?"

The prods zipped and zapped and I felt their heat at my kidneys. The shotgun tapped at the steel collar around my neck. "This does," Real Tim answered.

I elongated my neck and swallowed as if I was loosening a tie. "Yeah, I was wondering about that. No respect."

"Turn around. Slowly," Not Tim ordered.

I did. The three Tims stood like a defensive line, two arm lengths in front of me. Each of them had a shotgun pointed at the center of my face.

I tried to adjust the collar with both my hands. "What is this thing anyway?"

"Insurance," the always witty Not Tim said.

"Okay, I got that. What does it do? Does it shock me or something?"

The three Tims looked at each other and chuckled.

"Hardly," Not Tim returned, tugging on my shackles to make sure they were secured. He stepped backward, refocusing his gun on my face. "If you do anything, and I mean anything, that we're not sure about, we just say something into this—" he rubbed the lapel on his priest uniform, "— and it takes your head clean off."

"Lights on." He spoke into the mic. "Medium frequency." The beams on my side of the cells flicked on.

"Entire hallway." The lamps down the hall turned on as well. Almost immediately I felt the drain. Since Herman and I had been spared the light torture for a few days, the bite felt stronger than I remembered. Even if I didn't have the collar on, my sudden lack of energy prevented me from doing any damage to the three Tims before I ended up headless or with a cattle prod jammed up my cornhole. "Where are we going?"

"Father McAteer wants to speak with you," New Tim said.

"Are you taking me to a confession or something? I hope so; I have a shitload of sins. You know, being a demon and all."

Not Tim smacked me on the forehead with his gun. "Pipe down, smart guy. It's not a confession, I assure you."

Dismissive, I replied, "Yeah... I assure you."

We exited my cell, Real Tim and Not Tim on my sides with their guns still fixed on my skull and their prods grazing my rib cage. New Tim walked behind us, targeting the base of my neck and my lower back.

The walk was painful, but I sluggishly trekked onward to the door. Not Tim spoke into his microphone again as security cams above us feverishly scanned the scene for any funny business. "Door," he said clearly.

The industrial freezer-sized door disengaged and opened into a small, caged-in clearance room. There was another guard sipping coffee as he watched the monitors—and, believe it or not, a rerun of *Dag Nabbit*.

Real Tim patted the top of the television. "You know that little girl is the junky bitch who you've seen around here."

"No shit," the vigilant guard said, looking more closely at the set.

"I kid you not," Real Tim said.

Deciding that cute little Dag Nabbit was indeed The Habit, the guard bit into a piece of toast. "Wow. I was thinking about getting me some of that."

I moved my bloated and dried-out tongue to the side of my mouth. "No you weren't, loser. Even that bitch would kick your shiftless ass. What kind of priest talk is that anyway?"

Not Tim tugged at my shackles. "Keep moving."

Next to the security monitors there were several other colored screens that appeared to be tracking heart rates and body heat and the like. To the right of the main observation area there were around twenty blue lockers. Every locker that I could see had an Irish or Scottish surname taped across the front. *Pretty diverse bunch, The Cloth*, I thought to myself.

Not Tim took the lead after tapping the fat ass guard on the shoulder. He swiped a key card across a black security panel that opened the cage. The card reader flipped from a red light to green.

I looked over to the less talkative Real Tim and said, "What is this, a Radisson? Are you kidding me? Don't you guys have like retinal or fingerprint scanners? How do you expect to keep us in here with this nickel and dime shit?"

He blew a strand of sandy blonde hair out of his eyes. "It's managed to keep you locked in here for weeks, smart guy."

We proceeded into another hall. As we made our way across the gate's threshold, UV lamps hummed on before we reached them. It was a nice touch and pretty high tech, even though I knew fat boy at the TV was timing our steps, but it still didn't make up for the archaic key card technology. I mean seriously, was there an advertisement for a Pizza Hut on the back of that thing? With my mind drifting away from reality, my walking became more and more lumpish as we neared the end of the second hall.

"Door two," New Tim said into his microphone. I guessed it had to be a tag team effort to open the labyrinth from the inside out. Just like the first major obstacle, the door released and coasted open using hydraulics.

I stared at Real Tim's microphone. "Do these mics at least have vocal recognition?" I blew toward the round mesh ball.

He tapped my collar with his finger. "Don't get any ideas. We are always in control. There is a microphone on the front of this. We turn them on and off depending on what Fat Mac wants us to do."

"Is it on right now?"

To this, Not Tim clubbed me with his cattle prod across my thighs.

I fell to my knees.

"Fuck, dude. Why?"

They dragged me back to my feet, and we entered a large gymnasium with basketball hoops at either end. It looked more like a homeless shelter than a recreation center. On one side of the court were ten more cots like the dream bed I had been sleeping on every night. On the other side, there were approximately five rusted incubators. They were older and looked as if they hadn't been turned on in over ten years.

Past the incubators was a secured and barricaded set of double doors that had a large *Do Not Enter* sign. Yellow caution tape zigzagged everywhere. It didn't take Matlock to deduce that it was the makeshift hospital where I was born. Short on breath from the UV lighting dangling from fixtures above us, I kept my cynical observations and conclusions to myself.

We passed through one more secured steel door that led to a staircase, going up. As Real Tim and Not Tim shoved me up the stairs with their shotguns in my armpits, New Tim supported my back with his hands. "Owww, his skin is on fire," he said, pulling his sweaty hands away.

After venturing through the central worship area of the Catholic church that resided atop the stairs, we arrived at a series of unsecured doorways. Each of the doors was plated with the name of the corresponding Irish Catholic priest who worked inside. At the end of a long line of O'Malleys and Sullivans, we reached the doorway to Father McAteer's office.

Exhausted from supporting me as we walked up the stairs, New Tim rounded me from the side and pressed a button on an intercom. "Father McAteer," he said.

"Yes," Fat Mac's voice came through the intercom.

"We have the white one."

We were buzzed into the office. New Tim looked at Not Tim and Real Tim and said, "I'll catch up with you later. I have to work my other security job tonight."

Not Tim and Real Tim made the sign of the cross, clutched the beads around their necks and said, "We'll contact you when we need you again. Get some rest." Then they led me into the office.

Now, not to criticize the allocation process of the church donations, but to say Fat Mac's office was palatial was an understatement. Vintage bibles, books, and scrolls lined the walls, corner-to-corner, only ending every so often to expose the gleaming mahogany book cases that gave off an unmistakable blossomy scent that filled the room. When I say that Fat Mac had walls of bibles, I mean just that. Like an old-fashioned library, he had a ladder to get to those sometimes forgotten top-shelf books.

Several museum-quality chairs surrounded a similarly chiseled, glossy desk. The sky opened to a stained-glass ceiling that looked traced and blown from the prototype at the Sistine Chapel. The two remaining Tims stood at the door as I continued into the literary Promised Land.

"Please, Mr. Reynolds," Fat Mac said, inviting me to sit down. He looked across the room to the guards. "You can go, my sons." The Tims did the cross thing again and left the room.

I studied the microphone on Mac's priest garb.

"Lights. Low," he said. My throat gulped inside the metal collar as three production lights on boom stands triggered. "Sorry about the lights. I can never be too cautious."

"That's fine. I'm working on my tan."

As I lethargically clumped my way to the desk, I noticed that Fat Mac was setting up dominoes.

"Please, give me a minute and enjoy the seat. I'm sure it will be much more comfortable than the accommodations downstairs."

I lumped into one of the chairs. Even though I shouldn't have cared, I actually was worried I was going to soil or break the chair. It was that nice.

He looked over his reading glasses that rested on his globular nose. "You do know why you're here, correct?"

"Not really. Please don't keep me in suspense. You've already beaten the life out of me and dumped acid all over my chest. On top of all that, methadone isn't really a replacement for heroin. It tastes like soy milk by comparison to the real shit."

"Fair enough. Some precautions are unavoidable. I'm sure you can understand."

Refusing to make eye contact with my captor, I surveyed the room. "Whatever," I said.

He continued to set up his dominoes, seemingly as unfazed by me as I was by him. "You understand the Catholic Church's stance on abortion, do you not?"

"Yeah, I get it. Is that what the cots and incubators in the gym are for?"

"That is what they were for, Mr. Reynolds. *Were.*"

Fat Mac moved down the line, making sure that all of his dominoes were aligned correctly. He then reversed to the end and began placing more bones.

"You see, a long time ago, this parish became a safe house for drug-addicted prostitutes and battered, homeless women. You know, women in abusive relationships. You, your friends, and your enemies are a by-product of our somewhat well-meaning yet misguided efforts."

I turned away from the bookshelves. "Misguided? I don't follow."

He stopped with a domino pinched between his thumb and index finger. "The former cardinal of this church, God rest his soul, decided to take the word of our Lord a step further than most." He returned to his construction. "Father Herlihy was a great man, but like all of us, he misinterpreted the Good Word. He gave life to those who did not have life."

I looked up at the stained glass. It barely shaded me from the approaching noon sun, almost booming through. I pushed my seat back a little. As if the stage lights weren't tormenting enough.

Fat Mac pointed to the ceiling. "Precautions." He paused, assessed the domino set-up again and continued.

"You see, Mr. Reynolds, you are alive because we gave you a gift that we now know should never have been given."

Filthy sweat dripped from the ends of my hair. "It doesn't feel like a gift. You have my friend... errr... me and Cobra... chained up in your torture chamber downstairs. What are you going to give me for Christmas? A crucifixion?"

"Yes, yes. We have been a tad malicious toward you."

"Cut to the chase... you delivered us from evil by bringing us into this world?"

"Close," he said, paying more attention to his stacking game. "You are, or were, a stillborn child. You, like many of the others, were born addicted to heroin. Your birth mother came to the church as many other hopeless teenagers before her. She searched for guidance from God because she wanted to terminate the pregnancy. She also wanted somewhere to sleep. We took in as many as we could and gave them shelter. We gave you life as a result."

Any romanticized theories I had about my existence, whether it was being bitten by a Baron from Transylvania or being the spawn of Lucifer, were quickly swept behind the bookcases that surrounded me.

I dabbed the back of my hand on my blistering forehead. "How is that possible?"

"Not all of you were stillborn. Some of you were premature while others were just born addicted. That's why you need the narcotics, Mr. Reynolds. Quite simply, your hunger for heroin is why you live."

I scooted further back, away from the glaring rays slam dancing from above.

"That's still impossible. It doesn't explain why I'm a living, breathing, thinking being. If I were stillborn, how am I alive? On top of that, why am

I so strong? Why am I so sensitive to light? Why can I hear shit that regular people can't? I'm a vampire. If I wasn't alive when I was born, then how are we talking right now? And be careful what you say, Mac. The will and love of God isn't the correct answer."

He rubbed his nose a little, causing his glasses to slip down. He pushed them back to an approved domino-setting level.

"I assure you, it is nothing that spiritual. After we delivered you, we incubated you and gave you strength by feeding your addictions. At the same time, we gave you constant blood transfusions from clean members of our congregation."

"What about the fucking strength, asshole?"

"Your strength is a side effect. To counter your inability to grow normally, we gave you growth hormones and steroids. The stimulants caused an overactive blood system and heart rate that constantly, but slowly, drained your life cycle." He fumbled and dropped a domino on the floor. "Let me ask you a question."

I crossed my legs, uncrossed them, and put my elbows on my knees. "Shoot."

"Can you use without the help of warm blood?" He carelessly set up the domino he dropped on the floor. It almost tumbled backward. Using his pinky, he narrowly avoided complete destruction.

Smoke started to ignite from my pores. "I can. It depends on how much blood I have in my body, I guess. Is that the answer you're looking for?"

"It is the exact answer. Your body does not produce hemoglobin on its own. It only eats it because of the enhancing drugs. The drugs have since become unavailable, thankfully. They were a test drug to control the effects of Progeria in children, the disease that causes them to age too fast. They failed to counter the aging process, however. They sped up the circulatory system.

"Anyway, they spun your bodies into an uncontrollable spiral that it cannot break out of. As you have seen over the past few weeks, we can cure you from the heroin addiction. However, we can't cure you from your bodily disease. The need for your body to be constantly replenished with fresh blood is irreversible. I am sorry."

As the sun reached noon, I tried to poke holes in his story, wishing it weren't the truth. "So, what about the Battlesnakes? They can't be addicted to marijuana."

Ignoring my pain, Fat Mac continued wrapping another outer wall to his now circular structure.

"As far I know, you cannot become addicted to cannabis. We didn't give them marijuana while nurturing them, though. We gave them whatever drug their birth mothers were addicted to. Like most things in our modern society, smoking marijuana was a learned behavior that suited them and their lifestyle."

It was all so tidy, so *not* paranormal or alien or supernatural. I was correct when I told Herman that I was the product of the streets. "Jesus. Is this the only church that did this?"

"No, other churches in North America participated."

My skin tightened to my insides as a dark cloud rolled over the sun. I exhaled, relieved, and let out a huge puff of smoke. "Are you telling me that the Vatican is involved with this? Are you kidding me?"

"I am afraid not, Mr. Reynolds. We acted as The Order of The Cloth. We would have told the Vatican if our pro-life crusades hadn't gone so terribly awry."

Overwhelmed by the bombardment of information, I continued to throw low-numbered cards at him, bluffing and hoping to maybe win a hand. "So, why can't any of us remember anything before we were teens?"

He flipped a block in line on his desk and then took off his reading glasses. "We kept you here on life support and in several closely guarded locations around Los Angeles until I felt you were at the age to survive on your own."

"So, you dumped us on the streets without a user's manual? What kind of shit is that, you fucking hypocrite?" As I looked up to see my savior cloud rolling away, I put my arms over my face for protection.

Mac paced around his structure, checking to see if any pieces were out of line. "Be thankful, my son."

"Thankful? Be thankful for what? For being a living dumpster abortion?"

"Life is a gift from God. Accept it in your heart while you can."

I stood and kicked the chair back behind me. It smashed into wood chips as I blasted it against the wall.

Unfazed, Mac cleared his throat and yelled. *"Adstringo gutter."*

The microphone on the necktie was on.

The collar turned like a screw and constricted around my neck. My body broke down into spasms as I flipped onto my back. I gasped for air and tried in vain to loosen the steel device.

"Please," I begged.

"Labefactum gutter."

Instantly, the collar choker reversed. I remained on the floor, sucking in huge lungfuls of oxygen. Defeated, broken and clearly not of uncanny origin, I asked, "What do you want?"

"That should be clear, Mr. Reynolds. We need you to right the Church's mistakes."

As somewhat predicted, he recited the narrative for his ridiculous demonstration. "The Lord giveth." He then flicked at the first domino in line. His dramatic climax to the dreadful explanation of my life was short lived as the toppling effect only lasted under a quarter of the way through the progression. He rushed to the roadblock that was delaying the fully-realized potential of easily the lamest denouement in history. He swatted the disobedient block over.

"The Lord taketh away," he concluded. As the last brick toppled in the center, he made the sign of the cross.

Even though I felt my glands swell into the neckband, I had to say something. "Do you think I'm fucking retarded? What was all that?"

Unsure if I was questioning the context of his stupid performance or if I just didn't understand it at all, he answered, "A demonstration?"

I rolled under one of the chair backs to shield my body from the light. "Why?"

Embarrassed at himself, he opened a drawer on his desk and began sashaying the dominos inside. "I don't know. You are the first one of your kind that I've ever spoken to beyond phone calls. I mean, tried to convey this delicate situation to."

Disgusted, I asked, "By using toys and games?"

He tried to plead innocent. "It... It... It was just..." he stuttered.

"I get it, asshole. Please take me back to my cell."

XXI

ORPHANS

The Tims transplanted me back to my cell. I was physically and emotionally debilitated. Barely able to focus on the quaint manger where I was given new life, the same question wrapped around my thoughts: does everyone deserve to live? If so, what if the baby knew before they popped out of some drug addict's womb how shitty their life was going to be and decided that they didn't want to live?

They threw me back in my cell with a parting goodbye that was somewhere along the lines of "That will keep you in line, demon," as if I had lost a wrestling match with Fat Mac.

I dumped myself onto my cot and plunged the methadone and blood I.V. back into my arm. Delirious and exhausted, I rested my head on the edge of my pillow-less bed and vomited over the edge.

Herman banged the plexiglass table against the bars that separated us.

"Hey, you're up," I said, spitting pigskin through my two front teeth.

"Yeah. I'm up. Where did they take you? It looks like they kicked your ass again."

I cranked myself upright, using my left arm as if it were a flimsy jack under a car. I rubbed my neck above and below the dog collar. Dusty skin fell on my shoulders. "Do you really want to know?"

He stepped backward and plugged his nose, still trying to avoid my stink. "Of course I do."

Catching a whiff of myself, I put my arm over my nose. "Are you sure you're good to stand up?" I stretched out the wrinkled skin under the collar, trying my best to straighten it out underneath the grip.

Herman patted the pillow taped to his back. "I'm still jacked up, but I'm healing."

"Good to hear. Can I have a pillow please?"

Delicately, as if moving with the help of an invisible walker, he scuffed across the cement to his bed and grabbed his pillow. He reached toward the bars and pulled himself toward me, then pressed the pillow through the cells.

Steadying myself and mindful not to slip on my own vomit, I latched onto the I.V. stand and dragged it with me across my cell. I snatched the pillow from him and hugged it with both arms.

"Holy shit. They gave you a real pillow. That's lame."

He pulled the pillow on his back down a notch like he was stretching out a tight shirt to cover his ass crack. "I wish that was the pillow taped to my back." He turned around and showed me his rear. The once white pillow was drenched red. It looked like he was carrying a burnt rock on his back. "So?"

I threw Herman's superior quality pillow down and I put my arms under it to support my tight neck and then crossed my legs behind me. I faced him. "So... we're not vampires or anything like that."

"What does that mean, fool? Of course we are."

I picked some pig out from under my tongue and wiped it on the back of my jeans. "Well, we're different, but there isn't anything miraculous about us."

"So, we're like super soldiers gone bad? Right? That's what I always figured."

I scratched my feet together. "What the hell is a super soldier?"

Herman glanced at the operating table next to him. "You know, like we were created by Hitler's army or something."

"That's even dumber than what we really are. Look, Herman. I don't know if you want me to tell you any of this. As a matter of fact, I wish Fat Mac didn't even tell me. It's like the end of a shit mystery movie where the butler was the killer and the film was five minutes long."

He kicked at the table. "Just tell me."

Reluctant, I started delivering Fat Mac's message. "We were still-born, addicted babies that this Catholic church brought to life with some unapproved steroids. We spent about twelve to thirteen years on life support, with steroids and drugs to support our addictions. Then, when these assholes felt that we were ready to live on our own, they dumped us on the streets to fend for ourselves."

Herman was silent. As if he were ignoring me, he repeatedly picked things up off the operating table, studied them and put them back down.

"I'm sorry," I told him.

"You're telling me that we're orphans?"

I wanted to turn away from him, imagining what it felt like to have a self-illusion you were a super soldier or an extraterrestrial only to have the tablecloth yanked, revealing you were nothing more than a drug-addicted orphan. "I don't know what to tell you. I feel the same way. Yesterday, I felt like I was something special. Now I feel like a bum."

Without responding, Herman swatted the flimsy tray next to the table, knocking all its contents out of his cell. He paced to the wall opposite me and grabbed onto the bars with both his fists.

"You'd better be careful," I advised.

He shot around. "Why, Reynolds? Why should I be careful?" He stumbled for more answers like I had with Fat Mac. "What about the strength?"

"A side effect of the hormones and the steroids."

Desperately, he continued to poke holes. I felt his dejection as he tried to reelevate our existence to the level of magnificence.

"The blood? What about the need and hunger for the warm blood?"

"Can we stop talking about this?"

He bent one of his own fingers backwards and then flicked the broken bone back into place. "The blood?"

"Another side effect of the steroids. From what I understood, our organs, glands and circulatory system are overly active but they don't produce any blood. Our bodies eat anything that's inside of us."

His shoulders dropped with a sigh as if the glory was fading. I, on the other hand, was beginning to feel how I felt around Bait when she was curious about how I was alive.

"The sun?" he asked.

"We didn't really touch on that but I imagine it's either another side effect or photophobia caused by being born premature or dead. Probably."

Herman began bending the bars inward, toward each other. I saw the muscles on his back flex through the transparent lining of the pillow.

"The hearing?"

"I don't know, Herman. I'm guessing our senses are more evolved because of the drugs and the steroids. It might have something to do with our repulsion to light. They say that blind people develop sensitive hearing." I rubbed at the blank real estate on my chest where my Faction tattoo used to be. "I mean, think about bats." For some reason, that sounded too vampiric, so I revoked the suggestion that we were somehow related to bats. "Not bats. It's the drugs."

He didn't turn back around. Rather, he pumped the jail bars in and out. He still questioned though, wishing for a grandiose loophole. "The healing?"

"It has something to do with a sped-up immune system from all the steroids. Don't bother asking about your need for pot. I asked for you."

179

"And?"

"Rather than bringing you to life by making you smoke blunts in your crib, they filled you with high doses of THC. It's a combination of overexposure to cannabis and base or sherm or heroin. You picked up all the Rasta shit on your own."

"There has to be more to it. There has to be. We're fucking vampires. Why are they keeping us here? Why are they studying us? If they have all the answers, smartass, why do they want to know more? They are observing us... aren't they?"

I rolled over so I was facing the back wall of my cell. "They aren't studying us. They don't want to make any more of us at all."

He left the bars bent and walked back to the table. "Then, why are we here? Why do I have pins in my brain, bitch?

"They aren't studying us. They're torturing us, Herman. I think they want to fix their mistake. They want us to wipe out the rest. Before you ask me another twenty questions about why we would do that..." I walked over to bars between us, "we'll do it because of this." I flicked at the dog collar. "This little prick will screw your head right off your neck."

He gave me the finger. "I'd rather die, bitch."

"Why? All your Battlesnakes are already dead, except for Copperhead and those dancehall queers. I know you want to kill him. I know you hate the Mexicans. They're gonna kill us anyway. Why not use the chance to get away?"

"Are you really considering this, Reynolds? Why?"

I held onto to the I.V. stand. "Bait." I felt her ID in my back pocket.

Astonished, he wiped his hand across his eyes. "The little whore? Who cares?"

"I care. I brought her into this shit and I also know I can use her as a bargaining chip for our lives."

"How so? She's a stupid little bitch?"

"Because one of us got her pregnant. If The Cloth wants to wipe us all out, they are going to need to know which one of us did it so they can make sure that prick and any other mutants running around are dead."

Fat Mac stood in front of our cells. "You are looking better, Cobra," he said.

"Call me Herman." I didn't know if his response was a means of being difficult or if he was coming to terms with the fact that he was just another piece of street shit.

Mac pulled his small notebook from his pocket and took notes to the request. "Okay, Herman."

I cut to the chase. "Look, we'll do it. We would have all killed each other for drugs or territory eventually, so let's expedite the process without any more torture."

Herman butted in. "What happens to us?" He pointed to his exposed skull.

Fat Mac shoved his reading glasses from the end of his nose up to his eyes. "We will cover that for you."

"With what?" Herman bombed back at him. "A blankie?"

I increased the sincerity of my tone. "Stop, Herman." I turned to address Mac. "I think he means do we live?"

"Yes, you'll live here."

Herman started walking back toward his cot. "Are you kidding me?"

"Wait a second," I said. "Fat Mac, there is more to this."

The priest started balancing a domino on his index finger, clearly hoping I shared his presentation in the office with Herman. "How so?"

"There was this little girl living with me," I started. I grabbed Bait's ID out of my pocket and tossed it out of my cell.

"And?" He bent over to pick up the ID card as he cascaded the single brick down his hand like a slinky on stairs.

"One of us—I mean, not us." I pointed to Herman and myself. "But one of the Knucklers got the little girl pregnant."

Mac caught the domino in his palm and looked at her picture. "Impossible." He threw the card back into my cell.

"I swear. She gave herself an abortion a few days before you assholes kidnapped me."

"It is not possible, Mr. Reynolds. Even if enough blood was available to you in your bodies to become erect, we sterilized every one of you before we assimilated you back into society."

Herman rushed back to the bars as he ripped the pillow off his back. "Assimilate? Society? You dumped us on the streets."

Quietly, Fat Mac spoke into his mic. "Lights. Medium."

Herman tried to cover his exposed head with his hands. Not preventing the light from singeing him, he retreated to his cot, grabbing a pillow off the floor on the way back. He shaded his face and head with it like an umbrella.

"Be that as it may," Mac continued, "it is impossible for you to breed."

"Wait, wait, wait," I interrupted. "So, we were brought to life because your lame church thinks that abortion is a sin, but you sterilized us and now you want us to kill each other because giving us life to begin with was wrong? Are you kidding me? Aren't birth control and killing also Catholic sins?"

He put his notepad back in his pocket and then tossed the domino in the air from his thumb like a coin and caught it on the opposite index finger.

"Put the domino away. We offered to help you, asshole. At least show us the respect we deserve for surrendering to your torture. We don't need your visual aids. We'll clean up your mess. Even if the mess is... well... us."

I turned around and walked back to my cot. I picked the nice pillow off my bed and shoved it through the bars.

"Here, Herman. Cover yourself with this."

He reached his long arms to the bars and grabbed the pillow from me.

"Don't get too used to it," I warned him. "I want that pillow back."

Fat Mac spoke into his microphone again. "Lights. Off."

As if he were a little boy not getting his way, Herman spit on the pillow and chucked it back at the bars. "Here, fool."

"Thanks, jerk." I tossed the pillow up onto my bed with my foot.

I looked back at Mac. He dropped the domino into his breast pocket.

"Thanks for putting away your toy. How is this going to work, anyway?"

Mac scratched the blotchy whiskers on his chin. "Hmmmmm."

Herman got out of bed and relaxed on the plexiglass table. "That doesn't put me at ease. You trapped our asses in here to kill for you and you don't even have a plan."

"Come on, Mac. Throw us a bone. Jesus."

His scratching progressed up his face to his temple. "The only plan is that you two get us in the doors and The Cloth and girl—"

Herman steadied his forearm across the table. "What girl?"

Mac looked fully at him. "The girl who calls herself The Habit. I do not remember her real name. The one from the TV show—"

"Hell no!" Herman yelled as he pounded his arm directly through the table, breaking it right down the middle. "The next words out of your mouth better be that we get to rape and kill her, or I choose death... now."

"*Adstringo gutter,*" Mac shouted. The collars constricted. As I fell forward, I heard Herman spit up blood. He remained stoic, reluctant to back down to the priest and his weapons. At that point, it didn't matter to him whether he lived or died. He swished some blood around in his mouth and spit it at Mac.

Struggling for air and trying to breach the collar with my fingertips, I pleaded with him. "For Christ's sake, Herman!"

Knowing that Herman chose death, Fat Mac released the collars. "*Labefactum gutter.*"

Herman cleared his throat while I coughed up pieces of my esophagus. "Herman, we're going to kill a bunch of people. You don't have any more followers. This isn't going to ruin your street cred. Neither of us will have any pride and streets or gangs to lead anymore. We're orphans. Abandoned. Addicts. Who cares?" I said.

"Ahem. Continuing," Fat Mac said. "You get us in and we put the mistakes to rest. May God have mercy on their souls."

Herman rolled his head, trying to fully loosen the collar. "Don't care anymore, Reynolds. This is your show now. As long as I get Copperhead's traitor ass, I don't care."

I got back to my feet and looked at Fat Mac. "How do we know if we've killed all of them? I mean there are a lot of us. You told me that we were all over the world."

"You needn't bother with the rest of the world. We only want to correct the mistakes of this parish. We have records for all of you."

I built up a big ball of phlegm in my mouth and swallowed it, attempting to lubricate my throat. "You do? Can we see them?"

I looked into Herman's cell to see if our genesis interested him. He had checked out completely. To him, it was a kamikaze mission and nothing more. He wanted to hold on to as much of the grandeur of which he was as he could. If a serial killer druggie was all that Herman was meant to be in life, then he was going to die being the greatest serial killer druggie the world ever saw.

Fat Mac debated with himself for a minute. "I can show you," he decided.

Maybe I'd find something in my file that suggested my lineage could be traced back to cannibal kings or something. Something more than a dishonorable discharge from the land of the living that had *Stillborn* stamped on the front of it.

And if not, I could die knowing that I was going through with the suicide mission to help a troubled little girl whose only feeling of love was being raped.

XXIII
NUMBERS

As requested for the records, The Tims came for me the next morning. Herman ignored us.

I yawned, still waking up. "Herman, are you sure you aren't a little curious?"

He didn't answer.

Not Tim clicked his car alarm key chain. "White guy, face the back wall." The three stooges entered my cell and ran me through the same security drill as before. We then headed to the gymnasium.

We walked beyond the cots and past the yellow-stained, mildewed incubators to the double doors. Not Tim grabbed a crowbar and peeled back the wooden "Do Not Enter" sign. He pulled the police tape off the doors and wrapped it around his forearm.

New Tim slapped his cattle prod against a pole. "We'll wait here for Father McAteer," he said.

"No need to zap me, assface," I said, brushing the sparks off my lower back.

"Sorry," he apologized. "My hand slipped."

Disgusted, I bent my head around to look at his much-in-need-of-the-gym body. "Great. I hope you're not a part of the crew we're rolling with to take out Los Angeles' most dangerous gangs."

None of them responded. To me, that suggested The Cloth wasn't the deepest posse in town. To this day, I have no idea how they managed to storm the Battlesnakes compound and kill every single thug there. On top of that, they somehow managed to capture a seven-foot-tall Rasta psychopath. Sure, Dez and Copperhead loosened the pickle jar for them, but it amazed me that they carried Herman from their doorstep to the jail without being mangled.

I tapped my foot impatiently. "Well, it looks like we're going to be working together. I hope you've made peace with your God. If any of us make it back alive, it isn't going to be many."

Fat Mac called across the gymnasium as if he were arriving at a party fashionably late.

"Sorry for the hold up," he said. "I had some details to sort through." He walked up to us. "Are you ready, Mr. Reynolds?"

Still tapping my feet, I answered, "I'm as ready as I'm ever going to be."

He pointed to the chipped parquet floor. "Please wait for us here," he instructed The Tims. "If I need you, you'll hear me."

Surprised, I asked, "You trust me enough to go in there with me alone?"

"Precautions," Mac said as he tapped his microphone. "If I feel I am in danger, I will not hesitate to use this. And, Mr. Reynolds..."

"Yeah?"

He blew into the mic to make sure it was responding. "This time, I will not reverse the process."

I rubbed at my collar. "I understand."

"I will tell you before we enter that it is not very exciting. What we did... giving you life... that was the exciting part. However, we both know now that we should never have played God."

"Don't give yourself so much credit, Fat Mac. Your experiment wasn't as successful as the real human race."

"It is, though. Don't you see, Mr. Reynolds? We aided you in your will to live. We helped God bring you into this world."

I rolled my eyes. "And now you want to take it away."

Mac fogged up his reading glasses with his breath and then wiped them off on his sleeve. "I have to pay the price for participating and following Father Herlihy, as do all the workers at St. Matthews."

As he unlocked the bolted double doors and pulled back the curtain to my personal Wizard of Oz, I said, "You have not and will never pay as much as your victims have, Mac."

"Only the Lord will be the judge," he returned, putting his glasses back on their roost. "I ask forgiveness every minute of every day."

"That's quite a few Hail Marys," I said.

We entered the top-secret room and Mac flipped on the florescent bulbs. It took several moments for them to flicker to life. Some of the bulbs only half illuminated. Others just fused on and off one last time. The lab was less than half the size of the gymnasium. The floor was checker-tiled with a bad grout job. It was so dirty that the white squares were almost as dark as their black counterparts.

The first objects that caught my eye were more large incubators, about twenty or so. Worse for wear than the incubators in the main gym, the oxygen lines were corroded and all the electrical wiring had long since fizzled out. It wasn't quite the majesty you'd expect from a mad scientist's laboratory. Analogue life support systems that appeared to be donations from old hospitals remained beside about thirty percent of the incubators. At the far end, there was a collection of abandoned and decayed wheelchairs, crutches, and I.V. stands.

"You were right," I remarked.

Mac looked around the room. "How so?"

"This is pretty depressing."

A burst pipe under the sterilization sink by the main doors had flooded the right front quarter of the room. The black water served as a swimming hole for a variety of insects. The stale aroma smelled like a combination of discounted cleansers, burnt hair, and moldy food.

I waved my hand in front of my nose, the shackles around my wrists rattled loudly in the quiet room. "How long has it been since you cleaned this place?"

McAteer counted on his fingers. "It has been sealed now for about twelve years. There is no reason to come down here anymore."

"All joking aside," I said, "if you knew you were going to shut down your project, why leave all this evidence here to prove you were guilty of something?"

He looked back at me confused and somewhat shocked. "What were we guilty of? We were housing and caring for homeless and abused women. The only thing we were actually guilty of was trying to clean up the community."

I rubbed my hand across the build-up of filth on a bubble of one of the incubators. "You really believe that, don't you? Look inside this casket. That's where I spent my childhood. I was unaware of the world and I was kept alive by machines, steroids, blood, and drugs. How the hell did you get the drugs, anyway?"

"Some of our part-time deacons worked as police officers. They were paid to misplace evidence."

I looked further under the stain of the bubble inside the incubator to see another synthetic pillow. Unlike the cot in my cell, this bed had sheets and a blanket. However, it wasn't exactly a rich kid's racecar bed.

Frustrated, I asked, "And you never saw anything morally wrong with misplacing narcotics?"

"The drugs were the fruit that gave life; otherwise there would have been nothing. The drugs were the key, Mr. Reynolds. The steroids alone did not bring you back from the afterlife. Every one of the children that began to live and breathe did not become conscious until they were exposed to the same drug nourishment provided by their mothers in the womb. As you took form, you were bombarded with narcotics, sometimes as a replacement for food. Simply put, your bodies grew inside your mothers' infested bodies and you developed a need for the drugs like most forming humans need food and water. Our theory from day one was that once you children were born into this world, you lacked that one element to stay alive. As soon as the mothers' sour milk was taken away, so was the will to live."

"Then why the steroids at all?"

"In most cases," he continued, "the narcotics weren't enough because many of the births were third-trimester miscarriages. The growth hormone was a mistake, which we realized after it was too late. It helped your bodies develop rapidly. It sped up the nurturing process."

A rat crawled out from under the pillow inside the broken-down incubator I was surveying. "How did you know any of it would work?"

"We didn't," Fat Mac admitted. "In our quest to follow our pro-life beliefs, we ran into a lot of trial and error."

I scratched on the bubble. The rat investigated my finger by getting on his hind legs and sniffing the inside of the bubble. "How much error?" I asked.

"The first subject we gave life to after treatments was your friend Pico. To our dismay, we didn't give him a large enough dose of the hormone. That is why he is weaker and much frailer than the rest of you. With our second child, we had the opposite reaction."

"Herman?"

"Yes, your cellmate. Several others around that same time were the product of an overdose to the hormones. For several years, we figured we were being guided by the hand of God to create all sizes, shapes, and colors of children. You fell into this stage of the project. We found that the problem with heroin-addicted children was that they took more and more to the drugs, casually ignoring the steroids. Simply put, although the steroids eventually processed and your life system was kick-started, the need for more and more heroin was imminent."

"Did you ever figure out a balance, Mac?"

"At one point, we felt we had found the perfect balance with a child whose mother was severely addicted to several narcotics. We monitored him closely and he seemed to sustain a relatively normal balance between the drugs and growth. His system didn't devour blood at the rapid pace of the others. On top of that, his aversion to sunlight was more limited than most of you. Right up until the day we fought to have the experiment shut down, he was our prototype."

Uninterested in my finger, the rat went back down on all fours and crawled under the pillow. "I'm sure you know all of our names somehow. I'll guess that the prototype was Dez."

"How did you know?"

"Because all the white kids younger than him pretty much look and act exactly like him. I have another question."

He swatted a fly off his arm. "Okay."

I moved toward the rusted door hinges to the records room at the far-right end of the laboratory. Fat Mac followed about ten feet behind me. Even though we were having a peaceful conversation, it made sense that he didn't want to put himself in harm's way. Me being harm.

"When you used Dez as a prototype for the younger subjects, did you use his genetic makeup to help them survive?"

He hesitated for a second and then confessed. "Yes, I guess we did."

It became clear that my line of questioning served a purpose because The Cloth overlooked a rather large sidebar to their project. "Are you sure that he was sterilized as well? You don't think that maybe Dez could have evolved the ability to reproduce? Let me take that back. I'm sure you don't believe in evolution. Do you think maybe he figured out a way to reproduce?"

Fat Mac toweled up some sweat on his neck using the back of his wrist. "We would never have made that irresponsible of a mistake. As far as manifesting the ability to reproduce on his own... like I said, everything about his life was a miracle."

"But you said he was a prototype. Those were your exact words. Do you think maybe someone else figured they could play God further and let loose a breeding being? The fact is that I've never seen a female one of us."

"No females in Los Angeles survived the re-birthing process," he said.

"Right. So, if Dez was able to impregnate the girl, and I know from her mouth that he raped her, then he is the one we need to track down. He's the most dangerous one of us out there."

McAteer wheezed. "I still don't believe you, Mr. Reynolds."

I raised my fists and chains. "Look motherfucker!"

Mac readied his lapel to engage the corkscrew around my neck.

I retreated, showing him my palms. "Don't do it. I'm calming down. I'm not going to hurt you."

He let the microphone fall back into place.

"Dez got the girl pregnant. I'm almost sure of it. All we need to do is find him and the girl and no one else needs to die."

He swiped away at another fly. "I will believe you enough to let you find Dez and this girl, but the plague we created still needs to be resolved." He approached me carefully and put his hand across my chest. "I'm sorry, Mr. Reynolds, this needs to be set right in the eyes of God."

Understandably, I lightly brushed off his attempt to comfort me and make me understand his stance and tiptoed deeper into the records room. As I looked around not knowing where to begin, I noticed the folders that were still legible were numbered. "What number am I, Mac?"

"You're number fourteen."

Ignoring any attempt to console me further, I picked through a stack of folders.

"Really," I said. "I was hoping I was thirteen."

Confused, Mac responded, "Why?"

"Because, I'm superstitious."

"If that is true, then that would make you unlucky, would it not?"

I dumped some folders on the floor outside the door as I grabbed a handful more from the top shelf. "You don't even know the half of it. I am the unluckiest person alive."

"You have an hour, Mr. Reynolds. Although I would like to say I hope you find whatever it is you are looking for, I don't think there is anything in this room beyond the forgotten ideas, people, and places we misguidedly made." He turned around and exited the laboratory.

It didn't take me that long to find my case file. I pulled up a withered wheelchair from the corner outside the records room and read the mini-biography of the first twelve years of my life.

My name is Subject Fourteen.

I was stillborn on October twenty-first, nineteen hundred and seventy-six at five thirty-nine p.m. I was revived, breathing and reborn at eight twelve p.m.

I was born with blonde hair and blue eyes at three pounds, two ounces.

My birth mother's name was Cheryl McKensie. She came to St. Matthews seeking shelter from her abusive boyfriend. During her second stay at the church, she lost her left arm to gangrene at twenty-one years of age, which she contracted from the effects of chronic intravenous heroin addiction. No name was listed for my father.

Struggling to stay alive during the first six months after my rebirth, I was constantly monitored by a young Father McAteer who called for increased levels of heroin and hormone supplements.

During the transfer from my original incubator in the shelter to my childhood incubator in the lab, I bit one of the doctors. Although this doctor called for my immediate disposal, the rest of the care staff insisted that I be kept under constant supervision.

At five years, the doctors attempted to wean me off the heroin mixed into my life support supplements and replace it with dolaphine for the first time. My body did not adjust to the new treatment, and I was switched back to heroin.

Yearly monitoring of my growth inside and out showed that although the steroids were doing their job, they were overactive and attacking my blood cells. Not unusual, as similar activity was cited in all the subjects.

A sidebar was clipped on to the fifth page of my file. It read, "Seems to exhibit emotional and hyperactive rapid eye movement. Might be more aware than the rest."

As I flipped through the pages, the side notes ended and the reports diminished to weekly, then monthly, then yearly reports. The chronicles became less about my care and more about my vital signs, growth, and overall stability.

The very last page in my childhood manifesto simply read, "August fourteenth, nineteen hundred and eighty-eight: Subject Fourteen discharged. May God watch over him."

I closed the file, tapped it on my knee and threw it on the floor.

During the trek back to my cell, Fat Mac and The Tims were silent. Even if they had asked me anything, I didn't hear them.

I didn't as much feel like a dead man walking as I did a live man walking. Under the circumstances, being alive felt worse. As much as I would spit on the delusional glory of my existence, I always hoped in the back of my mind that it was more than being the product of a drug addict convinced not to have an abortion. So, just like Eldritch, Nomi and Herman, I was just putting on a vampire variety show.

Fat Mac patted me on the shoulder one last time and dropped me off at my cell. I didn't take comfort in the fact that my cell was located adjacent to my childhood home. I lay down on the bed and faced the back wall… it was after all, the closest thing to a window to the outside world that I'd ever have again.

"So, how was it? What was it?" Herman asked quietly, sensing my despair. Apparently, he was more curious than he let on earlier.

I closed my eyes, fighting the words on the pages of my file. "It was nothing. The files were all but destroyed a long time ago. You were number two, though. I found that out."

He popped his nose and mouth into my cell through the bars. "Number two what?"

"You were the second one of us, Herman."

"Bullshit. Who the hell was number one?"

I continued my fixation with the back wall. "It was Pico."

"It figures that worthless bag of shit would be number one."

"There's nothing to it. We're just as human as everyone else, dude."

He stuck his head out of the bars. "They're lyin' to you, Reynolds."

"It's true. We're a bunch of worthless orphans and druggies. The only reason we have any kind of extraordinary abilities is because of some mysterious steroids and our God-given lust for drugs. It's just like I told you before."

Probably because he didn't see his file, Herman remained unrattled. He grabbed the bars with both his hands and inched his face further into my cell.

"What are you all pussy about, Reynolds? We are extraordinary. We're vampires. I know I'm a goddamn vampire. So, we're not the dickheads in movies and shit. We're strong as all hell and we live on blood. That's a vampire."

"No, we're not." I gave him a go-away gesture with my hand. "Fat Mac told me that the reason you're so enormous is because they were still testing out the dosage of steroids when you were born. They gave Pico too little and they gave you too much. Now, leave me alone."

"What did they give you then?"

"A headache."

The gospels piped in, signaling midnight. Coming up empty, Herman eventually strolled back to his bed. Although I didn't sleep, I didn't talk for the rest of the night.

XXIV
TRAITORS

Dark and early the next morning, Fat Mac made his way into our jail. Herman greeted him between pushups. It was safe to say that beyond his exposed skull the Rasta was fully ready to reclaim his throne as King of the Vampires.

Father McAteer instructed Not Tim to open Herman's food hole at the bottom of the front of his bars as he reached into a Saint Matthew's duffle bag. Interested, I sat up on my cot to get a scenic view of the surprise gift. The priest bent over and kicked the plastic object from the bag into Herman's cell. It slid across the filth-covered floor.

Mid-push-up, Herman trapped it with his left hand. "What the fuck is this?"

"Protection and precautions," Fat Mac responded.

Acrobatically, my cellmate snapped to his feet gripping the present between his hands. He took a second to study it like Hamlet talking to the Jester's skull. Then, he projected the object back at the bars. "No chance. No way!"

Through the bars, Fat Mac punted it back to him. "I'm afraid it's all we have to protect you at such short notice. We did not realize that you were going to be scalped when we apprehended you."

Like a soccer striker, Herman stopped the object again and then rested his size twenty-two foot on top of it.

"I would not drop your weight on it," Mac warned. "If you do not wear it, you will not be allowed to leave here."

Incensed at what he thought Fat Mac was saying about him, Herman flipped the object on top of his foot and kicked it up to his hand again. "I ain't some special needs kid."

As he continued to holler, I got a good look at The Cloth's gift. It was a hockey helmet with two bolts on either side. From what I made out, it had a halo of wires and soft bandages jury-rigged on top to brace his head. Rather than any facemask, the headgear had three sharp hacksaw blades soldered across the front. On top of the corkscrew collar, The Cloth wanted to provide themselves with extra precautions when dealing with Herman.

Mac attempted to appeal to Herman's sense of safety. "If we send you out there without it, you are worthless to us. The helmet will secure onto your head and onto the bandages inside, only lightly grazing the vulnerable portion of your cranium. It will not be comfortable but it just might save you."

My self-pity about my youth suddenly escaped me. "Hey, look at that Herman," I chuckled. "It's an L.A. Kings helmet. Now you're really a king."

"Shut the hell up, Reynolds," he sneered, throwing the helmet toward my cell.

"Indeed," Mac continued, trying to sweeten a salty deal. "The Los Angeles Kings donated a lot of equipment for a roller hockey league that St. Matthews created for underprivileged children in the surrounding neighborhoods. One of the former players was quite portly and his head was too big for any of the professional-grade helmets. As a gift, they had that helmet custom made."

"Come on, Herms, The Cloth needs us for one thing and one thing only."

Fat Mac nodded approvingly.

I picked the helmet up again and tossed it to him. "You're no good to me or yourself if we go into a house filled with others like us; if they see your head looking all humpty-dumpty, we're screwed. Do you want to kill these bastards and get to Copperhead or do you want to sit in that cell and wait for these assholes—" I pointed to Fat Mac, Real Tim and Not Tim, "—to kill you when they realize you're not doing jack or shit for them? We're as good as dead no matter what. You might as well get even with that traitor." I winked at him with my left eye, letting him know that our escape was still in play.

He slapped it to the concrete floor again and mumbled. "What was that?" I asked. "I didn't catch that."

"I'm not a Kings fan," he whined as he bent over, picked it up, and tossed it onto his bed. "I'm a Blackhawks fan."

Somewhat satisfied that we'd convinced Herman that the helmet was mandatory, Fat Mac shifted gears. "We decided that we want you to find Dez and this girl."

Without hesitating, I questioned his sudden change of heart. "Don't you mean you want them dead?"

"No, we want them here," he assured me.

With no intention of fulfilling that end of the new bargain, I played along. "Okay. When and where are we going?"

"Tonight," Mac responded. "West Hollywood. You said the girl was with the homosexuals. After we get her to safety, we will seek out Dez."

Speaking without thinking, I asked. "And what if Eldritch is there?"

Confused, Real Tim and Not Tim looked at each other.

Fat Mac lowered his head. "Eldritch?"

It hadn't occurred to me that Eldritch wasn't even on The Cloth's radar. He was, after all, raised by wolves in the mountain regions of Northern Canada.

Herman started, "Yeah, you know—"

"He's the door man there… at the Batwangers's whorehouse," I cut him off before we caused too much damage. "The guy doesn't have a lot of love for Battlesnakes or Knucklers." I shifted my eyes at Herman to play along.

Herman bumbled his way through the lie. "Yeah. I mean, yeah, I hate that fairy homo."

I clenched my teeth together to get him to shut up.

Fat Mac looked at both of us, debating if something was afoot. Satisfied, however, he reached into his duffle bag and tossed each of us a large bag of fresh blood. "Please be ready."

As the three of them headed back down the hall to leave, Not Tim turned and pointed to his eyes with his index finger and middle finger and then flipped his hand around to point to us. *I'm watching you*, he mouthed.

Herman turned around, pulled his pants down, bent over and shoved his balls backward. "Watch this, bitch."

We looked at each other and erupted into laughter. I fell over, knocking my I.V. stand on the floor. I think we might even have high-fived.

XXV

BUTCHERS

The Cloth loaded Hockey Herman and me into two separate church bookmobiles, packed with five Catholic soldiers plus a driver and a co-pilot in each. Inside the trucks, used books were stacked everywhere, creating makeshift chairs for all of us. Although we were shackled for the trip, they didn't seem too spooked by us because not only did they constantly point out the kill devices around our necks, they were armed like Nicaraguan Contras.

The rent-a-priests were dressed in a strange variation of their standard Cloth attire. The outfits were more military-inspired with pockets for shotgun shells and knife caddies and the like.

"How much money do you guys actually put toward the church?" I asked.

The fake priest directly across from me wiped his nose on his sleeve. "What does that mean?"

"Well, I know we're not rolling up in tanks or anything but these—" I picked at my collar, "—and these outfits." I pointed down the line at all five of them. "And the jail, the shelter… it also seems kind of expensive. Do your parishioners know you waste money on demon-slaying?"

"We are the parishioners of St. Matthews," Not Tim said, riding shotgun. "We're the police."

Figures, I thought to myself. "The actual police or like the Dream Police?"

"Keep him quiet," the driver injected.

"It's okay, Shane," the priest across from me answered before turning to me. "We use our own money for the good of the city and the believers."

We hit a bump and a book fell off a stack into my lap. I read the title aloud. *"The Nightshayde Chronicles: The Night Bringeth Life."*

The cover had L. Byron Nightshayde crouching with his lover dying in his arms. He was wearing a vest but no shirt. His six-pack was airbrushed to protrude beyond anything humanly or inhumanly possible. With a gleam, I asked, "Why would you give this garbage out to kids if you kill vampires?"

The priest across from me pressed his gun against my head as he took the book out of my hand. "These are good. The author is a very charitable member of the Catholic Church."

"Why? So you can create more characters?"

The priests all looked at each other, confused. Obviously, they didn't know the truth about the demons they were hunting. I suppose in Fat Mac's defense, it was easier to keep his soldiers hunting Satan's children without letting them know he let us loose on the world.

I changed gears. "Where's The Habit? I thought she was coming along for the trip."

"The junkie? She's meeting us there." The priest that spoke laughed and nudged his neighbor.

"What was that for?" I asked.

"What was what for?" the neighbor chuckled.

I mimicked their actions. "You just elbowed your buddy and laughed. It doesn't take a top-notch detective to know something is up."

"Don't worry about it, demon," he said, almost unable to control his chuckling.

"Okay," I said rolling my eyes. If I didn't have so much hate for that low-life bitch and everything she had done to Herman and me, I would have told her that she was being led to the slaughter just like the rest of us.

I only hoped that Pico and Bait were still there. Since I convinced Fat Mac that she was a necessary and innocent life to be spared, I figured Herman and me would go in and nab her as we annihilated the 'Wangers.

Our truck came to a stop and the driver and Not Tim exited the vehicle. I watched the weekend deacons across from me let down their guard for a split second to pray. Each of them made the sign of the cross like a Mexican soccer team before they ran onto the field. The roll-up door opened on my left side. One by one they began leaping from their seats out of the back.

One of them stayed in the truck with me. "No funny stuff." He started toward me with keys in one hand and a .357 Magnum pointed between my eyes in the other. All the guards outside the truck readied their microphones to their lips. One false move and my neck would have become a Dixie Cup in a mosh pit. The priest in the truck with me unlocked the cuffs on my feet quickly, almost carelessly dropping his keys and then rebounded to unlock the cuffs around my wrists.

I rubbed the sweat build-up off my arms. As he scraped the revolver's scope across my cheek, he exited the bookmobile.

"You guys have nothing to worry about," I assured them as they continued to chaperone me. "I want this to be done just as much as you do."

"Get out. Slowly," Not Tim instructed.

With my hands in the air, I hopped off the back gate of the truck. From behind them, seven more fake priests approached us with Herman.

A few laser pointers lit up on my body. "Turn away from them," Shane coached me as he nudged me with a cattle prod.

As I turned, Herman lowered his head into a circle of guns. He didn't make a sound. His lumbering body settled in the center of the army.

The Habit's stumbling caught my ear. I heard her run her cokehead bullet fingernails down Herman's reef-like skin. "Looks like the big monkey is under control, boys. Good job."

"Hey, bitch!" a black priest yelled. His shotgun cocked, I guessed at her and not Herman.

"Sorry," she spat at him. "I didn't mean it like it that."

"Man. I know who you are bitch," he continued. "I've seen that Amos and Andy show you were on. Racist bitch."

I was shuffled around by two of the priests from my mobile. One of the other soldiers grabbed the barrel of the black priest's gun and pointed it back at Herman.

The big man's shoulders twitched a little. I don't know if he was laughing because he knew she was about to get hers or if he was trying to balance the fury that he was almost certainly about to unleash.

"Hey, RJ," The Habit said. She didn't look as muddy-minded as she had the night she paid us a visit in jail, but she was still wearing the dumb nun's habit like it was a uniform. I think it had a couple of barf stains on it.

Fat Mac probably spent that last couple of days trying to wean her off the shit, much like he had with me. He also probably made her all kinds of dishonest promises. Her stench and sounds made me wish that I had never gotten involved with her. I wished that I never wanted to screw her either; even a hate fuck was too good for that ignorant gash.

The Habit stayed further away from me, behind my captors. "How does it feel, RJ?" she asked.

I yawned. "How does what feel?"

"How does it feel that it's come down to this? You working for me, ordered to kill your own kind? Working for the star that captured the imagination of America's little girls. Daaaaaag naaaaaaabbit."

197

The black priest followed her with his eyes, waiting patiently for the right moment to crack her little neck. Rather than alert her to the fact that she was being thrown to the bats herself, I simply answered: "Lame." I ignored her and addressed Shane. "What's the plan?"

He pointed between Herman and me with his gun. "You two are going to get them to open the door. Then after you enter from the front, half of us will follow and sweep from behind, while the rest of us come in through the rear once we know it's safe to enter."

I licked my teeth. "So, we're doing all the leg work? There are at least fifteen of them in there. All of them are just as tough as..." I looked at Herman. "Well, as tough as me. Can we get a little more support than that? Their leader, Nomi, is going to have the girl somewhere I won't be able to get at her."

Declaring her allegiance to the real monsters, The Habit raised her hand off one of The Cloth's members she was using as a crutch and made her signature pouty TV face. "I wanna help, dag nabbit."

The black priest curled his lips, disgusted. I turned a deaf ear to her and asked Shane for a stick. Following my lead, he broke off a limb from a nearby tree and handed it to me. I began drawing in the sand between us.

"There is a long hall that leads to Nomi's room. On both sides of the hall are four to five fuck rooms. When we burst through the door, which is never heavily guarded by anyone other than a tranny hostess, I will make my way toward the end of the hall. As you all follow, rush the back and cover a different room."

Herman lifted his head. "What about me, Reynolds?"

"You're going to follow directly behind me and just wreck everything that comes near us." I pointed to the priests and The Habit. "The less of us who die in the first five seconds, the better chance we have of getting the kid. And the kid is what Fat Mac wants."

Herman nodded and asked. "What if he is there?"

Knowing he was referring to Eldritch, I said, "Why? Are you afraid of him? The guy is the biggest pussy I know."

The Habit twirled a gun around her finger, then stopped. "Wait. Who is 'he'? Are we walking into some kind of ambush?"

I dropped the stick. "Yeah, dumbass. We communicate with each other telepathically. This has been our plan since you trapped us." I rolled my eyes. "We're just as likely to die here as all of you."

The priests looked at each other as if I was informing them of some special vampire powers they hadn't been briefed on.

The Habit licked the end of her gun. "Fuck you, RJ."

"And Herman," I said picking the stick back up, "he's not in there. It's too late for him not to be bar hopping or holding a super-secret meeting with his agent or something."

Herman didn't laugh.

"Do they have security cameras around the perimeter?" Real Tim asked.

"No. They are a bunch of wasted, transvestite prostitutes. Why would they have security cameras?"

"I just…" He stumbled over the words.

"Trust me. They don't need any security besides themselves."

As stealthy as fourteen guards in priest outfits, a junkie nun-impersonator, a seven-foot Rasta in a hockey helmet, and dopey old me could be walking across the lawn of a recreation center, we approached the house. One of the priests signaled for half of the group and The Habit to go around the tree line next to the house, park-side. The rest of us prepped ourselves curbside.

Herman and I walked toward the door.

"You ready, my man?" I asked, flicking his hockey helmet.

"What's up with the jive, Reynolds? Talk normally and quit frontin'." He looked at me through the razors covering most of his face. "We don't really have a choice other than being dead, do we? You better not be under the control of The Gooch, Reynolds."

I sighed, realizing that I made a mistake telling Cobra about the voice. "There is no Gooch."

"The Gooch tol' you to say that."

I shook my head no and knocked on the door.

Platform shoes snapped down the tile toward us and stopped just on the other side of the door.

The hostess sang out. "Who is it?"

I looked at Herman.

"It's King Cobra, motherfucker. Open the door."

The hostess hesitated. Herman began beating his fists against the wood. After ten seconds passed, he said, "We can't wait any longer, Reynolds." He stepped in front of me, tore off the Christmas lights and, using his fists like sledgehammers, he barreled through the door. Quickly set in motion like a linebacker, he plowed over the door and the hostess became trapped under it.

Not ready to be announced at a party we weren't invited to, I called out. "Herman, wait."

It was too late; the game clock had started. Play ball. It would just be a matter of seconds before the Batwangers swallowed us.

I stepped on the door. The hostess peered out from underneath. I stomped my right boot into his face, shifting my heel under his neck and popped his head off. The insides of his neck jumped out as I put more pressure on the door, like his body was a novelty can of nuts filled with snakes.

I skated off the door and followed Herman, who was knocking on every door he passed as he made his way to Nomi's lair. One by one, the fuck rooms opened as we ran past. Shotguns exploded behind me as my half of the posse unloaded into the open doors; crumbs of buckshot whizzed all around my head.

Before Herman reached Nomi's door, two naked 'Wangers vaulted from their doors and positioned themselves in front of him. Herman locked onto both of their necks with his giant hands and pulled them down to his legs. He simply crushed their skulls by dropping his knees to the floor. Their cerebellums waterfalled off his muscles on to his shoes as he got back up.

Shaking myself away from his hypnotic violence, I noticed that the rest of the drones had come out of their rooms. One jumped on Herman's back as the others headed toward the priests and me. Empty shotgun shells bounced off the floor and thumped at my calves as heads were picked off the trannies in front of me.

Two 'Wangers who avoided the firefight jumped toward me and grappled me to the ground. Still stimulated from pleasing the fetishists cowering in their rooms, both 'Wangers's hard dicks folded as they touched my stomach. I grabbed onto one of the cocks and tore it off. I shoved it into his mouth and I kicked him away from me. He fell backward in shock.

Immediately, one of the priests leapt on top of him and filled his face with lead. I fixated on my other assailant who was trying desperately to wrap his arms around my neck and snap it.

The Cloth, still startled by the suddenness of the attack, shot up the walls and the furniture, blowing up refinished alien accessories rather than people. They probably thought the furniture was alive.

I got into a crouching counter move to my aggressor's attempts and pivoted him under me.

He cried out. "Why? Why, RJ? Why are you doing this?"

My body fell cold. I knew him. He grew up in the same stinky alley as me.

"I'm sorry," I said.

As he begged for answers and mercy, I trampled his cries by pinning his head to the ground sideways. I closed my eyes and then clobbered away at his face with my forearm. I felt squirts of his blood drench my face as his begs for mercy fell silent. I opened my eyes. In my mission to quiet him and forget who he was, I had completely severed his face in half below his nose.

Two of the priests rolled up in front of me and began clearing the rooms. I heard shots and figured they were deliveries from God to sinning humans who sought the company of transvestite vampires. "There's no back door," a voice rang out into our bedlam.

"Just stay there," I yelled back. While I kicked the dead tranny aside, I saw Herman crash through the door to the center of the hive. I raced down the hall to search for Bait, looking in every room I passed.

"Fuck you, Cobra!" Nomi shrieked. I made my way into the Queen's realm. Herman stood at the end of the bed. Nomi lay on his side in a metallic-silver teddy reading a magazine and smoking one of his long cigarettes.

Herman turned to me. *Should I?* he mouthed.

I held up my hand for him to be patient. "Where's Bait?" I asked, entering farther into the room.

Nomi licked his fingers and paged through the magazine. Next to him was the corpse of his latest lonely victim and an empty syringe. He put down the magazine and sank his teeth into a testicle.

"RJ. I thought you were dead." He swayed, blasé to our storming of his castle. His eyelashes flickered over his half-closed lids and eyes that rolled in ecstasy. "What do you two want?"

I turned my hand backward to the door behind me, holding it up like a stop sign to signal The Cloth to stay away. The alien tentacles lit up the room and the weavings above the canopy spun its web.

"Well?" he asked.

Herman studied the room as if he'd never been inside the belly of the beast and then backed down from the edge of the bed, giving me a clear shot at Nomi.

I asked again, "Where's Bait?"

Nomi crunched away on the gonad. "That little hooker?"

"Yeah, Nomi. Where is she?"

He swallowed his treat, took a drag off his cigarette and then ashed on the dead John. Before he brought the smoke back to his mouth for another puff, he dipped the holder into the guy's missing pelvis. "Hmmmm," he thought for a second. "I think I turned that bitch out, RJ."

I stretched my neck and readied my fists. "I told you not to."

I made my way to the bed, scratching my arms after seeing another syringe—this one half full of heroin—wrapped up in the satin bedcover.

"I run this town now, RJ. You've been like… gone or something."

I avoided looking at the heroin. "Where's the girl, Nomi?"

"Don't know. I gave her to the Perrys or something. You know, those boys." He patted his hand against the mattress. "Now get over here, slave. I'm your master now."

As he exited the room, Herman called back. "C'mon, Reynolds. He's too wasted to do anything for us. The girl ain't here."

He was right. Bait wasn't there anymore. I turned from Nomi and followed Herman back through the hallway where The Cloth stood diligently waiting.

Shane shrugged and said, "There is no human teenager here. We checked all the rooms and a shed out back."

"Where's the bitch?" Herman asked him.

"She took off a lot earlier. Probably knew we were going to kill her," the black priest answered.

I stepped over the bullet-ridden bodies on the floor.

"Get back here, RJ. Suck my tits, faggot," Nomi screeched from the bed, delirious. "I own you, RJ. Who's the faggot now?" Unaware that all his friends and worker bees had been dismantled in less than five minutes and that The Cloth was standing inside his house, Nomi continued to yell. "I own you, asshole. I own Hollywood now."

"Have at it," I said to the black priest and Shane. They surged into the Queen's lair and, without hesitation, unloaded every single piece of ammo they had left in their guns.

Before they reloaded us into our separate bookmobiles, The Cloth lit the whorehouse on fire.

To the cheers of his comrades, one of the priests whooped. "Begone, demons!"

XXVI
KINGS

I didn't try to resist the ass beating The Cloth unleashed upon me when we got back to St. Matthews. I deserved it.

But not for the reasons The Cloth thought.

I deserved it because I knew the person whose face I bisected. We had struggled together with all the other vamp junkies on the streets. He was part of the group I ran with while we learned about how to take care of ourselves, building makeshift tents to ward off the sun, learning how to roll drug dealers, testing our strengths and weaknesses. We had all been the same, trying to find our way in this nightmare existence, simply trying to figure out how we would survive each day. This guy had given me my first pack of cigarettes and had inadvertently given me my name.

The day that Pico came to fish me out of the alley, not everyone wanted to leave and start anew. They insisted they would find their own way, their own packs. So, I said my sincere goodbyes and rarely saw any of them again unless I somehow found myself at the various vampire lairs, collecting money for King Cobra. It was like we had all forgotten what we'd done for each other. Our communication became less and less, and tonight it ended in me silencing forever one of those first friends I ever had.

Even after I did their bidding, the demon-hunters laughed while cattle prods, hammers and guns pummeled me in my cell. Reminding me that I would still never be human, and how worthless I really was.

Trying to lick the latest gratuitous wounds inflicted on us by The Cloth, I rubbed my arms under the flow of water from my sink's faucet. "I don't want to do this," I told Herman. I could hear the merriment of the rent-a-priests die down as they left for the gymnasium until their voices finally ended altogether. Assholes.

Herman caressed the top of his helmet. "I have to ask you again, Reynolds: why do you care? Those 'Wanger fools never did anything for you or anybody else. You heard Nomi. He's dead now and guess what: you aren't his bitch. Let's just get this all done."

He didn't get it. There was no way he understood or would ever understand what happened back at the whorehouse. My body was filled with resentment and loneliness instead of blood and life. All I could hear in my head were the screams of the people I just helped massacre. If I hadn't been so loose-lipped about Bait being left at the Bat-Cave, the trannies wouldn't have even been a blip on The Cloth radar.

"What's wrong with you? You act like you've never killed anyone before. Pull your pants up and deal with it. You wanted this. You were the one convincing me."

He was right. I splashed water into a deep laceration on my arm. "It's more than that. They didn't do anything to us. They didn't do anything to The Cloth other than exist."

"Whatever," he replied, fluffing his pillow for bed. He had taken a lighter beating than me for some reason. "They turned your little bitch out and they were thinking that they ran my streets. I heard what he said. He said since we've been out of the scene, there's a new way."

Defeated, I leaned forward on the sink. "Who cares about that street bullshit?"

"I care, bitch. I run Los Angeles."

"You don't anymore, Herman."

"I will, fool." Herman brushed the quickly-formed scabs off his body. It was shocking that he never had a heart attack from healing at such a rapid pace. "So, I guess the BBPs are next. I hate them more. I can't wait to rip their smug little faces off."

"I already told you. I'm out. If they kill me or leave me locked in here, I don't care. You're on your own."

"Didn't it feel good, Reynolds? Didn't it feel good to kill somebody? We've been in here so long now, it felt like jumping back on a bike. It felt natural."

The door opened at the end of the hall.

Herman rubbed his hands together as if our guest was room service and he was starving. "Shit, are they ready for more?"

I heard Fat Mac's soft footfalls nearing us. He was accompanied by the familiar sound of clicking, dragging and wavering high heels.

Knowing that The Cloth was too busy with their post-kill fiesta to mind the lights, Herman pressed up against his bars. "Yo, Fat Mac. Are we going out again? Are we gonna get some more of our kill on?"

With The Habit walking in front of him, he crossed my cell, heading toward Herman. He had a gun to her head. Even though she tried to bitch and moan, she was muffled by a sock duct taped to her mouth. At least I wouldn't have to hear that lame catch phrase.

"What's all this about, Mac?" I asked as I splashed water on The Habit.

"There's been a change of plans," he answered, pushing The Habit dangerously close to Herman's bars. "Or, at least, I have reconsidered the plans."

Herman reached out of his cell and tickled at The Habit's nose with his fingernail. "Hi," he whispered.

"What do you mean? You're gonna kill us all now?"

McAteer pulled The Habit away from the bars and threw her against the wall. "*Patefacio duos,*" he said into his microphone.

As if fresh air had entered my body for the first time in my life, the corkscrew unlatched from my neck and dropped to my feet. I cracked my neck on both sides and felt the imprint left by the collar.

"I don't get it." I stepped backward, expecting to be torched by the lights.

"Holy shit, Reynolds." Herman hopped around like he was doing jumping jacks. His collar was still firmly attached. "They're going to let us go now. See, I told you."

"Shut up, Herman." I headed back to my bed and dragged the mattress over by the toilet where I planned to dunk my head as soon as the UV lamps flamed on.

"He is partly correct, Mr. Reynolds. The guards are off duty. There is nothing stopping you from escaping."

Herman raised his hand. "What about me?"

Fat Mac ignored him and continued. "You are human, Mr. Reynolds. You are more human than I am."

Not being ignored, Herman shook at his bars, much to my unease of the latest development. "What about me, motherfucker?"

"What right did we have to do the work of God?" Mac intensified his voice. "What right do we have to take it away?"

"Turn around, fool!" Herman screamed as he reached out of his cell and tried to grab Mac's arm.

From behind, The Habit quickly disarmed the priest and without hesitation, blasted him near the heart. He cascaded to the floor like he'd just been rag-dolled at a biker bar. Unable to move his right arm, he began praying with his left.

I raced to the bars and started bending an opening. Herman did the same. The Habit rose up behind Fat Mac, wobbly from whatever drugs she was currently on, and popped off a few rounds at Herman and then at me. Her drug-enhanced targeting system didn't lend itself to accuracy. A bullet breezed my jugular and knocked me over the sink. I tried to stem the blood emptying out of my neck as best I could and crawled back to the bars.

Several more shots scattered into Herman's cell. "You ruined my life!" she screamed after ripping off the tape and spitting out the gag.

Fat Mac pulled himself to my cell, continuing to pray.

The Habit raised the gun to the preacher's head. "See you in Hell, asshole."

She squeezed the trigger and the bullet pierced directly into his head.

Not letting a few bullets slow him down, Herman was back at the bars, trying to break them open. She fired more bullets his way, stopping only to shoot into my cell every five or so rounds. Despite her horrible marksmanship, one bullet nailed me in the upper thigh and another skinned my shoulder.

Without taking her eyes off Herman, she dropped the first clip out of the 9mm and nabbed another from under her nun's garb. Even though I didn't get a good look at its origin, I imagined she hid it in her ass or her vagina.

"I'm gonna finally kill you, bitch!" Herman shouted. Not surrendering to his threats, she continued to unload round after round into him.

The bullets did little to deter the massive Rasta, and he was almost out of the cell. Thinking quickly, The Habit grabbed Fat Mac's collar and pulled him up from the ground. Gray matter vomited up from the hole in his head. She bent down, sneering, and cleared her throat.

"No," I screamed, racing back to the bars. I tried to shred the metal, pawing through the bars at her head. Herman was oblivious to anything other than getting out of his cell.

Then, in what seemed like a split second, she hissed into Fat Mac's microphone: "*Adstringo gutter.*"

She kicked the dead priest at my cell and ran away down the hall toward the exit.

As the gunsmoke cleared and blood pooled into my cell from Mac and Herman, I saw the Rasta King sitting with his back against one half of his table. The corkscrew tightened around his neck. But he wasn't struggling. He wasn't even twitching. I dragged myself to the bars that no longer divided us.

He looked at me squarely as his eyes clogged with blood that spilled down his cheeks like tears. His breathing slowed, and I felt his life departing from the basement of the Church where he was born Subject Two. I felt everything about the person that I feared most in the world.

I didn't reach into his cell to help. If I had listened to the voice commands to disengage the collars, I could have saved him. Like he said weeks before though, I never listened to anybody but myself.

His lips quivered and his nostrils flared as his tongue scratched away at the roof of his mouth.

"I read your file. You did come from royalty," I said to him. "You are a king, brother. King Fucking Cobra."

One last smile etched on his face as more blood bubbled out. Before his life ended completely, he looked at me like I was his sibling and said, "Thanks, RJ."

XXVII

LEPERS

I stumbled through downtown Los Angeles. I knew The Habit wouldn't come after me. She had already made her point. Hopefully, the cops would investigate the house. As far as The Cloth was concerned, when they sobered up, they were going to be too busy trying to explain to their friends at the LAPD how Father McAteer was killed.

The scene left there was beyond ugly. There was a good chance they were going to just burn down the entire place and suck a little more money out of their tax-exempt status and whatever insurance company would cover a radical cult like theirs.

Every few steps, I looked for rats, possums, anything I could, all the while keeping my eyes peeled for a red cross tag. There were several downtown, but since I never really paid attention to them, I only had a vague memory of their whereabouts.

Downtown Los Angeles at night, at least in the shit area I was in, was dead. And I was about to become another victim of its streets if I didn't find blood to heal myself with soon. My body was still riddled with lacerations and my skull was nearly caved in from being beaten by the-rent-a-priests of The Cloth. I stopped next to a dumpster and tried to pull out the multiple bullets that The Habit knocked off at me. Even though I risked losing more blood by opening my wounds, the bullets weren't going to just fall out of my body.

I was coming down from my methadone blahs. The heroin "replacement" only bottled up the withdrawal long enough for you to need it; causing lethargy, rather than euphoria. The Cloth knew just the right dosage to keep me a Blood Hound during the hunt and a Chihuahua the rest of the time. I looked into the dumpster and began my dive to find any kind of vermin that would provide even a little bit of sustenance. Nothing. I shook my head and focused my eyes.

You Need Heroin.

I tried to ignore The Gooch until, finally, I spotted a condemned building with a red cross tag about a half a block away. I needed shelter as much as I needed blood, so I bunny-hopped on my left leg, using my arm to brace myself against a brick wall.

I clenched my hand into a fist as much as I was able to and hammered on the Master Lock security latch on the front door. Then I realized the lock was on the outside. I didn't find it too strange I guess. Just a small deterrent from squatters. After all, anyone walking into this place was going to be in more trouble than the vampire owners inside.

I stumbled into the decrepit old building. Though I couldn't see much, I judged from the molding and auditorium ceiling that it must have been a theater before downtown died and relocated to Hollywood.

Using a handrail for support, I began dragging myself up the stairs hoping to find an opera box. The degenerating steps creaked and almost gave out with every stride I took. Pigeon shit made the stairs slippery and at one point I fumbled to my knees. All I knew was that I had to get out of that main area and safely hide myself because the sun was coming up fast. I wouldn't die from direct contact with the light, but I would die from dehydration, lack of blood and that whole sobriety thing.

I reached the top stair, snapping the neck of a dead pigeon open as I stomped to my final destination. I looked around. It wasn't completely dark because of some painted glass panes on both sides of the large attic, but it was gloomy and empty enough for me to lay low. I was sure I could find a blanket to cover myself.

"Whadda you want?" a raspy voice questioned from the far corner. "You a cop?"

I shielded my eyes from the colored rays beginning to filter into the room like a disco ball's reflection. I couldn't make out the figure. "I'm not a cop," I said, and collapsed.

My face hit bird shit and caught splinters from the wood floor. I heard shuffling. As the shape got closer, I noticed that it was a bearded man using his hands to drag what was left of his torso toward me. He got closer and spoke, trying to keep conscious. "You okay, man? We haven't had anyone new come up here for a while."

"I need to get out of this light," I croaked.

He picked my head up and pried my eyes open, looking inside like a doctor. "Don't we all, brother? Makes you wish you were a human, huh?"

"How did you know I was…"

"No need to explain. We all end up here at one point or another." The man's breath reeked of MD 20/20 and the only teeth that were left behind his filthy cracked lips dangled by roots. Whiskers popped from almost every busted pore on his face and his lash-less eyes were so bulged that his eyelids didn't fully close when he blinked.

"Here," he said, planting where his body ended at the pelvis directly under him. He bent his shoulders backward to support my weight and I used both my arms to bring myself up. When he was sure I was on my feet he fell to his hands and began dragging himself back to the corner. "Follow me," he advised. "What's your name?"

I didn't answer.

"That's okay, buddy. There will be plenty of time for that."

"You said there were others," I asked.

"Yeah, some are still out hunting, getting high, whatever, the rest are passed out. Long day. There is a lot going on in L.A. for our kind right now."

"What does that mean?"

"Yeah, let's just get you some blood and I'll tell you all about it, buddy."

I limped along behind him.

"Down this hall. We got some decent blood down here."

I followed him down the hall, still shielding my eyes and trying to keep as much of my skin from the light as I could. He opened a curtain into the opera box. In one corner was a tent and in the other was a cooler. Two beach chairs and a fake campfire served as the centerpiece of my new friend's crib.

He pointed at the campfire. "Found this in the prop room. Pretty cool, huh, buddy? It works on four batteries." He dragged himself over to the cooler and opened it. "Shit man. Running a little low. I hope the hunters come back with some good food tonight," he said, handing me a Mason jar filled with blood.

I took a swig and passed it back to him. He rejected my offering. "You're in worse shape than me right now, buddy. You can get me back some other time."

I took back the bottle and sucked it down to the last drop. It hurt passing over the line of my throat where the dog collar had been clamped just hours earlier.

"Who are you?" I asked, licking my lips.

"They call me Shaver." He scratched at his beard. "I think it's on account of that I have this prickly pear beard. Could be because I'm shaved in half though."

I swept my gums clean of blood. "How did that happen?"

"I was fucked up on PCP, trying to drink some bitch's blood in a Safeway parking lot and her husband ran me over with a car. I guess they figured they were in the wrong, or they were drunk, because they took off. I made my way back to Skid Row and they brought me here."

"Who are they? A gang?"

"Hell. No more gangs around here, buddy. This is where all the screwball vamp people come. It's kind of like a veteran's hospital for the fuck ups who can't really hunt no more."

"Then where does the blood come from?"

"We work together. The ones who ain't got no legs use the legs of the ones who ain't got no arms. The one's with no eyes, them is the fucked-up ones, buddy. We usually drop them off on the curb at night as bait."

Bait, I thought to myself. I had to find Bait.

"What was that talk about changes in L.A.?"

I started licking the rim of the Mason jar. I felt some of my strength coming back.

"It's neither here nor there for me, buddy. Some stuff about a new way and all that. Heard that King Cobra is dead."

A nail hammered into my spine. "You know about King Cobra?"

"Sure. That black bastard ran L.A. since I can remember. Some of them other gangs come by here and pay for information about shit we've seen with blood."

"What gang is that?"

"Damn son, I don't know or care. They give me blood. I'm tired. Take that there blanket and get some sleep. Looks like you had a bad day."

As instructed, I grabbed the blanket and pulled it over my head. I was too weak to go anywhere near the light, so I was trapped in the opera box with that smelly transient at least until sundown. What little he did know, or cared to know, he had told me. It was enough. I was being hunted.

He ended the night with: "Have a good day, buddy," and turned off the faux campfire. I decided I had better get some sleep and prepare for the worst.

A filthy hand tugged at my arm. "Wake up, buddy. Feedin' time."

I covered my head, momentarily forgetting where I was.

"It's okay. I'll get us some rations and then introduce you to the boys later."

"Shaver," a voice called out from behind the curtain.

"I'm comin'," the whiskered cripple said. Shaver crawled across the room, his tied pant leg brushed across my feet.

I heard the curtain pull back. I hid under the blanket, hoping that this was an ask questions later halfway house.

"Can I get some extra for my buddy here? He came in early this morning... really bad shape. Looks like someone tried to hang him." I rubbed at the burn mark around my neck. "He's real shy, but I'll introduce you later."

A boot kicked me in the leg. I let out a grunt. I imagine they were checking to see if there was a living body under the blanket or if Shaver was just making shit up so he could get more blood.

The voice stuttered, "I don't know, Shaver. We only have enough for the people already here. You know the rules of bringing in newbies."

Shaver patted my leg. "My buddy here is in bad shape. I promise you, I'll bring him to a meet and greet before the hunt. Looks like he can pack a punch. Could be a big help around here."

The boot kicked at me again. I grunted louder.

"This time only," the voice said. The curtain closed.

I peeked out from underneath the blanket.

"Thanks, Shaver, I appreciate your help."

I backed my body up against the inside of the curved opera box as Shaver turned on the fake campfire and handed me a cocktail. My body still ached and the pain in my neck had only worsened from sleeping in the cramped corner. I drank the blood slowly.

"This is good shit today, huh, buddy?"

The sour taste of the cold blood tasted like pissed-out lemonade mixed with Ragu.

"It's great," I said, hiding my true feelings. "So, Shaver, what do you do around here? I mean, since you don't hunt."

"That's the thing; I'm the eyes and ears of this place. I have eyes for the sad saps that don't and I have the ears for those who don't like to hear. I keep lookout. Watch the place. Make sure no cops are around. They make me feel pretty important."

"I guess you're lucky after all. What time do you have to start your post?" The second he left the box I was going to get the fuck out of there.

"I'm running a little late now, but they'll understand. I got someone new to help us out, right, buddy?" He slapped me on the back.

"That's right, Shaver. Listen, I'm going to get back to sleep and let you get to your 'eyes and ears'. Wake me up when you get back so I can meet your boys. Hopefully by then I'll be feeling better." I slumped back down into my cocoon but before I covered my head, I added, "Thanks, Shaver."

Ask him for heroin, stupid.

"Ain't no thing, buddy. Just like I said, everyone ends up here at one point or another. Kind of surprised King Cobra never ended up here." He turned off the campfire.

I pretended to rub my eyes like I was nodding off.

"It is kind of a surprise."

I pulled the blanket over my head again as Shaver started his journey into a night's worth of bulldogging the theater. When I heard the swinging door at the end of the hall push open and then close, I started to make my move.

I slugged down what was left of my blood and looked into the cooler for more. Nothing. I really didn't want to steal from this poor guy anyway. As I slid my combat boots on, I patted around the inside of the tent to see if I could find anything. I came across a small baggy of something.

Since I didn't recognize it, I decided to leave it. Shaver said he did PCP and I had no interest in flying off the building after being sober for however long. I slowly pulled back the edge of the curtain and glanced down the hallway. No one was there. I guessed that they were all out doing their nightly duties on the streets. If all I had to worry about was Shaver and the jerk that kicked me, I was home free. Besides, the guy sounded kind of like a pussy.

Cautiously, I made my way down the hall, the opposite way Shaver exited. I hovered next to the wall, sideways so I could monitor activity from both directions. It was silent. Then again, The Habit deafened one of my eardrums with all her gunfire. I started down the stairs, then stopped when I faintly heard voices. Hopefully, I would find a stage at the bottom of the back staircase to conceal my movements.

I continued my descent quietly, eyes darting to every corner as I made my way to the bottom of the stairs. The moldy carpeting smelled like death twice over. The first was the decay of the building, and the second was the decay of the displaced transients that moved in and called it home.

As expected, the staircase took me backstage. The curtain was spray painted black with several different tags from several different gangs, some of which had been retired a long time before I was in the Knucklers. I walked parallel to the curtain without getting too close. I didn't want to disturb any of the pleats on the opposite side. Rat traps layered the floor. I guess they were for dinner, even though I doubted any living rodent had roamed around there in ages.

People were on the other side of the curtain; I heard them mumble and could feel their hunger.

As I looked around backstage, I noticed something. Limbless theater mannequins everywhere. The only body parts remaining were torsos and heads, most of which were nailed to the wall or hung from chains. All the eyes were dug out.

And then, *snap!*

Not paying attention to where I was walking, I became the rat caught in a trap. On both sides of the stage, two legless figures, harnessed with rope, descended like sandbags. The crusty curtains pulled back and a spotlight nailed me directly in the eyes. I covered my face and fell to the ground, setting off a domino effect of mousetraps around the stage. Laughter erupted from the audience.

Trying to avoid the light by bobbing my head from side-to-side, I picked the traps off my jeans and looked into the crowd. All I could see were silhouettes of misshaped figures. Twisted, stumped, and ragged.

The laughter raged on and Shaver slithered into the house lights reserved for the orchestra pit's pre-performance preparation.

His eyes scrunched in the light as he pointed at me. "That's him, right?" he yelled, begging for the adoration of his tangled brood. "That's RJ-fucking-Reynolds. I'd know that sonabitch anywhere." He kicked out his legless backside like a starving donkey.

Another figure stepped out of the darkness that engulfed the back of the theater and patted Shaver on the head with some kind of claw-shaped appendage. "I would clap," his smug, little voice whimpered, "but as you can see I have no hands." He lifted two steel hooks into the light.

Catching me off-guard, the two disfigured rejects acting as sandbags clamped onto my legs. Their arms were powerhouses, strengthened by years of dragging themselves around.

The hook-handed figure proceeded toward me. "Remember me, RJ?" he asked, sharpening his hook blades on each other. He didn't have to tell me his name… probably because I never bothered to learn it or care what it was. It was the Dezien bottom feeder. More accurately, it was the bottom feeder that I force-fed his own hands to.

Behind him, the congregation of deformities limped, crept, shuffled, and moaned their way into the pit lights. Each wave of atrocities that emerged from the shadows was more horrible and disfigured than the row that preceded them. It was as if they were arranged by rank from totally fucked up to so fucked up that they were simply the crumbs of something that at one time might have been a cookie.

Hook Hands stood over me as the sandbags pulled me down to my knees. Then, he licked his right hook. As the stainless steel left his tongue, he plunged it into my left shoulder, hooking it underneath the bone.

"*Fuuuuuuuuck you!*" I screamed.

His face became overly delighted and then he pompously pouted and asked, "Does it hurt, motherfucker?" He then licked the second hook, stating, "I'm guessing that it hurts more the first time."

He hammered the curved nail into my right shoulder, once again locking it in position under my shoulder. I bit into my tongue. He was wrong; it hurt just as much the second time.

He pulled me up to his waist. The legion of forgotten, deader-than-already-being-dead army continued their march toward us. They formed a circle. I didn't cry, I didn't beg. Other than wanting to save Bait, I really didn't care if this dick and his loser friends killed me or not.

"Unbutton them." He pointed to his jeans.

"Why?"

"*Unbutton them!*" he commanded, turning from right-to-left, delighting the spectators. Some of them hopped on one leg while other eyeless faces giggled as their blow-by-blow translators whispered the gory details to them. The Dezien pulled tightly on my shoulders.

Reluctantly, I unbuttoned the front of his pants.

He stopped playing to the crowd and he motioned his head downward. "And the zipper."

One of the blind ones was escorted over to me. He petted at my hair, inflaming the wound in my ear. "He's scared," he told the guide.

To that, the guide returned, "You should see his face. I think he's going to cry."

Plaster rained from the ceiling as the laughter boomed through the opera house.

"*The zipper!*" the finger-eater let out again.

I looked at the front of his pants. He jerked at my frame with the hooks. I didn't know how long I had been in captivity at The Cloth compound, but it didn't seem long enough for this guy to become the leader of any group, even this scrap yard of has-beens. The hooks elevated me further as they stretched the bones from their ligaments. I did as I was told. He had the upper hook at this point.

"Now pull them down, RJ." He shook his hips, initiating the pants to slump down below his pelvis. I shrugged, trying to doze off. "Open your fucking eyes and pull them all the way down, boy!"

The group of misfits tightened their circle and the Dezien turned the hooks inward, relieving the shoulders but condensing my ribcage. It became increasingly difficult to breathe so once again I did as I was told.

"Commando?" I wheezed. "Me too."

I don't need to elaborate on what limp pleasantry sat asleep directly in front of my mouth. I can say this: it was pretty cold in the theater.

"Shut up! Shaver, get over here."

The Dezien opened the center of his legs. With a syringe in his mouth,

Shaver crept under him and flipped over on his back like he was a mechanic checking this idiot's brakes.

"You ready?" Shaver cringed, as if seeing a taint was as bad as kneeling in front of a limp cock with two hooks in his body.

"Yeah," the Dezien sighed. Shaver released the needle from his teeth and dropped it into his hand. He took a deep breath to avoid the stench of fumunda and pierced a vein on the shaft. As the plunger reached the bottom of the syringe casing, I felt the hooks in my arms tense up. I tried to close my eyes again. I knew what was in that needle, and it wasn't a narcotic. It was really difficult to try and make happy thoughts while vomit ripened in my throat and started gushing from the sides of my mouth. Shaver exited as soon as his deed was complete.

"Open your eyes, RJ!" The excitement streaming through his body made him turn the hooks in my shoulders like he was adjusting knobs on a stereo. "You know what I want now, don't you?"

"Sing?" I asked, trying to avoid the pencil expanding under my nose.

"Suck my dick, motherfucker. I want you to know what being disgraced feels like before we rip you to pieces and take your body parts as our own."

In an attempt to appeal my conviction in the court of misfit vampires, I looked to the circle. As his member inched its way toward my face, I tried to fill my mouth with more vomit. It would taste better than the other thing inside there. I looked up at him. His face was filled with satisfaction and he smiled from ear to ear. Getting more sickened by his vainglorious air, I tried to pull away. The hooks had me anchored on my knees. *This is it*, I thought to myself. *This is the end of RJ Reynolds.*

Just as I was ready to throw in the towel, I looked once again to the circle of beasties. Just beyond them was a tower. It was a tower so dark that it actually stood out from the rest of the pitch-black stadium. A shadow broke from the tower, hovering toward the circle. As the shadowy figure converged, a fervor of whispering commenced in the room and the circle broke open. The Dezien who was too proud of his accomplishment at my expense and paid his followers no mind. Like a retreating horde, the sideshow panicked back into their holes.

The figure stopped about twenty feet behind the show. Black hair swirled around it like a tornado. Letting me sweat, the shape watched as the Dezien's cock entered my mouth. After a few seconds, it had enough and proceeded. A shadow swelled over us, showing a sword unsheathed from behind it's back. The sandbags let go of my legs and yanked on their ropes to be pulled back up to the rafters. The curtains began to close.

The Dezien looked down, furiously not aware that the matinee was about to end. "Keep sucking mother—"

Before he could finish his sentence, the tension from the hooks in my shoulders eased. I reached up and used all my remaining strength to clamp on to his arms at the elbow and bust them off, leaving the hooks and his bodiless arms in my shoulders. His eyes started to twitch as his head turned around to see the assailant.

It was too late. His head broke at the neck, slid off his left shoulder and onto the ground, rolling under the curtain. The rest of his body folded like a squeezebox. I spat the barf in my mouth on his corpse.

Eldritch extended his hand. "Need any help, my friend?"

I spun my right shoulder and slipped the hook out. I grabbed Eldritch's forearm and pulled myself to my feet, then slid the second hook out, using the massive vampire's body to steady myself.

"No need to thank me," Eldritch continued.

"To tell you the truth, Eldritch, I wish you would have let them kill me."

"You're already dead," he returned.

"Not as dead as you're going to be if I live through this and anyone else ever hears about it." I let go of him and stood on my own.

After a couple of lame tricks that one might expect to see at a peewee karate demonstration, he spun his sword over his shoulder and back into its sheath behind his hair.

"Nice sword, dude."

"It is a katana, said to be crafted during the Muromachi Dynasty—"

Too tired to argue or listen, I blacked out.

XXVIII
CONFIDANTES

When I regained consciousness, I was slung over Eldritch's back. He had apparently carried me all the way from downtown… or at the very least, from his car.

Activated by a Clapper rather than black magic or telekinesis, classical music reverberated inside Eldritch's loft. After dropping me in front of the human hookah, Lord Drugula made his way to the kitchen to warm me up some fresh blood, stopping only at his fanciful display cabinet to re-present his sword. My shoulders desperately thirsted for blood. My mouth, on the other hand, needed to be disinfected.

I crawled over to the comatose human sacrifice. His left toes twitched as if he knew it was feeding time.

"Do you have any Listerine or rubbing alcohol or anything, Eldritch?" I spit out a lump of vomit stuck in my teeth. I guess I was lucky to have teeth. If the Dezien kid had any sense at all, he would have beaten my teeth out jailhouse-style before he made me suck his cock.

"In the bathroom. Don't worry about that now. You need to get those wounds healed."

"How come none of those weirdoes in the Opera House tried to attack you?"

I looked toward the kitchen. Any other person would have just nuked the blood for me, but Eldritch always did things his way. In the center of his kitchen was a cast-iron wood burning stove. He poured the blood into an old copper teakettle. I noticed that he never owned anything made from silver. I suppose it was due to his Lycan upbringing.

"I am their friend. I bring them food and blood all the time."

I picked up the main tube from the hookah. "Kind of like working in a soup kitchen? Meals on Wheels and shit?"

Eldritch pondered for a second and simply said, "Yes, I suppose it is. Don't use that one."

I looked at the pipe. "Why?"

"Do I have to supply you with an answer to that? I use that pipe."

Rather than engaging in any conversation that would eventually lead to the reason why he didn't want me smoking from his pipe, I dropped it and exchanged it for one of the shabbier ones that came from the victim's thigh.

Eldritch returned to me and handed me an antiqued and bejeweled chalice. I took a huge swig out of it and chased it with a puff from the living pipe. "How did you find me anyway?" I asked.

From behind one of his many curio cabinets he produced a mop. He walked behind me and sponged up the slug trail I had left.

"One of those unfortunates is a very good friend of mine. He called me just after you arrived there this morning."

He returned the mop to its secret pantry, hiding it from view. God forbid he let anyone know that he cleaned up after himself, rather than having a loyal Renfield do those things for him. I wished that Bait were there to see him in action. Eldritch sat down on the sofa, crossed his legs, and blew vile clove smoke in my direction.

I coughed, using my hand to loft the sweet-smelling stench back his way. "Do you have any real cigarettes, Eldritch?"

"Have you not smoked enough today?" His face lit up as if he had just told a joke that brought down the house at the Improv.

"Really, dude? Lucky that I like you and you're also lucky you saved me. Do me a favor, Cinderfella, and leave the jokes to the pros." I sat on the floor Indian-style, rubbing my shoulders. I felt the skin start to seal up from where the hooks had pierced me. The opium felt good as it streamed through my veins, reminding me why I needed narcotics. I was, after all, born addicted.

"I knew you weren't gone, RJ. The question is, where have you been?"

"Dez and Copperhead set me up and fed me to The Cloth. I've been in their religious rehab center."

Eldritch produced a file from the side table next to him and began sharpening his claws.

"So that makes it okay to kill the Batwangers? Have you learned nothing of the vampire code? There aren't that many of us. Why kill your brothers? On top of that, why do you hate those who are not like you? Why do you hate gay people? You're just not a nice person."

He was right. Even though trannies and gays had helped me when I was first learning the trade, all they ever heard from me was hateful words.

For some dumb reason, I decided that I was better than them solely because they were different from me.

My right ear was still pounding from The Habit's mad artillery show. Unlike the rest of my body, my hearing wasn't going to be healed anytime soon.

"You tell me what you would have done. They were training me to kill for them like an animal. They force-fed me blood from like Cardinals and shit and they only gave me drugs after I did what they told me to do for them. When I say drugs, I mean methadone. I had a dog collar around my neck that was programmed to slice my head off, for God's sake."

He extended his fingers and blew the metal shavings into the air. "I would have fallen on my sword."

"Maybe I didn't have a sword in my fucking jail cell that was tripped with a gigantic ultraviolet sunbeam. Besides bro, the Batwangers were supposed to keep Bait away from Dez. They turned her out. I have no idea where she is or if she's even alive."

"And King Cobra?"

"He's dead."

"By...?"

I continued rubbing my shoulders and drinking the blood. "Why the fucking inquisition?"

"Because you killed a lot of my friends, RJ. They might not have been like you or I—"

"No one is like you."

"Be that as it may," he continued, ignoring my comments, "you have broken an unspoken code of conduct set forth by the undead."

"I'm not going to justify myself for this. First off, there is no code of conduct. We're in gangs. We fight to sell and do drugs. Secondly, I mangled them because if I didn't I was going to be killed."

He blew some steel flakes from his filing off his nails. "There is a code. You don't kill others like you."

"What is this code shit?" I pulled the pipe out of my mouth and lifted the foot of the hookah. "Is this your code? This fucking guy is alive right here and he is your bong."

"Hookah."

"Whatever. Where is the line drawn in this holy code of yours? This guy has more of a right to live than a bunch of killers who are already dead."

Eldritch, getting a little perturbed, threw his clove on the floor, stood up and extinguished it under his boot. He marched across the room and opened a vintage desk by the staircase. He put on a pair of eighteenth century reading glasses and rested them on his nose, then picked out a stack of parchment papers and a raven's feather quill. Still a little excited, he rustled through the documents.

"Ah, here it is," he finally stated. He placed the other pages back into the desk and brought the page of interest over to me. "It clearly states here, 'I, Thomas Anthony Buchanan, do give my body and soul to thee Baron Eldritch III, for a reward in the life after.'" He pointed to the document with the quill. "It's all here."

I snatched the sheet from his hand and read it. "What is this?"

"A contract, signed in the blood of the man you are feeding from."

"Dude, you make these people sign contracts? Who's going to bust you? How are you going to be sued? Look at this guy." I picked up his hand and dropped it. "He's never going to be right again."

"It is a part of my personal code of vampire ethics. These individuals willingly give themselves to me."

"You're no better than me, pal. Just because they gave themselves to you doesn't make it right."

Frustrated, he nabbed the contract from me and returned to his desk. He looked back and shook the piece of paper. "This is my contract. It is proof that my transgressions are not those of a heathen."

I rolled my eyes. "I also had Cobra to worry about; they completely fucked that guy up."

"For someone who places little-to-no value on life, you sure wanted to live. Why is that?"

"I don't know really. I guess I figured that if I ever got out of there I could find Bait. I thought about her a lot while I was trapped, and since Nomi told me that the BPPs bought her and took her to wherever, I wanted to save her."

"What if I told you that she is still alive and that I know where she is?"

"How would you know that, Baron?"

Not detecting the sarcasm in my voice, he said, "I met Dez and Copperhead to give them the money. I gave them the bag, no questions asked."

"You gave them my money? Why?"

"It would seem that your present state answers that riddle for you. Ever since that bag of heroin came to be in your hands, nothing but horrible things have happened. They told me that you were looking to kill my Nightcrawler friends and me. They asked me to join them in their crusade toward a new way. I honorably declined."

I walked over to him. "Is she okay?

"I did not see her. But I do know that Dez and Copperhead are now running all the drugs through the Skinland Invasion compound."

"You've gotta be kidding me. Meth?"

"Not just meth… everything. There is no longer a division of the street trade. One group. One source. The police will not even step foot on their land because they have made it very clear what they are and what their intentions are."

"How deep is this group?"

"Deep? I do not think they are a very enlightened bunch."

"Not deep like that, Eldritch. Deep like how big of a gang is it?"

"From what I judged, twenty SIs, Dez and his followers, Copperhead, and what is left from the rest of the gangs. A rough estimate would be about forty."

"But they're mostly pussies like Dez, right? Like you and I could rip them to shreds?"

"Have you looked at yourself in the mirror?"

"That's a stupid question, Eldritch. You don't have any mirrors in the house; that would give away the mystery behind whether vampires give off reflections."

"Why are you such a mean person? I just saved you from certain death and all you continue to do is pick and pry at my very existence."

"Can we get her back or not?"

"I do not kill others like myself. It is an oath."

"You chopped the head off that guy today. He was a vampire."

"I killed him because he was about to kill you. I am not proud of my actions."

I stood up, walked over to his desk, and placed my hand on his shoulder. "Look, I'm not trying to make you do anything that jeopardizes your beliefs." I looked into his eyes, realizing that he had skull contact lenses in. "She's a thirteen-year-old girl who, if still alive, is being raped, beaten and tortured. Please, look beyond your code of ethics and do this for the greater good." I appealed to his senses by pleading in the flowery context of his worldview. "She's a human child. These monsters are performing unspeakable atrocities on a child. She needs our help."

Eldritch nodded his head and cupped my hand into his. "I am with you, brother. You are correct. She cries out for our rescue."

"Besides, I don't have a car and I don't know if an MTA line can get me to the Inland Empire."

Eldritch dropped my hand, smirked and said, "Please go use some mouthwash now. Your breath is heinous."

I squirmed around in the red vinyl seats of Eldritch's hearse, creating as much gassy noise as a five-hundred-pound chili-eating champion the night after a day's worth of competition.

I looked over at Eldritch, slouching over the wheel to fit his lumbering frame into the driver's seat. His razor fingernail spikes pawed at the steering wheel as his steel fangs bounced off his tongue. Every few minutes when a section of a song excited him, he grabbed the right section of his ass-length, raven-colored hair and flung it back behind the headrest. I wanted to tell him to wrap his mane up into a scrunchie or something, but what would be the use of that? I'm sure having his hair covering his face made him look more vampir-ific.

I hesitated for a few minutes, shuffled around in the fart seat and blurted out, "Is this all really necessary, Eldritch?" Of course, I was referring to the hearse filled with more vampire clichés than the last-stop gift shop outside of Vlad the Impaler's castle.

He swung his eyes to me without turning his head from the highway. "I don't know, RJ. Is this scarlet woman worth it?"

"Scarlet woman?" I searched my brain for a reference. "It's called a hooker, Eldritch. And Bait isn't even that. I was supposed to be her first John."

"We act one way, you act another," he declared. "Just because we come from different eggs doesn't mean we're not all the same. We are all creatures of the night."

"Oh my God, dude." I picked at my ear. "You're killin' me."

Eldritch turned the stereo off and downshifted the car, screeching it beyond the shoulder and into the desert. A sandstorm blasted from his tires through the open windows of the hearse; I shot forward, and barely escaped plowing through the windshield by bracing my arms against the dashboard.

The sand dissipated, falling into the Count's hair and all over his black leather trench coat. He sat still for a moment, silently looking forward. He then blew the hair out of his eyes, spraying California Inland's dirty ashes.

He tapped his razor claws on the steering wheel. "Well?" he finally challenged.

I spit onto my finger and rubbed the sand out of my eyes. As I licked it out of my gums and spit it back into my hand, I returned, "Well, what?"

He sat still for another moment, then shifted his body around in the driver's seat and clutched my neck where my dog collar burn remained. Without any visible anger in his tone or his eyes, he quietly asked again. "Well?"

The sand trickled down my throat like I was an hourglass about to be timed out. I squeezed out, "I'm sorry." But, Eldritch didn't release his grip.

"You know that I shan't need to do this, correct, RJ? I could easily collect my belongings and leave Los Angeles," he continued. "I do have a debt owed to me. The chances that either of us will walk away are faint. I am doing this for you… a friend." He released me.

I hacked up some of the sand for a minute and looked at him squarely. "I'm sorry."

Eldritch threw the hearse back into gear and crept back on to the I-10.

Still choking a little on the sand, I said, "Where exactly are we going? I don't know anything about the SIs, except for the fact they're white supremacists and that they do a shitload of crank. As a matter of fact, I've only met the leader once. What's his name, Zits or something?"

"His name is Pox and their dominion is on the outskirts of the Salton Sea." Eldritch produced a clove cigarette from behind his left ear. "It's an old, destitute hotel called the Sea and Sun Oasis." By flicking his thumb against his index claw he sparked it. Unsurprisingly, the flame disappeared when he snapped his fingers.

Thinking he couldn't see me, I rolled my eyes and let a soft giggle out of my nose.

A smirk lifted over the corner of Eldritch's pale, sunken cheekbones. "It is rather ostentatious, is it not?"

I doubled over laughing as sand from my hair fell into my lap. "It's all really, really lame, dude. You know what though?"

He blew cloves into the already smoky and dusty car.

"No matter how lame you can be, King Cobra was terrified of you."

He smiled.

It was dark as Eldritch cautiously drove through what was left of the Salton Sea with the stereo low and the lights on the hearse off. The buildings in the tortured town looked like they would crumble at the slightest movement, such as us bouncing over a crack in the road. Graffiti camouflaged the faded pastel colors of the art deco architecture.

I rolled up my window. It smelled like the wharf had been shoved into suitcases and someone was opening them as we passed. I kid you not: the air was so thick with the perfume of rotting fish and birds that I couldn't help but pull my shirt over my face and inhale my own body odor rather than catch the slightest whiff.

"What the fuck happened here?" I asked as I wiped spittle off my face. I rubbed it into the fibers of my jeans.

"It was quite a tourist attraction in the 1950s. However, it was a man-made sea, and since it's nothing more than a hole filled with old water that has nowhere to escape to, agricultural runoff and pollutants are trapped, killing all the wildlife. The sea is nothing more than another one of man's unwanted atrocities.

"Open the glove compartment. We cannot drive any farther." Eldritch pulled the hearse into a covered parking area next to a hotel and cut the engine.

Following his orders, I opened the glove compartment. Rolled into a leather rig kit were six needles. "Heroin?" I asked.

"Hardly," he said. "It's 'poor man', a nice combination of 80 percent speed and 20 percent heroin. The only reason I put heroin in it at all was to keep us focused slightly. It will also feed your hunger for both drugs."

I unfastened one of the needles from the case and held it up to a flickering old light above the garage where we parked. The greasy brown gas station toilet water color affirmed Eldritch's chemical mix: garbage.

"Are you kidding me, dude? Even if I wanted this in my body, how in the hell are we supposed to get it in there? This place is a ghost town."

Eldritch pointed off to a rusted Airstream a block from the hotel that was surrounded by a six-foot-tall barbed wire fence. Behind the fence, a mad pack of Rottweilers was gnawing on the razor wire like it was made of rawhide.

Remembering the fates of Leroy and Skillet, I grabbed Eldritch by his boney shoulder.

"Are you kidding me? Come on, dude. I can't kill someone's pet. Copperhead killed both my dogs. How about some nice clean heroin and some dude on steroids or something?"

"That is not going to work, RJ. I do not think you realize what we are about to do. Not only is this area flooded with SIs, we also have to worry about Dez, Copperhead, and the rest of the followers. So just like I asked before: is this worth it?"

I remembered Leroy and Skillet unable to play with me after Copperhead maimed them. Then I thought about Bait. I didn't even know if she was still alive. On top of that, what chance did Eldritch and I have to take on these second-rate psychopaths?

I held the needle up to the light again; I opened the car door and kicked my combat boot out onto the marsh of the Salton Sea.

I remembered Bait in the bathroom, giving herself an abortion. I remembered Leroy and Skillet with their heads bobbling around. Bait wanted less to bring another unwanted little monster into this world than I wanted to be alive. For that and the fact that I think I felt some type of fatherly obligation to her, I needed to help her.

Reluctantly, I said, "It's worth it."

I stayed in the hearse as Eldritch got out and closed his door. He swung his charcoaled hair back, dusting out more sand as he shifted the tail end of his leather trench coat to the side, revealing his bare chest, his pinstriped trousers, and his patent leather creepers. He flipped a clove into his mouth and immediately clapped both his hands, spawning fire from all his fingers. He lit the sugary grit. Finally, he waved his flaming hands in circular motions over his face; the blaze smothered, creating the illusion of smoke rising from his shoulders.

I looked at the door handle to the hearse, wanting to close it. My boot sank further into the swampland outside as I stood up and shut the door behind me.

"Jesus-fucking-Christ," I grumbled.

Our shadows moved side by side to the dog pen, looking like those of an adult with his child. I hadn't realized that Eldritch was so much more massive than me. If he had been more muscular—he was quite lanky—he would have easily been the size of Herman.

Herman. Another reason I had to kill these bastards.

The dogs bit at the barbed wire and each other the closer we got. At one point, one of the bulkier, more agitated Rotts bit into one of his brother's hides, tearing a hole into its hindquarters. That was my dog, I decided. Leave the Poodles for Eldritch. The guy was already huge.

"Are you ready? Which one do you want?"

I pointed at the savage who had just crippled his little brother. "The big one."

"Good choice." Eldritch lunged his right arm through the barbed wire, grasped a stout neck and yanked the dog out, stripping fur off as he pulled. The dog wailed as it tried desperately to clamp its jaws onto Eldritch's gigantic hand. "You ready?"

"What am I supposed to do? I only know how to kill humans." The dog squirmed more as it yelped and kicked its dangling rear legs at the leather trench coat.

"It is almost the same thing." The Rott slung slobber across Eldritch's bare chest.

"No, it's not. Asshole humans don't deserve to live. These dogs—"

He interrupted and catapulted the hound at me. "Dammit, man! Catch."

The ravenous animal propelled through the air and caught me on the forearm. Its teeth sunk in with no intention of letting go.

"Put the dog down!" Eldritch commanded. I dropped the dog down to the wet ground under my forearm as Eldritch made his way over to me to open the dog vice consuming my arm. The dog released. "Hold him down by the throat and drop your leg into its chest." As I had with the 'Wanger, I turned away from my victim.

"Where are the drugs?"

I motioned with my head as I held the dog at bay. "In my back pocket."

Eldritch grabbed the rig kit out of the pocket and pulled a syringe out. He tapped at it and squeezed the air out, squirting just a bit of the brown sludge from the top. When he knew it was ready, he plunged the needle into the dog's heart.

"Get ready," he advised.

Making sure he depleted everything in the spike, he pulled it out, threw it and instantaneously dug his razor claws into the animal's chest cavity. As the kicking and fighting from the dog turned into trance-like movements and its tongue dangled to the side, Eldritch tugged the heart out, shattering the sternum outward.

"Eat it," he said softly.

I closed my eyes and did as he said. As soon as I had the snack in my mouth, Eldritch headed back to the dog cage. The dogs backed up and tried to snuggle underneath the trailer. Their attempt to hide was fruitless however, because the leather-coated nightcrawler ripped his way through the wire fence and grabbed two of them by their bobbed tails. He dragged the animals out and collapsed on top of them, his knees crushing their chests. He produced a needle in both his hands, plunged them into the dogs and then withdrew their hearts.

I was filled with the amped feeling of the terror ahead. The animal blood and meth in my system made me shake and vibrate, ready to kill.

XXIX

SULTANS

Eldritch and I huddled behind a big rock in front of a wasteland of abandoned mobile homes. While Eldritch jerked his head in all directions, making sure the coast was clear, I fidgeted and panted, feeling the dog blood and speed course though my veins, electrifying my heart and brain.

His unsteady finger pointed to the compound, about a mile away, that was surrounded by a six-foot brick wall. He reached into his patent leather purse and unfolded a swashbuckler-style, single lens scope. His lips bled from unsuccessfully grinding his fangs.

"Take a look at the perimeter." He handed me the scope and pointed to the four corners of the wall.

At all four corners were skinhead mules with AK-47 machine guns slung over their shoulders. At the entrance was a guard station set up to secure the once prominent gated community. Beyond the gate, at the center of the colony, was a clubhouse surrounded by several crumbled homes and rusted trailers.

"They keep all the drugs in the country club; they sleep and socialize in the trailers and houses. I'm guessing that Dez and Copperhead are in the stucco ranch home." He pointed off to the left side of the clubhouse. "And I believe your friend is with them there. It appears to be the most fitting home on the property."

Unnecessarily annoyed, I put down the archaic scope because I could see better without it. "Where did you meet with Dez when you came here before?"

Eldritch's head jerked and twitched, the speed eliciting him to tug on his own hair. "We met in the clubhouse." With his claw, Eldritch began unsteadily mapping the area in the sand.

I scratched the side of my head. "How the fuck do you expect us to get in there? I mean, Jesus, how can we get through undetected by the guards? Goddammit, Eldritch." I felt like there were sand fleas crawling all over me.

"I am going to drive directly up to the front gate and be let in. While I create a diversion for the guards, you are going to edge around the back, climb the fence, and make your way down the backside of the silo."

I chewed on my cuticles and scratched at my cheek. Boy, speed was a hell of a lot different than my cherished heroin. "Are you fucking crazy, Eldritch? As soon as you drive up there, they're going to rip you into a thousand pieces with those machine guns."

He sucked his clove down to the filter. I smelled the burning plastic. It made my nose itch.

"Not likely, RJ. They want me to participate in their new business."

"They have to know that you saved me at the opera house. That place was filled with snitches. Fucking snitch cripples." I felt like I was moving a million miles an hour doing nothing, like I was running on my knees, full-speed down a never-ending hallway.

"Trust me. Not one person there is telling these philistines anything. My presence at the opera house is known, trusted, and respected. Besides, I must get the hearse into the compound. All my weapons are concealed inside the casket in back."

Using his talon, he drew a circle around the outskirts of the gated area to establish the mountains surrounding the valley. Before he finished the circumference, his steel nail fell off from all his trembling.

"We'll use the dark cover of the mountains behind us to advance behind the clubhouse. As you can see, that area is much closer to the back gate than it is here." He marked an X on the ground representing our current position with another one of his claws.

I tried to focus on the mountains circling the Skinhead Invasion valley. The horizon tunneled inward and outward, making it difficult to judge the depth of the land directly in front of me. Ignoring the racing of my heart, I acknowledged that he was right. The range spiraled inward to the back of the clubhouse. The only way into or out of the basin was the route we took that was filled with the deserted dwellings of the Salton Sea.

"I don't know about this, Eldritch. Like you said, this is a complete suicide mission. If we're going to do this commando, let's just bum rush them straight up. You know? Do you know what the fuck I'm talking about? Do you hear me? Goddammit! Can you hear me?"

He grabbed my shoulders and shook them. "We cannot back down now. Our destiny is to save this young woman. We have to do this right or we are dead."

"This is so cheesy."

Out of nowhere, I felt an object belt me on the back of the head.

"Owww!" I yelped, deciding at first that it was nothing more than the overdose of speed in my system. I looked down at my chest cavity. The center of my body expanded and collapsed trying to keep pace with my heart. Slobber whizzed around me everywhere as I flapped my head around, releasing my jowls. Another object smacked me in the back of the head, driving my face into the rock formation in front of us. I shoved Eldritch. He fell back on the scope.

"Why are you pushing me?" He picked up the pirate-looking glass. It dangled around, broken. "This cost me a fortune."

"I pushed you because you just nailed me in the back of the head, asshole. And who cares about that stupid thing. It doesn't even work."

A Caribbean twang sang out from behind us. "So, I guess Dez was correct in tinking that you weren't dead, huh, RJ?"

We both spun around. Copperhead and three Deziens stood on top of one of the busted-ass airstreams behind us.

Arrogantly, Copperhead flicked dust off his shoulder. "Good ting we were out 'unting. Dez is going to love this." He picked up his cell phone and began dialing and pointed to Eldritch. "Eldritch? Come on, RJ, why bring dis pussy?"

Before I had the chance to leap into a brawl, Eldritch dropped two smoke bombs in front of him and screamed, "Mine!"

He pounced toward the trailers on all fours, unintentionally knocking me over the rock with his back leg. He rocketed toward them, vaulting his massive body into the warzone.

Without missing a beat, Copperhead jumped and met him mid-flight. Rather than be bothered with a collision, Eldritch simply grabbed Copper by the head, spun it around like a baseball and pitched him further back toward the mountains. I got to my feet and bounded in Copperhead's direction.

Eldritch descended directly between two of the Deziens. A thunderous boom rang out as the über vamp's boots landed on the aluminum trailer. His talons dug into each of their skulls, locking in securely as if they were bowling balls. Not wanting to be the next victim, the third Dezien jumped off the trailer, trying to escape. Viciously, Eldritch scooped the scalps, brains, and spines out of his first two victims and then one after another fired them like meteorites across the desert, tripping up the fleeing Dezien.

I made my way back to the canyon wall where I expected to find Copperhead. Eldritch clearly had those three covered. Rumors of his pacifistic demeanor were grossly misrepresented. That was the most barbaric display I had ever seen. At that point, I wanted to join his gang.

Like a jackal in a spin cycle, I leapt from trailer top to trailer top, looking between the openings for Copperhead. I smelled his pot-stench everywhere, but the speed made it increasingly difficult for me to hone in on an exact location. Bubbles blew out of my nostrils as I tried to slow my heart. An intense vibration grappled onto my body and carried me around like a Mexican jumping bean.

"Focus, RJ," I kept telling myself.

Tree limbs crackling, rocks rolling from the cliffs, and random pops in my bad ear came at me from every direction. As I made my way between the two last trailers, I was hit by a tree branch and lost my footing. I flipped backwards, hitting the edge of the trailer. I slid down the side, catching a railroad spike on my back that was being used to cover a window with wood. The ragged skewer bumped up my vertebrae like a playing card clicking through bike spokes. I felt it breaking bones in its path, until it reluctantly stopped on my recently healed shoulder bone.

"*Fuck!*" I wailed. I steadied my palms flush against the Air Stream and released myself from the spike. I stumbled to the next trailer, checking to see if Copperhead was above me. I didn't know if the tree I whacked into was his doing or if it was just my exaggerated alertness that was blinding me rather than servicing me.

He wasn't there. I scurried around the maze of campers, looking for a way out. I shook around my jowls again as mounds of spit whizzed everywhere. The dryness of my eyes was killing me because I hadn't blinked since I shot up.

A wave of twitching transferred from one of my arms to the other and then back, and my fingers contorted like they were all independently trying to escape from my hands. I clenched my fists to try and stop the disobedient behavior only to notice the blood vessels from my elbows to my wrists popping out and collapsing. There were sand fleas all fucking over me, so I tried to scratch at every inch of my flesh.

Finally, I made my way out to the boundary between the trailer maze and the open air. I looked over at Eldritch who was tugging organs and innards from the fresh carcass of the third Dezien. I looked to the top of the trailers and saw Copperhead. With long strides, he skipped over the top of the aluminum graveyard. Rather than bother with me, he made his way toward the unaware Eldritch who was squeezing an intestine to his mouth like a beer bong, trying to siphon what little blood was left.

I immediately began galloping like a quadruped toward the scene. What was left of the disks in my back slid around and separated. With not even a second to spare, I hurdled my frame at Copperhead, clipping his legs before he started his descent on Eldritch. We hit the ground while Eldritch continued to feast, paying our scrimmage no mind. I snorted away as the combination of Rot blood and meth continued to pull the strings, puppeteering my body and mind. I sunk Copperhead's face into the sand, beat in his cheekbone with my knuckles and kneed at his annihilated ribcage.

He spat sand and weeds out of his mouth trying to create a passage. "Okay! Okay!" He cringed like a tabby cat.

I remained relentless, breaking him open like a piñata at his center with my leg. I shifted my knuckles to my forearm and clubbed him so hard in the face that his nose became an indiscernible blob. His eye popped out of the socket and dangled from the spaghetti behind it. A clear fluid dripped from the jumbled ball.

The phony Jamaican accent magically disappeared. "Please stop, RJ. I'm sorry. I'm so fucking sorry, man. I didn't do anything. It was Dez's ideas. It was all Dez."

It was too easy to just let him go. I thought about Herman and the downfall Copperhead had plotted against him. They force-fed us to the enemy and handed Herman a pink slip at the hands of The Cloth and The Habit. I relaxed on the chest cavity and pinned his thighs down with both knees. I felt his pants fill with piss and shit.

"Please, RJ," he pleaded. He begged just like the tranny and the bus driver had, but I wanted to see him suffer. I was excited to kill him.

I tried to grab a breath and looked up to Eldritch, who was still paying no attention to us. He continued his fixation on the organs of his casualties.

"The w-w-whore," Copperhead stammered.

I placed my fingers around his skullcap and rotated his head out of the sand.

"You w-w-want the wh-wh-whore, right?"

I didn't answer. I grinded my teeth, panting every few seconds.

"Come on, RJ. Please let me live. I-I-I'll take you to the wh-wh-whore." He closed his intact eye and tried to inhale, hoping he would suck the other one back into the socket. His actions reminded me more and more of Herman. He was a cheap imitation of a great man.

"RJ, she's alive. I never touched her. I-I-It was Dez. I had nothing to do with it." He tried harder to inhale. The eye slowly started to move.

Halting his attempt, I snatched the eye and shoved it into his mouth.

"She's alive?" I asked.

Copperhead nodded, not sure what to do about being able to see the inside of his own mouth.

"Well then, I have no need for you, motherfucker. This is for King Cobra."

I fastened his head down in the sand behind him. He squinched his eyelids closed and bit into the eyeball in his mouth. With a powerful uppercut from my free hand, I compounded his chin all the way up to the middle of his face. I dug in farther, making his skull wrap around my fist like a boxing glove. I pulled my arm back for a moment and then plowed directly through the center of his cranium, spray-painting his brains all over the sand. I stood up, still breathing ravenously, and pulled his head off my fist with my boot.

Eldritch peeked over his shoulder at the mess. "No need for you to do me any favors, RJ. It does not appear like he was much of a contest anyway. Look over there, though."

Eldritch pointed off in the distance to Copperhead's black Cadillac Escalade. I reached into the front pocket of the former Battlesnake's jeans. Sure enough, the keys were there, and we had our ticket into the compound.

XXX

PROGENIES

I cleared a tube from the head-bong-vice-thing that was sitting on the floor under the passenger seat of Copperhead's Escalade. Around the rearview mirror were the braided remains of Herman's dreadlocks.

"You should take a hit, Eldritch," I said, offering the glass pipe over the center console. Bad dancehall music thumped away inside the vehicle, almost lifting the rear end as it boomed from the enormous subwoofer in the back. I blew out the smoke. "It will take the edge off the meth."

"No." With eyes bulging, he focused on driving.

"What's the plan here? These windows are pretty well tinted, but I think they will stop us at the gate into the compound."

He gunned the car, frequently stomping the brakes whenever he saw any obstruction on the dirt road. Sweat flooded his skeletal face. He didn't answer. His head twitched a little, but I don't think he was confirming any plan. I think he was just shaking from the speed and eating the vampire insides. I'd never really seen anyone suck down on that sewage and love it.

I took another pull from the bong. The pot fought against the speed in my system, calming me and helping me focus. The lights from the compound lit up the middle of the desert like it was Las Vegas. It agitated my eyes like the sunlamps at St. Matthews.

Eldritch grinned. "Hold tight, RJ." He floored the gas pedal and licked his chops.

"What the fuck are you doing? I thought all the weapons were in your hearse?"

"It's better to catch them off guard."

"Are you nuts? You said there were a bunch of these skinhead idiots."

The Escalade crashed through the main gate of the bloodsucker Auschwitz, splattering it, the two guards and the security station everywhere. Two skinheads rolled up the hood. One of them leapt over the top of the other which had been clipped off with such a velocity it embedded itself into the windshield.

"Eldritch? What are you doing?"

Before he could answer we heard SIs landing on the roof like golf ball-sized hail knocking on the metal. They started punching their way into the cabin as Eldritch continued to drive. An arm tugged at my shirt from above. I snapped off the arm and threw it out the passenger window. The SI fell off the top of the truck. Meanwhile, Eldritch snapped the steering wheel left and right, shaking off more skinheads. That didn't deter them though; more and more latched on to the vehicle.

"Are you ready, RJ?"

"Ready for what?"

With his clawed index finger, he pointed in front of us to a gas pump. "That," he said. Without missing a beat, Eldritch threw the truck into cruise control and opened his door. He looked over at me. "You had better jump."

Feverishly, I pushed my door open as SIs began pouring into the vehicle. I jumped and rolled out; seconds later, the SUV climbed up the gas pump, ripping open the protective plate on the bottom and the wiring beneath. A sudden spark and everything around it was consumed by a huge fireball. I sheltered my eyes from the explosion. Somehow, Eldritch had already made it over to me, and he picked me up by my neck and ripped my jacket off because it caught fire.

"No time to jerk around," he said, turning me to face behind us. Standing there was a motley crew of skinheads, Deziens, and other riffraff. They charged us. "Get out of here. I can handle these children." He pointed across the compound. "She has got to be in that building."

"Eldritch, you can't—"

"Go!" He shoved me away. "We knew this was a blasted *seppuku*." He drew two swords from behind his back and bowed his head in prayer.

Rather than ask what *seppuku* meant, I took off running. I turned around once to debate his decision, but it was too late. The Lycan-raised, would-be Hollywood star was gobbled up by the army of convicts. A tornado of sand and blood rose from the ground. I had made several bad decisions in my life... not calling Eldritch my best friend and my strongest ally is something that I would most likely regret for the rest of it.

Eldritch and Herman. They both sacrificed what little semblance of lives they had for me. The two people I respected the least in the entire world gladly gave themselves so that I could make things right. Maybe it was all the humanity that came from shots of Bait's blood, or maybe it was the holy blood force fed to me by McAteer, but at that moment, I understood human compassion. I felt something much deeper than the drugs and blood that I needed to stay alive. I felt like there was a reason, a mission. I was a living creature and I had to prove myself by not letting their deaths go unanswered.

A warning siren filled the compound as I made my way into the building where Eldritch thought they were keeping Bait. That was if she were still alive.

⚸

The entire compound filled with the blistering heat of our flamboyant entrance. Gas and smoke billowed across the desert. I took off my shirt and put it over my head. As I took it off, my palm ran against the former home of my Faction tattoo. My heart pounded away at the scarred cross on my chest, almost pumping itself free from the nothingness inside.

I ducked into the cove of a hallway as two SIs ran down the hall past me.

"What the fuck is going on?" one asked.

"That nigger drove his truck into the gas station."

"Where's Dez?"

"I think he's already over there. He's the only one who can keep that porch monkey in line."

"I hear that."

They seemed to think that Copperhead had turned Judas on them, which bought me a little more time. I didn't know how far the pack that took down Eldritch was behind me, but they had to be closing in quick. It was also only a matter of time before Dez got wind of my arrival.

What didn't make any sense to me at all was why a militant black dude and a bunch of intolerant, illiterate cunts were working together in the first place. I guessed they saw eye-to-eye on their sheer hatred for everything human. Either that or they simply saw a way to make more money with Herman and get me out of the way. It's amazing how money can make people hypocritical.

After I was sure they had exited the building, I slipped down the hall in the direction they came from. I passed room after room in the forgotten clubhouse and didn't hear a peep. By the end of the hallway, in what I believed was once a ballroom during the heydays of the Salton Sea, I finally heard a TV, some laughter, and the faint whimpering of a little girl. I crept closer, knowing that this was my destination and, most likely, my grave.

The foyer area in front of the ballroom had two doors on opposite sides of the room. A little farther down the hallways branched. One had a sign that read *Kitchen*. The other read *Backstage*. Not really wanting to relive my stage performance at the opera house for obvious reasons, I took the route to the kitchen.

The laughter increased and I was sure that only two people were in the ballroom with Bait. To camouflage my footsteps, I sat down on the permanently clammy carpet and took off my boots. The pot had worn off and my heart resumed its uncontrollable rush from the meth. I gagged on the smells in the air. The combination of a dead wharf smell and a gas fire was such an overwhelming mix that it tasted like a rotten fish fry at a soup kitchen as the scent made its way from my nose down to my throat.

I got back to my feet and pushed the swinging kitchen door open only to be knocked back by another smell. A gust of nail polish remover, burnt household and noxious eggs overpowered the rotten fish fry. The kitchen had been converted into a makeshift meth lab. What seemed like hundreds of bathtubs lined the room and even more test tubes cooked over Bunsen burners. It was the largest drug lab I had ever seen.

I shuffled through the labyrinth of bathtubs bubbling with off-yellow repurposed decongestants and 99 Cent Store disinfectants. The concoctions snapped, crackled, and popped, ready to ignite at any second. It was amazing that the place hadn't already gone up in flames. It disturbed me that a gang with the collective intelligence of a slow five-year-old had constructed a room full of liquid dynamite. Thankfully, Eldritch hadn't aimed his joyride here. The whole place would have gone up like Hiroshima and we all would have died. I pulled my t-shirt from my head and covered my nose and mouth instead.

I made my way to the end of the nuclear cookery to the swinging door that led into the main ballroom. I peered through the round observation window. Mountainous big-screen TVs filled the room, each screen showing a different sporting event. Two SIs sat by the stage, not interested in the feast of athletics that surrounded them.

Sure enough, I spotted Bait. She was centerstage in front of an enormous drooping curtain that was tagged with the SI swastika symbol. She looked exhausted, and was half-suspended and half-standing barefoot on a saguaro cactus that was laying on its side. She struggled to stay awake and alert; her toes trembling to find purchase on the plant in the safe, green spaces between its large needle clusters.

Around her neck, both supporting and choking her, was a noose, poorly tied to a light fixture over the stage. Worst of all, the safety lever of a live grenade was held between her blood-drenched inner thighs. The two wretched neo-Nazis threw darts at her, seeing who would be the first to knock her off and blow her inside out. I didn't have much time.

I backpedaled through the meth lab, deciding that I wanted to get behind her on the stage. If I was going to be the hero, I had to put my dick sucking incident behind me. Meth liquid continued to crackle and one of the bigger bubbles exploded and singed my right arm, nearly melting a hole all the way through my bicep. Clamping my mouth shut so I wouldn't let out a pained yelp, I ripped the shirt off my face and wrapped it around my arm like a tourniquet, pulling it tight with my teeth.

As cautiously as I had entered the kitchen I slipped out. The alarms and disorder from outside grew louder. I shuffled to the other side of the intermission area in front of the ballroom and beelined down the other hall.

"She's getting close," one of the skinheads delighted.

"Shit, this is like Jenga, only way cooler," returned the other.

I jumbled my way up the small staircase that led backstage, trying my best to keep the badly mildewed, parquet flooring from creaking. When I reached the center of the curtains, I knelt on one knee in a starting gate running position. Trying to remain undetected, I slid my hand through the parted curtains. The roaring of the televisions helped too.

As soon as I had my hand positioned, I let out a calming whisper. "Drop the grenade, Bait," I said. "Don't turn around." A dart flew through the curtain, barely brushing the wound on my arm. Bait's legs opened and the grenade fell into my hand as she plunged into the grip of the rope around her neck. The skinheads cheered as her neck slipped sideways and they covered their sensitive ears, preparing for the impending explosion.

Bait gagged on the rope as the quick asphyxiation began. I jumped into action, vaulting myself through the curtains and snagging Bait off the line with my injured right arm. I curled her inward and then dropped her to the floor before jumping toward the SIs who stood up in shock, hands still covering their ears.

"Holy shit," the dirtier of the two let out. The other turned around, tripping at first but finding his balance quickly and then headed toward the doors, arms and legs thrashing around in fear. I landed with my cupped hand directly onto the face of the first dirtbag. Without hesitating, I pounded the grenade through his crooked meth teeth and down into his throat. His eyes crossed as I let go of the safety lever. I then flipped his entire body over my shoulder and threw him toward his fleeing colleague. His chicken-shit buddy turned around only to be clobbered by the human projectile. He scratched at his friend's face for a split second, trying to release the grenade and save his own life before both their bodies exploded in a mixture of body parts and theatre shrapnel. Flesh and bone confetti snowed around the room as the smoke that delivered them set off the sprinkler system.

I rushed back to Bait and tried to cradle her back to life in my arms. "RJ?" She sniffled.

"Yeah, it's me, Bait."

She looked beyond me back toward the resting place of the two skinheads. "Look out."

Carelessly, I dropped her head on the floor as I turned and sprung back to my feet, bracing myself for an attack. Pouncing toward me, naked, was my old protégé, Dez. With bloodlust in his eyes, Dez hissed and growled like a mountain lion whose den had just been disgraced by a pack of coyotes.

He knocked me backward into one of the televisions, then pounded his head into Bait's chest cavity. I crashed into the TV and sparks pricked at my eyeballs, fizzled out and smoked. I tried blinking to stop the storm of broken electronics, but my sight became increasingly blurry as tears welled up to prevent damage. Dez landed on top of me, crunching down on my shoulder with his teeth and dug his thumb into the meth-inflicted trauma on my arm. He grabbed a huge hunk of glass off the floor and plunged it into my sternum. Always with the weapons.

"Who's the fucking leader now, RJ?" he shrieked. My blood coated his face and smeared his grimace from the tips of his ivories straight up into his gums. "Who's the fucking leader!"

Dez bit me again with his locking jaw, this time to my other shoulder. He clamped down harder, sensing the tender flesh from where the armless Dezien had locked his hooks into me. He grabbed the front of my hair and savagely beat me into the glass display of the TV.

In his madness, Dez's voice slipped and changed pitch. His teeth tugged on my clavicle as he howled and salty tears dripped into my ravaged lacerations. He shuffled into a kill position by releasing his mouth and pinning me down with his knees. I felt like the dogs that Eldritch and I had eaten alive earlier that night.

"She's dead, motherfucker!" He beamed like a shit-eating bastard kid. "I kept her alive because I knew you'd be back. I wanted you to see me kill her, you piece of shit." He withdrew the glass shard from my face and then, as quickly as he had attacked, he retreated. He bounced back across the room and pounded through a window. The shattered glass smashed to the floor directly on top of Bait.

She coughed. "RJ?"

I tried to blink but the burns on my eyes caught my lids, making it impossible for me to close them.

Bait coughed again. "RJ? Are you alive?"

"I'm here, Bait." I flopped myself over, out of the frame of the TV. I dug my fingers into the ballroom floor and gradually towed myself away from the mess. "Hang on."

"RJ. Hurry." She wheezed, choking on blood.

I pulled myself farther, breaking both sides of my vulnerable clavicle and ignoring the mauling I had just suffered at the hands of my so-called best friend. "I'm coming, Bait."

I reached her, cradling her frail body again in my arms. Shards of glass stuck into her like a pincushion. Without being able to see clearly, I did my best to pull out the larger pieces.

"Stop, RJ."

"It's okay. I'm going to help you. I'm going to get you to a hospital or something. I can get you to Pico. He can help."

"Stop. You don't need to do that."

"Goddammit, Bait. You can't die."

"You don't need to do that, RJ." She coughed out a huge clot of blood as I held her close. She shivered.

I felt around the glass. Dez managed to cave in her chest when he landed on her. I put my left wrist behind her neck and slipped my right forearm under her legs.

"You don't need to do that," she said again, spitting out her two front buckteeth.

"Why do you keep saying that? I need to help you."

"Where have you been, RJ?"

"Bait, shut up. I need to get you some help."

"You don't need to do that," she whispered again for the umpteenth time. She was more delirious than me. "Come here."

I bent the side of my head down to her lips.

"Make me like you. Bite my neck." Her legs started thumping against the ground. "You can make me live forever. You're a vampire."

"I can't do that, Bait. That's not how it works."

"RJ, come here."

I put my ear to her convulsing face.

"Make me one of you. I want to be a vampire."

As I felt her breathing freeze up and her soul begin to escape, I turned her head sideways. My vision started to clear just enough to see her smile under her skunky, greasy hair.

"I'm going to be a vampire," she said as I bit down into her neck.

I took my mouth off her neck and whispered back. "I want to be like you, Bait."

"Hi, hot guy," she said as I felt a comforting hand grasp my shoulder. And then, she went limp in my arms.

I sunk my teeth back into her neck, hoping maybe I could save her.

Her blood tasted innocent and naïve. She was the greatest tasting human in the world. She was everything right and wrong with the universe. She was my only tie to a normal life, a life I knew I could never have, and I was her tie to a world she wanted so desperately to fit into.

"Can you give me a second, Eldritch?"

"Yes, my friend." He released his hand from my drooping right shoulder. His creepers slowly tapped across the floor as he walked away.

Another explosion went off outside and the power shut down in the ballroom. As I pulled a dart out of her face, I gazed into Bait's eyes for one last look at what she would never become.

"It's over now." I crossed her arms across her chest and closed her eyelids.

"RJ," Eldritch yelled across the room. "Catch."

I didn't bother to attempt to catch the object without looking. Nothing that cool ever seemed to work for me. It landed on the ballroom floor next to me. It was the keys to the hearse.

"I'm too fucked up to drive," he said.

I hugged Bait all the way to sleep. I knew what had to be done.

XXXI

DEMONS

Peoria, Arizona was hot. I kind of felt like my skin was melting again, and it probably was. As the sun started to go down, Eldritch and I lathered ourselves up with sunscreen and rolled up the windows on his hearse. After I let him know where I wanted to go, he took over the driving.

"Can you turn off the vampire music, Eldritch? I've had enough doom and gloom to last me the rest of my life."

He pulled out the USB cord from his iPhone and turned up the radio. The talk radio host spoke.

"*A giant methamphetamine fire erupted out at the abandoned Salton Sea resort last night that police are blaming on a neo-Nazi street gang named The Skinland Invasion. According to area police chief, Timothy O'Malley, they were poised to strike the operation and had been investigating it for months.*"

"Is that always the way these things are explained, Eldritch?"

"For the most part. I heard the other day that a respected and charitable priest downtown was shot through the head by Satanists."

Neither of us really had much to say to each other so we just listened to the radio. I didn't even bother telling him The Cloth's experiments to create me. It was less about shame than it was trivial at that point.

The radio host continued with the day's headlines as the last of the desert sun sunk behind a mountain.

"*In entertainment news, more information is surfacing about the heroin overdose of the overly-private and secluded actor Stephan Rodderick.*"

The co-host laughed her way into the conversation. "*Ha. The guy who plays lead vampire in those* Nightshayde *films? The one who takes himself way too seriously, right?"*

"That's him. We told you last week that he takes his role so seriously, that he insists all his scenes be shot after dark. He won't even take a studio executive meeting during the day."

The co-host giggled. *"Go on."*

"It's really not that funny. It's serious."

She held in her laughter. *"Okay. Okay. I'm serious now."*

"Anyway, Rodderick apparently overdosed yesterday and insiders say that he was a heroin addict."

"Big deal," the co-host sighed. *"Another druggy movie star? Is that what shocks you?"*

"No. No. Wait. It's gets so much better. Rodderick recovered from the overdose and police say he refuses to leave his home in Austin, Texas; his handlers have only brought in his personal physicians to treat him."

Both hosts roared with laughter. The co-host said, *"Talk about someone who takes themselves too seriously."*

I turned off the radio.

"Rodderick is one of us, you know," Eldritch said.

"I'm not sure I know what you are, Eldritch." Without looking at him I said, "Pull over."

I snatched Eldritch's iPhone and searched for Bait's name. Surely, there had to be a record of a missing twelve-year-old on the Internet.

I found an article. *Parents Beg for the Return of Runaway Teen, Bailia Jenkins.* And in the very first sentence were their names: *Mother Roberta Jenkins and stepfather Thomas Fries.*

I walked to the door. I knocked.

I knocked again.

I heard fiddling with the doorknob. Then… nothing. After two more minutes of pounding, the white door finally crept open to the Arizona outside.

"What do you want?" Thomas was way slimier than I imagined in my head. Shirt off. Ponytail. Boxer briefs.

For a second, I shook off the image of Bait begging me to bite her neck. "Sir, I found your daughter."

"Who the fuck are you, faggot?" He wiped the coke snot off his irritated nose.

I scrubbed my forearm wanting more than anything to take him down. I wasn't a vampire. I didn't need to be invited into his house.

Time to get me high.

"I'm from... ahh shit." I grabbed his head from the back, dug my pinky into the base of his skull and twirled his George Carlin ponytail around my index finger. "Do you like to finger little girls, motherfucker?" I pulled his head into my chest. "One last chance: I found your daughter. Tell her you're sorry. I really don't want to do this. I don't want to kill you unless you did something wrong."

But I did. I was a serial killer and I was the world's greatest aftermarket abortion. Not all trash deserves to live and breathe.

Bait's voice seemed to be inside of me. I felt her pain. The pain she suffered at the hands of some shitbag who made her masturbate while he jerked off into her asshole. I rolled my fingers down and dug farther into his skull. I just wanted to rip his head off. I got my mouth right next to his ear. I tried to whisper, but at this point, talking was over.

"Do you think it's cool to fuck and finger little girls, asshole?"

He sniffed and searched his dense brain for some wise retort. Nothing came out. He didn't even care enough about his own life to plead for it.

"Who are you?"

The ringing in my ear from The Habit's bullets drove thumbtack pains into my brain. I couldn't hear shit. I just wanted to kill; no matter what he said to me, he was going to die.

I quit speaking. I took my index finger and jammed it into his left eye and started finger-fucking his brain. You know when something is just out of reach? You tickle it. I pulled him closer, fully penetrating his brain. His other eye rolled back, bleeding. I took my index finger and jammed out the other eye. All I could hear was *please* and *no* and *why?*

"*Why?*" I screamed. I moved him away from my chest and picked him up through his eyeholes. "You don't finger fuck little girls!"

He shook out one last worthless breath and quivered. For a second, I felt like a real vampire. I dug my mouth into his neck and just rocked his jugular. Then I balanced the top of his skull with my free hand as I broke through it with the hand I was using to dig around inside. I pushed upward and tore off his head. And I wasn't fucking around either; I beat it twenty-four times on the coffee table. I counted.

I threw his face across the room.

Disheveled, I wandered around the wood paneled house a little. Then, I heard, "Oh my God."

In lingerie, the worst human being in the world stood across the room from me with a toothbrush in her mouth. It was her. It was mom. Roberta.

"Are you Roberta Jenkins?" I didn't wait for an answer as I stormed across and seized her vocal chords and esophagus. The toothbrush fell out.

Using her voice box as a towrope, I yanked her to the floor, smacking her chin against my fist and the carpet. As I pulled on the insides of her neck, her shrieks became more and more high pitched until the stringy cords severed like the strings on a guitar tuned too far. As I reached the complete threshold, her voice let out a kazooed rumble and then fizzled away completely.

I snatched her tongue in my fingers. She didn't like to talk. What was the use? I ripped that thing out, right from the stem and threw it towards daddy's head. I picked up her electric toothbrush and brow beat the fuck out of her. The bristles cut into her forehead and the power of the beating made the batteries from the brush fall out. I grabbed one off the floor and pushed it into her ear until the eardrum popped. Red fudge slugged in and out of her triple chins. I picked up what was left of the toothbrush and drove it through her eye sockets.

This was the person who let her daughter get fucked by a molester and just sat there. She brushed her teeth and turned the other way.

The bitch squirmed around as her belly shirt gut brushed across my arm. She tried to beg for mercy but only came up empty.

I clinched my eyes and tried to shake it off. All I wanted from them was an apology. All I wanted from Dez was an apology. All I wanted from my mother was an apology.

"I know what I am!" I yelled. "You know what, you evil cunt?" Her last seconds of fear and life escaped her. I spun her head off and then punted it through a window that was taped over with a black garbage bag.

Her body continued to wriggle around. Good thing I still had a fix. I planted my foot in her sternum and ripped her arm off.

Shot to the wrist.

I squeezed every last drop of blood out of her arm like a towel. No knuckle this time. I went reverse-style and showered myself in her worthless blood.

I lifted up the arm like a trophy. It was my first straight fix since rehab.

I stumbled around for a minute. Well, stumbling would imply that I was in control of what I was doing. Realistically, I fell through the same window that I threw momma's head out of. I pulled myself back into the house, only to crash face first into the screen of an old school rear-projection TV.

And then, after several attempts at trying to pick myself up, I heard a peep from across the room. Drunk on misery, I slung around. Ready to kill.

Then I saw her.

"Hey," I said, as the mellowing drugs vibrated through my body. Under the kitchen table was a little girl.

I tried to smile when I remembered something that Bait told me.

He pins her down and makes her lick his balls.

"Pinball?"

She hid her face behind her hands and didn't say a word.

My legs collapsed Indian-style and I scratched my belly. A Pit Bull came over, licked some blood off my knee and curled up next to me.

I petted him. He hated his parents just as much as everyone else did.

I pulled Bait's ID card out of my pocket and tossed it to the little girl. She looked at it but didn't pick it up. Then, she pulled the tablecloth from above her head and hid her face.

The hot desert nightfall caused sweat to drip out of my eyes. Everyone knows that vampire-gangsters don't cry.

Oh, the humanity.

t

KNUCKLE SUPPER

ABOUT THE AUTHOR

For more than 20 years, Drew Stepek has written, produced, and directed for the publishing, online and entertainment industries. Drew has worked for Film Threat, Sci-Fi Universe, Wild Cartoon Kingdom, *The Tonight Show with Jay Leno, Late Night with Conan O'Brien, Saturday Night Live, The Profiler, The Pretender, Buffy the Vampire Slayer,* and ESPN.

In the past ten years, the author ventured into creative directing and ideation roles involving entertainment and technology marketing for Davie Brown Entertainment and Straight Up Technologies. In 2012, Stepek took a position as the Head of Branded Entertainment for Machinima. He has also been a Creative Director at AwesomenessTV.

Born in Royal Oak, Michigan, Drew moved around a bit as a young man and finally found his home base in Hollywood, California in 1994. Drew attended Rollins College in Winter Park, Florida. His first novel Godless (ISBN# 0978602498) was released 666 (June 6th, 2006) and has since captured a strong underground following.

Currently, Stepek is working on the sequels to *Knuckle Supper*.

Lloyd Kaufman
Bentley Little
Kristopher Triana
Shane McKenzie
Alistair Rennie
Jack Ketchum
Ryan Harding
Edward Lee
John McNee
AND MANY MORE...

YOU'LL LAUGH...YOU'LL CRY...YOU'LL VOMIT
DON'T SAY WE DIDN'T WARN YOU.

"Take one part Sid Vicious, one part H.P. Lovecraft and shake.
Throw in a dash of the thrill kill thug life and you have *Mother's Boys*."

~ David C. Hayes, author of *Cannibal Fat Camp*

Available through Blood Bound Books
www.bloodboundbooks.net

"*Pretty Pretty Princess* is disgusting, offensive,
and absolutely hilarious."
~ *Sci-Fi and Scary*

"Shane McKenzie has the kind of imagination
that should take a license to operate."
~ Ray Garton, author of *Live Girls* and *Ravenous*

DON'T MISS THIS TWISTED FAIRY TALE FOR ADULTS!

Available through Blood Bound Books ~ www.bloodboundbooks.net

Made in the USA
Columbia, SC
24 March 2021